PRAISE FOR *WINTER COTTAGE*

"Offering a look into bygone days of the gentrified from the early 1900s up until the present time, mystery and romance are included along with a multifaceted tale that is sure to please."

—*New York Journal of Books*

"There is mystery and intrigue as the author weaves a tale that pulls you in . . . This is a story of strong women, who persevere . . . It's a love story, the truest, deepest kind . . . And it's the story of a woman who years later was able to right a wrong and give a home to the people who really needed it. It's layered brilliantly, hints are revealed subtly, allowing the reader to form conclusions and fall in love."

—*Smexy Books*

PRAISE FOR MARY ELLEN TAYLOR

"[A] complex tale . . . grounded in fascinating history and emotional turmoil that is intense yet subtle. An intelligent, heartwarming exploration of the powers of forgiveness, compassion, and new beginnings."

—*Kirkus Reviews*

"Absorbing characters, a hint of mystery, and touching self-discovery elevate this novel above many others in the genre."

—*RT Book Reviews*

Spring House

OTHER TITLES BY MARY ELLEN TAYLOR

Winter Cottage

Union Street Bakery Novels
The Union Street Bakery
Sweet Expectations

Alexandria Series
At the Corner of King Street
The View from Prince Street

Spring House

MARY ELLEN TAYLOR

Published by Montlake Romance, Seattle

www.apub.com

Amazon, the Amazon logo, and Montlake Romance are trademarks of Amazon.com, Inc., or its affiliates.

ISBN-13: 9781503905320
ISBN-10: 1503905322

Cover photography and design by Laura Klynstra

Printed in the United States of America

Spring House

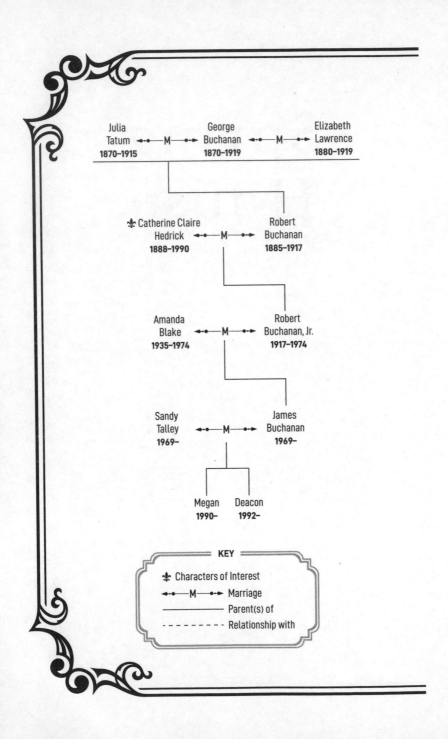

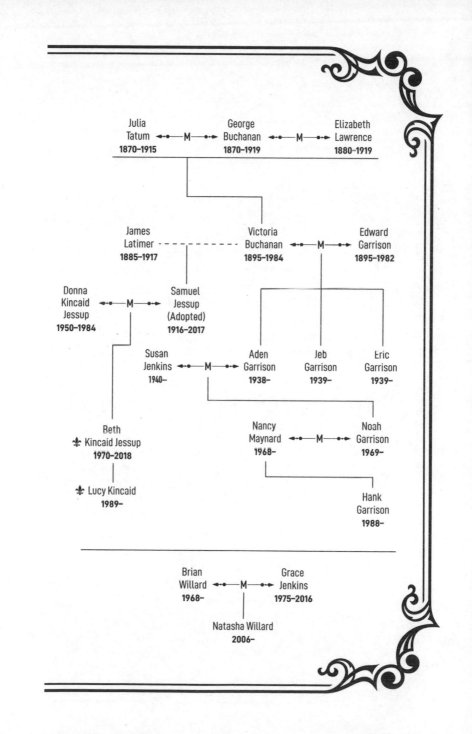

All houses are haunted.

All persons are haunted.

Throngs of spirits follow us everywhere.

We are never alone.

—Barney Sarecky

PROLOGUE

Adele

Tuesday, September 19, 2017
Cape Hudson, Virginia, in the Chesapeake Bay
11:00 a.m.

In Adele Jessup's almost one hundred years of living, she had learned that blessings and curses came hand in hand. Love and birth were always counterbalanced by pain and death.

She sat in her wheelchair, watching the dozens of mourners gathered around the casket draped with an American flag. The overcast sky hovered above as strong winds thick with the promise of rain swirled and teased the edges of her black skirt.

She shifted her attention away from the scene before her to the headstones that surrounded the freshly dug hole. These graves belonged to her husband and his brothers. The Jessup boys had all been born and raised on Virginia's Eastern Shore. Good, proud men, they had remained loyal to each other all their lives.

Sitting beside her now was Samuel Jessup, her brother-in-law, the last of the Jessup siblings. He had shaved and had his hair cut. His black merchant marine captain's uniform was freshly cleaned, its brass buttons polished. However, he wore none of the medals he had earned in more than five decades of service. His tall, lean frame had grown frail, and his right hand trembled constantly, but he had refused his wheelchair. Always too proud and stubborn for his own good.

How many times had the two of them sat here over the years, mourning the loss of one of their own? Like her, Samuel surely must feel closer to the dead now than to the living.

Today, they had gathered to honor the life of her great-grandson, Scott Jessup, a marine who had died five days earlier when his helicopter crashed in the Atlantic Ocean during a storm. He had been on a rescue mission, searching for lost seamen whose ship had been taking on water. He had saved one, deposited him safely on a naval vessel, and then returned to search for more.

Scott, like all the Jessup men, had been drawn to the water. He had grown up hearing the talks of the brave seafaring men in his family, and he fully understood that the weather and ocean gave as easily as they took. Scott had been good, brave, and sometimes too self-indulgent, but then he had been only twenty-seven when he died.

A flicker of movement beyond the mourners caught her gaze, and she looked toward the wrought iron fence that surrounded the small family cemetery on the Eastern Shore.

A young man stood there alone. Her failing eyes could not make out his face. She assumed he was another mourner until he began to move forward, but then she realized it was Scott.

Adele was not surprised to see him. The veil separating her from death was so painfully thin now that spirits were just as easy to see as the living.

Scott walked up to his mother, Helen Jessup, seated in front of her son's casket. She clutched a worn Bible and openly wept. Helen had adored her only child, and his death had sliced her heart so completely that no words or deeds would mend it.

Scott laid his hand on his mother's shoulder, but she did not seem to notice. But Samuel saw him, and when the two locked gazes, a faint smile tweaked the edges of Scott's lips. Samuel placed his hand softly over Adele's and gently squeezed.

Next to Helen sat a grim-faced man dressed in a US Marines uniform. Rick Markham had not only served with Scott and all the pallbearers, but they had also been good friends. His dark hair was closely cropped and accentuated stern features. Though he could not have been much older than Scott, he seemed to carry the burden of Atlas on his shoulders.

Scott offered Rick a reassuring smile, but that too went unseen. Adele took it all in.

Finally, Scott moved beyond the crowd toward a woman who stood outside the fence. She was alone and looked lost. Adele knew the look all too well.

Although she had never met the girl formally, Adele knew her name was Megan Buchanan. She had been Scott's fiancée but had broken up with him two weeks earlier. Although no one had shared the details of their relationship with Adele, she knew the young woman had abruptly canceled the wedding.

If Scott had been angry with Megan in life, he did not appear to be in death. He stared at her with loving eyes that held no hint of blame. When he kissed her tenderly on the cheek, her eyes widened and she raised her hand. Slowly, she looked around as if she expected to see him.

Adele studied the young woman more closely, deciding there was no single thing particularly remarkable about her. Her round face, full lips, and green eyes were fairly ordinary as individual features. Yet combined, they created a striking appearance. There was something special about Megan Buchanan.

Another native son, Hank Garrison, also dressed in his US Marines uniform, ordered five enlisted men to raise their rifles toward the sky and fire three volleys. Samuel gripped the edges of his walker and pushed himself to a standing position. Rick quickly rose and tried to steady Samuel, but the stubborn old man refused help.

A solemn stillness settled over the crowd, and for several moments no one moved.

Rick helped Samuel back into his chair and then walked with the marines single file to the casket, where the group dispersed equally to either side. They folded the flag with neat, crisp precision until it was a sharp triangle, which Rick presented to Helen on behalf of a grateful nation.

Scott hovered close to his mother as she pressed the flag to her chest and drew in a shuddering breath. The ceremony ended, and the next few moments were filled with more tears, people lingering around Helen, and some acknowledging Adele and Samuel before they all slowly walked out through the old iron gate.

"I'll be right back," Helen said.

Adele raised her gaze as Scott looked toward her. He tossed her an impish grin that reminded her of when he was a boy stealing cookies from her kitchen. "There's no rush," she told Helen.

For a moment, the living left Adele and Samuel alone with Scott. Content to sit in silence, Adele was grateful for this moment, for she was certain it would be her last with either man.

"You see me, don't you?" Scott asked.

She shifted her gaze from the stand of trees ringing the small cemetery back to his sun-weathered face. "Yes," she said.

"I'm not too far behind you myself, boy," Samuel said.

"Yes, sir," Scott said.

"There's no sense waiting on me," Samuel said. "I'll find my own way."

"He's not waiting on you," Adele said.

"Then who?" Samuel asked.

She watched as Helen approached Megan. Whatever they were saying to each other did not look pleasant. "Them. He's waiting on them."

Samuel drew in a breath and nodded. If Samuel and she understood any truth, it was the power of unfinished business and secrets, which anchored the living as well as the dead.

CHAPTER ONE

Megan

Monday, March 5, 2018
Norfolk, Virginia
8:00 a.m.

A blustery wind flapped the edges of Megan Buchanan's coat and brushed back freshly cut and frightfully short bangs as she hurried toward Ragland's Mariner Antique Shop. She opened the door to a rush of warmth and the chiming of a ship's bell that jingled overhead to announce her arrival.

As the heat seeped into her bones, she drank in the atmosphere and savored the clutter of the old lanterns, buoys, and ropes that seemed to fill every bit of open space. Mounted on the back wall was a large collection of wooden figureheads carved into shapes ranging from unicorns to full-breasted mermaids. Each ornament had once been mounted on a ship's bow and meant to capture her spirit and prowess.

Tracing her fingers over the iron of an ancient anchor, Megan angled her pregnant belly down a narrow aisle toward the counter. As she waited, her attention was drawn to an eclectic collection ranging from board games to a large jar of red and white marbles and a box of dominoes. None really fit the seaman's theme, but shop owner Duncan

Travis never passed up any item that could be purchased for pennies and sold for dollars.

When she reached the counter, she tapped a small bell. "Duncan, it's Megan."

Footsteps shuffled behind the curtain separating the front of the store from a desk that she knew sported a brand-new computer and piles of books, papers, and magazines. Though Duncan maintained a retail front, his bread and butter came from the items he scouted for private clients, collectors, and designers.

"Megan?" A gnarled hand gripped the edge of the purple curtain. The pause reminded her that Duncan enjoyed making an entrance.

"Yes, it's me."

The parting curtain revealed a tiny old man with a thin body, hunched shoulders, and sparse, graying hair tied back in a ponytail. Seventy-plus years in the sun had left his tanned face etched with deep lines.

He wore a striped, collared shirt, faded jeans cinched with a worn leather belt, and black shoes. A Masonic onyx ring winked from his left index finger, though Megan was fairly certain he had chosen the ring for its dramatic effect rather than its symbolic origins. A gold watch that had stopped working decades ago wrapped smartly around his wrist.

"You're early," he said.

"I finished up early at my doctor's appointment."

He glanced at her round belly. "You look mighty ripe."

"I feel like a beached whale." Everyone talked to her about the baby and her belly as if both were public property. Though she appreciated the interest, talk of the baby reminded her that she had no idea how to raise a child alone. "I'd rather talk about the artifacts you said you found for me."

Megan had been hired in January to oversee the renovation of a historic hunting lodge called Winter Cottage. Her great-great-grandfather, George Buchanan, had built the massive, twenty-one-thousand-square-foot structure for his second wife, who'd shared his love of duck hunting on the Eastern Shore. Construction of the house had been completed in 1901, but in 1916, George had gifted it to his daughter-in-law, Claire Hedrick Buchanan. Claire had lived in the house until her death in 1990.

Duncan studied her a moment, his eyes narrowed. "You changed your hair."

She brushed back her diminutive bangs, sorry now that she'd filled the gap between the ob-gyn and the antique shop with an impromptu visit to a hair salon. The instant the hairdresser had snipped the bangs from her long, straight hair, Megan realized she had made yet another terrible mistake. "I feel a bit like the little Dutch Boy."

A smile tugged at the edges of his lips. "I'd say more like Friar Tuck."

She laughed and reminded herself short hair was not a forever mistake. "I shouldn't come into town. I'm safer on the Eastern Shore."

Duncan chuckled. "The bangs ain't that bad."

"Liar."

He shrugged as he reached under the counter. "I have an object for you. Can you tell me what it is?"

"Duncan, don't you ever get tired of this game?"

"Never."

They played this game every time she came into the shop. If he had an unusual item, he would ask her to deduce its history. She was rarely wrong, but then again, she had built a reputation in the art-restoration world as an expert in the odd and unusual.

"Come on," he coaxed. "Show me what you know."

She held out her hand. "I'll have to make this quick. I'm due back home within the hour."

From a red velvet box he removed a gold pocket watch covered in a fine patina and scrolls that looped around the letter *S*.

"I thought maybe you could give me an idea of who owned it," Duncan said.

The locket was the size of a silver dollar, and its finely worn gold facing felt cool to the touch. She rubbed her thumb over the engraved

S and then pressed her finger against the tiny latch. The top popped open.

Made by French watchmaker Cartier around 1850, the watch had a champagne face and roman numerals. The time had stopped at 11:20, and engraved on the inside were the words *To my dearest wife*. In 1850, few in the region could have afforded such an expensive timepiece.

"Where was this watch found?" she asked.

"I bought it in an estate sale in Alexandria, Virginia. The family had no information on it."

She closed the locket and ran her thumbs over the delicate scrolls carved on its outside. "You said Alexandria?"

His eyes narrowed. "That's right."

Alexandria had been a thriving port city from the colonial days when tobacco was king through the mid-1800s. The city had a population of roughly eight thousand, and of those, twenty-five hundred were African American. There had been a financial crisis in 1819, but by 1850, the town was again booming.

Megan had a working knowledge of the city elite of the time. "Search the name Captain Robert Stewart."

He scribbled the name. "Why him?"

"A wealthy ship's captain who had a fascination with watches. Over two hundred were listed in his last will and testament."

He shook his head. "You're right. You must be psychic."

She wasn't psychic, but she was blessed with a mind crammed full of endless historical facts that she never forgot. She was accessing that database and not the spiritual realm.

Her keen memory for historical facts had been a great icebreaker when she'd landed in a new school. Her father had worked for the shipping arm of the Buchanan Corporation, and he'd been transferred ten times during his years with them. For her and her brother, Deacon, that had translated to as many schools. By elementary school, they were both expert at packing toys and books, saying goodbye to friends, and finding something to dislike about where they had been and something to love about where they were going.

Her athletic brother never had trouble finding a place in a new school, but for her, transitions were always awkward and unsettling. Somewhere along the way, she had learned if she spun a vivid story featuring a new friend's lunchbox, piece of jewelry, or picture, she could entertain and win the hearts of her peers. Her assessments, which some of her friends said were spookily accurate, were always harmless and diverting. It had been a quirky way to fit into new crowds, but it worked for her.

She handed him the watch. "Your message said you found information on Winter Cottage."

Megan had written her PhD dissertation on Winter Cottage, which had been her lone anchor in a childhood spent adrift. Growing up, she could not count on where she would be living in any given year, but she could rely on a summer vacation to the Eastern Shore in the shadow of Winter Cottage. Her great-grandmother Catherine Buchanan had hosted her father here each summer from the age of five until he left for college. According to her dad, Claire had been loving and kind to him, and he'd always spoken fondly of her and the old house.

Megan had assumed her great-grandmother would leave Winter Cottage to her father, but the property had gone to Samuel Jessup, a merchant marine. Though the Jessups made their living either as watermen or merchant marines, or in the military service, their lives were closely intertwined with the wealthy Buchanans'. Samuel, in fact, had been her late fiancé's great-great-uncle.

Megan had thought the land would revert back to the Buchanans after Samuel's death, but his will had been clear that Winter Cottage should go to his grandchild. And Lucy Kincaid, a Nashville bartender, had been located.

Thanks to a generous trust established by Claire, Lucy had the means to renovate Winter Cottage and its surrounding buildings. Lucy, perhaps reluctant at first to live on the Eastern Shore, had quickly embraced ownership and all the restoration. Six weeks ago, she had hired Megan to oversee the operation.

"I hear you moved into Winter Cottage," Duncan said.

"It's easier to be on-site during the renovation," Megan said.

"How's it going so far?" he asked.

"As much as I love history, I do prefer modern plumbing and electrical systems that won't short-circuit over a hair dryer or microwave oven."

He nodded ruefully. "Those were the good old days."

"Perhaps, but I'm very happy in the world of epidural blocks and antibiotics."

"What will you renovate first?"

"Spring House. It was Samuel Jessup's house. He was the property's caretaker before Claire died. Once we have Spring House renovated, Lucy, her sister, and I will move into it. Then the work on Winter Cottage begins."

His gaze flickered to her swollen belly. "You got a lot on your plate."

"Nothing I can't handle." She hoped that was true. "What do you have for me?"

He reached under the counter, pulled out a box, and laid a bent hand on top. A vaudevillian devotee to the core, he tipped the edge of the box back a fraction so that only he could peek inside. "Have you ever heard of Thomas Delany's photography?"

The name sparked her interest. "Sure. He was a cold plate photographer and did most of his work in the 1890s."

"Well, a treasure trove of his photographs surfaced at an estate sale a few weeks ago. I received the call and bought them all up. I spent the last week going through the glass plates as well as the photos."

She resisted the urge to tell him to hurry up. Duncan loved the suspense. "Keep talking."

"I came across a series of photographs of Spring House before Winter Cottage was built."

"Late 1890s?"

"Exactly."

He removed the lid, pulled out the first picture, and slowly placed it on the counter. It was a black-and-white picture of Spring House.

The center section of Spring House was basically a two-story log cabin that had been built circa 1700 by a local merchant named Stuart Wentworth, who had been awarded the property by a grant from the king of England. Wentworth went on to grow corn and beans, which he shipped along the East Coast and to England via the deepwater port of Onancock, located twenty miles north.

The house was sold around 1870 to an engineer who had been sent by the railroad company to survey the extension of the rail line south to Cape Charles.

George Buchanan purchased Spring House in 1895 and used it as a hunting lodge until Winter Cottage could be built five years later.

Standing on the porch of Spring House was a young girl who couldn't have been more than five. She had dark hair and wore a calico dress that looked two sizes too big for her small frame. To the right of the clapboard house was the brick foundation of an outbuilding that Megan guessed had once been a kitchen, which were often built away from the main house to guard against fire.

Her gaze shifted to the shoreline and the expanse of the Chesapeake Bay. Two ships were on the horizon. A thick gaggle of geese flew past fluffy white clouds.

The land was stark, barren, with no hint of the grand mansion that would soon come to dominate the Eastern Shore and the neighboring town of Cape Hudson.

"It's interesting. Do you know who the girl is?" she asked.

"I have no idea. I wonder what brought Mr. Delany to the shores?"

"No doubt George Buchanan. He enjoyed having his picture taken." She tore her gaze from the girl. "It's fascinating. Historical context is always valuable in restoration work."

"Do you really think I'd have called you here if it were only that picture?"

She grinned. "I was hoping for more."

He removed another picture from his box. The image featured four young girls standing by their pregnant mother. The girls ranged in age from about eleven to eight. "The oldest girl is your great-grandmother, Claire Buchanan."

"Really?" She leaned in, searching for resemblances and finding eyes shaped like her father's. "How can you be sure?"

"Flip it over."

Written on the back was *The Hedrick Women*. Hedrick had been Claire's maiden name.

"Look at the youngest girl and then back at the first picture."

She glanced between the two images. "They're the same girl."

"Yep. Kind of odd, isn't it?"

"The youngest Hedrick girl was named Diane." Megan had been able to trace the lineage of the three oldest Hedrick sisters, but Diane had vanished from history.

"One last picture," Duncan said. He reached under the counter and pulled out a framed photograph of a stunning woman with clear blue eyes and blonde hair coiled in a style fashionable in the early 1940s. Megan did not need Duncan to tell her who this woman was. It was Victoria Buchanan Garrison, Claire's sister-in-law.

Victoria had married Edward Garrison in 1920, and the couple had traveled the world while Edward served in multiple Foreign Service posts. They moved among the elite, and it was not until their sons were born in the pair's later years that the couple returned home. Victoria, according to family lore, had credited her belated pregnancies to a fertility goddess she had met in North Africa shortly before World War II broke out.

Megan's great-grandmother Claire had left behind videotapes that Lucy had found recently. In the tapes, Claire stated that Victoria had given birth to a son at Winter Cottage, and Claire had turned the child, Samuel, over to the Jessups. Claire had been nearly one hundred years old when she made the tape and had no reason to lie. Adding credence to the baby's birth was Victoria's own behavior. Before the summer of 1916, she had lived a very public life and was often seen at the theater or dinner parties. After her marriage, she became very private. When she and her husband finally had children, they withdrew even more without a hint of explanation.

"An interesting collection, Duncan. Can I buy these from you?" Eventually, Winter Cottage would be set up as a museum, and these pieces would be of great interest to its visitors.

"I'm thinking two hundred bucks a picture."

"How about two hundred for all three?" she countered.

"I hear Winter Cottage has a large trust fund behind it dedicated to the renovation."

"That doesn't mean I'm going to pay a crazy high price."

"Four hundred for all three," the old man whispered.

"Three fifty for all three. Final offer, Duncan."

He stared at her as if peering over a hand of poker, wondering whether she was bluffing. If attending ten schools before the age of seventeen had taught her any lesson, it was to keep her emotions to herself. She said nothing and waited.

"Fine. But only because I don't feel like haggling with a pregnant woman. Makes me look bad."

"Can I take these and have you bill me?"

"I'll send the bill out this morning."

"If you find more pictures as you go through those glass-plate negatives, call me."

"You'll be the first."

As he collected and boxed the pictures, she said, "May I also buy these games?" She fished a couple of twenties out of her purse. "They're for me."

"What do you want with a bunch of old games?"

"Lucy's sister, Natasha, likes games."

"Kids today don't care about these games."

"I'm trying to teach her that not all fun is had online."

He snorted. "Good luck with that."

"If the Mystery Date board game doesn't do the trick, then the Ouija board will."

"I'll sell them all to you for ten bucks."

"What? You're giving me a deal without haggling."

"Getting soft in my old age."

"Thanks, and remember, I'm looking to buy furnishings for Winter Cottage. You find any other Winter Cottage items, call me."

"Oh, don't you worry. Half the antique vendors on or near the bay know you're looking. Word of that trust fund has spread."

"Thanks."

He bagged up the games and pictures into a large paper satchel, and Megan carried her new treasures out the front door. After settling the bag carefully on the back seat of the truck, she slid behind the wheel, her belly barely fitting.

She drove through town and finally along North Hampton Boulevard toward the Chesapeake Bay Bridge–Tunnel, which connected Virginia's mainland to the Eastern Shore. She paid the toll and set off for the seventeen-mile bridge and tunnel.

Megan rolled down her window, and the salt air funneled into the truck's cab, brushing the tips of those too-short bangs off her very round face. The breeze from the bay coaxed some of the tension from her shoulders, but when she flipped down her visor, she did not see a posh woman staring back, but rather—as Duncan had suggested—Friar Tuck. She groaned. "It's hair, for God's sake."

The horizon was painted a rich blue and dotted with the occasional plump white cloud. The waters were calm today, but hints of whitecaps foretold that bad weather was coming soon.

As the bridge descended over the grasslands of the Eastern Shore, her phone rang. One glance at the display sent fresh waves of stress crashing over her.

Megan tightened her hold on the steering wheel and then answered the call. "Hello, Mom."

"How did the appointment go with the obstetrician?" Sandy asked.

"It went well. The baby is doing fine. How did you know I was in town today?"

"The geo-tracker on your phone. These days you only go into Norfolk for baby checkups."

Megan downshifted, sorry she had agreed to allow her mother to track her. But her parents had been on the verge of canceling their trip to Australia if she refused. They were due home just before her delivery date. And if they were going to be a world away from their only daughter while she was pregnant, they expected stalking rights. "It all went well. The baby is fine."

"Are you still on target for a late April delivery?"

"That's the plan." The doctor had said she and the baby were doing great. There had been the usual warnings to slow down and put her feet up more often, but with normal blood pressure and more energy than she'd had in months, she took these as only suggestions.

"Your father and I will be back in plenty of time for the delivery."

Megan straightened in her seat, working the tension from her back. "See, it's all working out fine."

"How's the restoration project going?" her mother asked.

"Phase one begins today. The dumpster will arrive, and Lucy and I will start going through her grandfather's study."

Megan had pitched the restoration idea of Spring House and then Winter Cottage to Lucy a couple of months ago, and to her delight, Lucy had accepted it. Thanks to the substantial endowment from Claire, Megan had the freedom to do an accurate and full restoration of Winter Cottage, plus she could upgrade Spring House to a modern home.

"I received another call from Helen," her mother said.

Helen Jessup was Megan's almost mother-in-law and her baby's grandmother. Helen had wanted her son to marry a woman adept at entertaining and capable of fully supporting his naval career, but she had been gracious and welcoming to bookish Megan when Scott had told her about the engagement. Days after the wedding announcement, Helen had set about reinventing her son's fiancée, who was more interested in dusty books than making nice with an admiral's wife. Soon Helen was taking her clothes shopping or for pedicures and manicures. Megan had loved Scott, so she had tried to please Helen.

And then it all fell apart when Megan abruptly ended their engagement two weeks before the wedding. She had barely begun to process the breakup when Rick Markham, Scott's almost best man, called and told her that Scott was dead. Rick explained that Scott had been on a rescue mission when his helicopter crashed.

Megan should have stayed away from the funeral, but she had really loved Scott. So she had driven to the Jessup family plot near Winter Cottage on that hot and humid September day. The country cemetery had been packed with mourners from near and far.

It would have been better to remain on the periphery of the ceremony, but when Helen approached her, Megan had seen it as her chance to express her condolences. But Helen had taken one look at her and, in a voice only Megan could hear, hissed, *"Get away from me. You killed my son."*

"What?" Megan had whispered.

"If you'd been grown-up enough to make your relationship work and be the woman Scott needed, he'd be alive."

Megan had stayed silent, but she'd cried all the way back to Norfolk.

"What did Helen want?" Megan asked.

"She made a lot of small talk. I think she was hoping I would mention you. When I didn't, she asked me directly about the baby. I didn't realize she'd not seen you in so long."

Megan had visited Scott's grave. Helen had been there, sitting quietly on the ground, rearranging fresh flowers in a stone vase. She had been crying, and Megan had wanted to give the poor woman some hope to buoy her through the choppy waters ready to pull her under. So she had told her about the baby, thinking she might be tossing Helen a lifeline.

Helen had stared at her for a long, tense moment. "If you think you're going to pawn that baby off as Scott's, you are mistaken."

They had not communicated since. "I'm not sure she believed me, Mom."

"Cut her some slack, kiddo. She's in a lot of pain. Scott was the world to her."

Megan shifted in her seat, away from the annoying ache in her lower back. "What did you tell Helen?"

"She knows you're back in Cape Hudson and working on Winter Cottage. It's a small town. Word gets around. I told her the baby and you are fine."

"So she has the basic update."

There was a long pause. Then: "Helen wants the baby to take a paternity test."

"A what?"

"She wants proof that the baby is Scott's."

Megan rolled her head from side to side. "I don't have time for these kinds of games. I told her the baby was Scott's."

"I know. I know. That's what I told her several times. I think she's looking for an excuse to see you."

"She'd have better luck reaching me if she'd stop insulting me." Intellectually, she understood the woman's pain far surpassed her own. But her rejection also made Megan angry. "I have to go, Mom. I have to get to work."

"Megan, there are chemicals in old homes. Asbestos is highly toxic to the unborn child."

"There's no asbestos in this house," she said. "The house was finished in 1901."

"Renovation work is also strenuous. It's too big a job, and it's not the least bit good for the baby," her mother warned.

"The baby's fine. And I can do this job." This project was her chance to prove herself. Her history degree wasn't an expensive hobby, as her father had once called it, and she could give up her online baking business and still make a living.

"It's a big job, Megan. And with the baby coming, I'm worried. Maybe you should tackle a smaller project."

"Mom, stop."

Sandy sighed, a last-ditch effort to maybe guilt her daughter to her side. When Megan didn't budge, she said, "Well, on the bright side, if the renovation doesn't work out, you can go back to catering."

She was not going backward. She couldn't. As much as the future scared her, her past was too painful and filled with disappointments to revisit. "Mom, I need to let you go. I've got contractors to meet at Spring House today."

"I can see you're almost across the Bay Bridge–Tunnel," her mother said. "Good. I don't like seeing you make that drive."

On a good day, the bridge offered stunning views of the bay. On a bad day, it could get dicey, but she was careful to watch the weather. "I've made this drive countless times. I'll be fine." And before her mother could answer, she said, "Take care. Talk to you soon."

The bright sky had her fumbling for her sunglasses from her purse. As she put more distance between her and the bridge, the knot in her back eased.

Ending the call so abruptly shoveled more guilt onto a growing pile. She needed to be kinder and more openhearted to Helen, but Megan herself felt as if she were on the verge of drowning. She simply did not have the reserves to save the woman.

CHAPTER TWO

Megan

Monday, March 5, 2018
Cape Hudson, Virginia
10:00 a.m.

Megan drove up Route 13 past the turnoff to Cape Hudson, a pictur-
esque town that bordered the Chesapeake Bay. In the off-season, the
surrounding area sported close to ten thousand residents, but in the
summer, that number grew tenfold.

Cape Hudson consisted of a central street where the majority of its
businesses were located. In the winter, some would close shop, while
others cut back on their hours. In recent years, beachfront property on
the Virginia mainland had become excessively expensive, causing more
folks to turn to Cape Hudson for an affordable vacation option. The
summer season that had once begun on Memorial Day and run through
Labor Day now extended from mid-April through Thanksgiving. The
first of the early-bird tourists would arrive in a couple of weeks.

Megan continued driving a few more miles before spotting the fifty
acres of vines that belonged to Beacon Vineyards. The land had been
leased to the Garrisons for years through the Winter Cottage trust, and
now her third cousin Hank Garrison had taken over and was expanding

the operation. Hank, who had served with Scott in the marines, had left a promising military career shortly after Scott's death and moved back home. He was now in the process of building the Eastern Shore's largest winery.

Megan and Hank shared the same great-great-grandparents, George and Julia Buchanan. Whereas Megan descended from their son, Robert, Hank's line extended from the Buchanans' daughter, Victoria. Megan and Hank, along with Deacon and Hank's sister, Rebecca, spent summers on the Chesapeake Bay, and the four remained close.

Hank wanted Winter Cottage renovated not so much for its historical significance but because the house would eventually become a tourist attraction that would also help his soon-to-be-launched winery. Hank's girlfriend, Lucy, the new caretaker of Winter Cottage, had more sentimental reasons for the renovation, but she too saw the business potential. In Lucy's mind, Winter Cottage was destined to be a thriving wedding venue.

Lucy and Hank had big plans for the property and were betting large that it would be stunning when it was complete. All this boiled down to Megan's successful completion of the restoration on time and within budget.

She turned right at the newly constructed twin brick pillars, each sporting a metal plaque that read BEACON VINEYARDS. Winter Cottage was located up ahead on the shore of the Chesapeake Bay. As dust kicked up around the wheels of her truck, she spotted Winter Cottage's copper roof, which peeked out from behind the trees. To the right, the spire of an 1840s brick lighthouse jutted up toward blue sky. The lighthouse had been dark for seventy years and, like Winter Cottage, was in need of an extensive restoration. If somehow she managed to have this baby and restore both Spring House and Winter Cottage, then the lighthouse would be next on her list.

If, if, if.

All the restoration work began with Spring House, which would become Lucy and Natasha's home. Spring House would be the base of operations for all the projects for several years to come. So it had to be not only preserved but also dragged into the twenty-first century to serve as a proper home.

Megan was the champion of big dreams and had had a lot of them over the years. So far, though, her follow-through hadn't kept pace.

"One problem at a time, Megan," she said to herself.

She ignored her growing to-do list for Winter Cottage and the lighthouse and kept her focus on Spring House.

She followed the dirt road to the left, veering away from the lighthouse and the old hunting lodge toward a stand of tall brush that wrapped around shorter fruit trees twisted by years of wind from the bay. Nestled among the trees was the white clapboard house she had seen in Delany's photograph.

It now appeared much the same, though the weather-beaten red tin roof had been damaged in several storms, and the ten-foot-wide porch that wrapped around the exterior had so much rot it would have to be torn off or replaced eventually. The floor-to-ceiling windows and dark storm shutters remained intact, as did the front door, which was outfitted with a brass pineapple knocker.

She was pleased to see the arrival of the big blue dumpster that she had ordered the previous week. It had a capacity of thirteen hundred cubic feet with a sixteen-thousand-pound weight limit. And she knew after her multiple tours through the house that she would need every bit of that space. The house was crammed with clutter from floor to ceiling, and judging by the faint smell of mildew, there was water damage that meant walls would have to come out along with an outdated kitchen and bathroom. No doubt that blue dumpster would be filled to the brim by the time she was finished with this place.

Megan pressed her hand to the small of her back as she gathered her purse and climbed the steps. She crossed the wooden porch to a red front door faded and streaked by salt air. As sweet smelling as Chesapeake Bay's air could be, it was brutal on houses. Without maintenance, paint peeled, hinges rusted, and boards split in the briny shore air. She only prayed the damage to Spring House didn't extend to its foundation.

Megan fumbled with iron keys that dated back a century and then slid the one shaped like a large F into the lock. It took a little twisting, turning, and some jiggling to get the lock to give. When its tumblers reluctantly clicked into place, the door creaked open.

Stale air drifted out of Spring House like a tired yawn as sunlight streaked in and dust danced and swirled in the beams of light. "Time to rise and shine."

The house almost moaned like a sleeping giant, and she sensed it was not the least bit interested in rising. It had been left alone for decades and was content to be forgotten.

"Leave me be," it seemed to whisper.

"No way, my friend," she said. "We're going to reinvent ourselves together."

The center hallway was packed with a collection of mismatched bookshelves that were crammed full of magazines, books, and papers. The limited remaining wall space was filled with photographs in inexpensive dime-store frames. The floor was covered in sailcloth painted in a black-and-white checkerboard tile pattern. The stiff cloth was covered in decades of dirt and stretched the length of the hallway. But despite its age and neglect, she suspected that, under the grime, the original cloth still might be salvaged with a good cleaning.

Once the clutter was stripped away, she knew there would be hardwood floors, crown moldings, and marble fireplaces aching to be rediscovered. Her excitement grew as she anticipated all the discoveries waiting for her. Regardless of the time involved, she would bring Spring House back to life.

The baby kicked hard against her ribs, reminding her that the best-laid plans often ventured off course.

The rumble of tires had her turning to see Lucy Kincaid pull up in her yellow Jeep. Blonde hair with a blue streak that matched her eyes made her a sight to see. She had turned more than a few heads in town. It would have been easy to resent Lucy if she were not so down to earth and kind. She had been living in this still, remote community for only four months, but already locals considered her, well, a local.

Not only had she won over the community but she was also tackling these restoration projects that were destined to stretch out for years. On top of that, she was now raising her half sister, Natasha, whom she was in the process of adopting.

Lucy's German shepherd, Dolly, bounded out of the Jeep and barked before dashing into a thicket of trees as Lucy's cowboy boots thudded across the front porch. "Tell me the party hasn't started without me," she said, grinning.

Her Tennessee-laced accent conjured images of the honky-tonks of Nashville's Lower Broadway and its aged bourbon that still stained her trademark blue cowboy boots.

Lucy sported a red Nashville T-shirt featuring a bucking bronco, and her worn jeans skimmed a slim, athletic figure. A spark in her gaze hinted at a life filled with fun that had always eluded Megan.

Dolly barked from the brush, reappeared, and then, catching the scent of a squirrel or deer, bounded back into the tall grass, happily barking.

"When did you get here?" Lucy asked. "I thought you had a doctor's appointment in Norfolk this morning."

"All done in record time, thankfully. I just arrived," Megan said.

"How did the checkup go?" Lucy asked.

"It's all good."

"Glad to hear it."

"Natasha and her history project arrive at school?"

"I left her at the school dressed as a Greek senator complete with laurels in her hair. She's ready to talk about Julius Caesar."

The toga was a white bedsheet, and the laurel was ivy from the surrounding woods. "She looked cute."

"She was worried it made her look stupid until she saw three other girls dressed just like her."

"Ah, we all want to fit in during middle school."

"Her more than most," Lucy said. "But I'm hoping that settles as soon as she figures out her big sister is not going anywhere."

Natasha's mother had died two years earlier, and the father she shared with Lucy had little interest in raising her. The girl had spent the last couple of years either being bounced between neighbors or hiding in Winter Cottage.

Lucy turned and called for Dolly, who quickly burst out of the undergrowth and up the stairs, wagging her tail and licking Megan's hands.

Megan scratched the dog's head. "Hey, girl."

"So what's your assessment?" As Lucy stepped closer, she studied Megan's swollen belly, patted it gently, and smiled. "Will we be finished by fall so the crew can gut Winter Cottage?"

"It's going to be tight." As Megan thought about the schedule and the baby, her constant hum of worry kicked up a notch. She had disappointed so many people in her life, and she did not want to add Lucy to her list.

As if sensing her thoughts, Lucy said, "We'll figure it out, Megan. Don't make that worried face."

Megan moistened her lips and relaxed her frown. "I'm not making a worried face."

Lucy scrunched hers up. "Yes, you are. Like I tell Natasha, your face is going to stick in a frown if you're not careful."

Megan smiled, hoping if she projected Lucy's relaxed attitude, she would unwind the tension knotted in her back. What was it that

Lucy called her life philosophy? The law of attraction? *"Our thoughts,"* she often said, *"manifest in our lives."* Megan certainly had never once thought about the troubles that had manifested with Scott, his death, or the baby, so she was tempted to call bullshit on the attracting-law theory.

Lucy cupped her hands on Megan's belly. "Don't let your mama's worries bother you, little spud. Life has a way of sorting itself out."

"The moving and construction contractor will be back here first thing in the morning along with his crew. I thought we'd need at least a day to get our bearings."

"I can't wait to get this place cleaned out and renovated. I miss a modern bathroom and shower."

Both women had been in the house a couple of weeks earlier as they walked the property with the contractor, Ron Tucker. As Lucy talked about what she wanted to see, he made notes occasionally, frowned, tapped on a calculator, and then promised to work up estimates.

The walk-through had not only confirmed this was going to be an expensive job but also convinced Megan that Samuel Jessup had been a pack rat.

Megan flipped the light switch. Two overhead bulbs barely spit out enough light along the entry hallway that stretched from the front door all the way to the back and into the kitchen addition.

"You met my grandfather several times," Lucy said. "Was he always collecting stuff?"

Megan had been hearing about her family history since she was a little girl. Her father always had a story about Claire or Samuel, and she knew those stories well.

But Lucy hadn't had the luxury of a family history until she moved back to Cape Hudson. Lucy's mother, Samuel's daughter, had left the shore when she was eighteen and pregnant with Lucy. She had never returned. Until her death, Lucy's mother, Beth, had never once mentioned Winter Cottage or her daughter's deep roots in this community.

"I never stepped inside this house," Megan said. "He always met us at Winter Cottage when I visited with my mom, my dad, and my brother."

"Was your dad close to Samuel?" Lucy asked.

Megan shrugged. "Claire called Samuel and Dad her boys. Dad said Samuel taught him how to fish when he was six and to sail on the bay when he was eight. He said Samuel was quiet but always a patient teacher."

"Did they see each other much?" Lucy asked.

"Until Dad was about ten. Then Claire decided Dad needed more education, so she enrolled him in a private high school in Alexandria. From then on he spent only summers or holiday breaks on the shore. And with Samuel sailing with the merchant marines, there were few times they crossed paths."

"But you met him once or twice. What did you think of Samuel?" Lucy asked.

"He was nice enough and talked to me about the history of Winter Cottage. When I was working on my dissertation, I interviewed him again. He was charming, but I got the sense there was a lot he wasn't telling me."

"Like what?"

"Things to do with the families. I think Samuel took a lot of secrets to his grave."

"Do you think he knew about Victoria?"

"I don't know."

Lucy leaned in toward a picture that featured Samuel standing on the bridge of a ship. She guessed it had been taken in the 1930s. Samuel Jessup in his prime was a very handsome man. Stark eyes were offset by suntanned skin and a shock of light hair. Looking at this picture, it was easy to see where Lucy had inherited her looks.

According to Claire's videotapes, Samuel's biological father had been a local waterman by the name of James Latimer. An internet search had produced a picture taken in 1916, the year Samuel was born. A side-by-side comparison of Samuel and James left no doubt that the men had been father and son.

"It's like James cloned himself," Lucy said.

"You look like James too."

"So did my mother," Lucy said. "Funny how genetics works." She moved to the next picture. "It's too bad I didn't know about this life on the Eastern Shore sooner. I feel like I missed so much."

Megan opened the tall oak pocket doors of Samuel Jessup's library and turned on the old light switch. A couple of lights flickered, their illumination barely reaching the corners. This was her first good look at Samuel's study in a couple of weeks, and it seemed worse than she remembered. Though she had always expected this renovation to be extensive, she was again unprepared for the level of memorabilia the old man had crammed into his life.

The room was filled with mounds of books, magazines, and newspapers that towered on either side of a central pathway, which branched to the left toward a chair and a fireplace framed in a carved wooden mantel. The trail went right and ended at a six-foot-long mahogany desk covered with more piles of yellowing papers, charts, and pictures.

Megan had done some research on organizing, knowing there were tried-and-true methods to taming madness like this. What she had learned was to start with the vertical surfaces. She would tackle the desk, side tables, and mantel first.

Lucy clicked on the black light switch on the wall, and more low-wattage bulbs spit out meager circles of light.

The study was a large room with high ceilings and four east-facing windows draped with dark curtains. By all rights, the room should have been light and airy, but the window treatments, coupled with dark paint covered by more framed photographs, brought the space crashing in.

She crossed the study, slowly navigating the narrow pathway to a tall set of curtains. She pulled each dusty panel back, allowing in bright sunshine. Dust particles danced in the sunbeams as the room illuminated.

Megan pulled a hair tie from around her wrist and, after combing her fingers through her dark hair, fastened it into a ponytail. "He certainly liked having his belongings around him," Megan said.

Lucy crossed to one of the walls and studied more pictures spanning from World War II through the Korean War and Vietnam. "Mom was like this. She hung on to more stuff. I must have donated or thrown out two dozen packed bags after she died."

"Your grandfather was one of the few merchant marines who requested work in war zones," Megan said.

Lucy picked up an old book and leafed through its yellowed pages. "So many memories. If there were ever a room with secrets, it's this one."

"You wanted to know about your family. This is the best way to learn."

Lucy swiped her finger over the edge of the dusty desk. "Be careful what you wish for, right?"

"Well then, buckle up, buttercup. Because we're going to find a few secrets in this time capsule."

Lucy picked up a *Time* magazine that dated back to the eighties. "Where do we start?"

"There are bins in the back of my truck. Let's line them up on the porch outside. We'll start with *Donate* and *Keep*. Trash goes straight into the dumpster. Then we'll decide what to do with whatever we keep."

Her identical plastic bins were sturdy, though they seemed inadequate the longer she stood in this room. But this project had to start somewhere.

"I'm also on the lookout for buried treasure to sell," Lucy said. "Claire might have left the house to me, but every dime in the trust is earmarked for property upkeep, not me. And I need cash. Twelve-year-old girls are expensive to raise."

"I'm sure we'll find a few treasures that fit the bill."

Lucy glanced at the clock. "Speaking of which, Natasha will be here by three. She's been anxious to get into all this."

"But you not so much? In fact, you look a little nervous."

Lucy smoothed her hands over her jeans. "I didn't like Samuel Jessup," she said.

"You never met him."

"Whatever happened between my mother and him drove her away from Cape Hudson. If not for that, I might have known more about where I came from." She shrugged, then picked up a book on maritime law and leafed through it. "I'll get the bins from the back of the truck and put them on the porch."

"Thanks."

Lucy left, and as Megan stood in the room alone, she could almost feel the hum of emotion and memories. She imagined Samuel sitting at the window, staring out toward a sunset, his stooped shoulders weighed down by loneliness. As she moved toward the desk, a rush of tears welled in her eyes. The one time she had ever experienced such a sense of loss was when Scott died.

Megan wiped away the tears and stepped back. Suddenly she needed to breathe and stepped out onto the porch. The sunshine and fresh air brushed away the foggy feeling and the last of the shadows. Closing her eyes, she tipped her face toward the sun and shook off the mood.

Lucy opened the tailgate of Megan's truck and grabbed the first five bins. As she climbed the stairs, Megan turned toward the side of the porch and blinked away the last of the tears.

"I don't think these bins are going to cut it," Lucy said.

Megan cleared her throat. "No. Not even close."

In the distance the sound of tires on the gravel driveway had her turning to see the sheriff's car rounding the corner. Lucy waved and walked casually down the steps toward Sheriff Rick Markham's vehicle.

He stepped out of his car, his gaze sweeping over the house and then settling on Megan in a quick, efficient way that made her think of a commander inspecting one of his marine infantrymen.

Lucy nodded. "Welcome to Operation Declutter."

Standing at six feet, Rick had broad shoulders and dark hair still cut tight on the sides and high on the top. He sported a freshly ironed uniform that managed to stay in pristine condition no matter what. Rick had escorted Scott's remains home and then relocated to Cape Hudson right after the funeral. Late last summer, the former sheriff had retired for health reasons, and Rick had won a special election.

Rick and Scott had been the best of friends, and it seemed he had been standing guard over Scott and her ever since.

"I've seen the inside and know you have your hands full," Rick said.

"I don't suppose you have a flamethrower in that police car of yours. I'm half tempted to scorch it and then start fresh."

"Law enforcement frowns upon arson," Rick said with a straight face.

"I'll keep that in mind," Lucy said.

Megan envied their easy banter. Anytime she tried to talk to Rick, her thoughts and words twisted, and she felt like she had said something wrong.

As if sensing her, his gaze shifted to her. Megan's cheeks warmed as she stared at Rick.

She quickly flicked back her bangs and jabbed her thumb over her shoulder. "Show's about to start."

Her lighthearted reference to the renovation skidded right by him like a pebble on the water. "Megan, how did the trip into Norfolk go?" he asked.

It did not surprise her that he knew she'd had a prenatal appointment. Like Helen, he was protecting Scott's legacy.

"Great. Heartbeat is strong, and she's growing like a weed. Estimates put her at nine pounds at delivery."

"And your blood pressure?"

"Always normal," she said.

Lucy glanced up toward the clear, blue sky. "We've been waiting for warm weather and a dry day. Thankfully, it'll last until Friday."

"I thought there was no rain in sight for ten days," Rick countered.

"Not according to Arlene at the diner," Lucy said. "She swears we'll have rain by Saturday."

"Then I suppose we will," Rick said. "She's never wrong."

"Let's get going," Megan said.

Rick looked up at the house and appeared pensive. Upon his return to Cape Hudson, he had taken it upon himself to check in with Samuel on a regular basis. He had tried several times to convince Samuel to consider assisted living, but the old man had refused, saying he had all he needed on the first floor of his house. Rick was the sheriff by the time he found Samuel dead in his chair in the room they were now cleaning out. "House may look like a disaster to us, but Samuel knew where every item was. Ask him about a book, he could find it on the shelf. A receipt, he had it. The man's mind was sharp as a tack until the end."

"Good to know," Lucy said.

He took the bins from Lucy and lined them up side by side on the porch. As he set them out and studied the neat labels marked on the sides, he frowned. "Try not to let Megan overdo it. I know she works for you and the estate now, but go easy on her."

"Not my habit to slave-drive pregnant women," Lucy said.

"I'm standing right here," Megan said. "And capable of answering questions."

Rick pinned Megan with his gaze. "I don't trust you to throttle back when you're tired. You've always pushed yourself too hard."

Suddenly, she felt crabbier, if that were possible, and when she spoke, her irritability hummed through her words. "I'm doing fine. And thank you for your concern."

Unfazed, he shifted his attention back to the house. "Samuel didn't use the upstairs. He was never really comfortable in this house, so he spent all his time in the den or the kitchen. But as you've already seen, he liked to read, and there wasn't a book or a magazine he could bring himself to throw out."

After Samuel retired from the sea, he had become a bit of a recluse and had rarely been in town. Few people under seventy knew much about him.

"Did he ever speak about my mom?" Lucy asked.

Rick pulled in a breath, holding it as if he wished he had better news. "He never said a word about family. I asked him a few times about relatives, but he was always tight lipped. Once he grumbled that he liked being on his own, though I don't think he meant it."

"Did he talk about anything?" Lucy asked.

"Only way to get Samuel talking was to talk about the merchant marines." Rick dug the tip of his boot into the chipped paint on the porch floor and watched it flake away. The paint had been a short-term fix to cover rotting wood. "Sometimes the wounds are so deep it's best to leave them be. Trying to repair them only makes it worse."

"Perhaps, but we've got to try." Lucy looked up at the peeling siding and the shutters with the broken slats. "I'd like to think anything could be mended."

Rick looked inside the house toward the clutter. "Not everything, Lucy."

Megan suspected they weren't talking about Beth's relationship with her father, Samuel, any longer.

CHAPTER THREE

Diane Hedrick

Age 9

Friday, August 24, 1900
Cape Hudson, Virginia
Noon

Wreaths wrapped in black crepe and decorated with sprigs of seagrass hung from the teak front doors of Addie and Isaac Hedrick's small bayside cottage. The thick scent of lilies blended with warm salt air streaming in through the windows. The smell of pies baked by the local women of Cape Hudson lingered as the grandfather clock ticked.

Diane sat on the fourth step on the small staircase and watched as her oldest sister, Claire, opened the pocket doors and beckoned her forward. "Diane, come in here, will you? Have a look at Mama."

"I don't want to remember her that way," Diane said. "She promised we'd go into town next week."

Though Claire was only twelve, her frown mimicked their mother's. "Please."

Their mother had gone into labor with her seventh child yesterday, and after hours of screams, she had grown silent.

Diane slowly rose from the steps and smoothed the wrinkles from the brown gingham skirt normally reserved for Sundays. The heavy fabric itched her skin, and the high collar made it tough for her to breathe.

Floorboards squeaked under her feet as she entered the parlor. Choking back tears, she turned toward the coffin resting on the dining table. Desperate to see her mother again, she rushed up to the edge, only to halt at the sight before her.

Her mother had never been fussy about her appearance in life. Seemingly always pregnant, she'd filled her days with children, gardening, and running a household alone while her husband traveled the seas as a merchant marine. Diane's mama barely had time to sit and eat a meal, let alone comb her hair or press a blouse.

However, Claire had seen to it that, in death, their mother was outfitted in her favorite blue dress, her salt-and-pepper hair was arranged in a neat topknot, and her favorite scrimshaw broach—given to her by her husband on their wedding day—was pinned above her heart.

"Diane, the others have said goodbye to Mama," Claire said. "It's your turn now."

She looked at her siblings clustered to the side. Jemma was a year younger than Claire and she held their newest baby brother, Michael, who squawked as she rocked him softly. Next to her was her sister Sarah, who held the hands of their one- and two-year-old brothers, Joseph and Stanley. Tears glistened from the girls' eyes as the little boys huddled close, knowing something was wrong but too afraid to ask.

As Diane stood by the coffin, aware of the ticking clock that clicked in time with her drumming heart. Ticktock. Bang. Ticktock. Bang. She kept her gaze downcast on her fingers threaded so tightly her knuckles were white. Her mother was so still. She wanted so much to jostle her and demand she wake up.

Ticktock. Bang.

"Say goodbye," Claire whispered. "This is your last chance. After today, she's gone forever."

"Gone where?" Diane asked.

"She's with God now."

Diane studied her mother's still, pale face. Her hands were folded, left hand over right on her chest so that her plain wedding band caught the afternoon light streaming in a window. Her face possessed a peace and serenity Diane had never remembered seeing before. Claire had said Mama was dead, but how could she be dead when she had been laughing and eating an apple just two days ago?

Diane had always feared the dead. But she was not afraid of her mother. She did not look scary at all. Instead, she looked so peaceful that Diane thought for a brief second she was teasing and any moment would sit up and smile. She reached inside the casket and brushed a stray strand away from her mother's cool face.

"Please, wake up, Mama," she whispered.

Claire laid a hand on her shoulder.

Diane reached for her mother's fingers. They weren't warm and soft but cold and stiff. Whatever she was touching now was not her mother, and she drew her fingers back. Any notion of Mama being alive shattered into a thousand tiny pieces.

Diane took Claire's hand, grateful it was warm and smooth, and tightened her grip. "What are we going to do without Mama? Who will take care of us?"

"We have to leave Cape Hudson," Claire whispered.

"Where will we go?"

"Jemma and Sarah are going to live with cousins. I'm going with the Buchanan family, and you're going to live with the LeBlanc family. The boys are going to move in with the Jessup family."

"Why can't we stay in this house with Papa?" When she looked up, she realized Claire's eyes were red rimmed and her face was as ashen as when she had become sick with the measles last year.

Claire slowly drew in a breath as if it hurt. "Papa can't keep us. He returns to sea in two weeks."

"Why can't he stay with us?"

"He has to work," she said in a rush of frustration and sadness. "We have to work now."

Diane turned to her mother and jostled her shoulder. If her mother could just wake up, then they could all stay together as a family. "Mama, get up. I need you. Wake up!"

Tears welled in her eyes and streamed over her cheeks. "Mama, please."

Claire wrapped her arms around Diane's shoulders and pulled her close. "She's gone."

Diane began to cry, letting all the fear trapped inside her flood out. She prayed to God to bring her mother back, swearing she would do her chores and take care of her younger brothers. She made bargain after bargain. But her mother's eyes did not open. She did not draw in a breath. She did not promise that everything would be all right.

"Why did she leave us?" Diane gasped between sobs. "Why? I thought she loved us."

"She would have stayed if she could."

"She could have tried harder."

"She tried. She fought," Claire whispered.

Diane fisted handfuls of Claire's sleeves. "Can't we stay? Please?"

A sob caught in Claire's throat as she kissed Diane on the top of the head. The scent of lilies and beeswax wafted about her. "I want us to stay together."

"Do you mean that?"

"Yes."

"I don't want to leave, Claire. Promise me we'll be a family forever."

"No matter what, I'll be there for you."

Miss Diane Hedrick
Baltimore, Maryland
December 2, 1902

Dear Claire,

You were wrong. I still do not love the city. It smells. There are too many people. Mr. LeBlanc is nice, but he has an endless number of visitors that come at all times of the day and night. He is constantly in meetings, and it seems someone always wants to collect money from him.

Madame LeBlanc talks of returning to France. She says her late husband's cousin owns a castle on the coast of Normandy. She says he is very rich and is sure to welcome his family and young charge with open arms. I suppose this is why she insists I learn French.

Madame LeBlanc also has a nephew, Pierre, who is an odd sort. He is five years older than me but is as moody as an old man. He stares at me in an odd way, but as long as Mr. LeBlanc is in the house, Pierre leaves me be.

The LeBlancs are nothing like our friends in Cape Hudson. They do not work. They play cards, go to parties, and worry about what each in their group is doing.

I am doing as you say and keeping my thoughts to myself. "Cheery faces," as Mama used to say.

I fear the times will never be better. Mama is dead, and Papa has sent you away, along with Jemma, Sarah, the boys, and me. We will never be a family again. I am an orphan and *alone* in this world. Promises are like butterflies. Beautiful. Colorful. Easily crushed and broken.

Your Dearest Sister,
Diane

Miss Claire Hedrick
New York, New York
December 16, 1902

Dearest Diane,
I have knitted you this scarf in the way Mama taught me. I may have worked the needles and yarn, but I felt her hands guiding me. So consider this *our* Christmas present to you.

Madame LeBlanc tells me you are a diligent worker, but that you are very quiet. I almost wrote her back and questioned whether she had the right girl because the Diane I remember never stopped talking. The Buchanans will be sailing to Paris in the spring, and they mean to take me along with them so that I can attend to Miss Victoria. I wish you could come. I hear it is a city of lights, and the Eiffel Tower stands almost one thousand feet high. It is a sight to behold. Perhaps if Madame LeBlanc returns to France, our paths will cross.

Remember, the Buchanans recommended Madame LeBlanc. Being in her employ is sure to set you up for a better life. Mama wanted us to have more than Cape Hudson could offer, and you must not give up hope.

You and I will never be orphans. We have each other, the girls and boys, as well as Papa, who promised we would be home for Christmas next year. We are rich in each other. Don't ever forget that. Have a very merry Christmas.

Your Devoted Sister,
Claire

January 18, 1903

Dear Claire,

Mr. LeBlanc died two weeks ago. The funeral was a quiet affair with only Madame LeBlanc, Pierre, and me in attendance. Madame LeBlanc says we need to get ready to pack our belongings and leave Baltimore. She has written to the cousin in France asking him for shelter. I don't belong in France any more than I belong in Baltimore. Home seems so far away, now.

Your Dearest Sister,

Diane

CHAPTER FOUR

Megan

Monday, March 5, 2018
Cape Hudson, Virginia
11:00 a.m.

"I'd forgotten how bad it was." Rick's frown deepened as his gaze trailed over the piles of clutter. "This is going to take forever."

Raising her chin, Megan moved behind the desk and lowered herself into the worn leather chair. From this vantage point, the piles looked more like fortifications.

"It's a miracle you found him at all," Lucy said as she surveyed the room.

"He was sitting by the fireplace in his recliner," Rick said. "He sat there almost all the time toward the end, and at first, I thought he was sleeping."

"I don't see a television," Lucy said.

"He never had much use for one. He liked to read, but when his eyesight began to fail, he'd walk up to Winter Cottage and sit on the porch and stare out over the water. In the last few weeks, he didn't even do that. Whenever I stopped by, he was mumbling like he was having a conversation."

"With whom?" Megan asked.

"He never would say, and I didn't ask. I just assumed he was getting old. He asked me several times to find some of his old journals and read them to him."

Lucy followed the path to a chair by the fireplace. She cleared off the stacks of books, sat, and selected an old bound green journal. "It's dated 1939," she said as she thumbed through it. "What was so special about that year?"

Rick shrugged. "He was running supplies to the English. With the German U-boats patrolling, it was dangerous work. World War II had just broken out in Europe."

Megan fanned through a stack of unopened junk mail. "Lucy, designate a box for Samuel's journals and any personal papers you can find. I'll start tossing junk mail."

Rick's radio buzzed with a call from his dispatcher summoning him to a car accident north of town. He responded back with a 10-4. "I'm going to have to go. When does the moving crew arrive?"

"Tomorrow morning," Megan said. "I thought we could get ahead of them today and start prioritizing what to save and to toss. I think we'll be lucky to get his desk cleared."

Lucy was still flipping through the pages of the journal. "The man had terrible handwriting. Just like Beth."

"Do me a favor and save the heavy lifting. Hank and I will be back around six," Rick said.

"You don't have to come back," Megan said.

"We'll save the tough stuff for you." Lucy faced Rick. "I'm not going to deliver a baby because she can't slow down."

"She doesn't know when to quit," Rick said.

Megan rose. "And I'm still here."

Rick pointed a finger at her. "No heavy lifting."

She straightened. "I know my limits."

"So do I," Lucy said. "Don't worry, Rick. She points, I lift."

"You're my boss," Megan said. "I work for you."

"Yeah, well, I was raised by a woman who didn't put much stock in labels, so you're just going to have to deal with a more casual relationship."

Megan shook her head, already feeling like she was letting Lucy down. A year ago, she would have dived into this project and been able to knock out twelve- to fourteen-hour days.

"The Buchanans have their pride," Rick said. "She's going to try to work when you're not looking."

"I've noticed that," Lucy said. "But I suppose that's a good thing. Every ship needs a captain, and if I were in charge of this project, I'd be ordering that flamethrower right now." She held up her hand when he frowned. "I promise the fire won't get out of hand. I'll drag the garden hose around for good measure."

"No arson," he warned.

Lucy shrugged. "If you insist."

"I do."

"Now, last I remember, you have a fender bender to see to," Lucy said. "So skedaddle, Sheriff, so Megan and I can get to work. Once Natasha gets home from school, it's going to be bedlam."

"Do you want me to pick her up?" Rick asked.

"Thanks, Hank's bringing her."

Like a century-old tree, Hank Garrison and his family had deep roots in this community. When he had moved back last year, he'd staked his claim. Megan envied that sense of permanence; however, her trip to Cape Hudson, like all the ones she'd made as a kid, would be short-lived. Though she would be here about a year, eventually the winds would shift, and she'd move on.

Megan looked around the room, feeling overwhelmed and wishing a stiff breeze would blow her to a place where she fit. "Scurry on then. The sooner we dive into this, the sooner we'll be done."

"If you return at six and can't find us, send in a search party. We've no doubt been swallowed up by a mountain of magazines," Lucy said.

Rick glanced toward Megan, and again she felt an annoying heat rise up her body. "Will do."

"Thanks, Rick," Lucy said.

Megan looked up from a stack of papers. "Thank you, Rick."

"Anytime," he said. He left, and the front door closed.

"Whatever history is in this room doesn't compare with whatever was between you two," Lucy said.

Megan shook her head. "It's not what you think."

Lucy grabbed a box and set it beside the desk. "Maybe not for you."

"He was Scott's best friend. I was engaged to Scott. That's all we have in the way of a connection."

Megan lifted a scrimshaw paperweight from the desk. Engraved in the yellowed ivory was a bluebird, its wings extended as if caught in a gust of wind. The bird mirrored a tattoo on Lucy's wrist. Lucy had said her mother sported a similar tattoo.

Megan placed the paperweight in the *Keep* box. She touched a stack of papers on the desk. "The desk alone is going to take days."

Lucy lifted a pile of yellowed newspapers. "My mother saved a lot of stuff that didn't make any sense to me. When I cleaned out her apartment after she died, it took me days."

"There's a lot of history in this room. At least let us get through this desk without a dumpster. This was the heart of your grandfather's life, and if there is something he'd have wanted you to have, it would be here."

"That's what I'm afraid of."

"Why are you afraid?" Megan asked.

"My mother left this house and this town when she was eighteen and pregnant. There had to be a very good reason."

"I thought that had to do with your birth father."

43

Lucy shook her head. "This town rallies around its own, and Beth was one of them. Samuel was her father. He should have protected her."

"I'll be very careful as I go through all this. If there is anything to be discovered, I'll find it."

Megan leafed through a magazine dating back to March 1971. A receipt fell out, and she carefully inspected it before placing it to the side.

Lucy set the *Trash* box by Megan. "I didn't mean for this to be an archeology dig, Megan. We don't have the time to scrutinize every receipt."

"It's history."

Lucy glanced at it. "That receipt is for groceries."

"From 1971. Have you looked at these prices?"

Lucy picked up the receipt and tossed it in the *Trash* box and then took the next magazine and quickly thumbed through it before tossing it. "I'll give you until four, and then I'm getting my gasoline can and match."

Megan removed the magazine and put it in the *Donate* box. "The library will want that."

"We can't save it all."

"But we can't have a scorched-earth policy either." She yanked open a side drawer and found it was crammed with stuff.

Lucy pulled the drawer out the remainder of the way and carried it to the front porch.

"What are you doing?"

"Sorting faster."

Megan followed Lucy, stepping outside to see her dump the packed drawer onto the porch deck and begin to sort. Paper clips, rubber-band balls, gum, glue, and old batteries.

"It's all trash." Lucy held up a handful of dried ink pens as proof.

"I see a glimmer of silver," Megan said. "Is that an ink pen?"

Lucy quickly studied the pen and then tossed it into the *Keep* box. "We'll look at it later. On to the next drawer."

Megan had started to reexamine what had been tossed away when Lucy headed back inside. Fearing she'd miss something, she hurried after Lucy.

Lucy worked the drawer back into the desk. "I'm ready for the next."

"It's not possible to sort this fast," Megan said.

"My grandfather and my mother were hoarders, Megan. Just because something is saved, or old for that matter, doesn't mean it's valuable. I'm sure George Washington had a trash pit."

"Sacrilege."

"Said the would-be hoarder to the sane woman." She pulled out the second drawer. "I shall return."

"Let me see what's in the *Trash* box."

"No. Keep thumbing through the magazines."

"Oh, no, I'm making sure you don't toss anything valuable," Megan said, following her back outside.

The second drawer was much like the first. More office supplies than any human man would ever use, empty ketchup packets from who knew where, bundles of crackers, and two cans of chicken soup that had expired in the eighties.

"Jesus, Samuel, did you think world famine was imminent?" Lucy asked.

She returned the drawer to the desk and reached for the third. Deeper than the top two, it was heavier and tougher to move. Outside, she dropped the drawer, and it landed with a hard thump.

"Careful," Megan said.

"Feels like he stored bricks in there."

On the top were letters to Samuel from the merchant marines. There were certificates along with a blue box that contained a gold watch, which caught the sunlight and shone as if it had been waiting to do that for a long time.

Megan turned the watch over. Its inscription read, SAMUEL JACKSON JESSUP. 1931–1981. FAITH, DUTY, AND HONOR. The sea had been his life for fifty years. Fifty years. She removed her glove and held the smooth, pristine gold in her palm. It retained its polish and looked as if it had just been removed from its original packaging. She doubted Samuel had even touched it. She carefully placed the watch in the empty *Keep* box.

Megan sat on the top step and then gently patted the floor of the porch. "I think this drawer might be interesting."

Lucy sat beside her and lifted the watch from the box. "This is stunning."

"Samuel's retirement watch." Megan traced the face. "It was shoved in the drawer."

"He probably hated receiving it. It marked the end for him."

"He lived another thirty-six years."

Lucy shook her head. "Can you imagine how awful that would have been for him? All those years on the sea and to be landlocked in this house." Claire, who had been trying to see to his welfare, had unwittingly imprisoned him by giving him Winter Cottage. "Why would he accept the responsibility?"

"Maybe because he wanted your mother and you to have it."

Lucy was silent for a moment. "Maybe."

Megan shifted through odd utility bills that covered the electric and water, which she tossed in the trash box. Next were more retirement documents and social security papers. She found five gold coins in a wooden box. "Now that's a nice find. Five ounces. That's at least five grand. What are you going to buy for yourself as a treat?"

The pieces appeared to be heavy in Lucy's hand as she turned them over before she tucked them in her pocket. "Braces for Natasha."

"Seriously?"

"The dentist recommended we have her teeth straightened, plus crooked teeth really bother her. The kid really wants to fit in." Lucy sighed as if her sister's insecurities bothered her more than the crooked teeth. "Hank assures me the contents of this house are mine to sell."

"And you are just going to sell your family history?" Megan asked.

"My little sister is very smart, and she's going to college. I'll sell every stick of furniture in this house if that's what it takes to get Natasha educated. One day this place will make money on its own, but I can't bank on turning a profit within five years and being able to afford college tuition."

"Natasha is smart. She might get a scholarship."

"She may, but again, I can't count on that. I'm not taking a chance."

"Winter Cottage, this house, and eventually the lighthouse are going to be showpieces," Megan said.

"I'm counting on it and the unlimited potential of the house and the vineyards."

"For your event business?" Megan asked.

"You bet. Once you've done your historical-restoration thing, the cottage will be a perfect wedding and event venue." Lucy's mind was always racing toward the future. "I've been on a few wedding-venue sites. You would be amazed what they can charge."

"If you build it, they will wed?" Megan asked, grinning.

"Yes. We could even do a historical angle. I have the wedding pictures from George and Julia, and I have Claire's wedding portrait and her gown. I'm telling you, this could be a good gig."

"Claire was an entrepreneur herself. With all her monies in a trust for her son, she was forced to make a living sewing and selling booze."

"Claire was a bootlegger?" Lucy asked.

"Apparently, she had quite the network in Maryland and Washington, DC. She kept many of the local establishments in business."

"How did she get the booze?"

"I don't know. All I know is she sold a distilled liqueur called Calvados as well as white sparkling wines. Her stash was never found."

"I tended enough bar to know that Calvados is French."

"From the Normandy region of France. That's why she was so popular. She had the good stuff."

"In all the videos my mother made with Claire, she looked so formal and traditional," Lucy said.

"I think she did what she had to do to keep her family together and to hang on to Winter Cottage." Megan dropped her gaze to a box in the drawer. "I would have done the same. Winter Cottage is a magnificent property."

"Maybe Claire did us both a favor. The house is an anchor for us both."

Megan opened the box and carefully removed a stack of letters. Thick black ink scrolled into an elegant handwriting that adorned each envelope.

"What's that?" Lucy asked.

"Letters to Claire Hedrick Buchanan."

"*Our* Claire?" Lucy asked.

"Yes." Whoever had written Claire had been prolific. "They appear to all be from *DH*. Claire did have a sister, Diane. Diane Hedrick. *DH*."

"It makes sense that the sisters would correspond. But why did Samuel Jessup end up with them?"

"No idea." The envelopes felt heavy in her hand. Given her druthers, Megan would have slipped away to a quiet room and read through each and every one of them now. But they would have to wait.

Megan reached in the back of the drawer and pulled out stacks of unused stationery with the initials *SJ* at the top. "Trash?"

Lucy accepted the stack. "I don't write letters, but Natasha has a thing for paper and nice pens. She'll use it all."

Megan lifted a burgundy velvet bag with a gold cord tied into a tight knot. She dusted it off and started on the knot, which would not give.

"Wait, I have four thousand paper clips in the trash box." Lucy dug one out, unfolded it, and handed it to Megan.

Megan wedged the metal paper clip between the silken strands and gently loosened the cords. "Important not to move too quickly."

Lucy flexed her fingers and reached for the bag. "I don't think you could move any slower."

Megan moved the bag out of reach. "Patience, grasshopper. The fabric is old and can tear."

Ignoring Lucy's raised brow, she coaxed the bag open. Setting the paper clip aside, she pulled out three spinning tops fashioned out of silver and encrusted with rubies. Each side was marked with a faded Hebrew letter. "Dreidels?"

"Were the Jessups Jewish?" Lucy asked.

"No." She lined each up carefully on the porch. "They were Methodist, as were the Buchanans and Hedricks."

"Samuel traveled the world and has a house full of memorabilia to prove it. Stands to reason he'd have something like this."

"These are very old and would have been prized in a family," Megan said. "Not the average thing someone would give a merchant marine."

She fished deeper in the bag and removed a wooden box. She opened the brass clip and found a finely crafted heart shaped from a piece of polished wood nestled in the velvet-lined interior. The piece was encrusted with red and clear glass stones that encircled a hollowed-out center. She flipped it over, and engraved on the back was *Paris, France*.

"It's a planchette," Megan said. "The word means *little plank*."

"Looks like the playing piece for a Ouija board," Lucy said.

"That's exactly what it is. Funny, I just bought a Ouija board set today at an antique store. I thought Natasha might get a kick out of a vintage game."

"We used to set up several Ouija boards and tarot cards in the bar at Halloween. It was amazing how freaked out both drunks and sober people got when a piece of wood levitated across a board and answered a question with a yes or no. If only I had a nickel for all the people asking if they'd find love or money."

"They are two of the greatest motivators of all time." She studied the pieces, wondering how two very different games had come to be together.

Lucy took the planchette from Megan and studied it. "You spend your life digging into the lives of dead people. I'd think you'd be interested in talking to a few."

"I study whatever they left behind."

"So you're not interested in talking to them directly?" Lucy asked.

"Are you?"

"Sure, why not?" Lucy held up the planchette to the sun, peering through the circular opening. "Talking to the dead would clear up a lot of mysteries in my life. Like why I have this house and Winter Cottage."

"Because Claire delivered Samuel, and she always had a soft spot for him. Perhaps she was also getting a bit of revenge against her late father-in-law. He didn't approve of his son having a child with her and would have been furious if he'd known his daughter had a child with a local waterman."

Lucy shook her head, looking up at the house that was as foreign to her as her mother and grandfather had been. "Dreidels and a planchette. What's it like to come from a normal family?"

Megan skimmed her fingers inside the drawer but found only dust. "You're asking me?"

"The Buchanans are about as conventional as they get."

"Yes, they are. Unfortunately, I am not."

"That sounds ominous."

"Not really. It's just that Mom would have liked me to be popular and be the girl that dated the football player. I wasn't interested. I was a bookworm more interested in meandering through historic homes."

"Aren't you the rebel?"

"What can I say? I walk on the wild side."

Lucy handed her the planchette. "Are your parents back in the country yet?"

Megan shook her head as she carefully placed the device back in the bag. "Not for several weeks. Mom is tracking me via my phone."

Lucy scratched her head as she shook it. "Nice."

"They're worried. Not only did I pass up law school for a PhD in history, but I also broke up with their idea of a dream guy. I'm sure they think I've lost my mind. And they now have a baby to worry about."

"You're stable," Lucy said. "God knows you've read enough baby books. I think you're pretty grounded and will make a great mom."

Megan brushed her bangs back. All the research in the world wasn't a guarantee that she would get it right with the kid. "I hope so. The future scares the hell out of me."

CHAPTER FIVE

Megan

Monday, March 5, 2018
Cape Hudson, Virginia
3:00 p.m.

Megan and Lucy spent the entire afternoon working on Samuel's desk. While Lucy cleared the stacks of magazines and books and hauled them out to the growing *Donate* bin, Megan dug through the drawers. It was amazing how a man could accumulate junk that spanned the globe and the better part of the last century. The *Keep* gems she discovered were a collection of pens encased in carved ivory, a small dented metal box filled with silver dollars that dated back to the 1930s, and several compasses engraved in gold. At the rate they were going, Lucy was going to be able to buy braces for Natasha and send her to a great school.

The thunder of footsteps had them both looking up to see Natasha standing in the doorway. Her dark, curly hair was pulled up into a ponytail, and her naturally mocha skin glowed from the sun she'd soaked up during soccer practice. She and Lucy were as different as night and day, but they both shared a grin that had to have come from the same father.

The girl wore green athletic shorts, a white shirt with the name KINCAID on the back, and black soccer cleats. Since Lucy had taken formal custody of her half sister, the girl's grades had improved, and she'd joined a sports team for the first time. The father they shared could be volatile, and though he had granted custody to Lucy in a clearheaded moment, there were no guarantees he would not challenge her when he was released from prison. Lucy was pressing the courts for a final adoption decree.

Natasha dropped her red backpack on the floor next to a pile of untouched magazines. "Did you find any buried treasure?"

"Found some awesome paper and pens," Megan said.

Natasha scooted along the single-access path across the room to the freshly cleared desktop. Immediately, she reached for the scrimshaw inlaid with silver. She pulled the top off and studied the pen's dry nib. "Does it work?"

"Once we fill it with ink, then it'll work," Megan said.

"You have to fill it?" Natasha asked as she shook it and held it up to the light.

"That's how they did it back in the day."

"Seems like a lot of work," Natasha said.

"I suppose they were used to it," Megan said.

Steadier footsteps mingled with the scratch of dog paws from the hallway, and Lucy straightened in time to see Hank Garrison appear. Dolly, having decided months ago Hank was the new leader of their patchwork gang, was at his side. Her tail was wagging.

Hank was a tall man with broad shoulders and a bearing that suggested a soul far older than his thirty-one years. Sunglasses set atop short, dark hair; dusty, faded jeans; and scuffed work boots suggested he'd left the field to pick Natasha up from practice. When Megan's cousin had moved back to Cape Hudson last year, he had taken the nearly orphaned girl under his wing, and though Lucy had legal custody, he continued to play an active role in Natasha's life. Now that

Lucy and Hank were dating, the kid had a stability she'd never had in her life.

Lucy shifted a stack of books in her arms as she walked up to Hank and kissed him. Megan watched as each leaned slightly toward the other. There was not only heat between them but also a strong connection.

Megan had loved Scott, and she'd thought they were going to have a perfect life. She had imagined that one day, they would move back to Cape Hudson and burrow deep roots into the sandy soil. She realized now, if they had married, they could very well have ended up like Samuel and his wife. Scott would have been traveling constantly, while she would have remained here alone to raise the baby.

"Looks like you've made some progress," Hank said.

"It's been slow going," Lucy said. "As tempted as I was to toss all this, Megan is making sure we treat it as an archeological dig."

"Megan treasures history," Hank said.

"That's exactly what it is," Megan said.

The sound of a car door shutting drew Megan's attention out the window to Rick's black pickup truck. He had changed into jeans and an old T-shirt. He opened the back door and rummaged out a six-pack of colas and a few pizzas. Despite herself, her stomach grumbled, and for the first time in a few days, she actually felt hungry. "Looks like Rick brought food."

"Thank God," Natasha said. "I'm starving to death."

"You're always starving to death," Lucy said, smiling.

"Are you saying I'm getting fat?" Natasha asked.

Lucy held up her hands. "Not at all."

"Then why did you say I'm always hungry?" Natasha challenged.

"Because you are. There's nothing wrong with that. Simply stating a fact," Lucy said.

Natasha rolled her eyes. "Let's eat on the porch. The air's a little fresher out there."

"Sounds like a plan," Lucy said as the girl ran out of the room.

Megan chuckled as the girl stomped off. "I drove my mom a little crazy when I was that age."

Lucy ran her fingers through her hair. "Tell me it didn't last long."

Megan shrugged. "You'll have to ask her. But I'd say right now I'm hitting an eleven on her stress meter."

Lucy rolled her head from side to side. "The kid challenges me at every corner."

"She's almost thirteen. It's kind of expected."

"But I'm not her mother."

"Technically, no. But in every other sense of the word, yes."

"I started off being the cool, hip older sister."

"She needs a mom."

"Until I tell her to pick up her dirty laundry, and then she reminds me that I'm not the boss of her."

Megan laughed. "She adores you. She gets angry at you because she feels safe enough to test you."

"Save me," Lucy groaned.

Laughing, Megan stepped out into the sun to watch Dolly race toward Rick, her nose sniffing the pizzas. Megan closed her eyes and tipped her face toward the warmth. She drew in a deep breath and pressed her fingers into her lower back.

Without a word Rick pulled out a chair for her and then flipped open several pizza boxes. He'd also set out paper plates, the sodas, and a roll of paper towels.

Natasha went directly for the pepperoni with onions and pulled several slices onto her plate. "Rick, how did you know I was starving?"

A slight grin softened an otherwise stern face. "I'm psychic."

Natasha bit off the tip of her first slice as she flopped into one of the four wrought iron chairs. "Why'd you get ginger ale? Grape soda goes the best with pizza."

"Who says?" Rick asked.

"I do," Natasha countered. The attitude in her tone had him raising a brow, and she immediately shrugged. "But I like ginger ale."

"Good," he said.

Rick had trained hundreds of marines, and though he had a reputation for being fair, Scott had said he was one of the toughest instructors in the corps. If Natasha thought she was going to get a rise out of Rick, she'd have to try a lot harder.

Rick nodded for Megan to sit, and, too tired to argue, she took a seat and reached for a slice. When she took a bite, she was tempted to close her eyes and moan. She wasn't sure if she'd ever tasted anything so good.

He popped open a ginger ale and set it in front of her.

Lucy took a seat beside Natasha and grabbed a slice. "How does the pizza taste, kiddo?"

Natasha shrugged. "Okay."

"Did you thank Rick?" Lucy asked.

Natasha stared at her as if the answer was obvious, but Lucy kept staring back at her. Finally, Natasha sighed. "Thank you for the pizza, Rick."

"You're welcome," he said.

Megan drank from the can and discovered she was really thirsty. She nearly drained the entire can.

Rick grabbed a soda and leaned against the railing. "Find anything interesting today?"

Megan reached for a paper towel and wiped her fingers. "Pens, coins, dreidels, and an old planchette." Responding to Natasha's curious stare, she added, "The triangular piece to a Ouija board."

"Those are kind of spooky," Natasha said. "Could we do it sometime?"

"Funny you should say that. I bought an old set of games today," Megan said. "I was thinking about your party. When do you want to have it?"

"Does Saturday work?" Natasha said.

"Works for me," Lucy said.

"I thought vintage games would be fun. One game is a Ouija board," Megan said.

"That sounds cool," Natasha said.

Lucy, who had had the same idea shot down by Natasha a week ago, arched a brow but stayed silent.

"Who are you going to invite?" Megan asked.

Natasha shrugged in a way that telegraphed worry more than it did indifference. "I dunno. There are some girls at school, but I don't know if they'll come."

"Game night with Mystery Date and magic?" Megan asked. "They won't say no."

"How do you know?" The girl suddenly sounded very unsure.

"Because you're great," Lucy said. "And it'll be fun."

"You have to say that," Natasha said.

Hank grabbed two slices of pizza and kissed Lucy. "Everyone wants to see Winter Cottage. Have the party there in the parlor. You could even do a sleepover."

Natasha chewed her bottom lip. "Maybe."

"I could draw up invitations," Lucy said. "A very Spook-tacular Party."

"It's not Halloween," Natasha said.

"All the more reason to have it," Rick offered. "I have fireworks left over from July 4. We could set them off over the water."

"That would be kind of cool." The girl's tone had softened, and interest now hummed under the words.

"Anybody can drive into Norfolk and go out to dinner. But not anybody can have a haunted sleepover," Megan said. "I could read fortunes."

Natasha nibbled her pizza. "Maybe we could also grill out."

Hank nudged Natasha gently on the shoulder. "I'm a grill master. So is Rick. We're at your service."

"That could be cool."

"It will be cool," Rick said.

Hank scooped up another slice of pizza. "Now I have to go back to the winery. Lucy, just tell me when and where."

"I can do that," Lucy said.

Hank kissed her on the forehead. "See you later?"

She smiled. "Yes."

Hank tugged Natasha's ponytail. "Homework before television."

"Yeah, I know."

"Rick, that stonemason friend of yours called me about a job," Hank said. "He's coming by in a few weeks. He's on the ball."

"He's a straight shooter," Rick said. "You won't be disappointed."

When Hank was out of earshot, Natasha handed Dolly a piece of pizza. "Ouija's kind of cool. What should we ask it?"

Megan listened as Lucy and Natasha chatted about the game and who they could potentially reach out to on the other side. There were also negotiations about homework and walking Dolly.

She marveled at Lucy's patience and how, at age thirty, she had effortlessly slipped into mothering a moody preteen girl who was now testing her at every turn.

"So, what are you going to name the baby?" Natasha asked.

"Herminie Periwinkle," Megan said with a straight face.

Natasha's eyes widened, and then her mouth stretched into a smile. "That name's going to be heavy lifting when she's in middle school."

They'd been playing this game for the last couple of weeks, and Megan's name choices were getting more outlandish. In truth, she had no idea what she was going to name the child.

"What about Princess Fairy Dust?" Natasha asked.

"Good choice," Megan said. "I'll add it to the list."

"Alicia Stardust," Lucy said.

"Another sage choice. But remember, girls, we can't name her until we meet her," Megan said.

"Megan," Rick said, "I made an official call to the Crawford house yesterday."

"Everything all right with Herman?" Lucy asked.

"He's fine. He has a boat for sale, and I went to look at it."

"You going to buy the boat?" Natasha asked.

"Nope. Too expensive. Anyway, Herman said he has pieces of furniture that once belonged to Winter Cottage. He said he'd be willing to show them to you. Apparently, he contacted an antique dealer named Duncan, who said you'd be interested." He dug a neatly folded piece of paper from his pocket and handed it to her.

"That would be great," Megan said. "Did he say what kind of pieces he had?" Rick's handwriting was bold, neat, and precise, conjuring images of self-confidence and direction.

"He said something about a table and chairs," Rick said.

"What kind of table?"

Rick shook his head. "I have no idea. I thought I would leave that to the two of you."

Rick was a details man, and for him not to know meant he'd been rushed or focused on something more important. "That's great. Thank you. I'll call him today."

"He did say he's leaving for a vacation tomorrow, so if you want to get over there today or tomorrow morning, that would be the time."

Megan never said no to historical artifacts, especially when they related to Winter Cottage. She appreciated that the universe was sending her so much abundance, but juggling it all was turning into a challenge. "Let me call him right now."

She dialed the number on the paper, and as the phone rang, she pushed to her feet and walked away from the group. The phone rang once, twice, and it kept ringing. She was on the verge of hanging up when she heard a rushed, "Yep, what do you want?" A television blared a game show in the background.

She tucked a thick strand of hair behind her ear. "Mr. Crawford, this is Megan Buchanan. Sheriff Markham said you might have furniture for Winter Cottage?"

"Who said what?" Crawford yelled as a dog started barking in the background.

"I hear you have furniture," Megan said. "For Winter Cottage."

"Winter Cottage? Yeah, I have a card table and four chairs. But I'm leaving at first light. Come and get it now or wait until December."

She checked her watch. The Crawford place was up Route 13, about fifteen or twenty minutes from here. It would be easy enough to assess the pieces and decide if she needed them. Getting them loaded and transported was another matter. "Can I come by now?"

"Yeah, sure."

"Okay. See you soon."

When she ended the call and turned back to the group, Lucy and Natasha were inspecting the planchette, but Rick was moving in her direction. "How about I ride over there with you and help?"

"Aren't you on duty?" Megan said.

"I'm always on duty. I can just as easily respond from the Crawford place as here."

"Aren't you supposed to be getting a deputy soon?"

"Town council has to approve it. And they don't always move fast."

Megan was tempted to refuse Rick. He'd helped her so much since she'd moved back to Cape Hudson, and if she wasn't careful, she'd end up relying on the guy. And that was destined not to end well when she and the baby moved on to the next job.

As if he saw the wheels moving in her head, he asked, "What's the downside of me helping?"

"None, I suppose. Sure, let me tell Lucy," she said.

"Do you want to finish your pizza?"

"I'm stuffed."

"You barely ate." Hints of censure hovered around the words.

Rick and her mother were on the same page. Her mother was looking out for her via satellite, and no doubt she had spoken to Rick.

Scott had often said that loyalty ran deep in Rick, and as soon as Rick had learned she was pregnant with Scott's baby, whatever loyalty he'd had for his old friend extended to his child.

Megan felt a pang of irritation, not liking the idea that she was some kind of obligation to him. "Let me get my purse," she said.

She explained to Lucy what was going on and within minutes had tossed her purse in the front seat of Rick's vehicle. She hiked her leg, grabbed hold of the open door, and, as she did with her own truck, counted to three as she lifted her round, awkward belly.

A steadying hand took hold of her arm and with little effort gave her the boost she needed to scoot onto the seat. It had been so long since a man had touched her, and the feel of his calloused hand on her bare skin sent unwelcome waves of desire through her body. She tried not to inhale his scent or wonder if his chest was as hard as it appeared. She scooted away, blaming all sexual desire on hormones.

A slight smile on Rick's face said more than words ever could. He, of course, was a man of the world and knew when a woman wanted him. Thankfully, he was too much of a gentleman to say so. He reached for the seat belt, handed it to her, and when she clicked it over her belly, he closed the door and walked around the front of the car, tossing his keys casually in his hands.

As he slid behind the wheel and started the engine, her gaze was drawn to his rope bracelet, which could be unraveled and used in an emergency. The faded-green color reminded her he had been wearing the bracelet since the first time she'd met him three years earlier.

She had been at a bar at Chic's Beach just outside Norfolk, overlooking the Chesapeake Bay from the mainland side. It had been girls' night, and drinks were half-price. The plan was for her brother to meet up with them so she could introduce him to her friends. Deacon had brought along Scott and Rick. Megan had been attracted to Rick, and she sensed he was also interested.

After a couple of drinks, the conversation had turned to politics, and it became very clear quickly that the two didn't agree on much. Not really a stretch if you considered her peasant top and braids and his marine haircut and straight-backed posture. She couldn't remember exactly what they had been arguing about, but the conversation was basically the third rail of whatever budding desire they had. He had made a crack about her getting a real job, and it was all downhill from there. Scott, always quick with a smile, had worked his way into the conversation and grabbed her attention. Whatever spark she had shared with Rick had been completely doused.

April 1, 1939
From the Journal of Samuel Jessup

SS *Mayhew* cut away from the convoy two days ago and shifted direction toward the harbor of Le Havre, France, three days away. We spotted a U-boat two days ago on radar, and my captain ordered me to drop depth charges. The underwater explosions detonated the U-boat's own arsenal, and when the seas calmed, the blip on the radar was gone. We apparently got her. We aren't at war, and some of my men think I overreacted, but I've heard tales of the U-boats and how fast they can sink a ship.

The Germans are again moving to expand their borders. I've got bets with a few of the men that the Krauts bust through the Maginot Line by next year. The French say it's impenetrable, but that kind of talk reminds me of all the chirping about the unsinkable ships that are now at the bottom of the ocean.

I expect the waters to grow more dangerous as we get closer to the coast of Africa. I'm not happy about this side trip, but someone far above my rank has ordered that we pick up Edward Garrison and his wife, Victoria. Like many rich people, they are clearing out of Europe and Africa ahead of the Germans. Once we get them on board, we are committed to make a call in the Port of Le Havre, and then it's back to the US. God bless America is all I got to say.

CHAPTER SIX

Megan

Monday, March 5, 2018
Cape Hudson, Virginia
4:00 p.m.

As Rick backed out of Spring House's driveway and onto the main road, his radio squawked. It was his dispatcher.

"Sheriff, Buddy Trice wants to know if you remember his court date. He said you were going to call the magistrate for him."

"Tell him it's May 18. He's to be in the county courthouse by 9:00 a.m. sharp."

"I'll pass it on."

"Ten-four."

"When did you start calling the magistrate for people you've arrested?" Megan asked.

"I don't make a habit of it. But Buddy has a hard time remembering. That's the third time he's asked, and he'll ask me at least a half dozen more times in the next few weeks."

Since moving to Cape Hudson in January, she had gotten to know all the players in the community. Buddy, she had learned at Arlene's diner, had been in a car accident a few years earlier. Since then, he hadn't been good about managing his alcohol or his time. The local bars knew to cut him off after two drinks, but occasionally he got it in his head to roam from bar to bar, buying up two drinks at each place along the way. Rick had arrested him for being drunk in public as he was coming out of the Rusty Nail in late February. He'd done it for Buddy's own good so the man would not do anything stupid.

Rick eased back in his seat, resting his hand on the steering wheel. That was Rick. So self-contained and together. Scott had told her that Rick had wanted to be a marine since he was knee high, and once he set his course, he was locked in. Now he had shifted his sights to Cape Hudson and would no doubt care for it as he had his men. He had met more people in the area in the last year than she had met in a lifetime of summer visits. He made lifelong relationships, whereas she saw them all as temporary.

"How do you like living in Winter Cottage?" he asked.

"It's been great. Nice not to make the trip in from Norfolk three times a week. Though a steady supply of hot water would be appreciated."

"You still delivering pies?" he asked.

"I have one last delivery in Norfolk on Friday. The pies are for a wedding rehearsal dinner. Apparently, the groom hates cake and wants pie. As soon as I fill that order, I'm suspending the business until after the baby is born."

"Why even pick the business up again? I would bet a month's salary Lucy is paying you well, and she'll keep you busy for at least the next year."

"She is paying me well."

"Then why even keep the catering business?"

"Because renovations are not a forever job. And I've got a nice online catering presence now, and it would be a shame to give it up. It's always smart to hedge your bets and have a fallback."

"You were juggling two jobs, or was it three, when we met at Chic's Beach?"

She was surprised he'd remembered. "Four. I suppose I'm the classic jack-of-all-trades and master of none."

"And your folks are due back in town soon."

"By mid-April."

He was silent for a moment, his jaw tightening as it had the night they'd dived into politics. "Helen called me."

Megan plucked at a thread on her blouse. "She's also called my mother."

"She wants to see you," he said.

The last time she had seen Helen, the older woman's eyes had been raw with anger. "She emphatically stated my baby wasn't Scott's and then recently asked my mother the same thing."

He frowned, tapping his index finger on the steering wheel. "She knows the baby is Scott's."

"Then why the theatrics?" She could feel her anger stirring.

"She's afraid. She's lost her husband and now her son. She's afraid of loving a baby that she could also lose."

"I wouldn't do that to her."

"Deep down, she knows that. But fear and pain are a powerful thing."

"She has never struck me as afraid."

"She's terrified."

Helen had been upbeat and smiling when she was around Megan and Scott. When she spoke about her late husband, she always did so with such tender affection. Helen had never let on about her suffering, and Megan had never looked beyond the smiles.

"I don't play games," Megan said. "I'm willing to let her be in this baby's life if she behaves."

"I know that."

He slowed his truck and pulled into a small gravel driveway. The tires rolled and crunched over the stones as the vehicle approached a one-story brick ranch house. Several flowering dogwood trees surrounded the house, along with clusters of weather-beaten crab pots beside two overturned green rowboats.

Mr. Crawford had retired from the Federal Reserve and moved back to Cape Hudson full time two years earlier. He had maintained property here all his life and fished, caught eels, and harvested oysters when he could. He now considered himself a true waterman, and thanks to a generous retirement plan, he wasn't beholden to the harvests or weather.

Parked in the driveway was a large truck attached to a trailer sporting a twenty-seven-foot boat. The bed of the truck was loaded with coolers, fishing rods, and nets, suggesting Mr. Crawford was in search of a new adventure.

"Where's he going fishing this time?" Megan asked.

Rick put the car in park. "The gulf coast of Texas. When I came out to see the boat I mentioned the renovation on Winter Cottage had begun. That reminded him of the furniture he had in storage. He thinks the piece he has is from Winter Cottage." He opened his door and came around the front of the car.

She grabbed her purse and reached for her door, only to have Rick open it and extend a hand. If she thought she could slide out of the seat and balance her big belly with some dignity, she might have refused his help. But with her center of balance totally skewed, she opted to accept rather than risk missing a step and falling.

"I am a beached whale," she said.

"You are not."

She cocked a brow. "You are a polite gentleman, Rick."

He closed the door behind her. "I'm being honest. You have a glow. Pregnancy suits you."

"That glow is from nausea, and if you think my Michelin Man figure is attractive, then you have been in Cape Hudson too long and had better visit the mainland soon."

He chuckled as she walked up to the front porch and rang the bell. A dog barked, and seconds later footsteps followed.

Mr. Crawford was in his late sixties and had a tall, wiry body and thinning gray hair. At his ankles was a black miniature dachshund with gray whiskers.

"I'm Megan Buchanan." She shook his hand.

The dog barked as it wagged its tail and sniffed her feet. She would have leaned over and petted him, but her body wasn't so flexible these days.

"Don't mind Shorty. He talks like that to everyone."

"No worries," she said. "I'd pet him if I could reach him."

He took one look at her belly and shook his head. Just like she knew his story and Buddy's and everyone else's in town, they knew hers. "Come on in. I'll show you what I have."

"Great." With Rick trailing behind, she followed the old man into the dimly lit house. They walked past a small living room with a wide-screen television broadcasting a game show toward the back room off the kitchen. "I was cleaning out my mother's storage unit a few weeks ago after she passed. The woman saved everything, and my brother and I didn't realize she even had the unit until the annual charge hit her credit card."

"It's been a while since your mother moved back to Norfolk," she said.

"About fifteen years ago, if you can believe it. She wanted to be closer to my sister. It took my brother and me the better part of a weekend to get that twenty-by-twenty space sorted out." He pushed open a side door that led to the garage.

"Was the storage shed climate controlled?" Megan asked. She'd seen too many lovely heirlooms destroyed by mold, heat, or water.

"It was. She paid a pretty penny for it, but seeing as the furniture was in such good shape, I suppose it was worth it."

"And you have how many pieces?"

"Just a few. My brother and sister took most of it. I didn't want more clutter. As far as I'm concerned, if it doesn't have to do with fishing, then it's not important."

He crossed to a worn cloth tarp covered with dried red, blue, and black paint splatters. Carefully, he pulled it free, revealing a late-nineteenth-century game table made of walnut and four matching chairs. Resting on a single pedestal base was a round tabletop inlaid with a checkerboard or chessboard. Though dusty, there were few scratches on the surface, and the patina was excellent.

Megan skimmed her fingertips over the smooth wood. "It's French, circa 1880 or 1890. It would have been the type of furniture that belonged to Julia or Elizabeth Buchanan." Both of her great-great-grandfather George's wives had loved all things French. Each had visited the country as often as she could.

Julia had come from money, and she had given George his children, Robert and Victoria. But shortly after her daughter's birth, Julia had lost interest in her husband's constant talk of hunting. She'd also tired of the responsibilities of children and managing a household. When she moved abroad for an extended stay, George met Elizabeth. A former actress and a widow, she shared George's love of hunting, and the two quickly hit it off. For years, the two lived as a couple, and when Julia finally passed, they married.

George and Elizabeth had been inseparable until their deaths in a motor accident in 1920. By then, Robert Buchanan, his father's sole male heir, was dead, and his younger sister, Victoria, though married, was still childless. The only male heir at that time was Robert Jr., Claire's son. The Buchanan fortune and company fell under the control of a trust until Robert Jr. turned twenty-one.

Later, Victoria would have three sons, but for whatever reason, her children had no interest in the Buchanan company and never placed a claim for an inheritance.

"There was also a picture in the drawer," Mr. Crawford said. "It's of two women." He opened a center drawer likely designed to hold playing pieces or cards and removed the black-and-white photo.

Megan flexed her fingers and accepted the picture of two young women sitting on a settee. Embossed on the bottom right corner was *DuPont Photographer, Le Havre, France.*

She flipped it over, but there was no notation about the women's identities. However, written in faded black ink was the year 1909. The date matched the women's long skirts, formal pinned hair, and straw hats.

The women appeared to be as opposite as night and day, and she recognized the woman on the left immediately. The pale peaches-and-cream complexion and round face gave her away as Claire Hedrick Buchanan, Megan's great-grandmother.

Claire's soft curls peeked out from a straw toque embellished with dainty flowers. Though the black-and-white image could never confirm this, Megan knew her great-grandmother's hair had been a rich auburn. There was a splash of freckles across Claire's nose, and her smile was warm and welcoming. She wore a high-collared white lace top that was drawn tight around her waist by a high-waist skirt that dipped over the tops of her black shoes. The skirt had a tunic effect and conjured images of a Russian peasant.

Megan didn't recognize the other woman, who had dark hair sweeping into a twisted coil set low on her head, which was adorned with a wide-brimmed hat. A high slash of cheekbones combined with a pointed chin created an angled face that looked more exotic than approachable. This woman's dress was made of a simpler fabric and resembled something a woman from the country would have worn.

Her skirt hit inches below her ankle, but polished black shoes peeked out from under the hem.

Both the women would have stood out, and she could see why they had caught the photographer's eye. Together they were an odd blend. A sense of giddiness rose up in her as it did whenever she stumbled onto an interesting find.

"I can see the wheels spinning in your head," Rick said.

"They're racing," Megan admitted. "There are so few pictures of Claire before her marriage."

"That's Claire? As in Winter Cottage?" Rick asked.

"One and the same. This is my great-grandmother, Claire Buchanan. I know from family records that she traveled with the Buchanan family all over the world around that time. Paris, only a few hours away by train, was a favorite stop. In 1909, Claire would have been twenty-one and a lady's maid. She was still eight years away from marrying Robert or having her one and only child, Robert Jr., in 1917."

"Who's the other woman?" Mr. Crawford asked.

"I don't know," Megan said. "As I mentioned, Claire worked primarily at that time as a lady's maid for Victoria Buchanan, but that's not Victoria. Victoria was an ice blonde who would have been in her teens about this time. She also would have been dressed more stylishly."

"The other woman is younger than Claire?" Rick asked.

"Yes."

"Their heads are slightly inclined toward each other," he said. "Their legs are crossed and angled toward each other, and their smiles are relaxed. Body language says they liked each other and knew each other well."

"I would agree." Megan shifted her gaze to the table. "I've pored over every picture I can find of Winter Cottage between 1900 and 1910, and I don't remember this table in Winter Cottage. That's not to say it wasn't in the house. Claire sold off several pieces during the Depression. Perhaps she didn't realize this picture was in the drawer."

"Or whoever owned the desk knew the Buchanans," Rick said. "The owner of the table could have been attached to the other woman."

Megan stared at the mystery woman's face. "Given the other woman's attire, I doubt she'd have owned such a fine piece. She's dressed as if she lives on a farm."

She wasn't sure where the piece would be placed in Winter Cottage once the house was redone, but she felt strongly that it needed to be there. "Do you know how your mother came across this piece?" she asked Mr. Crawford.

"She loved to go to yard sales and estate sales," he said. "I couldn't say for sure, but I can tell you her favorite antique dealer is in Norfolk. Her name is Pat Schmidt."

"I don't know the name," Megan said.

"I can ask my sister. I don't have a clue," he said.

Most pieces like this came with stories, and Megan wanted the story as much as the piece—it was the stories that would bring Winter Cottage and Spring House alive for the tourists.

"Do you have a price in mind?" Megan asked.

Mr. Crawford quoted a price that caused Rick to straighten. She imagined he was thinking the money would be better spent on a new truck or dash-cam video equipment for his squad car rather than a table and four chairs.

Megan, however, kept her expression stoic. She knew enough about the furniture to know its worth, and Mr. Crawford was asking triple its value. She smoothed her hand over the top, knowing that the piece needed to return to Winter Cottage where it belonged. But she was not a fool, and she was patient. "Knock off seventy-five percent and we have a deal."

"Seventy-five percent!" Mr. Crawford said. "That would take me down to . . ." He let the sentence trail as he quickly calculated the math.

She'd already come up with the number. As she waited for him to burrow down to it himself, she pulled out her cell phone and snapped several pictures of the image that had captured Claire and the mystery woman over a century earlier.

"That's robbery," Mr. Crawford said.

"It's a fair price." She handed him back his picture. He might get a few hundred dollars more from another antique dealer, but that would require him to shop the pieces around, and judging by the boat already hooked up to the packed truck, he didn't have the time now.

Mr. Crawford shook his head. "I can't go that low, no matter how sorry I feel for you."

If the comment was meant to throw her off her game, it did the opposite. In fact, it irritated her. "I don't expect you or anyone else to feel sorry for me, Mr. Crawford. In fact, instead of feeling desperate, I'm annoyed now. I'm not here for a handout but here to make a business deal. Do you accept my price or not?"

A redness spread over his gaunt cheeks, suggesting he had been properly chastised. But feeling chagrined was not enough to make him accept her offer. "No, I got to have double that."

Which put them at half of his original number, which was still too much. "I'm afraid that's too rich for my blood."

"It's not even your money that you're spending. We've all heard the old lady left a ton of money for the restoration projects."

"You're right, it's not my money, and that makes me all the more responsible." She dug a small business card from her purse, scribbled her offer on the back, and handed it to him. "I can promise you I'll buy it if you can change your mind."

"You're not willing to negotiate at all?" Mr. Crawford flicked the edge of the card, looking a little stunned and annoyed. Megan said nothing.

"Even the bald guy on *Pawn Stars* negotiates," he said with a chuckle.

She extended her hand. "Thank you, Mr. Crawford, for showing me the lovely pieces. And the picture was one of the best of Claire I've ever seen. You've made me curious about how the photograph and the desk came together, but I suppose I might not ever know that."

He shoved her card in his pocket. "You know I'm leaving town in the morning."

"I do. And I wish you safe travels," Megan said.

"I won't be back for at least six months," he warned.

His tone suggested she would regret not closing the deal, but Megan did not budge. She disliked the thought of losing out on the pieces, but she refused to be a pushover. "We'll have you over to Winter Cottage at Christmas."

CHAPTER SEVEN

Megan

Monday, March 5, 2018
Cape Hudson, Virginia
5:00 p.m.

The sun had dipped low in the sky as Megan walked straight to Rick's truck. She massaged her fingers deep into the small of her back as Rick thanked Mr. Crawford. Rick reached the truck first and opened her door. She hoisted herself up into the cab.

"Are you doing okay?" he asked.

"When you're the size of a barn, getting around ain't easy, Sheriff." When his expression remained worried, she smiled and added, "I'm fine."

"For the record, you're doing great." He leaned in, his arm resting on the top of the truck. His energy was warm and comforting, and she sat a little straighter and brushed her snub-nosed bangs away from her face. "You're a cool customer, Ms. Buchanan. I saw the way your eyes lit up when you saw that table and the picture. You wanted it. But you still walked away."

"That is the advantage to living through so many moves. I learned not to get too attached."

"Does that extend to people as well?" Rick asked.

"I suppose it does."

"There have to be places and people you miss."

She shrugged, shifting her gaze to the woods that ringed Mr. Crawford's property. Absently, she rubbed her hand on her belly. Even this baby would grow up and one day go off and discover her own life. But for now Megan was in Cape Hudson and determined to dig her roots as deeply as the sandy soil would allow. "I accept that few things last forever."

"You're too young to be so cynical."

"I'm not cynical. When I'm in a town or city, I make the most of what it has to offer. I really enjoy it, because I know I'll likely not see it again."

"Are you going to budge on your price with Crawford?"

His waist was lean and she suspected firm to the touch. Her libido was fully awake. "Nope. What I offered was fair, and he knows it."

"I'll bet you one of your apple pies he walks away from the deal."

Megan was feeling oddly optimistic and excited, as she always did when she was dealing in the past. "I'll bet you that apple pie and raise you a cherry. Mr. Crawford will call me before he leaves town. What are you offering up?"

"A few days' worth of labor at Spring House."

She held out her hand. "You have a deal, Sheriff."

He wrapped strong, calloused hands around hers and shook. "Mighty cocky, Ms. Megan."

She liked the way his deep voice curved around her name. She cleared her throat as she pulled her hand free. "Wear your tool belt when you come."

Smiling, he tapped the top of the truck with his hand and closed her door. As he walked around to the driver's side, she opened the image on her phone. She stared at the two women and found herself drawn not to Claire but to the other one.

When Rick slid behind the wheel, she turned to him. "Even if Mr. Crawford says no to the sale, I'm grateful for the chance to see this picture. Piecing together Claire Buchanan's life has been a challenge. The woman was intensely private."

"Who do you think the other woman was?" he asked.

"I'm not sure." She thought back to the pictures she'd bought from Duncan. The photo that came to mind was the one of the little girl with dark hair. "She could have been a domestic in the Buchanans' house." She stared at the young woman's dress, her shoes, and the scarf that did not quite match. Her eyes were bright, her skin clear, and she sat with an erect posture that suggested she'd been raised with standards. "She didn't have money."

"Didn't Claire have sisters?" he asked.

"A sister?" she said, more to herself. She looked beyond the dark hair and bright eyes to the shape of her mouth, the tilt of her head, and the way she clasped her hands in her lap. She scrolled through her pictures and found the image of the four Hedrick sisters with their mother. The youngest had to be the other girl with Claire. "You might be right, Sheriff. Good detective work."

"I like to think I haven't lost some of my best moves."

"Do you feel like you've lost some moves?" she asked.

"Maybe a few. Small-town life takes some getting used to."

"You could be anywhere, Rick. You don't have to stay in Cape Hudson. I picture you as a big-city detective."

"I'm not sure that's for me."

"But are calls for people locked out of houses, missing dogs, and wandering elderly residents for you? This all has to feel tame compared to commanding an artillery platoon."

"Definitely quieter." He tapped his finger on the steering wheel. "Out here I've gotten the chance to do more diving. There are wrecks along the bay and the Atlantic shore. I plan to hire help soon, and then I'll have time to maybe do some salvage work."

She shifted in her seat. They had skirted so many topics since they'd both landed in Cape Hudson, and she was tired of avoiding choppy waters. "Are you here for Scott?"

Rick adjusted his grip on the wheel and tossed her a sharp glance before looking back at the road. "He's why I came here, but he's not why I stayed. Like I said, this place is growing on me. After Winter Cottage is renovated, are you leaving?"

"I'll have to make a living somehow, and unless there's another project, the baby and I might have to move on."

"Baby." He spoke the word as if it still did not fit into the world he'd become accustomed to.

"I know. Sounds weird to be saying it."

"Scott would have been excited about the baby," he offered.

"I know. But it never would have worked between us."

Rick remained silent, but as he drove, a muscle pulsed in the side of his jaw.

Megan had not discussed with Rick or anyone else why she and Scott had broken up. By the time she could bring herself to talk about what had happened, Scott was dead, so she let the reasons behind their breakup die with him. She did not want the world, especially Helen or Rick, to know that Scott had been cheating on her. Even now, it was humiliating to think she'd misjudged him so badly.

He stared ahead as they passed more fields of green corn, rows of pine, cedar trees, and kudzu. Neither spoke for several minutes, and she realized she had likely offended him. He had moved to Cape Hudson out of tribute to a fallen friend, and she had just confessed she would have left Scott regardless.

"Do you mind if we swing by my house?" Rick asked. "I'm supposed to get a delivery of siding material. The company's been promising it for days, and I'm going to have to raise holy hell if they haven't come through this time."

Up ahead there was a small gas station and a convenience store. "I didn't realize you bought a house here."

"About a month ago. Like I said, the place is growing on me. It also made sense to make the investment."

"What house did you buy?" she asked.

"I bought it from Tom Brewster. He's owned the house about thirty years."

"The name's not familiar. What about before?"

"I didn't get a detailed history of the house, so I can't tell you much about it."

"What does it look like?"

"It's a Cape Cod located on a cove. Great view of the bay."

"Nice."

"We'll see about that. I think I bought the original homestead, because the place is going to take years to fix up." He took a right turn off the main road down a small side street that cut toward the ocean rather than the bay.

Megan, despite herself, was curious about his purchase. "What did Tom Brewster do?"

"He was a merchant marine. His son and two of his brothers were marines. Tom finally decided to move inland and be closer to his daughter."

"The name Brewster is starting to ring a bell." She laughed. "My father always called them the Brewster boys. Jeff, Mark, David, and Tom."

"I served under Tom. He's the youngest of the boys and just retired as a full-bird colonel."

"He didn't want to take over the house?"

"Said he'd seen a lifetime's worth of the ocean and wanted to head inland toward the Shenandoah Valley. Most of the family have scattered over the years."

"This isn't an easy place to live. Unless you're in the tourist trade, a farmer, or a waterman, there's not much to hold you here."

"And yet here we both are, making a living."

"The town will always need a sheriff. And I predict in a couple of years, you'll be county sheriff or have a thriving dive business."

Rick rounded the final bend and pulled up to a small Cape Cod–style house covered in graying shingles and a cedar roof. The front door was painted a faded red, and the windows looked as if they dated back a half century. Mentally, she calculated the cost of the renovation and tried not to wince when she realized the final tally. "I hope you got a deal on this house."

He shut off the truck. "I did."

She searched around for supplies but did not see any. "What are you having delivered?"

"Planks and siding. The spring project is to fix the back deck and replace the siding. Roof in the fall, and come winter, I'll move the show inside and redo the bathrooms, kitchen, and floors." He got out of the truck and opened her door. "You may give me your professional opinion."

A breeze blew off the water as she walked up to the front door. The garden beds had been stripped of both weeds and plants, leaving behind cracked oyster shells. "Who's going to do the work?"

"I am."

"In your spare time?"

He jangled his keys, and they walked around the side of the house. "I like to keep busy."

"Good. Because you will be." As the drive bent east and drew closer to the bay, the soil turned sandy, and the backyard opened onto a couple of white Adirondack chairs nestled on a small beach that overlooked the cove. The waters were calm and clear. In the distance two large tankers lumbered across the horizon toward northern ports.

"What do you think of the property in general?" he asked.

As inspiring as the view was, the house was not. "It'll take time and maybe a few years, but the house can be fixed, and the view will always be stunning." She studied a large bay window and imagined what the sunsets looked like over the water.

"I'd give you a tour of the inside, but it's a little depressing right now."

"I don't mind a mess. I'd like to see it."

"If you're sure. Okay. Watch your step." He opened the back door and switched on a light that was surprisingly bright.

She glanced up at new recessed lights. "I see you've already been busy with the ceiling. Good choice."

"Light had to be a priority."

She stepped into the kitchen and walked up to a white porcelain farmhouse sink with an original gooseneck faucet and porcelain cross knobs for the hot and cold water. She skimmed her fingers over the edge of the sink. Brewster had been a merchant marine, so he'd likely been gone for long stretches. It would have been a lonely life for Mrs. Brewster.

"What's that frown mean?" he asked.

"Nothing really." She shook her head, chagrined that he'd noticed her worry. "Just trying to picture Mrs. Brewster. Wives of the merchant marines were often alone nine to ten months out of the year."

"Scott told me you could deduce the history of just about anything."

"I have an encyclopedic knowledge of history. Touching items kind of jars my memory." Scott had considered this anomaly of hers a funny parlor trick, and he'd gotten a kick out of her "reading" objects at parties. She had always laughed along and played up the drama, as if she were psychic. "And pregnant women are moody, if you hadn't noticed."

"There had to be times when she was happy in this house."

"I'm sure that's very true. They had four sons and were married for decades."

He studied her as if he didn't buy whatever she was selling, but he let it pass. "Let me give you the grand tour."

As she moved through the house, she noticed he had upgraded the lighting in most of the rooms. Modern illumination didn't quite chase away the dreariness.

The architectural details of the house were amazing. Beadboard, crown molding, a stone fireplace topped with a broad beam mantel, and wide hardwood floors that would be stunning when they were sanded and polished.

Many might have passed on the house because of the work required. But Scott had said Rick was always the kind of guy who liked a challenge. "The bones of the house are solid, and that view will ensure you never have a problem selling it."

He stood by the window, and the late afternoon light silhouetted his broad shoulders. "Good to know."

She turned from the fireplace. "Make sure you take lots of pictures. The 'before' pictures will highlight the transformation. I can think of a couple of bloggers who would happily cover it. Again, a bonus for resell."

"Who says I'm selling?"

She laughed, deciding that he would have to learn the hard way how lonely it could be out here. She walked to the window. "I don't see any building supplies."

"Neither do I." He didn't look too perturbed. "I'll be making calls first thing in the morning."

"Speaking of calls, I have a few to make."

"It's the end of the day."

"I persuaded the contractor to give me his personal cell number. It's a big project, and I expect quick responses to my questions."

"I never pictured you as such a hard-driving boss."

"I have to be. My contractor and his crew have a lot to haul out of Spring House."

"Lead the way."

She made her way out of the house and across sandy soil that shifted under her feet. The more distance she gained from the house, the better she felt.

Rick followed, clearly slowing his pace to match hers.

"If I have a question about materials or historical detail, do you mind if I call you?" he asked. "I want to drag it into the modern world but hold on to as much charm as I can."

"Happy to lend my advice." He opened the truck door for her, and she slid into the passenger seat. "I have a very particular skill set that doesn't often come in handy unless you're renovating."

He grinned. "That's a lucky break for me."

Rick closed her door, and as he walked around the front of the truck, she found it hard not to admire the square set of his jaw or the span of his shoulders.

For a moment, she wished away the last couple of years and wondered where she would be now if she had gone with Rick.

CHAPTER EIGHT

Diane

Age 12

Tuesday, September 15, 1903
Baltimore, Maryland

Diane was always hungry.

Since Mr. LeBlanc had died almost eight months earlier, Madame LeBlanc rarely allowed Diane time for eating. When she did give her a moment, it was generally dried toast or broth. Pierre, free from Mr. LeBlanc's scrutiny, also had begun to lurk around her.

More and more often, Pierre would stand in the doorway and watch her while she ironed or polished a boot. Twice last week when she passed him in the hallway, he had stuck out his foot and tripped her. The first time had caught her so unaware that she had fallen hard, dropping her sewing kit. As buttons rolled over the tiled floor and she rubbed her bruised palms, he simply laughed.

"Clumsy fool," he had said.

Another time she had been on the last step of the staircase when she felt his hand on her shoulder. He had shoved hard, and again she had fallen. That time her shoulder had struck the floor and been deeply bruised for weeks.

Now each time he approached her, she flinched and drew away. This only seemed to please him.

Madame LeBlanc also had announced that the three of them would be departing on a steamer leaving Baltimore and bound for Le Havre, France. The decision to leave came quickly, and when Diane asked why they were rushing to pack trunks, Madame LeBlanc explained that her husband's dear cousin had finally answered her letter and agreed to meet them in Le Havre. Pierre, who was always so moody and withdrawn, actually looked happy.

Women continued to visit Madame LeBlanc, and she sat with them in a candlelit room, held their hands, and whispered words that often made the women cry. More and more, Madame LeBlanc requested that Diane be listening in the nearby room, and when Madame LeBlanc asked certain questions, Diane was instructed to tap on the wall.

Men also visited the house, but they were not looking for the same thing. Each one wanted money, and several threatened to call the police. Madame LeBlanc had a way of smiling, though, and after she took them into the study and closed the door behind her, she was able to convince them to give her a bit more time.

The morning they departed, Madame LeBlanc produced a dress made of white lace and muslin. When Diane showed only a slight interest, Madame LeBlanc announced it was for her. It was time Diane dressed as a young lady, she said. Diane rose and touched the soft fabric. Never had she felt anything so lovely.

"You are like a daughter to me now," Madame LeBlanc said. "And you should dress like you are my child." Madame LeBlanc had a bath drawn for Diane, and she washed the girl's hair, lathering in a lavender soap that smelled of spring.

As Diane's hair dried by a vent that blew warm air, she ate not only dry toast but also cheese and sausage—just like Madame LeBlanc.

"What is important is that going forward, I will introduce you as my daughter, and you must not contradict me," she said.

The butter tasted so good on the toast and the cheese was so ripe and creamy, she was not sure she cared, but still she asked, "Why?"

"Because it's best that way."

Diane frowned at the empty reply.

"I will also have you accompany me to some of my onboard appointments. I've heard the way the ladies speak about your eyes and how pretty you are."

Madame LeBlanc arranged Diane's hair in ringlets in front of her dressing table outfitted with pretty jars and delicate perfume bottles.

"Ah, to have such beautiful hair again," Madame LeBlanc said as their gazes met in the mirror. "And your eyes. They are like lavender gems. You are quite magical, child."

"Thank you, Madame LeBlanc."

"You must not call me Madame LeBlanc any longer," she said. "It's far too formal for a mother and daughter." She produced a white ribbon and coiled it around the hair she'd gathered at the crown of Diane's head. "Perhaps you could call me Mimi? It sounds so endearing, no? Would that work for you, my dear?"

Diane had loved her mother, father, sisters, and brothers, but after two years of separation from them, Madame LeBlanc was as close as she had to family now. "Yes, Mimi."

"Ah, I do like the sound of that. Good girl." She tied the ribbon in an elaborate bow and then got the dress for Diane to step into. Madame LeBlanc faced Diane away from the mirror as she carefully fastened each button. When she turned Diane to face the mirror, the girl was stunned by her reflection. She looked like a princess.

"Mimi, thank you," she said.

"But of course, my girl."

"Will Pierre be coming with us?" Diane asked.

"Yes, but we will not see him much on the ship. You seem to be quite clumsy when he's around, and it would not do for you to be black and blue all the time."

An undercurrent of worry roiled under her fleeting sense of relief. Pierre had been careful to obey Mr. LeBlanc, but she worried that he did not fear Madame LeBlanc in the least.

They boarded the ship that afternoon, and it turned into a frenzied affair. Madame LeBlanc had dressed in a brightly colored, fitted coat made of silk, and she wore a wide-brimmed hat. She was a handsome woman who painted her lips and cheeks a faint blush of pink and enjoyed the glances and nods she garnered from men.

Pierre was sent ahead to board the ship alone, and Madame LeBlanc and Diane followed in a hired carriage that was far finer than their normal modes of transportation. As they walked up the gangplank, Madame LeBlanc held her head high, as if she were from the wealthiest of families.

Diane had always thought the LeBlancs' Baltimore townhouse was so much finer than her parents' home in Cape Hudson and had found it strange that Madame LeBlanc complained about money all the time. But now, as she stared at the polished portholes, teak trim, and fine carpeting of the ship, she realized there were many far wealthier than the LeBlancs. Madame LeBlanc's eyes glistened as she looked around the ship and the finely dressed ladies and gentlemen.

"We'll have this life one day, Diane," Madame LeBlanc said. "We'll dress in the best and stay in the finest establishments as soon as I speak to Cousin Gilbert. But you must be very good and do exactly as I say." She softly brushed a curl from Diane's eyes.

"Yes, Mimi."

"Securing a prosperous future can be a delicate process for women in our station."

"Station?"

"Women who are too smart or too pretty to work the streets but still without real means. I had reasonable funds when Mr. LeBlanc was alive, but his passing has made it more difficult. But not to worry. I have an idea for us both."

Madame LeBlanc and Diane settled in their stateroom, which came equipped with a small sitting room, a bedroom for Madame LeBlanc, and a much smaller room for Diane. Their trunks had arrived and were stacked on top of each other in Madame LeBlanc's room.

"Where will Pierre sleep?" Diane asked.

"He has his own room. As I said, we won't be seeing him during this trip."

"Why not? He's always close to you."

"It is best we not associate with him now. Perhaps later when we are in France."

Diane hid her smile as she removed her hat and gloves.

"Diane, dear, if you will get us unpacked, then we can order some tea. Then I shall move about the ship and make our introduction. Though you better change out of that dress while you work. We want it nice and crisp."

Moments later, Madame LeBlanc had breezed out of the cabin with the promise to have a tray sent for Diane. As soon as the cabin door was closed, Diane walked to the porthole and watched as the coast grew more distant. How many times had she sat on the bay's shore with her sisters and watched the boats steam south from Baltimore? Eventually, the vessel would dip around the southern edge of the peninsula and cut out toward the open waters of the Atlantic.

The tray Madame LeBlanc had promised never came, and Diane, tired from their long day, slid under the sheets of her small cot. She dreamed of her mother, standing on the beach, her hair blowing in the wind. Her mother turned to Diane and said with a smile, "It will be all right. You'll see."

Diane awoke when she heard the cabin door open. A glance at the clock on the wall told her it was nearly one o'clock in the morning.

Rubbing her eyes, she rose and found Madame LeBlanc pulling the last of her pearl-studded hatpins free. She removed her hat and set it on the chair before she walked across the room and poured herself a cup of tea. She took a long, deep sip, and then, turning to Diane, she smiled. "We have a luncheon appointment today. You must wear your white dress."

Diane's stomach grumbled, and she quickly pressed her hand onto it. "I'm hungry."

"Oh, my. I didn't send up a plate for you, did I? But I didn't forget." She reached into her purse, pulled out a napkin, and handed it to Diane.

Diane carefully unwrapped the cloth napkin embossed with the ship's logo and found a sizable slice of cheese and sausage.

"That should hold you until our lunch."

Diane took a bit of the cheese, savoring the taste, which was far finer than they normally ate. "Will I be able to eat at lunch today?"

"Perhaps."

Moonlight streamed through the porthole, catching the diamonds in Madame LeBlanc's earrings, which were the last gift that Mr. LeBlanc had given her.

"Mrs. Howard is going to be our hostess. You must be very polite and speak only when spoken to."

"In English or French?"

"French, I think. And remember: if I should refer to you as my daughter, do not disagree with me. I know I shall never take the place of your mama, but Mrs. Howard, a woman I just met, looked so lonely. Her son passed last year, and I thought she would feel closer to me if she knew I was a mother too."

She yawned and glared at the night sky. "But that is not for hours, so until then I must sleep. Wake me at noon, and that should be enough time before our two o'clock lunch."

"Yes, Mimi."

"That's a good girl."

Diane helped Madame LeBlanc undress, and when Madame LeBlanc slipped into bed, Diane hung up her beaded blue dress and put her shoes inside her traveling trunk. As she picked up Madame LeBlanc's earrings from the nightstand, an odd sense of disappointment passed through her. Mr. LeBlanc had gifted his wife the earrings on her last birthday. Though she'd smiled for her husband, she had often lamented that the stones were so small. Carefully, Diane tucked them away in the silk bag that held all Madame LeBlanc's baubles.

Diane spent the morning reading and practicing her French letters. By two, both Diane and Madame LeBlanc were at Mrs. JoAnn Howard's stateroom, which was located on the top deck of the ship.

The room was ten times the size of theirs with portholes offering a lovely view of the open sea. There was a lush display of freshly cut yellow roses, and the portraits hanging on the walls looked as if they had come from a private collection.

Mrs. Howard appeared to be in her fifties and had thick swaths of gray hair woven through the chestnut brown. Her face was round, and though not remarkable in her looks, she didn't look unpleasant either. Mrs. Howard smiled at Diane and welcomed her and Madame LeBlanc into the suite.

Over a cold lunch of biscuits, roasted chicken, and fresh berries, Diane tried not to eat too quickly. Mrs. Howard spoke about how she had lost her husband and son in a typhoid epidemic a year earlier.

Madame LeBlanc was kind to Mrs. Howard, listening patiently to her sad tale. The older woman soon relaxed and began to chat easily with Madame LeBlanc.

The waiter delivered the women coffee and Diane a hot chocolate, which to her delight tasted more delicious than anything she'd ever had. After the waiter closed the suite's door, Madame LeBlanc reached into her small purse and removed a velvet bag with a gold drawstring.

"You are a lucky woman to have such a lovely daughter," Mrs. Howard said as she smiled at Diane. "She is a delight."

"Our children give our life such richness," Madame LeBlanc said.

"Yes," Mrs. Howard said. "I miss my Peter and our son more than I can say." The portly woman glanced toward the closed door. "You hinted at dinner last night that there might be a way to talk to them?"

Madame LeBlanc sipped her coffee, in no rush. "There is. But it's not easy."

"I am willing to do whatever it takes. Truly."

Diane licked the chocolate from her upper lip as she studied Madame LeBlanc. Speaking of spirits and the dead seemed like such a dangerous topic, and she was certain the minister in Cape Hudson would not approve. But she was not afraid—she was fascinated.

Madame LeBlanc calmly sipped her coffee, smiling at Diane and gently arranging a curl over the girl's shoulder. "You were right to summon me here today. The longer we travel over open water, the weaker my connection with the departed becomes. Most spirits are grounded to earth, and their energies are scattered by water."

Mrs. Howard tugged a small roll of bills from her purse and set it on the table. "If my husband were alive, he would be appalled if he knew we were talking."

"Ah, but he is not alive, and I think now he would not mind if you reached over the heavens to speak with him. I sense he misses you very much."

"Truly?"

"Yes. I'm certain."

"What else does he say? What about our son?" Mrs. Howard glanced out the porthole at the smooth waters of the open sea. "*Oh dear*, I hope we're not too late."

Madame LeBlanc tucked the money in her purse and smiled. "Our timing might be perfect. The day is lovely and the skies clear." She set her cup down. "Diane, my sweet, would you draw the curtains, please?"

Diane's cup rattled in her saucer as she set it on the satin-covered table. Carefully she rose, straightening her skirts, and walked to the round porthole. With a yank, she drew the velvet curtains closed. Immediately the room dimmed.

Madame LeBlanc pulled a small cloth folded into fourths from her bag and unfurled it on the table. It was covered in an arching alphabet written in scrolled letters, and under that were the words *yes* and *no*. Next, from a purple silk bag, Madame LeBlanc removed an odd device shaped like a pear and adorned with a red gem and black scrolls. Finally, she removed a candle from her bag and lit it.

"Diane, dear, would you dim the lanterns?"

Diane crossed the room and turned the gas dimmer down until the flame was barely visible. The candlelight flickered and glowed on the scalloped wallpaper and cast shadows into the corners.

When she sat, Madame LeBlanc extended her arms to Mrs. Howard, and the two clasped hands. She shifted in her seat and then announced, "It is good Diane is here. She is young energy. Spirits are attracted to it."

Diane perched on the edge of her seat, her hot chocolate nearly forgotten. She was anxious about what Madame LeBlanc was about to do. She knew Madame LeBlanc had clients and often visited them in their homes, but there was never any discussion about what happened. Had she been speaking to the dead all this time? Could Madame LeBlanc speak to Diane's mama? Nervous energy buzzed through her limbs, and sitting still as Madame LeBlanc had taught her was difficult.

"You must grasp our hands as well, Diane," Madame LeBlanc said. "The three of us must create a circle of trust. Spirits can be distrusting of the living, and they like it when we are clustered together."

"Why would they distrust us, Mimi?" Diane asked.

"Perhaps they are jealous because we are alive and they are not," Madame LeBlanc said. "Perhaps they need our combined energy to realize we can speak to them."

"How do you know when they are here?" Diane laid her right palm first in Mrs. Howard's and found it damp and soft. Her left hand went into Madame LeBlanc's dry, small hand that radiated with surprising strength. Madame LeBlanc's ringed fingers wrapped around hers.

"They are always here. It just takes someone like me to see them," Madame LeBlanc said.

"Your mama has a very special gift," Mrs. Howard whispered. "My dear friend Elizabeth Lawrence from New York was quite impressed with your skills. You might remember she is acquainted with George Buchanan."

The Buchanan name caught Diane's attention, and she nearly mentioned Claire. But when she looked up, Madame LeBlanc leveled a warning glance in her direction.

She pushed aside all the questions about the Buchanans for now. Later, she would ask Madame LeBlanc if there was news of Claire.

Diane's thoughts turned to all the women who'd visited their townhome, and she knew now that Madame LeBlanc had been speaking to their departed loved ones. Madame LeBlanc closed her eyes, and so did Mrs. Howard. Diane closed hers—almost. Her curiosity was too keen for her not to watch whatever she was about to see.

As the small woman began to hum and roll her head from side to side, Mrs. Howard drew in a deep breath as if she were trying to inhale whatever magic was spinning around Madame LeBlanc.

The humming turned into a kind of chanting, and then Madame LeBlanc returned to humming. Diane felt the vibrations in her chest and grew more curious by the second as she expected some specter to appear before them.

Madame LeBlanc called to Mr. Howard several times, pausing her chants to listen for any kind of answer. This went on for several minutes, and Diane felt her anticipation waning as Mrs. Howard also shifted in her seat.

"Men can be as stubborn in death as in life," Madame LeBlanc said. "Perhaps your son is more open to a visit. Call to him."

"Yes, my son was always such a sweet boy." Closing her eyes again and settling back in her chair, Mrs. Howard called out to the boy several times. Silence rose up and thickened the air.

Knock. Knock. Knock.

Mrs. Howard startled and opened her eyes. "Is it my son?"

Madame LeBlanc shook her head. "Shh. I feel something."

"Yes, yes, I do too," Mrs. Howard said.

Anticipation hummed in Diane, and she felt an excitement normally reserved for Christmas morning.

"Sebastian Jr., are you there?" Madame LeBlanc asked.

Knock. Knock. Knock.

The sound was faint at first, reverberating from the ceiling above. "Sebastian, are you there? Your mother wants to talk to you."

Diane peeked and noticed Madame LeBlanc now staring up at the ceiling, searching. All Diane saw was the white, freshly painted ceiling.

Knock. Knock. Knock.

The sounds were louder this time and came in a rapid-fire progression. Despite Diane's cynicism, her skin prickled with anticipation. If Sebastian could be summoned, then surely her mama could be.

"That is your son," Madame LeBlanc whispered.

"Sebastian, is that you?" Mrs. Howard asked.

Knock. Knock. Knock.

Tears welled in Mrs. Howard's eyes as if she were staring into the face of her son. "I knew you would come."

Diane's heart swelled with hope as she thought of all the questions she would ask her own mama. Claire would be so thrilled to know that their mama was watching over them. And that they were not alone. Any communication would have been welcome—it pained her to admit that she already could not remember what her mother's voice had sounded like.

As the minutes passed, Madame LeBlanc instructed Mrs. Howard to speak to her son, and the woman quickly began to chatter about her day. "Oh, Sebastian, I do miss you so much."

There was the occasional knocking to remind everyone that Sebastian was still around until the knocking stopped and there was only eerie silence. Madame LeBlanc sat back in her chair, pulling her hands free and breaking the circle.

She closed her eyes, removed a lace handkerchief from her shirt cuff, and dabbed her dry forehead. "Your son has returned to the other side of the veil."

"So soon?" Mrs. Howard choked back tears.

"Yes. Diane, could you turn up the lanterns? And pour me a glass of water?"

The girl rose, twisted the knob, and as the flame rose, blinked against the brightness.

Madame LeBlanc took a long sip from her water glass. "He enjoyed his visit with you."

"How do you know?" Mrs. Howard asked.

"I simply do."

"Can I speak to him again?" Mrs. Howard asked.

"Not today. I'm tired. Perhaps tomorrow."

"Yes, yes. That would be lovely. Would lunch work?"

"Perhaps dinner. My senses are keener at night."

"Of course." Mrs. Howard pressed her hands to her flushed face. "Thank you."

Out in the hallway, Madame LeBlanc seemed to recover some of her energy as she took Diane by the hand and the two returned to their cabin. As they neared the cabin, Pierre approached them. He looked sullen, as he normally did, and glanced from left to right as if to ensure no one was around before he acknowledged their presence.

"Madame LeBlanc. How do you do?" His thick accent had always been heavier than Madame LeBlanc's and more guttural. She had once said he had grown up rougher than most.

"Sir," she said, carefully. "How are you this fine day?"

His gaze shifted to Diane, and his scowl sharpened, as if he resented seeing her in the fine dress and with her dark curls arranged around her face.

Diane drew closer to Madame LeBlanc, grateful that he was not staying in their cabin.

"I trust everything is well," Madame LeBlanc said.

"It is." He bowed slightly as he looked at Diane. "You look pretty. Quite grown-up."

Madame LeBlanc stepped in front of Diane, blocking Pierre's view of her. "Have a good day."

"Of course," Pierre said.

Madame LeBlanc hurried Diane down the hallway and the staircase leading to their deck in the middle. When she closed the door, she quickly locked it. "I shall have to have a talk with Pierre. He's quite forward."

"Can you really speak to the dead?" Diane asked.

"What?" She cast a glance toward the door and then looked at her. "Of course, child. It's the gift the Lord above has given me."

"Can you speak to my mama?" Diane asked.

Madame LeBlanc sat in front of her dressing table and studied Diane as she removed her pins from her hat. "Perhaps I could."

Diane took the hat and set it on the bureau. "I need to talk to her."

"Why is that?" She removed her rings and reached for a jar of lotion.

"I want to know if she loves me."

Madame LeBlanc carefully worked the lotion into her long, elegant hands. She was silent for a moment and then turned, extending her hands to Diane.

The girl rushed to the porthole and closed the curtains and then returned to Madame LeBlanc and laid her hand over Madame LeBlanc's. The woman drew in a deep breath and released it slowly. "What was your mother's name?"

"Addie."

"Addie is a lovely name." She was silent for a moment and then began to hum.

As questions for her mother rushed around in Diane's head, she waited for a knocking sound or a sign that she was there. But she heard only the silence and the sound of her heart beating in her chest.

All the questions for her mama that had been swirling like a funnel cloud for three years bubbled to the surface. Did she miss her? Where was she? Would Diane ever see home again? How were her sisters and brothers?

Madame LeBlanc took Diane's hand and squeezed it gently. "Child, she loved you very much."

Tears she'd not allowed since her mother's death welled in Diane's eyes. Her anger melted away as her mind, starved for affection, replayed Madame LeBlanc's words over in her head.

Madame LeBlanc smiled and released her hand. Gently, she wiped the girl's tears. "You were very lucky to have such a lovely mother."

Diane sniffed. "Thank you."

"Of course, child. Go and lie down. I want you to come with me to dinner tonight. There is another woman who wishes to speak with the departed. You put Mrs. Howard at ease, and I think you will do the same for this woman. With those violet eyes of yours, I think you will be my lucky charm."

Diane nodded. "Could I have hot chocolate?"

"Yes, of course."

————— ◦◦◦◦◦ —————

The next week fell into a predictable pattern. Diane accompanied Madame LeBlanc to meetings in the private cabins, and she helped the lonely living speak to their dead. She always received payment either in coin or sometimes jewelry such as rings, pendants, or bracelets. Diane didn't know what happened to the items, as Madame LeBlanc was careful to keep them well hidden.

Diane was always on the lookout for Pierre, but he never approached them in the hallway again. A couple of times she saw him across a crowded room, staring at her in a way that made her skin prickle and her belly tighten with fear.

Madame LeBlanc continued to teach French to Diane and almost never spoke to her again in English. The sounds soon rolled off the girl's own lips as if they were her natural tongue, and there were nights when she dreamed in French. Claire and her family, even her old mama's memory, faded as the ship gained more distance from the American shores.

CHAPTER NINE

Diane

Wednesday, September 23, 1903
Le Havre, France

When land was sighted, Diane welcomed the news. She had grown tired of the rocking ship and the late nights listening to Madame LeBlanc speak to the departed.

Last night, Madame LeBlanc had gone out alone and stayed out until dawn. When she returned, her right wrist was bruised, and she didn't smile with her usual confidence. She was sharp with Diane and suddenly anxious to leave the ship.

When they departed down the gangplank, the docks were crowded with people dressed in drab clothes who had pale, grim faces. There was a man playing a trumpet, his hat at his feet filled with a few small coins. The smell of fried cakes and fish whirled as crowds jostled each other and pushed toward the street, where carriages waited.

On the street beyond the dock, the chaos did not ease up as carriages rumbled by little boys dressed in shabby clothes begging for coins. Girls not much older than Diane wore brightly colored dresses and hats with weather-beaten feathers. Their faces were painted, and none seemed to mind that their sleeves slipped off their shoulders as men approached.

"Is this where Mr. LeBlanc's cousin lives?" Diane asked.

"No, he lives in the country." Madame LeBlanc rubbed her bruised wrist, now covered with a white glove. "It's a boring place, but I think a good one for us to stay at for a while. Pierre would never think to look for us there."

"Why are you sending him away?"

"Because our cousin would never accept us if we had him."

"Why?"

"Child, you ask too many questions."

Diane tightened her hold on Madame LeBlanc's skirt, hurrying to keep pace. When they reached the street corner, Madame LeBlanc paid a carriage driver to take them to the hotel in Le Havre where they were to wait for her cousin, Gilbert. Madame LeBlanc said he had pledged to escort them home to the Bernard château downriver in the Normandy region.

"If you don't like the country, then why go there?" Diane said.

"Sometimes situations dictate our actions."

"Why isn't Cousin Gilbert here now?" Diane asked.

"It's harvesttime in the orchards. He's working in the fields. He shouldn't be delayed more than a few days."

The idea of being lost in this chaotic city alone terrified Diane. Until now, her world had been lived in small boxes.

"All will be well," Madame LeBlanc said to Diane, though it sounded as if she were trying to buoy her own spirits. "It's not the style to which I am accustomed, but it will have to do."

When they were settled in a coach, Diane scooted closer to the window and peered out. She started when her gaze locked on Pierre's. He stood on the street corner, staring at them. He was always sullen, but now he looked furious.

"Is he going to join us now?" Diane asked, unable to hide her fear.

"No, he has his own accommodations. As I said, I have told Pierre he must now take care of himself. We are done with him."

Diane shrank back against the cushions, glad she would never see Pierre again. "He'll not like that, I think." It had been weeks since he had tripped or pushed her, but the memory of the pain lingered.

"That's too bad for him," Madame LeBlanc said.

Diane peeked past the velvet curtains covering the window, expecting to see him, but he had vanished as if the chaos and crowds had swallowed him up.

———— ❧❧ ————

Diane remained overwhelmed by all the sights and smells of this foreign city as they rode through the streets. The houses were made of gray stone and topped with red tile. The doors were slim and narrow. Windows were often decorated with flower boxes filled with late-season greenery. Churches sported tall spires and stained-glass windows that caught the surrounding light. Narrow streets were paved with cobblestones smoothed and rutted by the endless cart traffic.

Their carriage slowed and pulled under a set of stone arches adorned with monsterlike creatures that stared at Diane as if daring her to enter. The wagon's wheels rumbled over cobblestones and jostled the pair in their seats before it came to a stop in front of a large wooden door. She felt as if history were yanking her back through the centuries.

She'd never seen a building so large and with such thick walls that seemed as ancient as the earth. The driver carried Madame LeBlanc's trunks up into a first-floor hallway, where a man with narrowly set eyes and thinning black hair greeted them. He opened the door to their rooms and spoke so quickly Diane caught only a few words. Madame LeBlanc gave him and the driver a coin each.

A fire crackled in a tall hearth, light from the gaslit sconces flickered up toward roughly hewn beams crisscrossing a high ceiling, and a ragged red rug did what it could to warm the wide-planked floor. Two doors led off the main sitting area to sleeping chambers and a kitchen outfitted with a sink and a worn, narrow counter.

"Certainly not to our standards," Madame LeBlanc said. "But we will manage until Cousin Gilbert can come to our aid."

"When will he be here?" Diane asked.

Madame LeBlanc appeared nervous, as if she expected trouble. "Soon. In the meantime, let us go to the café for a brief repast."

"Do you think Pierre will find us?" Diane asked.

The older woman shook her head. "No. He has been paid well, and he has known for weeks that we would have to go our separate ways."

Madame LeBlanc turned from the room, locked the door behind them, and hurried down the stairs. Diane rushed to keep up with her through the building and along the cobblestone sidewalk. They settled in the bistro on the corner.

Madame LeBlanc relaxed back in her chair and ordered a pair of coffees and two macarons. Conversations mingled with the rattle of cups and the hiss of a kettle.

When their order arrived, Diane stared at the glistening cookies, her stomach grumbling. However, she waited with her hands in her lap as Madame LeBlanc had instructed. Finally, Madame LeBlanc nodded and told her she could have her coffee, but not the macaron. The cookies sat between them untouched.

"You must become accustomed to not eating," Madame LeBlanc said. "I know it sounds harsh, but it is not seemly for a woman to eat too much, and when you reach my age, you will thank me."

The woman sipped her coffee, chatting about Cousin Gilbert and his fine château nestled near the cliffs overlooking the ocean. She had never been to the house, but her dear late husband had often spoken of it as a prosperous and rich estate.

"I have told Cousin Gilbert about you," Madame LeBlanc said. "He is anxious to meet you."

Her coffee gone, Diane's thoughts drifted back to the cookies. "Why?"

"Gilbert is a man who values family. It is why he helped his dear uncle, Mr. LeBlanc, from time to time. I have suggested that you are Gilbert's family as well."

"I don't understand."

"Your eyes reminded Mr. LeBlanc of his first wife. He said many times you could have been their dearly departed daughter, Eva."

Diane traced the edge of her saucer as her stomach grumbled. "I'm not her daughter."

"But it might be kinder to let Cousin Gilbert believe that you are."

"Why?"

"Does it matter? I want you to let me do all the talking, but if Gilbert is to ask you about your dear mama, say that you do not remember her."

"But I do."

Madame LeBlanc's eyes hardened as her patience thinned. "If you want to eat, then you will have to be flexible with the truth."

Madame LeBlanc dug several coins from her purse and put them on the white tablecloth beside the untouched cookies. The two rose, but Diane left her gloves behind on the table. "It is time we returned to the apartment," Madame LeBlanc said. "I am tired."

She beckoned Diane to follow. As Madame LeBlanc summoned a carriage, Diane said quickly, "My gloves. I left them on the table."

Annoyance flickered. "Hurry. I'll not buy you another pair."

Diane hurried back to the table, and as she scooped up her gloves, she grabbed the two cookies and tucked them in her pocket.

Madame LeBlanc approached a carriage and haggled about the price with the driver, and when they could not come to an agreement, she took Diane by the hand, and the two strolled down the street. Several people openly stared at them, and one woman even reached out and tried to touch Diane's coat sleeve.

"I do not like this place," Diane said.

"Neither do I. That is why it is important that Gilbert believe you are his cousin—so that he gives us an allowance."

Thunderclouds rumbled overhead, and when they reached their building, Diane saw Pierre step from the shadows. Diane gasped and drew closer to Madame LeBlanc as he strolled toward them. He had purchased a fine dark suit, a blue silk cravat that wrapped around his neck and then tucked into a fitted vest, and a top hat.

Pierre glanced at Diane, grinned at her surprise, just as he did after he tripped her. "It took a little tracking and a few coins to find you, Madame LeBlanc."

"Pierre." Madame LeBlanc's expression tensed, but she squared her shoulders as she faced him. "I can see you've spent most of the coins I gave you."

"About time I looked like a man destined for better things," he said.

"If you are looking for more money, I have none."

"I don't believe you."

"That is not my concern."

He shook his head, a hardness settling in his angled jaw. "I won't have you toss me away to be replaced by a girl."

"You knew our arrangement wasn't forever," Madame LeBlanc said.

The two began to speak so quickly to each other in French Diane struggled to keep up. Though some of the words escaped her, the tone grew harsher by the moment. Finally Madame LeBlanc pushed him away and told him to leave or she would summon the authorities.

Pierre speared Diane with his gaze. "I will not be tossed aside for you."

As a uniformed officer approached, Pierre took a step back, turned, and vanished down a dark alley. Madame LeBlanc smiled toward the officer, took Diane by the hand, and together they hurried back to their room.

"Why is Pierre so angry?" Diane asked. "I thought he liked you."

"He has grown into a greedy young man. He was well taken care of. I taught him many things, but now it's time for him to get on with his life."

"Is he going away?" Diane looked over her shoulder toward the alley where he'd vanished like a spider into a crack.

"Yes."

"What if he returns?" Diane rubbed her arm, remembering the last fall down the stairs. If he came back into their lives, she was certain he would harm her again. "He looked so angry."

Madame LeBlanc's grip tightened on her hand, and she pulled Diane along. "Do not worry. I'll always be able to handle Pierre."

CHAPTER TEN

Megan

Monday, March 5, 2018
Cape Hudson, Virginia
6:30 p.m.

When Rick parked in front of Spring House, Megan noticed furniture had been moved onto the lawn and the dumpster filled with molded curtains, water-soaked magazines, and old towels. She checked her watch, realizing they'd been gone more than two hours.

"Looks like Natasha and Lucy got a lot done," Rick said.

"God, I hope they didn't throw out anything valuable," she said.

"Don't go rummaging in the dumpster, okay?" Rick asked.

Megan shrugged just as Natasha had earlier that day. "I just might."

"Lucy's under orders to call if you get carried away."

"Funny."

"Not kidding. Do you have it from here?" Rick asked.

"I do. Thanks for the lift. And thanks for the tip on the table."

As he turned, he paused. "What do you think the odds are that Mr. Crawford will call you before he leaves town?"

"Eighty percent," she said.

"That's downright cocky, Ms. Buchanan."

"Not really. He's packed and ready to take an extended trip. He strikes me as a man who has no patience for haggling."

"I'd forgotten how well you could dig in your heels."

She smiled, remembering how his eyes had flared when they had taken opposite sides of that long-ago political debate. He'd pushed, chided a little, but she'd stood toe to toe with him. "Well, I look forward to seeing what comes of it."

Megan slid out of the truck feeling more energized than she had when they'd left to inspect the table. As Rick drove off, Megan spotted Lucy wearing a coconut-bikini top and grass skirt over her work clothes and doing the hula with a big grin. Natasha stood beside her, looking just a little mortified.

"Am I missing a party?" Megan asked, climbing the stairs. Dolly rose up from a blanket where she'd been chewing on a rawhide bone.

Lucy took an armload of debris straight to the dumpster. "Looks like Samuel had a leaky pipe or roof, probably both at some point. A corner of his office is soaked, and it's all going to have to be tossed. But in the digging, we found a trunk full of costumes."

"Explains the mildew smell." Too much of history was lost to fire, flood, and neglect, so she supposed she should be grateful they were saving as much as they were. "Let me start grabbing trash."

"It was super moldy," Lucy said. "I dropped it all in the dumpster, and I've opened the windows."

Megan walked to the dumpster and peered over the edge.

"I promise nothing valuable was tossed." Lucy followed a few steps behind.

Megan surveyed a collection of old *Time* magazines, the discarded green curtains, broken fishing gear, and several sets of old, worn boots. It took a chunk of willpower to turn away and let whatever was ruined go.

"You didn't buy the table?" Lucy asked.

"I made him an offer," Megan said. "He's mulling it over."

"You know there's enough money in the trust to cover the renovations and also furnishings."

"It's going to be the first piece of many. I've got to be a good steward of your money."

"And that's why I chose you," Lucy said.

Lucy's trust and confidence always humbled Megan. She'd been entrusted with renovating not only Winter Cottage but also Lucy's home. "Thanks."

"Aren't you going to say anything about Lucy?" Natasha said.

Megan raised a brow as she studied the girl. "Is there something different about her?"

Natasha rolled her eyes.

Megan asked Lucy, "Are you parting your hair differently?"

"No, hair is the same," Lucy said.

Natasha groaned as she walked toward the house. Dolly followed on her heels. "You two are hiiii-larious."

Lucy thumped the coconut bra with her index finger. "What happened to the sweet little girl I used to know?"

"Hormones."

Megan and Lucy returned to Samuel's study, which was now actually looking somewhat like a study. A weight had lifted, and the room felt light. Maybe the crabby old house did not mind a bit of attention after all.

"So what took you so long?" Natasha asked.

"Rick took me by his place. He wanted to make sure construction supplies had been delivered."

"He's excited about that house," Lucy said. "I know it's not much to look at yet, but Hank tells me Rick is very handy. He helped Hank finish installing the last of the plumbing at the vineyard."

Scott had referred to Rick as a jack-of-all-trades once. "I could tell."

"It really means something to Rick to have a place of his own. He and his family never owned a house."

"He's already made progress. If he ever decides to flip the place, he'll make a profit," Megan said. "Have you learned anything new about your grandfather?"

"He had an odd fascination with coconut bras," Lucy said.

"You mean there are more where those came from?" Megan asked.

"She already has a set for you," Natasha said. "I'm not putting on mine." The girl held up a pair of half coconuts and jiggled them until they clanked together.

Megan smiled. "So, that's what different about you, Lucy? I knew there was something."

Natasha fished the two remaining sets from a cardboard box. Megan took the larger of the two sets and held them up for inspection. "Natasha, I'm thinking your sleepover party should have a tropical theme."

"No way," the girl said. "The girls would laugh me out of school if they saw me wearing those things."

Megan slipped the halter strap over her head and motioned for Lucy to tie the back. "I don't know. I think they're kind of hot. Though I'm not sure if they'll fit me. My breasts are spilling over my bra."

Lucy fastened the back. "You're spilling over the top. But believe me, I'm jealous."

"Be careful what you wish for," Megan said, laughing. It took a little more maneuvering to get her expanded bustline into the cups. She thumped each coconut with her index fingers. "What do you think, Natasha?"

Poor Natasha tried to remain sullen, but as tough as she pretended to be, the kid just was not that jaded. A smile spread across her face, and she looked away quickly to hide it.

"Is that a smile I see?" Megan asked.

Natasha rummaged in the box. "No."

"Is there a grass skirt in there too?" Megan peered inside the box and, seeing a skirt, plucked it out. She stepped into the center and, thanks to an adjustable waistband, pulled it over her belly. Dolly sniffed the skirt and barked.

Megan glanced at the coconuts. "What's so funny? I think I'm pretty sexy."

Lucy pulled out her phone, and Megan grabbed Natasha as Lucy moved closer. She took several selfies featuring Megan's grinning, round face; Lucy's brilliant smile; and Natasha's grimace.

"Please do not post that," Natasha said.

"What? Coconut boobs don't help build your reputation?" Megan asked.

"Nooooo!"

"They'd not do much for a historical scholar either. There's something about coconut bras that stab at credibility."

"Point taken," Lucy said. "Our private moment."

Natasha giggled as she studied the pictures. "We are the craziest family." She grabbed another armload of stuff and walked out of the room.

Lucy stilled as Natasha's footsteps echoed through the house. "Family," she whispered. "Did you hear that? Nothing lately I've said is right, but now we're family."

"You're the safe place for her to show her frustrations," Megan said. "She trusts you enough to be moody."

Lucy studied the picture, enlarging their faces with the swipe of her fingers. "Thanks for playing along. She's so worried about being seen as different."

"I know your family isn't conventional, but I can promise you, this is all normal. She's about to turn thirteen, and I can attest to the power of raging hormones." Megan couldn't remember the last time she'd had a really good laugh. For the first time since Scott had died, she thought she might actually get back to feeling like herself again.

"I keep telling her she's great, but she's having a hard time believing it. I have a whole new respect for my mom and being a single mother."

Megan rubbed her hand over her belly. "Has her father contacted her?"

"He hasn't spoken to her directly. I wrote him a letter and reminded him that she'd like to hear from him, but I haven't heard back from him. And before you make up an excuse for him, I put money in his phone and cantina accounts at the jail."

"Then he'll call."

Lucy wrangled off the coconut bra as if her good mood had evaporated. "He won't call, but he signed the adoption papers without comment."

"That's a good thing, right?" Megan asked.

Lucy sighed, staring out the window toward Natasha, who was throwing a stick for Dolly. "It is a good thing. But Natasha cried when she saw her father's signature. He spent most of his life ignoring her, and now he's officially given her up. She's been in a foul mood since."

"But he's given her to her sister, a woman who clearly loves her."

Lucy shook her head. "You're trying to reason away emotions that are impossible to understand."

"When will the adoption be final?"

"The court promised I'd have the final decree in a few days."

"Maybe we could make it a celebration and fold it into the sleepover party."

"I don't know if she'd like that," Lucy said.

"I wouldn't be so sure about that. Her soccer jersey says *Kincaid*, not *Willard*, on the back. She's already chosen your name over her father's."

"Yeah, you're right." Nodding, Lucy considered the idea. "Let's make it a blowout."

"I have a few cake recipes in my arsenal."

"I thought you were all about pies," Lucy said.

"I'm multifaceted."

"Thanks, but I'll make the cake. It'll mean more to Natasha."

Megan envied Lucy's ease at this entire situation. Lucy had made single parenthood look effortless.

She rapped her knuckles against the hard coconuts. "A tropical vacation sleepover adoption party with a Ouija board."

It was past seven, and they had put a good dent in the initial cleanup. The crew would arrive in the morning, and then they would really start to make progress. For now, they were all starving, and Natasha had math homework.

Megan drove down the long driveway that rolled away from Spring House toward the bay where Winter Cottage nestled on the sandy bank. She opened the front door, pausing as her fingers wrapped around the brass doorknob. A wave of pride and energy flowed through her, and she imagined the countless times Claire had walked into this house and felt the same rush.

Her footsteps echoed in the main hallway as she walked toward the collection of tall windows that faced the Chesapeake Bay. The sun had dipped toward the horizon, but it stayed bright a little longer every day. Soon it would be summer. Soon she would be a mother.

"Baby girl, I sure hope I don't screw this up for you."

A car door slammed shut, and Dolly barked seconds before she bounded around the side of the house toward the reeds rimming the shore.

"No, homework first," Lucy said.

Natasha thumped up the stairs. "I *know!*"

Lucy went into the kitchen and flipped on the lights. Pots and pans clanged.

"What can I do to help?" Megan asked as she entered the room.

"You can sit. I'm making an easy supper for us."

Megan sat at the kitchen table, running her hands over the smooth wood. "Is Natasha okay?"

"She wants to watch television and do her homework later." Lucy pulled a head of lettuce and some tomatoes and cucumbers from the refrigerator.

"I always loved doing my history homework. But when it came to math and science, it was like pulling teeth. I remember when we were living in Portland and I was in a new middle school and hating it. My mother promised me a trip to a living-history museum if I got an A in math."

"Did you?"

"Not even close. A C minus," she said.

Lucy set a pot of water on the stove and turned on the gas before she started chopping. "My mom and I had our problems, but it was usually me reading her the riot act. Since I was five, I had been the adult in our relationship. Hell, she'd even insisted I call her Beth."

Within fifteen minutes, Lucy had made a simple salad to accompany pasta and heated up bread she'd made the day before.

The smell of food lured Natasha into the kitchen, and she plopped into a chair, her gaze on the tablet that Hank had given her.

"Homework done?" Lucy asked.

"Yep, it was super easy."

"Electronics off."

Natasha did not look up. "Okay. Okay."

"Now," Lucy said.

When Natasha seemed to slow-walk closing down the video, Lucy took the tablet from her. "Hey, that's mine!" the girl yelped.

Lucy shut it off and set it on top of the refrigerator. "One more comment, and it's mine for a week."

Natasha's eyes widened with shock and frustration. "Hank gave it to me. You can't just take it."

"Two weeks."

"You're not the boss of me."

"Three weeks, Natasha."

114

She thrust out her bottom lip in what could be described only as a power pout.

"I can call Hank right now and ask him what he thinks about you watching a video at the dinner table."

Natasha scrunched her face and then flounced back in her chair. "No."

"Thought so. Let's eat." Lucy's grin was forced and stiff.

"I'm not hungry," Natasha said.

"Then you may sit there and watch while Megan and I eat."

"I don't see why I have to," Natasha said.

"Because I said so."

The classic mother words tripped off Lucy's lips so easily, Megan almost smiled . . . until she thought about wrangling a preteen girl alone one day. Her heart beat a little faster, and all her worries and doubts doubled in an instant.

Without a word, Lucy made a plate of spaghetti with extra sauce, salad, and bread with double butter for Natasha, before she made a plate for herself.

Natasha shrugged, clearly doing her best to be defiant.

Megan sneaked a quick look her way and winked. "I've been thinking about the planchette and the dreidels and how they came to be together," she said. "The items really don't go together. I keep wondering why Samuel would have them."

"You're asking the wrong person. I don't know anything about my family," Lucy said.

Remembering the picture Mr. Crawford had found in the desk, Megan pulled the image up on her phone. "Have a look at this. I think the woman on the left is Claire."

Lucy set down her fork and took the phone. With the swipe of her fingers, she enlarged the photo. "That's Claire."

"I know my great-grandmother spent time in Paris with the Buchanans," Megan said.

"Who do you think the woman is with her?" Lucy asked.

"Rick theorized it's her sister."

"She had three of them. And three brothers. I know a little about the brothers because they stayed on the peninsula, but the sisters were scattered to the wind after their mother died."

Natasha reached for a second slice of bread and took great care pulling it apart. She was paying attention.

"Stands to reason Claire would make friends while she was in France," Lucy said, handing back the phone. "This woman could be anyone."

"Agreed. I have another picture that I thought you might like to see." She scrolled through her phone. "This was taken on the front porch of Spring House. But as you can see, Winter Cottage had not yet been built."

Lucy wiped her fingers on a paper towel and took the phone again. "She has dark hair, and her eyes are light just like the woman in the Le Havre picture."

"Which supports the theory that the woman is Claire's sister."

"Which one would she be?" Lucy asked.

Megan reached out and swiped the screen to the next picture taken of the four Hedrick girls. "I think she was the youngest sister, Diane."

Lucy studied the image. "The four Hedrick sisters all together. And that's their mother sitting between them?"

"Addie Hedrick," Megan said.

"From what I know about Claire, she was quite traumatized after her mother died and she was sent away," Lucy said.

"I'm sure that was true for all the girls," Megan said.

"Do we know where the other sisters were sent?"

"Jemma and Sarah went to farms in the western part of Virginia, but Diane vanished. I've not been able to find records of her."

Natasha rose and looked over Lucy's shoulder. "She looks like a witch."

The girl's response surprised Megan. "Why do you say that?"

Natasha shrugged. "Her hair, her eyes, and that wild scarf around her neck. She'd have been the kind of person to work that triangle thingy on the Ouija board."

"But how did it end up in my grandfather's desk?" Lucy asked. "He wasn't even born when this picture was taken."

Natasha sat, popped a torn piece of bread in her mouth, and then wound thick strands of spaghetti around her fork. "Can we break out the Ouija board?"

"Finish up your dinner," Lucy said.

"And then we can do it?" Natasha asked.

"You did finish your homework?" Lucy asked.

"And the extra credit," Natasha replied.

The girl was smart, especially in math, where she was already outpacing her teacher. Lucy had confided in Megan that she worried Natasha wouldn't get the challenge she needed in her regular math class, but she'd already spoken to the school about all advanced classes in the fall.

Megan dropped her gaze to the image of the two women. She felt drawn to the exotic young woman's face with her sly smile. The tilt of her head suggested independence, uncommon to women in that era.

Diane Hedrick. *What happened to you?*

Natasha cleared her voice, coughed, and said, "Cell phone at the table."

"Touché." Megan closed her phone and laid it facedown.

"So are we agreed we'll do a magical game night kind of sleepover party?" Lucy asked. "I can read fortunes and decorate the house to make it look haunted."

Natasha shook her head. "I don't know. Brittany had a pool party for her thirteenth, but it's too cold."

Lucy nodded thoughtfully. "We could dress up like the people that used to live at Winter Cottage in the 1920s."

"Or we could dress as zombies," Natasha countered.

"I'll throw in 1920s cuisine and music, and we'll sketch portraits."

"I know some great secondhand stores," Megan offered. "I could get a deal on clothes from the era, so if the girls don't have anything, we can have it here."

"Tempting," Natasha said. "I think I'd rather dress modern."

"What if we did a scavenger hunt?" Megan asked. "Or solved a murder mystery."

"I like the murder idea," Natasha said.

"Think about it." Lucy kept her tone casual, as if she'd learned the harder she pushed, the more her sister resisted an idea. Lucy had the bait in the water and a few nibbles; now all she had to do was wait before she reeled her in.

It took another hour for the trio to finish up dinner, which was filled with chatter about Brittany's new outfit, the math teacher who was so lame, and a discussion about tomorrow's moving logistics.

When the dishes were put away and the table cleared, Megan brought out the old Ouija board set she had found in the antique shop. It was cracked and torn in several places, adding more mystery to where it had been before.

"Cool," Natasha said.

Megan touched the edges, amazed it was in such good shape. "Let's fire this sucker up."

Megan removed the planchette from the wooden box and set it on the table. It felt heavy in her hands, which surprised her. Usually these devices were designed to be light so they could be easily manipulated. Carefully, she handed the piece to Lucy.

"It's been a while, but I think I can do this." Lucy made a show of flexing her fingers. "Who wants to ask the first question?"

Megan then shifted in her seat, suddenly nervous at the idea of talking to anyone who had crossed over. It was one thing to research the lives of people who had passed, but another to have a conversation with the other side. There were so many things that had remained unsaid between Scott and her, and as much as they needed saying, she could not bring herself to do it yet.

Natasha's eyes widened, and she looked at the board and then at Lucy and Megan. "What do I ask?"

"Anything you want," Lucy said.

"Anything?"

"That's right."

Natasha sat back in her chair, and as she sighed, her brow furrowed, forming a deep wrinkle over the bridge of her nose. "I dunno."

"I know who I'd be talking to, if it were me," Lucy said.

"Who?"

"My mom. I'd want to know why she never told me about this place. If she had, I might have come here sooner and gotten the chance to meet Samuel and maybe your mom."

"You should ask her why she left," Natasha said. "She might have a really good reason."

"I might," Lucy said, thoughtfully. "One day."

Megan realized then that she did not have a lock on unfinished business. *Everyone should be playing this game,* she thought.

"Ask your mother if you were a good baby," Lucy said.

"Okay," Natasha said. "Let's do this."

Lucy nodded, her face solemn. "Megan, can you dim the lights?"

"Sure." Megan rose and reached for the lights. She hesitated before she turned the central light off, leaving the one over the sink on to cast a soft glow of light over the room. Out the window, the full moon bathed the property and the bay in a delicate silver hue.

Megan sat back down and scooted her chair close to the table. The baby kicked the side of her belly several times, as if she too felt the energy pulse around them.

"Remember each of us needs to not break contact with the top of the planchette," Lucy said.

Megan looked at Natasha's wide-eyed expression, which reflected a youthful excitement. In this instant she too felt like she was twelve again, at a sleepover and staying up long past curfew to whisper secrets in the glow of a dime-store flashlight.

"Everyone needs to close their eyes and try to summon Natasha's mother, Grace," Lucy said.

Nervous giggles rumbled from Natasha as she closed her eyes and then quickly opened them. "What if no one is home?"

"You won't know unless you ask," Lucy said.

The three closed their eyes, and Natasha began to call out to her mother in soft, even tones as if she were coaxing a fawn toward her. Her soft, melodic voice called out and then paused before she asked, "Mom, it's me, Natasha. Do you miss me?"

The planchette didn't move at first, but Megan could feel energy shooting through her own body. And then the wooden device moved barely a fraction, but it was enough to make Natasha hiss in a breath.

Megan peeked and saw that the girl's eyes were squeezed shut tightly while Lucy's face looked serene.

The piece suddenly jerked to the *yes* and then to the *no*, and then quickly it returned back to the *yes*, where it settled. After several beats, Lucy opened her eyes and met Megan's gaze.

"Natasha, open your eyes," Lucy said.

The girl slowly opened one, and then both sprang open. "It says *yes!*"

Lucy nodded. "So it does."

Natasha picked up the piece and looked under it. "You guys did that. You moved it."

"I did not," Lucy said.

"Then Megan did."

Megan held up three fingers. "Nope, scout's honor."

"This thing can't be real," Natasha said.

"Why not?" Lucy countered. "It makes perfect sense to me that your mother would miss you. I know I would."

"You would not," she said. "I drive you crazy."

A smile tugged at the edge of Lucy's lips. "Yes, you do. But I would miss you if you were gone."

Natasha stood up abruptly, came around the table, and hugged Lucy. "I would miss you too."

"Good thing we're stuck like glue," Lucy said. Dolly barked and wagged her tail. "It's getting late. She needs to go out, and you need to go to bed."

"I'll take her," Natasha said. "Can we do this again?"

"Sure," Lucy said.

"I like talking to dead people."

The girl and dog bounded out of the room. When Megan heard the door slam closed, she asked, "You did that?"

Lucy smiled. "It was the power of the universe."

A breeze blew outside, rattling the old windows. "Come on. You said yourself you did this in the bars on Halloween."

"And I was good at it. I had repeat customers because some thought I was psychic."

Megan laughed as she rose. "Right."

She crossed to the counter and set up the coffeemaker for the next morning. As Lucy cleared the table, Megan stared out the kitchen window toward the waters of the bay now glistening in the moonlight.

Rick's new home had a similar view, though there was something more settled about the view of the cove than the one of the open waters of the bay. He was trying to fit into Cape Hudson because of Scott. He looked out for her out of a sense of duty and honor. But he had a gypsy spirit much like Scott had. Though dedicated and brave, no place or woman would ever hold him down for long. Her body vibrated with sexual tension when she thought about him standing in his house. Her body ached to kiss him and to feel his rough hands on her skin.

Megan watched a tanker appear on the horizon. Its bow was nosed south, and the lights slowly crawled along the horizon, away from Baltimore and toward the Atlantic Ocean.

Her attraction to Rick was clearly being fueled by hormones in overdrive and by the fact that he had been Scott's best friend. They shared a history, and if there was anything she liked, it was history.

April 7, 1939
From the Journal of Samuel Jessup
The Port of Tunis, Tunisia

Mr. and Mrs. Edward Garrison appeared out of place on the old, weathered dock. Husband and wife were finely dressed and looked more suited for the grand avenues of New York rather than a dock crummed full of sweaty men, stacks of cargo, and livestock. Like all the men, I was curious about the couple we'd been sent to fetch. But instead of crowding against the railing like the others, I stood back, oddly nervous.

As Mrs. Garrison boarded the ship, her gaze caught mine, and for a moment she stopped and stared at me as if she'd seen a ghost. I knew enough history of Cape Hudson to understand she had vacationed there when she was younger. But that would have been years before I was born. When her husband finally caught her attention, she smiled quickly and continued to their rooms.

The ship's captain greeted the Garrisons like they were royalty.

Mrs. Garrison's sister-in-law, Mrs. Claire Buchanan, met me in Norfolk, Virginia, one month ago. It was good to see Miss Claire, and when she asked me to deliver a letter to Mrs. Garrison, I agreed. It seemed a routine task until Miss Claire cautioned me not to read the letter. It was for Mrs. Garrison only. I'm not sure why all the secrecy, but rich people are an odd lot in general. I do not pretend to understand them now, or ever.

CHAPTER ELEVEN

Megan

Tuesday, March 6, 2018
Cape Hudson, Virginia
8:00 a.m.

Megan, Lucy, and Dolly dropped Natasha off at school and waited until the girl vanished into the building before driving back to Spring House and arriving at a quarter past eight.

Megan got out of the Jeep, wrangling her big belly out of the tight space. She opened the back door for Dolly, who jumped out and put her nose to the ground immediately, following a scent into the overgrowth.

As Megan walked toward the house, her phone chimed with a text. The contractor reported that his movers were caught in traffic in Norfolk and would be several hours late. The extra time turned into a boon for Lucy, who spent the time removing the books from the floor-to-ceiling shelves while Megan sat in a chair, thumbing through each volume. She knew from experience that important stray papers or letters often found themselves tucked into a book, and she did not want to miss one.

After an hour, she had a small pile of papers, including a stub for the movie *Jaws*, receipts for groceries purchased in 2005, a political pamphlet dating back to a congressional election in 2000, and a receipt for property taxes on a 1989 truck.

Samuel's reading tastes were indeed varied, ranging from historical military biographies and classics such as *Oliver Twist* and *Silas Marner* to political histories that covered the Bay of Pigs invasion as well as the fall of the shah in Iran. Samuel had not graduated high school, but clearly he'd had a thirst for learning that had spanned his entire life.

At ten in the morning, the moving crew arrived, and three burly men climbed out of the cab. Lucy turned from a now empty shelf and breathed a sigh of relief. "Thank God. The cavalry has arrived. We can get those guys to box all this up and haul it away."

Piles of books stood like sentries around Megan's chair as freshly stirred dust danced in the sunlight streaming through the window. "We're making real progress. Once they get the books out of here and the furniture, then the demo can begin."

With a hand cupping her belly, Megan rose and gingerly tiptoed her way around the books and out the front door. A man dressed in faded jeans and a Tucker's Moving & Construction T-shirt approached. His gaze went directly to her round belly as he stuck out his hand toward her. "Ms. Buchanan."

"Yes. Mr. Tucker."

"You can call me Ron, and these two fellows are Dave and Bill." He looked past her toward the house and the porch cluttered with *Keep* boxes nearly bursting.

"All those need to be loaded so we can clear the porch and work our way into the study."

"Will do. I understand Mr. Jessup was over one hundred when he died."

"He was, and the last century of stuff is all right here."

Mr. Tucker laughed while shaking his head. "We specialize in houses like this. Clutter is our bread and butter."

"It's not all junk," Megan said, a bit defensively.

"No, ma'am."

Mr. Tucker and his guys got to work, and soon the porch was cleared. Lucy came outside and, tipping her face toward the sun, stretched. She crossed the yard to her Jeep, opened the back door, and removed a cooler she'd packed earlier.

"Time to take a load off, Megan."

"I think I'll stand here and make sure they don't damage the furniture. Some of it is quite valuable."

"It's going to take at least an hour before they can clear the room enough to attempt furniture removal. Sit and eat." She pulled a water bottle and sandwich from the cooler and handed both to Megan.

"Technically, I should be doing this for you," Megan said. "You're the boss. I'm the employee."

Lucy laughed as she pulled two folding chairs from the truck bed and opened them. She cracked open a water bottle, stretched out her legs, and took a long drink. "You're right. As your boss, I'm telling you to sit, eat, drink some water. Otherwise, one of these three guys is going to be delivering your baby on this front porch."

"Yes, ma'am," she said with a grin.

The sandwich was ham and cheese with a slice of tomato. Mustard, not mayo, just as Megan liked it. Lucy noticed the little things.

"I got a call yesterday about a potential wedding on Winter Cottage property," Lucy said.

"Really?" She drank from her bottled water, not realizing how thirsty she'd become.

"The event is scheduled for August."

"Four months in the wedding world is short notice for a venue."

"So I've been told."

"Who's the client?"

"Her name is Zoe Bradford, and she has been to the Eastern Shore before and seen the property. She has always dreamed of getting married here and just got engaged." Lucy rolled her neck from side to side. "I hear it's really hot here in the summer."

"It's beautiful, but you're right. It's hot. And it's hurricane season. If you schedule it for the evening, some of the day's heat may have cooled. When's she coming to look the place over?"

"Saturday. I don't know if I can help her out, but what the heck, it doesn't hurt to talk, right?"

"There's going to be a lot of transition in August. We won't have Spring House finished."

"I know. It might not work out, but who knows? The extra cash would be welcome."

"So she called you out of the blue?"

"Not exactly. I posted my notice on a wedding website. Plenty of parking and room to pitch a tent. Limited kitchen access. Portable potties a must. You can bring your own caterer. Discounts on wine from Beacon Vineyards."

"How much are you going to charge?"

"I don't know. I've got to figure wear and tear and insurance—see if Rick wants to earn a few extra bucks working security."

"Sounds like you have it all sorted out," Megan said.

"I planned a few events back in Nashville. My claim to fame was a music festival last year. I'm thinking a bride can't be much worse than a bunch of temperamental musicians."

Megan chuckled. "I have my last pie delivery to make in Norfolk on Friday. Come with me, and I'll introduce you to the coordinator. She knows everyone in the wedding world."

"Cool. I'll do that."

Lucy tore off the crust of her bread, and they both ate in silence. The rumble of tires on gravel had them turning to find a dark sedan with Virginia plates driving their way. The car pulled up and came to a stop. Helen Jessup stepped out.

Helen was a tall, slim woman who kept her graying, thick hair short and her makeup minimal, but her features were striking.

She was dressed in crisp slacks, a white blouse with a vintage Hermès scarf wrapped around her neck, and tasteful, chunky pumps. Helen took meticulous care of her clothes. Her salt-and-pepper hair was swept into a low ponytail, and diamond studs winked from her ears. Her blue eyes reminded Megan of Scott's, and for an instant, Megan's heart squeezed with pain.

Tension rippled up her body. The easy relaxation she had shared with Lucy vanished.

"What's wrong?" Lucy asked.

"It's Helen Jessup. Scott's mother."

"Is that a bad thing?"

"We didn't part on good terms." She smoothed her palms over her jeans. "Helen, what are you doing here so early?"

Helen tipped her chin up. "I was just visiting Scott's grave. I visit him often."

Megan's throat tightened as she thought about the endless supply of fresh flowers that always adorned his grave.

"Your mother said you were working here now," Helen said.

"Yes. I'll be here for at least a year."

"Please tell me you're having the baby in Norfolk and not here at the clinic."

"That's the plan."

Helen slid her finger under a thick gold bracelet sporting a gold star. Megan could not read the writing on the charm but suspected it bore Scott's name.

Her baby kicked hard, and for a second, Megan allowed herself to imagine what it would be like losing her child. The thought squeezed her chest, making it impossible for her to speak without her voice cracking.

When she and Scott had been together, she had known almost from the beginning they were not really suited. He was on the go constantly, always needing to ride his motorcycle, swim, or hike a trail. No such thing as too much adrenaline. In fact, sitting was torture for him. She, however, was always content to curl up with a new biography or historical research project. But the one place they had been compatible had been the bedroom. That had lulled them both into thinking that great sex translated into lifelong compatibility.

Helen's expression just then softened in a way that made her look vulnerable, and it caught Megan off guard. Helen's gaze dropped to Megan's belly. Seconds passed before she raised her eyes. "How are you doing?"

"Well."

"And the baby?"

"The baby is fine. Likes to kick a lot."

Plucked eyebrows rose as regret and pain darkened Helen's blue eyes. "Scott was like that when I was pregnant. I barely slept a wink that last month."

Helen was not a woman who apologized. She was not a hugger, and according to Scott, she had never been comfortable with deep emotions. For her to associate this child with Scott was about as close as Megan was going to get to any kind of apology or acknowledgment that Scott was the father.

"My mom said you called her," Megan said.

"She wrote me a lovely note, and I wanted to touch base with her and see how you were doing."

Considering her mother was in Australia, it could not have been an easy call to coordinate. "How are you doing, Helen?" Megan asked.

"Restless, angry, tired of staying with my husband's grandmother, who is pushing one hundred and really does not need me hovering around all the time." She paused and cleared her throat as if this utterly raw moment embarrassed her.

Megan had received some of those looks blended with curious stares and a few angry glances. And those who shoved pity her way usually got an earful from her.

Helen cleared her throat again. "Renovating Winter Cottage and Spring House is quite the undertaking."

Megan accepted the change of subject, reminding herself again that Helen was living a mother's nightmare. Scott had said when his father had died, Helen had gotten very angry and turned that rage on Scott. Now, she knew, thanks to Rick, that all Helen had was an aging grandmother-in-law.

"We've only just begun to scratch the surface. It's going to take days to clear it out."

"Is that good for you to be working so hard?"

"I'm taking it easy."

Lucy stepped forward and extended her hand. "I'm Lucy Kincaid."

Helen shook her hand. "You're Samuel's granddaughter, correct?"

"That's right. Did you know him?" Lucy asked.

"Not well, but he came to Scott's funeral dressed in full uniform. Polished shoes, shaved. They tell me he rarely left this house, but he was there for Scott."

Lucy's eyes glistened. "I'm glad to hear it."

Helen cleared her throat. "I knew your mother, Beth, also. We went to high school together."

"Everyone who knew my mother has some kind of story," Lucy responded.

A faint smile tugged at Helen's lips. "I do have a few, yes. She was a lively girl. I understand she passed away."

"Yes."

"I'm sorry to hear that," Helen said. "I lost my mother when I was about your age."

Megan could hear the sadness and pain in Helen's voice. But how could she offer comfort to a woman who held her responsible for her son's death?

If Lucy sensed the tension, she skated around it. "Can I offer you a water, Mrs. Jessup?"

"No, I don't want to impose. And please call me Helen."

Helen looked up toward the house as if struggling to find some reason to stay. Though she could simply ask, she was a prideful woman, and despite her pain, she would not intrude.

Whatever anger Megan had hung on to since last fall abandoned her, leaving instead an empty, exposed sensation. "Would you like to see the house?" she asked.

Helen's eyes softened, and she released a breath she was holding. "Yes, Megan, I would. Thank you."

Mr. Tucker and his two men each carried out boxes filled with books. "If you ladies go inside, let us know if you need anything."

"Thank you," Megan said.

As the three women climbed the front steps, Helen looked around, clearly curious about the project. "I guess you remember that Samuel was my late husband's granduncle. Samuel didn't move to this property until the mid-1990s. He was quite the man of the world."

"He waited fairly late in life to marry my grandmother," Lucy said. "My mom was born a year later."

"My father-in-law said once that Samuel, as a young man, was in love with another woman and pined for her most of his life. Your grandmother apparently reminded him of his lost love. I understand he asked her to marry him on their second date."

"Really?" Lucy said. "Do you know who the lost love was?"

"No. I never pressed for details."

"Do you know where he lived when he was married?" Lucy asked.

"The house on Cove Lane," Helen said.

"The sheriff just bought a house on Cove Lane," Megan said.

Helen stepped closer. "I'm the one who told Rick about it. I'd heard it was for sale and knew he would be the kind of man to bring it back to life."

"That was Samuel's house?" Lucy asked.

"Samuel bought the house for his wife and your mother. Though from what I remember, he wasn't around much."

"You and Rick talk often?" Megan asked.

"Yes," Helen said. "He's a good man. He's one of the few people who still talks about Scott. And I miss that. I don't want him forgotten. And I want the baby to know about her father."

"I haven't forgotten Scott," Megan said softly.

Helen was quiet, as if the words were trapped in her chest. She shifted her gaze to a picture on the wall of Samuel in southeast Asia. "I'm not angry with you, Megan. I want there to be peace. I want to know my grandchild."

Tears welled in Megan's eyes, and as much as she tried to will them away, they spilled down her cheeks. "I want that too, Helen."

The conversation petered out, and an awkward silence settled between them. It was Lucy, as always, who steered them toward calm waters. "Helen, you really do have to help us. I want to know more about my grandfather. You're the one person I know who knew him the longest."

"Are you sure?" Helen asked.

"Of course we're sure," Lucy said.

"I can also introduce you to my grandmother-in-law," Helen offered. "She's ninety-eight. Samuel would have been a young man when she married Aaron, and they must have crossed paths many times. She might know who Samuel was in love with all those years ago."

"That would be awesome," Lucy said.

"Megan, is it all right with you?" Helen asked.

Megan could almost feel Scott standing beside her, nudging her to speak. *Come on, Meg. Be the bigger person.*

He had said the same words to her when she had pushed through the front door of his apartment. She had just found out she was pregnant and wanted to share the news with him. Instead, she had found one of her bridesmaids wearing only his shirt.

Scott had tried to talk to her, but she'd run from the building. That had been the last time she had seen him. He had called and texted her a dozen times with no answer.

She had contacted her mother, announced she was canceling the wedding and needed a vacation. Her mother had been stunned, angry, and had reminded her of the costs involved. Megan had vowed to pay it all back. Better to be a runaway bride than the gullible woman.

To her parents' credit, they had recovered from the shock and rolled with the sudden change. While Megan had gone into hiding in the Blue Ridge Mountains, her mother had canceled everything and eaten the cost of the rental space and half the catering fee.

Two weeks later, Scott was dead.

"Helen, of course you're welcome," Megan said. "We could use the help going through this house." Even as she made the statement, she tried to picture interacting with Helen on a daily basis. They had always been polite to each other, but they had never landed on a connection beyond Scott.

Helen's face softened. "I do like to organize."

Megan turned to Lucy, who quickly picked up the ball. "It'll take us a week to dig through the office alone."

Mr. Tucker and his men pushed through the front door and onto the porch with a dolly full of boxes. With each new box removed, the house felt a shade lighter.

Helen faced them, her eyes brightening with hope. Death had taken away her husband and her son, and it was clear she was desperately lonely. "I need to drive into Norfolk to check in on Grandmother, but I can be back here bright and early tomorrow." Her shoulders straightened a fraction. "I think I have arrived just in time. I can see you two girls are going to need my help."

———— ❧~~ஒ ————

By 4:00 p.m. Mr. Tucker and his men had cleared the front hallway of books and the makeshift set of bookshelves that Samuel had hammered into the wall. Their truck loaded, they drove off to make stops at the local library with the books and then the landfill with the trash.

Megan cringed as she saw the nail holes and dents in the wainscoting that must be nearly a century old. But the addition of the shelves was just one of many questionable improvements that had been foisted onto the house over the decades.

"It baffles me why homeowners cover up such lovely wood with fake paneling or a bad paint job," Megan said.

"Take a deep breath," Lucy said. "We'll make it all better."

"It's so unnecessary."

"Think of it as job security," Lucy said.

When Rick pulled up in his sheriff's car shortly after four, he had Natasha in the front seat.

"Judging by the way the girl is chatting and grinning, her hormones have dialed down from raging to calm," Megan said.

"Like the weather on the bay, both can turn on a dime," Lucy said, peeking out a salt-streaked window. "I wonder what new ideas she has for her party."

Megan smiled as she watched the kid bound across the front lawn. Dolly, sleeping on the front porch for the last hour, rose up and rushed toward her.

When Rick rose out of the vehicle, Megan felt a familiar knot coil in her stomach. His muscled, lean frame moved with the grace and confidence of a lion, and she suffered another jolt of sexual desire that was almost comical considering her pear-shaped body.

Rick followed Natasha across the front lawn and up the stairs, and when he looked up, his gaze caught Megan's and she felt a flush of heat warm her cheeks. That smile tugged at the edge of his lips, and she could only imagine how ridiculous he thought she was.

"Wow, this place looks amazing," Natasha said. "It doesn't stink near as bad as it did yesterday."

"Musty books have their own unique scent," Megan said. "But I wouldn't stay *stink*."

Natasha shrugged. "Did you find any buried treasure or anything cool?"

"Nothing but books and more books," Lucy said. "We went through them all, hoping to find something, but so far, nada. Maybe we'll get lucky later today."

"I can totally go through books," Natasha said. "If I find treasure, can I keep it?"

Lucy laughed. "No. But I'll tell anyone who asks that you were the one that found it."

"And I can tell the kids at school?" Natasha asked.

"Absolutely," Megan said.

"Megan, did Mr. Crawford show up today?" Rick asked.

"He did not."

"Well, then I believe you owe me a couple of pies, Miss Megan." She grinned. "I'll pay up."

"I'm holding you to it." Rick picked up an edition of Winston Churchill's biography, and as he leafed through it, he said almost conversationally, "I hear Helen is in town."

"Who's Helen?" Natasha asked.

"She's the mother of the guy I was engaged to," Megan said.

"Baby daddy?" Natasha asked.

As a historian Megan was in the business of uncovering secrets, but she had promised this baby it would not be that way between them.

What she knew, her daughter would know as soon as it was age appropriate. "Correct. Helen stopped by, and she has agreed to help us work on the house."

Rick's gaze lifted to Megan. "You asked for her help?"

"I did." Megan had heard pregnant women lost their minds a little toward the end of pregnancy. This had to be a symptom of diminished mental capacity. "She's a whiz at organizing, and this job is bigger than it looks."

Rick did not speak, but she saw the slight pulse in his jaw. "A project like Spring House will be good for her."

"Because her son died?" Natasha asked.

"Yes." Megan hoped Helen wouldn't drive her insane and her brain would return to full capacity after the baby was born.

"It can be pretty lonely after someone dies," Natasha said. "I'm glad she's going to have us now."

Lucy laid her hand on Natasha's shoulder. "For all the drama, kid, you're pretty amazing."

Natasha shrugged. "Obviously."

Rick cleared his throat. "You've made a lot of progress."

"We have," Megan said. "Mr. Tucker just took his first truckload of books away. Most will go to the library for their spring sale, and any others that couldn't be saved to the dumpster."

"That might be a lot of stuff," Rick said.

"Wait until the construction crew arrives tomorrow. There's no telling what they'll find when they start ripping down these walls."

"Like a dead body?" Natasha asked.

"I hope not," Megan said.

"Might be cool."

"Come on, kid," Lucy said. "Help me with some of the stuff in the bedroom."

"Okay."

When the two moved toward the door, Megan started to follow until Rick gently took hold of her arm. The contact surprised her and once again churned up warmth that spread through her body.

"What you're doing for Helen is very kind," he said quietly. "I know she said some pretty harsh things to you at Scott's funeral."

She straightened, wondering who had heard the exchange between Helen and her. She'd certainly told no one. "If you see me running down the road screaming like a madwoman and pulling out my hair, all I ask is that you keep me from jumping in the bay."

Rick smiled in a way that was far too charming. "She can be intense. But she needs you more than you realize."

"Hey!" Natasha yelled. "We found something!"

Megan and Rick followed, arriving as Lucy set several books on the floor. Beyond the dusty outline of books on the shelf was a small hatch secured by a latch and a lock.

"Can we open it?" Natasha asked.

Megan inspected the hidey-hole. The lock was made by Dudley and appeared to date back to the 1920s or 1930s. She hesitated, curling her fingers into a fist.

"Everything all right?" Rick asked.

"Rick, you think you could open this?" she asked.

"Sure." He gripped the lock and tugged, but when it did not budge, he fished a folding knife from his pocket and flicked it open with practiced ease. Very carefully, he wedged the tip under the lock and carefully pried the nails attaching the door to the wall. The brittle wood finally gave way, splitting around the hinges.

The small door popped open, and he wedged it back and forth until the screws securing the hinges worked free. Rick handed the door to Megan and, taking a flashlight from his belt, peered into the opening.

"Is there anything good in there?" Natasha asked.

"Natasha, I think we might have found your buried treasure," Rick said.

CHAPTER TWELVE

Diane

Age 12

Thursday, October 8, 1903
Le Havre, France

By the afternoon, Madame LeBlanc had not changed out of her dress-ing gown, and remained by the fire. She held the planchette in her hands, rubbing her thumb over the smooth surface as she stared into the flames.

They had eaten all the bread and cheese, and Madame LeBlanc had drunk the last bottle of wine. "Diane, you must post a letter for me to Gilbert. The wine merchant can take care of it for you."

Diane's stomach grumbled. "Can I buy bread and cheese?"

"A little, yes. And I require more wine. Grab your coat and hurry. It'll be dark in a couple of hours."

Diane looked out the slender window toward the gray sky. "Alone?"

"You're a clever girl. You're used to a rougher sort of life than I, and you are far more attuned to the streets. You can run these errands without being noticed."

Diane's heart pounded in her chest as Madame LeBlanc motioned for her to slip on her coat. "You know what kind of wine I like. You know the shop on the corner we passed when we arrived."

"No, Madame LeBlanc, I'm not sure which one it is."

"Out the main door and to the right. It should be easy enough."

"Can I post my letters to my sister?" She had written several letters to her sister on the crossing but had been unable to post any.

"You may post one," Madame LeBlanc said as she fastened Diane's topcoat button. "But it's critical that you send Gilbert's letter."

Wrestling with the tightness in her chest, Diane considered refusing. "What if Pierre finds me?"

"He won't." She rose out of her chair and slid on her own coat.

"But he's out there."

"If you're no use to me, then I shall have to put you out on the street, Diane. There is no place for laziness in my household. You wouldn't want to earn your living like the girls on the street, would you?"

Diane stepped back, shocked by Madame LeBlanc's sudden crossness. She had seen the wretched creatures whose thin, painted faces projected a mixture of bravado and fear. As much as she did not like living with Madame LeBlanc, the streets were far worse.

Madame LeBlanc recovered her smile quickly. "I'm tired, Diane. Pay no attention to me. Now hurry."

"I'll run the errands," Diane said.

"That's good, girl."

"What if Cousin Gilbert doesn't answer you?"

"Gilbert is a man bound by honor," she said. "He'll see to our safety."

Diane, with her coins pushed deep in her pockets, hurried outside past the girls who lingered on the street corner and past the men who leered. Several men called out to her, as they did each day. *Mademoiselle, un moment, s'il vous plaît.* But she ducked her face, refusing to look at anyone. Laughter chased her down the cobblestone streets, blending with the sound of her beating heart and the rush of the city in her ears.

When she rounded the final corner and saw the wine merchant's shop, she felt such relief. She crossed the street and pushed through the front door. The warmth from a potbelly stove in the corner of the shop made her realize just how cold it had been outside. The heat drew her closer, and she extended her hands toward the hot grate.

The dimly lit shop was a curious place, stocked with bottles of wine from more places than she could ever imagine visiting. There were slabs of sausage hanging from the ceiling and wheels of cheese piled high. Earthy smells of old stone mingled with the scents of cinnamon, blackberries, and licorice. Her skirts brushed against the casks and bottles of wine shelved carefully on their sides as she made her way to the front counter made of roughly hewn wood still showing the ax marks from medieval serfs who had felled the tree.

The curtains behind the counter flickered, and a man appeared. She guessed he was not very old judging by the faintest of wrinkles creasing the corners of his eyes when he smiled. Dark eyes glowed with an almost otherworldly brightness as he watched her approach.

"I need to mail a letter," she said. "Where do I go?"

"I can post it for you," he said. "Let me see."

She handed the two letters to him. He read each address and frowned.

"Is something wrong?" she asked.

"No." He looked up at her. "New York is in America."

"My sister lives there."

"Ah."

Diane ordered bread and a bottle of wine. The man placed her purchases in her bag and then counted out several pennies in change. As Diane reached for the coins, she noticed the small display of macarons. Realizing she had enough for two, she placed her order.

The man raised a brow but after an indolent shrug wrapped the two largest macarons in white paper. She held the cookies up to her nose, inhaling the scents of rose and lavender. Her mouth watered. She would eat one on the way home and hide the other in her room.

"Bon appétit," he said.

"Merci."

With her bottle and bread in her sack, she stepped outside under a darkening sky. Thunder clapped as if the heavens needed to emphasize the point. Raindrops fell, striking her on the face and the lace collar Claire had sent to her before they departed from Baltimore.

She turned to the side and saw a young, wiry dog regarding her with his one good eye. Though he was a ragged-looking fellow, he appeared adequately fed and seemed good natured.

"Bonjour."

The dog wagged his tail but did not approach.

Again, thunderclouds rumbled. "The rain isn't going to wait for me," she said.

Smiling at the dog, she glanced down the alley by the wine shop, knowing it cut through the long block. Shortcuts came with their own risks, but this one would save her five minutes, and she knew Madame LeBlanc would be cross if Diane got caught in a downpour and ruined her shoes.

Thunder rumbling, she stared down the narrow, dark, crooked lane that zigzagged between two old stone buildings. Lines loaded with drying clothes crisscrossed above, and as she passed, a woman peered out of a window and frowned at the sky and then down at her. From another window, she heard a man and woman fighting, and to her left, a rat scurried behind a broken barrel. Her heart beat faster when she sensed someone behind her, but instead of glancing back, she hurried toward the light at the end of the alley. When she reached the sidewalk, she released the breath she had been holding.

She found her way back to the arches marking Madame LeBlanc's apartment and again felt a wave of relief. As she moved to the front door, she remembered the macarons in her pocket and quickly fished out one. She ate it in two bites, and when it was gone, she was annoyed she had not savored it. She was ready to eat more when a dog barked. She turned to see the mutt from the wine shop regarding her with his one good eye. His tail thumped.

"Ah, so you followed me here?" She approached the dog and scratched him between the ears.

The dog licked her hands and then began to sniff near her pocket.

"Ah, you smell the cookie?" she said. "I don't think dogs like cookies, do they?"

The dog cocked his head as if to refute her claim. She reached in her pocket and pulled out the macaron. She broke it and gave half to him. He gobbled it up and looked toward the remaining half. "I thought we would share this one," she said.

He lifted his gaze, looking as doleful as her younger brothers once had when they wanted extra attention. Remembering her brothers, she suddenly missed her home. "I wonder if the boys even remember they have a sister," she said in English to no one.

The dog nudged her hand, and she relented just as she had always done with her brothers and gave him the rest of her cookie.

She heard footsteps to her right, and when she straightened, she realized a man wearing a dark coat was now only feet from her. His hair was dark, his eyes a dark shade of green, and his jaw shadowed with dark stubble.

The man was leaving the landlord's apartment and quickly striding toward her as the dog chomped on the cookie. He lifted a brow.

"You are feeding my dog," he said in French.

Diane lifted her chin, not the least set back by his tone. He was younger than she'd first thought, perhaps in his early twenties. "He looked hungry."

Her accent must have caught his attention, and he regarded her more closely. "He wasn't."

Unsettled, she quickly patted the dog on the head and gathered her bag before hurrying up the stairs to the apartment. When she pushed through the front door, Pierre was standing over Madame LeBlanc, who lay on the floor.

Too stunned to move, Diane dropped her gaze to Madame LeBlanc's pale, still face. A thin red mark ringed her neck. The figure stared sightlessly toward Diane.

Diane's stunned shock appeared to please Pierre. "Hello, Diane."

"What have you done?" she asked.

"She thought she could toss me aside like trash."

Diane dropped her bag, and the bottle inside clunked against the stone floor. "Pierre, do you realize what you have done?"

His fingers clenched around a coiled section of brown rope. "I told you both I would not be cast aside."

"I didn't . . ."

"She said over and over that she saved me from the streets, and if I didn't behave she would toss me right back. I feared that day, and it has stalked me in my dreams." He flexed his fingers as he glanced down at Madame LeBlanc. "I gave her one last chance to take me back, but she laughed. So today it was my turn to see the fear in *her* eyes."

"What have you done?" Diane asked.

Amusement danced in his darkening gaze. "You're a smart girl. You tell me."

"She's dead?" Diane whispered.

"Very."

The weight of his words sent energy racking through her body. She had to get away. Turning, she raced toward the door, but it took only a few steps before a rough hand grabbed her and yanked her back so hard she thought her arm would snap.

"Where's the money?" Pierre's breath smelled of cheap wine and tobacco.

Panicked, she could not find her words and in English whimpered, "I spent my last pennies on cookies."

"I'm not talking about pennies," he said. "Where is the real money? I know Madame LeBlanc made far more money on that trip than she told me."

Her breathing quickened as her thoughts turned to survival and the closed apartment door behind her. She had not locked it, and if she could get away, then perhaps someone would help her.

Pierre said something else to her in French about money, but her addled brain understood even less this time. "I don't know!"

He grabbed her by the shoulders, dragged her past Madame LeBlanc's body, and slammed her against the stone wall. Pain radiated through her, jumbled her thoughts, and for an instant, her body went limp.

Pierre smiled as he always had when she suffered. "You made me do that. It's all your fault."

He cupped her face in his hands, forcing her to stare at him. Slowly he spoke, as if he wanted her to understand every word. "She said not to touch you. She said she had bigger plans for you. What was she planning?"

"I don't know," Diane sobbed. "Let me go!"

"She may have had plans for you, but I have a few of my own." He gripped her arm and twisted until she cried out.

He whirled her around, and before she could catch her breath, he pushed her hard against the rough stone, again knocking the breath from her. She tried to pull away, but he pushed her so hard this time, her face slammed against the rough surface.

She screamed, "No!"

He grabbed her by the hair and yanked hard. Before she could draw in a breath to scream again, he clamped his hand over her mouth and pressed his face close to hers. A grin of even white teeth materialized in her peripheral vision as his gaze roamed down to the budding curve of her breasts. His gaze darkened, and he licked his lips.

"As long as she paid me, I didn't touch you. You flaunted yourself in front of me. I held back."

"Let me go!"

"I should have seen this betrayal coming, but Madame LeBlanc was very good at making me believe. Now you can pay me what she owed me."

She grimaced as fresh agony coiled around her arm. "I had nothing to do with that!"

"Of course you did. I bet you were the one who told her to leave me behind. Well, it's my turn to collect from you."

"No."

"Don't make me hurt you."

Diane clenched the fist of her free hand and brought it around as hard as she could. Knuckles connected with the side of his nose and came with enough force to surprise and hurt her attacker. The gaslight flickered on the rough contours of his face as a clap of thunder cracked outside. His fingers captured her hand and tore into her flesh, twisting.

"Help!" she shouted. "Save me!"

His mouth came down on hers, and she had never tasted anything so foul. The one person whom she had trusted was dead, and again she was all alone in the world. She could feel herself drawing inward, wondering how she would ever be able to hide this terrible shame.

In the distance, thunder mingled with the sound of footsteps, and before she could cry out, her attacker's weight was yanked from her. The man from the courtyard stood in the room. His thick arms bulged as he clenched his fist and faced her attacker, ready for a fight.

Her attacker scrambled to his feet and, assessing her defender and likely the prospect of the police, hurried away as the dog chased him. The man let him go.

He grabbed Diane by the wrist and pulled her away from the wall. "Who was that?"

"I don't know." The lie rolled off her tongue in an instant because she was fearful he would step aside if he realized she knew Pierre.

She wiped the back of her hand over her bruised lips, and her attention shifted to Madame LeBlanc. Diane moved toward her slowly and then knelt beside the woman. Gently she touched her bruised neck. The cold stillness reminded her of the last time she had seen her mother in the casket. Madame LeBlanc was dead.

Tears welled in her eyes. She was the last remaining lifeline Diane felt that she had.

"Are you all right?"

She nodded, raising a trembling hand to her neck. "Yes."

"You're a fool." His French was heavily accented in a dialect she didn't recognize. "What are you doing with Louise LeBlanc?"

Diane swallowed, wincing as her throat burned. Pointing at the body, she said, "She told my father she would take care of me."

"Who is your father?"

"Isaac Hedrick."

"It is not Antoine LeBlanc."

"No."

He mumbled words that had the hard edge of curses. "Gather your things."

"Why?"

"Do you wish to stay here?" he demanded.

"No!"

"Wise girl. If that man doesn't come for you first, the police will."

She scrambled to her feet, wobbling a little as she tried to steady herself. "Police. But I didn't do anything."

He grabbed one of Madame LeBlanc's carpet satchels and handed it to her. "They won't care. And there's no telling what the police will do to you when they have you alone."

Pierre's scent still lingered on her flesh, and without thinking, she wiped the back of a trembling hand over her lips. "Who are you? Why should I trust you?"

"I am Gilbert Bernard, Monsieur Antoine LeBlanc's nephew."

Hearing a name she recognized offered a small measure of comfort. "The man Madame LeBlanc has been writing?"

"Yes." He nodded to the bag. "Pack."

She numbly walked into her tiny room and put in the few meager items she had been given by Madame LeBlanc. There was her mother's handkerchief. She raised it to her nose and caught only the faintest hint of home.

"We must go," Gilbert said.

"Where?"

He was silent for a beat. "I can't leave you here. You will come with me."

"Where?"

"To the family estate. My housekeeper will know what to do with you. Come. *Now.*"

She rose, clutching her bag. As she turned toward Madame LeBlanc, she cringed.

"Don't look at her."

"Why would he kill her?" she asked.

There had been times when Madame LeBlanc had made her feel safe and loved, but more often the woman had left her scared or feeling alone.

"Whatever kindness she extended you was only because she wanted something." Outside, a dog barked, and the shouts of men echoed up the old building's stone walls. "Now, we must *go.*"

Diane thought about the planchette that Madame LeBlanc had used to speak to her mother. Perhaps it had been a lie, but if she left it behind, whatever chance she might have had of talking to her mother would be gone forever. She raced across the room and found the ornate wooden box where Madame LeBlanc stored it. She shoved the box in her bag and hurried out the door to find Gilbert standing just outside looking for the police.

He frantically beckoned her forward, his rough hand outstretched. His dog beside him began barking.

She did not trust Gilbert Bernard, but in this moment, he was all she had. She took his hand, and he wrapped calloused fingers around hers as he took her bag in the other.

She struggled to match his quick pace and hurried down the worn stairs and out across the courtyard. Beyond the arch a whistle blew, and the shouts of the men grew louder.

Gilbert turned them both, and they started walking in the opposite direction. "Go slow and easy. Give them no reason to chase us."

"They'll see us if we do not hurry."

"They will see a man and a girl walking." He issued an order to the dog, who raced ahead and then darted to the left.

They followed along the road, moving slowly to the right. "Easy," he said. "Look as if you have nothing to hide."

She glanced up at his hard features that remarkably looked as if he did not have a care in the world. As they rounded the corner, she saw the wine shop where she had been less than an hour earlier. He opened the door and pulled her inside.

"Max," he said.

The man who had sold her wine less than an hour ago looked at Gilbert and then her. "What are you doing with her? She works for Madame LeBlanc."

"I know. Madame LeBlanc is dead, and the man who killed her appears to have summoned the police."

Max motioned them around the counter and into the back room. "What is her name?"

"I don't know."

Max muttered a curse. "Girl, your name?"

"Diane."

He eyed her. "How old are you?"

"Twelve."

"A child," Max said.

"The woman had no heart," Gilbert said.

Max nodded. "Gilbert, you can go out the back door, down the alley, and to the right. You'll be at the river. You came by boat as you always do, I assume?"

"Yes."

"Then go," Max said. "I'll stall whoever shows up on my doorstep with a moderately good bottle of wine."

"Thank you," Gilbert said.

"Wait." Max dashed behind the curtain to the front counter, and when he returned, he held a small package wrapped in paper. He gently handed it to Diane. "Cookies. Don't feed them all to the dog. He would eat them all if he could."

"Thank you," she whispered.

Max waved them out the back door, and Gilbert quickly led them through a series of alleys until she had no idea where they were.

Thick clouds above grew darker and heavier with moisture, and when they stepped out of the alley, fat rain droplets began to fall. They kept moving, crossing a damp cobblestone street filled with people who appeared to be seeking cover. As they continued west, the rain grew heavier and the scent of saltwater grew stronger, along with the sound of seagulls. When they rounded the final corner, she spotted several tall ships moored to the dock. The rain allowed them to rush without being noticed down a long pier to where his dog patiently waited for them.

There was a young boy standing on the dock. Gilbert pulled several coins from his pocket and dropped half in the boy's grimy hand. "If anyone asks about us, tell them we went east."

"East," the boy said, eyeing the closed fist.

"Yes." He then dropped the last of the coins in the boy's hand.

The boy clamped his fingers down hard against the metal. "You can count on me."

Gilbert hoisted Diane quickly up and into the boat as the dog wagged his tail and barked.

"How did he know where to find you?" Diane asked.

A small smile tugged at the edge of Gilbert's lips. "Because he is smarter than most people. Sit in the cabin. No one needs to see you."

She ducked into the cabin and sat down as the raindrops fell even heavier upon the roof. The dog shook off rain from his coat and then sat beside her, making himself comfortable as if he had done this many times before. An engine stirred and rumbled. The boy from the dock then unfastened the ropes and tossed them toward Gilbert.

She was silent as she watched Gilbert maneuver away from the dock. The engine puttered as he slowly directed them past the other vessels, steering with the experience of the skilled watermen she had seen on the Eastern Shore.

"What's the dog's name?" she asked.

"His name is Oscar. And guard your cookies close. He will eat them all and ask for more."

In the distance, more whistles blew, and men shouted. Gilbert kept his gaze forward, his expression blank. He was a man without a care in the world on a short boat trip.

CHAPTER THIRTEEN

Diane

Age 12

Thursday, October 8, 1903
Bayeux, France
Normandy Region

Diane sat in the front seat of the boat, watching the lights of the shore drift farther away as Gilbert maneuvered down the river. She wrapped her arms around her midsection and nestled close to Oscar as waves of shivers ran through her body.

When Gilbert reached the end of the river, he guided the boat out into the open sea and what she guessed was south along the coast. She had grown up on the water and had memorized the constellations in the night sky. For the last three years, she had been landlocked with Madame LeBlanc, and there was so much light in the cities, it had been hard to see the night sky.

Now that she saw the sun peering out from behind the clouds, she did not feel any sense of relief. In the space of an hour, her life had flipped, and the uncertainty of traveling with this stranger chilled her to the bone. What if he was like Pierre? Madame LeBlanc had not always been kind, but Diane had grown accustomed to her moods, her odd-smelling potions, and men and women parading through their Baltimore home seeking a connection to their dead.

The surge of adrenaline she had felt abandoned her. She closed her eyes, trying to ignore the chill in the air and fight off fatigue and desperation.

A heavy cloth that smelled of apples and tobacco dropped around her shoulders, startling her awake. She blinked and looked up at Gilbert, who had already turned back toward the waters ahead. His hands clutched the wheel, and he looked more annoyed than ever.

The jacket warmed her skin and chased away the chill. She slid her arms into the sleeves, clutched the front folds, and nestled closer to Oscar.

Diane slipped into an uneasy sleep and dreamed of her mother and her sister Claire standing on the Virginia shore. She was on a boat that had been caught in a riptide, and she was being carried out farther to sea.

"Mama, Claire! Save me!" she shouted.

They both looked at her with their hands outstretched toward her. She called back to them and tried to grab hold, but they remained out of reach. They were all helpless, unable to reconnect.

Suddenly a dog licked her face, nudging her fully awake. When she opened her eyes, she realized Oscar sat beside her, his ears perked. She scratched him between the ears as the late-day sun hung low on the horizon.

Gilbert was standing before her with a small bit of cheese and bread. He handed half to her and half to the dog before turning back toward the wheel empty handed.

Oscar gobbled up his food, and though she had not intended to devour her portion, Diane was starving and consumed the entire bit in a few bites. The boat engine chugged, and the bow turned west.

"How much farther?" Diane asked.

"A few hours."

"Where are we going?"

"My home."

"Madame LeBlanc said you live in a castle."

His expression soured as if he now regretted her presence all the more. "How would she know? She has never been there."

"She said her husband was there many times and he spoke of it often," Diane said.

"My uncle was only at the estate once. He spent most of his time in Paris."

"And they fell in love, and he married her. Madame LeBlanc told this story many times."

"Madame LeBlanc was his third wife. I doubt love had anything to do with it. And my uncle is not related to me by blood but was married to my father's sister."

They did not speak after that comment. The boat engine rumbled as the sun dipped below the western horizon. Without the sun's warmth, an evening chill settled in and had her retreating back into her seat. He worked his way through the bay, which narrowed into a river that took them inland.

The sun had vanished, leaving only the light of the full moon to help him steer down the river for several hours. Finally, he slowed the engines and slid alongside a small dock. He tied the boat off. Gilbert got up, stretched, and lifted the dog onto the dock. He climbed out of the boat and then extended a hand to Diane. She took it, climbing out while looking about.

"Is this where you live?" she asked.

"No. Inland. A carriage ride away." He retrieved her bag from the boat.

She followed him down the dock and along a darkened, narrow path along the river. Several times she had to hurry her pace to match his long strides, and as tempted as she was to complain, she did not dare for fear he would leave her alone along the side of the river.

Soon, she spotted the spire of a church, and when they rounded the bend, she realized they had reached a small town. Gilbert kept walking past shops that were only just opening and toward what appeared to be stables.

He paused at large wooden doors. "Stay here."

"Where are you going?" Panic cut through her as she realized he might very well be leaving her.

"I'll return."

"Are you coming back for me?"

His brow wrinkled. "Yes, of course."

She did not trust him, but she had no choice but to hope he would help her.

And then, as if sensing her worry, he added, "Oscar will stay with you."

She nestled closer to the dog as Gilbert vanished into the barn and minutes later appeared with a horse and carriage. He lifted the dog into the front seat and then helped her climb up beside the animal before taking his seat along with the reins.

He maneuvered the carriage out of town, nodding to some of the residents, who watched him and her with blatant curiosity. She huddled closer to Oscar and focused on the gentle back-and-forth motion of the carriage.

The road took them past moonlit, freshly harvested fields and then finally toward twin carved pillars. He drove the cart down the driveway lined with tall trees surrounded by fallen apples.

"Mimi said you grew apples," she said.

"Yes."

"What do you do with them?"

"I press them into juice and distill it."

Diane straightened stiff shoulders as a large brick-and-stone house ringed by a strip of water and a limestone wall came into view. The house was three stories high with over a dozen tall windows. Broad chimneys that stretched up to a high-pitched roof covered in slate tiles stood on both ends of the house. Smoke rose lazily from the chimneys.

"Is that your house?" Diane said.

"Yes." He sat taller.

"Is this what a castle looks like?" Diane wondered.

He arched a brow. "No."

"It looks like a castle to me." In truth, she had never seen a place so lovely.

Gilbert extended a gloved hand to her, and she took it, wondering how it was possible to be so tired. He helped her to the ground and nodded toward a front door fashioned from wide planks and darkened iron.

"Are you sure it's not a castle?" Diane asked.

"Yes."

"How do you know?"

"Castles are too large and drafty."

Gilbert pounded on the door as the dog ran off into the woods barking. Another light flickered inside, and the knob twisted and then slowly opened to a small woman. She had gray hair braided into a thin plait, a pale face etched with deep lines, and gnarled hands that held a candle up. Images of Old Mother Hubbard from Diane's mother's nursery book came to mind.

"Gilbert, I was becoming concerned." The old woman's gaze never left Diane. "Who is this?"

"This is a girl," he said. "Girl, this is Madame Herbert."

The old woman's expression soured. "I can see this is a girl. Does she have a name? Is this the child Madame LeBlanc wrote about?"

"I suppose she is."

The woman pulled Diane inside and closer to the warm fire. Madame Herbert inspected her with a critical eye that grew more concerned when she saw the thin fabric of her coat and the soiled edges of her white dress. "She does look a little like your aunt. Those eyes could be hers. Oh my, I never believed it, but perhaps that terrible woman was right, and this girl is your cousin."

"She's not," Gilbert insisted.

"How old are you?" the woman asked.

"Twelve."

"Not ten?" Madame Herbert asked. "Are you sure?"

"Yes, I'm sure of my age," Diane said softly.

"You're so small," the old woman said.

"I think Madame LeBlanc did not feed her," Gilbert said. "When I gave her bread, she ate it as if she were half-starved."

The old woman tugged Diane into the kitchen. In the center of the room was a long wooden table, nicked and scarred by what must have been years' worth of meals. The scent of rising dough, cinnamon, and apples enveloped Diane as her stomach grumbled. There was a black metal oven with a teakettle on top, and several skinned chickens hung from a rafter over a worn slate floor.

The woman placed her at a table in front of a large brick hearth with its fire glowing inside. She uncovered a loaf of bread wrapped in a red-and-white-checkered cloth. Using a large knife with a carved wooden handle, she sliced the bread in a quick sawing motion. She set it on a blue-and-white porcelain plate along with a thick piece of cheese in front of Diane.

"You saw Max?" she asked Gilbert.

"Yes."

Motioning her to eat, the old woman said, "How is dear Max?"

"He's well." Gilbert walked toward the iron stove and reached for the kettle.

The old woman nudged him away. She made him a hot cup of tea and then handed it to him in a worn earthenware mug. "And where is that hateful Madame LeBlanc?"

"Dead," Gilbert said. "One of her own murdered her."

The old woman snorted as if she did not care, and then on second thought crossed herself. "How?"

He sipped his tea. "Strangled."

Hearing the word spoken so casually sent a dart of sadness through Diane.

"Girl, who was that man?" Gilbert asked.

"Pierre Laurent. He has been with Madame LeBlanc since I arrived three years ago."

Gilbert reached for Diane's wrist and pushed up the sleeve to reveal rings of bruises. The old woman gasped and cursed under her breath.

"Evil," she muttered.

Gilbert released Diane's wrist and closed his eyes as if the travel was finally catching up to him. "Do you know anything about Pierre?"

Diane swallowed a bite of bread. "He helped Mimi, Madame LeBlanc."

"Doing what?" Gilbert asked.

"Everything," Diane said. "He was always there when Madame LeBlanc helped her visitors speak to their dead relatives."

"The dead?" The old woman crossed herself again. "Evil woman. *No* shame."

Gilbert walked to the hearth and stretched out his hands. "I couldn't leave the girl in Le Havre."

"No, the city would have eaten her whole. It's good you brought her here." The old woman beckoned Diane forward. "Once she has eaten her fill, I'll put her to bed. We can figure out the rest in the morning."

"Can you send me up a cold plate?" Gilbert asked. "I've not slept in days."

The old woman helped him shrug off his coat. "Yes, of course. Get yourself into bed. I'll send up a warming pan to ease the chill in your sheets."

"Thank you."

As he turned to leave, Diane grabbed hold of his hand. "Are you going to leave?"

"For now, I'm going to sleep." And then softening his tone, he said, "I live here. This is my home. You will stay here for the time being until we can find your papa."

"My papa doesn't want me back," Diane said. "I've written him many times asking and he never writes back."

"Is there other family?" Gilbert's frown deepened.

"A sister. She lives in New York now, I think."

"Then we'll figure it out after I've had sleep." He gently pried her fingers from his hand and managed what passed as a smile. "Madame Herbert is kind. She'll take care of you."

As tempted as Diane was to follow Gilbert, she stood her ground. She might not know the man, but he at least had kept her safe and had fed her.

Madame Herbert lit several lanterns around the room.

"You must be hungry." The woman poured a small glass of cider before motioning again for Diane to sit at the table. "Didn't that woman feed you?"

"Mimi gave me bread and wine once a day."

The old woman poured hot water into a cup and dropped in some tea wrapped in cheesecloth. "Why did you call her Mimi?"

"Because she said it sounded like a nickname a child would have for a mother, and she said she was going to be a mother to me."

"Was she?" She sat at the table, her eyes alight with curiosity.

"Not always," she stammered.

Madame Herbert humphed. "When it suited her, no doubt."

Diane bit into the bread, which was as soft and warm as the bread her mother used to bake. "Did you ever meet Madame LeBlanc?"

"No. After Gilbert's aunt married Mr. LeBlanc a dozen years ago, they left for Paris. Two years would pass before he wrote and told us she had given birth to a girl and that his wife had died." Madame

Herbert arranged her lace collar over her full bosom. "He wrote nine years ago and said he'd married Madame Louise Girard, your Mimi, and announced he was moving to America. We heard nothing for years, and then Madame LeBlanc began to write about the girl child."

"Me?"

"Yes." She sniffed. "Hateful woman." Madame Herbert sat across from her, eyeing her closely. "That woman has no shame. She'd have been in for a real surprise when she realized the pot of gold was an apple farm. Your Mimi no doubt ran through her husband's money and needed more. She eats everything in her path."

Diane tore off a piece of bread and put a big slice of cheese on it. "Oh, she never ate."

"Child, I mean she uses people."

Diane knew this to be true. "What is this place? And why wouldn't Mimi like it? It's beautiful."

The old woman looked pleased by the question. "It's an apple orchard. We also make Calvados."

"What's that?"

"Stay more than a day, and you will learn." The old woman regarded her. "When I look at you, I think of my sweet little Émilie. She was Gilbert's aunt, and I knew her since she was a little girl. Very striking violet eyes like yours."

"Thank you."

"You speak French well."

"Mimi taught me. She said she wanted to show me the world."

"Humph." She sliced another piece of cheese for Diane. "You have no family other than the sister you mentioned?"

"I have brothers and sisters, but they're all scattered." She took another sip of cider, wanting nothing more right now than to close her eyes and get some sleep.

The old woman shook her head. "It's the way sometimes. I'll speak to Gilbert. He'll find someone who will take you back."

April 8, 1939
From the Journal of Samuel Jessup

I found Mrs. Garrison alone today. She was sitting on the deck in a chair with her feet propped up. Dressed in her furs and covered with a blanket, she had her eyes closed, and her face was tipped toward the sun. I was nervous about speaking to her, but Miss Claire had been clear that I give her the letter.

I walked up to stand beside her, and when she didn't open her eyes, I cleared my throat.

She started awake and looked up at me. For a moment she appeared confused and called me Jimmy.

"No, Mrs. Garrison. I'm Samuel." My throat felt dry. Though I never had a case of nerves in my life, that moment felt like I was staring into the eye of a hurricane.

Mrs. Garrison sat up quickly and then stood. She regarded me for a long moment and then said, "Yes, of course, Samuel. What can I do for you?"

I'd almost forgotten about the letter, now crushed in the grip of my fingers. I thrust the letter toward her. "From Mrs. Claire Buchanan."

Mrs. Garrison's face paled, and she hesitated before finally, raising her chin, she took it. "Thank you, young man."

CHAPTER FOURTEEN

Megan

Tuesday, March 6, 2018
Cape Hudson, Virginia
4:30 p.m.

Natasha's wide, excited smile crumpled when she saw the so-called treasure, which amounted to a leather-bound journal and a stack of letters. "Oh, man. That's just letters."

Excitement exploded in Megan at the prospect of reading the pages. "Not just a book or just letters, I think. Otherwise, why hide them?"

"Where's the gold?" Natasha leaned past Megan and peered into the tiny alcove, searching for anything that glittered. "Where are the diamonds?"

Megan's heart skipped a beat as she held the heavy stack of envelopes yellowed around the edges. They were bound together by a length of thin rope, carefully fastened into a seaman's knot. The first letter on top of the stack read *Miss Claire Hedrick* and was postmarked Baltimore, Maryland, 1902. As she riffled through the stack, she realized they were all addressed to Claire.

Rick reached behind the letters and pulled out another box. "Maybe your treasure is in here."

"What do you think is inside?" Natasha asked.

"Let's open it," he said.

"It's locked," Natasha said, frowning at the small padlock.

Megan's energy soared as she stared at the box. As much as she had tried to piece together the history of the Buchanan and Jessup families, there had been so many missing pieces. These were two families who guarded their secrets.

Rick wedged his pocketknife under the lock. It took a firm twist, but the lock popped open.

He hesitated before opening the box. "Are you sure you want to see what's inside?"

Natasha tried to look indifferent, but there was no missing the excitement in her eyes that frankly mirrored exactly what Megan felt.

"Yes!" Megan said. "Open it."

Rick glanced up at her, clearly enjoying himself. He pried open the lid and held up the box so that Megan could see. Folded up inside were what looked like identity papers. Megan reached for cloth gloves in her pocket and slid them on.

She laid the two sets of papers out on the desk. They were written in German. One was a set of papers for a young woman by the name of Elise Mandel. Her black-and-white picture featured a young woman with soft, blonde curls arranged about an oval-shaped face. Her skin was flawless, and she had striking, dark eyes and high cheekbones. Elise Mandel had been born in Le Havre in 1909.

The other set of papers was for Alexander Fontaine Mandel, born in 1938 in Edenkoben, Germany. He was a towhead with chubby cheeks.

"What are these doing here?" Lucy asked.

"I don't have a clue," Megan said. "But clearly they were important to Samuel, because he hid them with great care."

"Why hide them?" Natasha asked. "Why not just burn them or throw them out?"

"Because he recognized their importance," Rick said.

"I can get on my computer tonight," Megan said. "If these papers are official, then we might have a chance of finding out more about them."

"Why wouldn't they be correct?" Lucy asked.

Megan turned the pages until she found the final travel stamp with *Denied* over top of it. Beside it was the boldly written letter *J.*

"Why does it say *denied*?" Natasha asked.

"Edenkoben, Germany, is not far from the border of France and Germany. Before the war, people traveled back and forth between countries regularly. But by 1939 the Germans had severely tightened their hold on the Jews. See this *J*?"

"Yes," Natasha said.

"These two people were Jews and not permitted to leave the country."

"Why?" Natasha asked.

"Nazi Germany forbade it." Megan studied the young boy's sweet face. "Remember the dreidels?"

"You think they belonged to him?" Lucy asked.

"Perhaps," Megan said. "This woman and I guess her baby boy were trying to flee to safety."

"How did Samuel figure into this?" Lucy asked.

"I have no idea." She thought about Claire and Diane sitting in the Le Havre café circa 1909, thirty years earlier than this woman and her child. "Diane is the one Hedrick sister I was never able to track down. All I could ever figure was that her father had given her to a wealthy family just as he had done with his three other daughters."

"Maybe there's an answer in those letters," Rick said.

"Believe me, I'll read them all," Megan said.

Megan thought about the letters all afternoon, and when she finally arrived back at Winter Cottage about six, she could barely wait to read them and research Elise Mandel and the boy. After a quick supper, she hurried to her room and opened her laptop. An internet search of the Mandels revealed nothing, which was not surprising. So many historical documents were not posted online. As she stared at Elise's face, she realized she would have to find help in Europe to complete the search.

After Megan had graduated college, she had worked a summer in France as a tour guide. The job was nonstop for nearly four months, but at the end, she had had enough money to pay for her first year of graduate school. She returned for two more summers and, in the process, made several student friends who still lived in Europe. She emailed her friend Chloe, who lived on the outskirts of Paris, and asked if she might be interested in doing a little digging in the national records.

When she glanced up at the clock, she was surprised so much time had gotten away from her. If she did not start mixing her piecrusts tonight, the pies would never be ready for the Friday delivery.

Pushing off her bed, she changed into sweats and a large T-shirt and pulled her hair into a thick ponytail. Fifteen minutes later, she was standing in the kitchen. As she stared out over the calm waters of the bay, her mind drifted between the renovation schedule flowcharts and flour and sugar ratios for her crusts.

She dug her hands into the sticky dough, kneading the crumbling mixture until it formed a tight ball. If she stayed on schedule with these pies, she would see this order filled and make a nice chunk of change for her and the baby.

As she wiped her hands and wrapped the first batch in cling wrap, her thoughts kept drifting back to Elise, her baby boy, and the missing Hedrick sister. She measured more butter and flour into the large mixing bowl and began working it with a pastry blender. Why would Samuel have hidden the Mandels' travel papers? How had he come to know a young woman who lived near the border of Germany and France?

By 8:00 p.m. Megan's back ached, and she was beginning to shift her weight from foot to foot and wondering if she should sit.

When she had committed to this order, she had been three months pregnant and feeling good. Now plagued with aching muscles and swollen feet, she wondered what she had been thinking. But bloat and belly aside, she had made a promise to deliver one hundred pies for the Baugh-Smith rehearsal dinner on Friday, and that was exactly what she would do.

She measured out ten more cups of flour and dumped it into the bowl. Two or three batches to go, and she would have enough for the Thursday-night baking session that would begin about six and not end until midnight. Some bakers made their products ahead of time and froze them, but she had always stuck to her motto of handmade fresh. It was not as profitable and likely would not be sustainable after the baby came, but for now it felt right.

Footsteps had her looking over her shoulder to see Lucy yawning and rubbing the sleep from her eyes. "What are you still doing on your feet?"

"Making piecrust. I'll be done in an hour or so."

Lucy walked to the coffeemaker and poured herself a cup. "When do you plan to rest and put your feet up?"

"I'll sleep in tomorrow."

"Isn't Helen coming tomorrow?"

Megan sighed, irritated that she had already forgotten. "One hundred years ago pregnant women plowed the back fields and then went home and had a baby."

Lucy washed and dried her hands. "It isn't a hundred years ago. Wash your hands, I'm taking over this gig."

"That's ridiculous. I can finish this."

"I didn't say you couldn't, but you and the spud need to sit." She bumped her aside with her hip. "Sit."

The baby did a sudden somersault, punching her way around Megan's insides. Her back aching, she gave in, washed her hands, and after filling a glass with ice water, sat at the kitchen table.

Lucy began to cut the butter into the flour with a pastry blender. "Who's getting married?"

"Jessica Smith and Danny Baugh. Their venue is an old plantation outside of Norfolk. Thankfully, it's a moderately sized rehearsal dinner. There are only seventy-five people coming."

"So how many pies?"

"One hundred individual ones." The order had sounded relatively small when she had booked it months ago. Now it felt a little overwhelming.

Lucy winced. "How much dough have you made so far?"

"Enough for forty."

"Does Jessica know there's weather coming on Saturday? According to the old guys at Arlene's diner, it's going to be heavy rains and wind."

"Do I look like a weather woman? But I'll text her with a warning." Megan took a long sip of water and then typed a message to the wedding coordinator. "I did reach out to a friend in Paris who travels to Alsace a few times a year. She might find our Elise for us."

Lucy poured iced water into the dough and worked it into the butter-and-flour mixture with her fingers. "Do you think Elise knew Samuel?"

"She had to have known him. He would have been in his early twenties in 1939 and sailing with the merchant marines. He had a reputation for traveling the most dangerous waters, and some hinted he worked closely with the French Resistance."

"Could she be the woman he loved and lost?" Lucy asked.

"That would be as good a guess as any."

"So how does a sailor working for the merchant marines end up with the papers of a German woman and her son? Why hide them? What's the big deal?"

"No idea. How about I read some of the letters we found?"

"Yes. Dying to know more about Diane's life."

Megan rose up out of the chair and made her way to her room, where she collected the letters. She had sealed them in a plastic bag in her dresser. When she returned, Lucy was already dividing out the dough into smaller batches.

Megan laid the letters gently on the table and counted them. There were eighty-six total. As she created stacks according to each year, she discovered two-thirds of the letters were written between 1900 and 1903. There was a gap between 1903 and 1905, but then the letters resumed and remained steady until 1939. These sisters had stayed in close contact.

"I've never written a single letter," Lucy said, incredulously.

"It would have been the primary way the two sisters could have communicated," Megan said.

"I can't imagine living without text."

"I love to write letters. I used to have pen pals in middle and high school. In fact, one of them helped me get the job as a travel guide in Paris. She is looking into the travel papers for us. No matter where we lived, I would write to them. It was always exciting having a letter in the box with postage stamps from far away."

"Very old-fashioned," Lucy commented.

"I wrote Scott letters."

"Did he write back?"

"He texted back."

Megan removed the first letter dated 1903 from its envelope. She noted the author's thick, dark handwriting, which appeared childlike. She studied the envelopes and realized that the first quarter had been mailed from Baltimore and the remainder from France.

"I hope they're in English. I don't speak a word of French," Lucy said.

"I'm fluent."

"Really?"

"Someday I'll tell you about my work as a tour guide in France." Those days now felt like they were a lifetime ago.

Lucy grinned and arched a brow. "Why do I get the sense there is a mysterious side to Megan Buchanan?"

Megan could barely remember the carefree girl who had led hundreds of people through the French countryside. "I'll have to drink a good bit of wine to talk about those days."

"I'll hold you to that."

Megan cleared her throat before she read several letters that covered Diane's new life in France. As she laid them down, another letter caught her eye. It was postmarked from the western port city of Le Havre, France.

March 1, 1939

Dearest Claire,

I need a favor, dear sister. Stories from Germany are as bad as I thought. The Germans are on the march, and I know it's a matter of time before they . . .

"Are you reading the last letter?" Lucy asked.

"Yes. I kind of want to know how it works out for Diane."

"I bet you start with the last chapter of every book you read."

"I do."

Megan couldn't make out the next several words and skipped to the next line she could read.

We have agreed to take our dear friend Max's daughter, Elise Mandel, as well as her son. Though Max's daughter is French, he fears if his daughter and grandson delay in Germany much longer, they will be trapped. The Germans have already imprisoned her husband and charged him with treason, which of course is a lie. However, we all fear the government will arrest Elise and her son. Keep us in your thoughts and prayers.

Yours truly,

Diane

"That must have been a terrifying time," Lucy said.

"Diane was wise not to delay. Hitler's final solution was gearing up, and in a little over a year, the Germans would be in Paris. Half of France and the seacoast would be closed."

"*Mandel* sounds German," Lucy said.

"But Max was from Le Havre, and his daughter is French. A French girl married a German boy. It happened quite often."

"If Max was also a Jew, he was on the edge of being in real trouble himself."

"Le Havre would have been fully occupied within fourteen months by the Germans," Megan said. "The entire western coast became a restricted zone."

"So we know that Max sent his daughter to live with Diane and she reached out to Claire."

"Thanks to the Buchanan company holdings, Claire had many connections in the shipping industry by the late 1930s." Megan yawned. "I need to start at the beginning of the letters and read them properly."

"I'll finish the crusts."

"It's my job to make the pies."

Lucy shook her head. "I bake and you read. I want to hear the letters and Samuel's journal. The Buchanans and the Jessups certainly do have a twisted history."

"Yes, they do," Megan said. "I owe it to Claire to fill in the pieces of her life."

"And discover Diane's fate?"

"Yes. For some reason, that feels more important to me than ever."

"Why?"

"Just an odd sense that we're running out of time."

—— ⟡ ——

Over the next couple of hours, Megan read several of the letters to Lucy, and they now understood Diane had moved to an apple farm in the Normandy region of France. But now it was late, and Megan's eyes were too strained to read the faded ink. Plus her back was killing her.

With all the dough wrapped in cling wrap, she happily retired to bed. However, hers was not an easy night's sleep. In fact, it was very restless. The baby continued to toss in her belly as if she had her own worries.

Her mind kept conjuring the moment the four Hedrick girls were separated forever from their home on Cape Hudson. That was such a different time. Families often had to make hard decisions to survive. But that didn't stop them from missing their home and mourning what might have been.

She realized that she desperately wanted to set down roots in Cape Hudson and make a life here for her child. Like Claire and Diane, she never wanted to leave.

The Eastern Shore's rich, sandy loam was fertile, but like everything here, a shift in the winds could uproot the oldest of trees.

CHAPTER FIFTEEN

Megan

Wednesday, March 7, 2018
Cape Hudson, Virginia
6:40 a.m.

Megan gave up trying to get back to sleep, got up, and dressed. She went down to the kitchen and made herself a small cup of coffee—an indulgence she had not been able to give up. She rubbed her eyes and stared out over the calm water as the first hints of sun illuminated the sky.

As she stood at the kitchen sink, taking her first sip, she pressed her hand into her back. It ached and the muscles bunched. She had overdone it yesterday.

"Just a few more days," she whispered to the baby. "And then I'll put our feet up and take a long nap."

Her phone dinged with a text from her friend in Paris, who she imagined was already halfway through her day at the art history department. You have piqued my curiosity. I travel to Alsace this weekend. Stay tuned.

Megan smiled. Chloe would get answers.

Upstairs, Natasha's footsteps thundered as she ran around. "Has anyone seen my green shirt? Never mind, I found it!"

Lucy calmly cooked breakfast and made her sister's lunch. Natasha rushed past Megan and into the kitchen. Conversations about homework and after-school activities buzzed as Megan sipped her coffee. Dolly lay on her doggy bed chewing a rawhide stick.

The front doorbell rang, and Megan turned from the sink. "I'll get it. You two carry on."

She opened the front door to find Mr. Crawford's truck was parked in the circular drive in front of the house. Hooked to the trailer hitch was his massive blue-and-white fishing boat.

Mr. Crawford greeted her at the base of the front steps. "I have your table."

"I thought you left town yesterday." She wondered if she still owed Rick those pies.

"I was delayed," he grumbled.

"So you're selling it to me at my price?" she asked.

"It's one valuable table, but it belongs in Winter Cottage."

If Megan weren't eight months pregnant, she'd have jumped up and down. Instead, she politely smiled.

"Lucy is rushing to get her sister off to school, so it'll take me a couple of hours to get you a check."

"Just run the check by the First National Bank in town." He handed her a deposit slip. "They know me there, and you can just put the money in my account."

"Sure. I can do that." A flutter of excitement raced through her, and she sensed a piece of the puzzle drop into place.

He climbed up on the bed of his truck and tossed a tarp aside to reveal the table. "Want me to put it inside?"

"That would be great," Megan said. She hurried back to the front door, opening it wide as he carried the card table inside.

"Where do you want it?"

Without hesitating she said, "Follow me into the parlor. There's a corner."

She stayed a couple of steps ahead of him as she walked down the center hallway toward the parlor where she felt that it belonged. She would have to search out more photos of the house to determine where the piece might have been.

Mr. Crawford set the table in the corner by the window, and it seemed to fit almost immediately. "I asked my brother how we came to get the piece. He wasn't sure but promised he'd ask our aunt. If I hear of anything, I'll be sure to give you a call."

"I would appreciate that. Do you have any idea how long it's been in your family?"

"At least seventy-five years."

Which meant if the table had belonged to the house, Claire could have sold it during the Depression. He retrieved the chairs and carefully set them around the table before stepping back to study the entire set. "It looks right at home there."

"Yes, it does. Thank you."

The four chairs reminded Megan of the four Hedrick sisters who had been scattered after their mother died. Perhaps the table had not belonged to Winter House but to the Hedrick family. "And I'll get that money deposited by tomorrow," she said.

"No worries."

She followed him outside. "If your family comes across any other pieces, I'm happy to look at them."

He pulled off his cap and scratched his balding head. "I'll warn 'em you drive a hard bargain."

She laughed. "You do that."

Lucy and Natasha had already left for school, so Megan locked Winter Cottage's large door behind her and made the short drive to Spring House. As she looked at the dumpster nearly overflowing with years of junk, she sensed the house felt a brighter future in store and was ready to give up a few more secrets.

Helen pulled up in her Volvo, nearly an hour early. She parked and stepped out, dressed in jeans that looked pressed, a white sweatshirt, and sneakers. "I'm ready to work."

"There's still quite a bit to do," Megan said, smiling.

"You look pale. Did you sleep well last night?" Helen asked.

"The baby does her best aerobics at night. The kid is going to be a gymnast."

A small smile tugged at Helen's lips. "You might as well get used to that. Children take over our lives."

The bittersweetness in the words reminded Megan again that Helen had lost her only child. "How is your grandmother-in-law?"

"Doing well. A broken hip at her age can be quite dangerous, and healing can be almost impossible. But she has impressed all the doctors with her determination to walk again. I told her I was coming here and wouldn't see her for a couple of days, and she understood. She says when she can travel, she'll come to see the baby and might have a story or two to share about Samuel Jessup."

"Did she tell you what the stories were?"

"Not a hint. Adele can be quite coy when she chooses to be."

Scott hadn't spoken much about his great-grandmother, and Megan was surprised she had not pressed him for more details.

Lucy's Jeep rumbled up the driveway, and Megan released the breath she was holding as she always seemed to do when she and Helen were alone. Lucy hopped out with Dolly on her heels. The dog bounded up to Helen, who, to her credit, did not flinch but rubbed the animal between the ears. "We had a dog just like this when Scott was little. What's her name?"

"Dolly. She was my mom's dog," Lucy said. "Would you like to see what we've done with the place since you were here last? We're in the process of cleaning it out."

"I'd like that," Helen said. "Megan, do you mind?"

Megan didn't speak for a moment as Helen climbed the stairs. Her casual sneakers looked brand-new. "It's filthy in there."

"A little dirt never bothered anyone." Helen's tone was brisk as she paused at the doorway, peering into the dimly lit hallway. "My husband and I offered once to help Samuel organize this place, but he wouldn't hear of it. He liked it just the way it was."

"From what little I know about my grandfather's family, the Jessups had five boys," Lucy said.

"That's correct. Stanley, Joseph, Michael, Aaron, and Samuel. They called Aaron and Samuel the Irish Twins because they were born less than a year apart." Helen studied a picture on the wall. When she did not seem to recognize anyone, she moved on to the others as if hoping to see a picture of someone she knew. When she did not, she turned toward the study.

"You wouldn't believe the junk we've pulled out," Megan said.

"You've barely made a dent," Helen countered.

If her mother or Lucy had made that comment, Megan would have laughed it off. But from Helen, it felt like a reminder that no matter what she did, it was not good enough. "This place was stacked to the gills."

"Worse than I thought." Helen moved toward the wall of book-shelves. "I think this room is part of the original house that was built in 1775."

Megan's curiosity was piqued. Scott must have told his mother Megan could not care less about diamonds or roses, but toss a historical detail at her, and you had her heart. "The house was owned by a bean farmer."

"That's partly true," Helen said. "According to Samuel, the original owner made the bulk of his fortune running the English blockades during the American Revolution."

"Why is it called Spring House?" Lucy asked.

"Because Samuel was at sea ten months out of twelve for most of his career. He was only home in the spring. People good-naturedly ribbed him about 'vacationing' in his Spring House."

"If you went to high school with my mother, then you grew up on the Eastern Shore?" Lucy asked.

Helen skimmed a manicured finger down the length of a dusty leather spine. "I lived here through high school but didn't return after college. Both my husband and I wanted a bigger life than the Eastern Shore could offer."

"Could you see yourself living here again?" Lucy asked.

"For my granddaughter, yes," Helen said.

Megan hadn't really considered that Helen would be in her life beyond the birth of the baby, but now it was a real possibility. "We found letters from Claire's sister Diane. Did you know anything about her?"

"No. I only met Claire a couple of times. Again, Grandmother will be the one to ask. She and Claire knew each other for years."

"I'm very curious to meet Mrs. Jessup."

"As soon as I can transport her, I will. It'll be a few weeks, but she's very resilient and independent."

Megan too could be independent, but also solitary. She did not need activity or social networks as Scott and his mother did. She also realized, though she did not need Helen or her approval, Helen needed her. For her baby's sake, this was a good thing.

"Samuel was an avid reader," Helen offered. "He was also a very talented carver. He didn't graduate high school but was one of the smartest men I knew."

"He didn't graduate high school? Neither did my mother," Lucy said.

"He went to work in 1931. It was the Depression, and the entire area was feeling it. He said he wanted to help out and go to work like his older brothers. And back then, a fifteen-year-old boy was expected to do a man's work."

"He didn't mind going to sea?" Lucy said.

"He loved the sea. It was the only place he felt at home," Helen said.

"What's the deal with Samuel and my grandmother?" Lucy asked. "There was a massive age difference."

"Samuel was always young at heart and looked ten years his junior. He got along well with his young bride, even though he traveled— or perhaps because he traveled. When his wife died, he was truly heartbroken."

"So was my mother," Lucy said with a slight edge. "Why didn't he stick around for her?"

Helen was silent for a moment. "Grief makes us do stupid, hurtful things, Lucy. A wounded soul can be a very selfish one."

CHAPTER SIXTEEN

Megan

Wednesday, March 7, 2018
Cape Hudson, Virginia
10:00 a.m.

The three women quietly sorted more books over the next hour, and when Mr. Tucker and his crew arrived, Helen had neatly stacked the books into piles on the front porch and discarded the rest in the dumpster. The woman was fifty, but she worked with the energy of a woman half her age. Most importantly, by lunch the office was cleaned out of books. What remained was the furniture, oddities such as a large globe, several model ships mounted on the wall, a ship captain's desk, and a brightly painted, hand-carved mermaid figurehead that looked as if it had been yanked off an old ship.

"Ladies, I think we should take a break," Helen said. "Mr. Tucker and his men can remove the furniture and place it on the front lawn. Be good to air them out, and the rains are supposed to come on Saturday." She pulled a handkerchief from her pocket and wiped her hands. "I also have a cooler in the trunk of my car. There's enough food there to feed an army."

"That sounds pretty great," Megan said. "Thank you."

Helen pursed her lips as if reining in an unwanted emotion and nodded. As she walked out the front door, they heard her offering to feed the work crews as well.

"She's pretty amazing," Lucy said.

"I know."

When they came outside, Helen had organized the men, who had removed a folding table from the back of her car and set it up. She had Mr. Tucker putting a white plastic cloth on the table while two other men carried one of the coolers up to the porch. Inside it were waters, juices, milk boxes, and protein shakes. No sodas.

The second cooler contained a variety of sandwiches. "Helen, I think I love you," Lucy said as she selected a ham-and-cheese sandwich.

"This is what I did for years. I was always room mother or a soccer mom," Helen said. "I'd forgotten how much I missed it." She handed a roast-beef club to Mr. Tucker, who grinned as if he'd been given a golden nugget.

"I swear this is the tastiest-looking sandwich I've ever seen," he exclaimed.

"It's really nothing," Helen said. "Takes me seconds."

"That's because you have a lifetime of experience. You make the difficult look easy." He grabbed another bag of chips and a thick chocolate brownie. He winked at her, and if Megan had not been watching, she'd have missed the pink rising in Helen's cheeks.

———— ❧～❧ ————

By mid-afternoon, Mr. Tucker and his men had moved the furniture into the bright sunshine. Much of it was covered in a thick coat of dust, but it was obvious all the pieces had been handcrafted a century ago.

"Where do the pieces go?" Helen asked.

"I have a storage unit rented in Cape Hudson," Megan replied. "After the renovation is complete, we'll be able to bring some of it back. Lucy will sell what we don't."

"Make sure you contact me before you sell anything, Lucy," Helen said. "I love antiques."

Mr. Tucker and his two men carried out a rolled-up oriental carpet that smelled of mold and mildew. The back right corner of the carpet had been nibbled away by mice. "Is it worth saving?" Lucy said.

"It's a rare piece," Megan said. "It's a shame it was damaged."

"But can you save it?" Lucy asked.

"I'll call Duncan. He knows every restoration expert in the mid-Atlantic. Then we'll figure out if the restoration work is worth the cost."

The three women walked back into the study, which was now stripped bare, probably for the first time since Samuel had moved in.

Megan studied the wide-plank pine floors, which would need to be sanded down to bare wood and then refinished. Mr. Tucker walked into the room and went directly to the back corner and its water damage. He frowned as he looked up at the ceiling. "The plumbing and electrical were added in the 1940s. Neither is likely up to code. We won't know for sure until we get into it." He checked his watch. "It's three thirty and too late to start on the bathrooms and kitchen. We'll call it a day and make an early day of it tomorrow."

"Sounds good." The idea of a break thrilled Megan, who wanted nothing more than to prop up her swollen feet.

Helen walked across the empty room. "It feels a little lifeless."

"I thought you didn't like the clutter," Megan said.

"I didn't. It's just another change, and I've had far too many in the last few years."

Megan's baby gave her a hard kick, and as Megan studied Helen's lost expression, she found herself suddenly walking over to her. Without a word, she took the woman's hand and pressed it to her belly. The baby kicked hard and did what felt like a backflip. "Not all change is bad."

Helen's eyes widened and filled with tears. "My goodness. I suppose you're right! I just wish Scott were here for this."

"He would have loved this baby," Megan said.

"Yes, he would have."

———— ❧〜❧ ————

Megan's back was aching when she walked into the kitchen at Winter Cottage. She was once again overcome with the overwhelming desire to sit but was faced with a delivery deadline for her pies. "A few more days, kid," she said. "And then you and I are putting our feet up and binge-watching *Downton Abbey*."

She pulled the dough from the refrigerator and set it on the butcher-block countertop. She knuckled her fingers into the base of her back and stretched. "Baby B., life is going to be a lot easier when you aren't pressing on my kidneys."

"What're you doing? The deal was I bake and you read." Lucy's hair was damp from a shower, and she had changed into sweats and a BEACON VINEYARDS T-shirt. She wore thick wool socks, no shoes, and had scrubbed off what little makeup she normally wore.

"I thought I'd get a jump start on the work."

"As I stated before, I shall make the pies. You may sit and peel apples if you wish."

"I feel like I'm being a slacker."

"Why didn't you just cancel this gig when you got the chief historian job at Winter Cottage?"

"Because as much as I love this job, it won't last forever. Life demands a backup plan."

"You can plan all you want, but life has its own agenda. A year ago, I'd never have pictured this moment. What about you?"

"Never."

"So it's settled. Don't worry about plans right now." Lucy reached for the large bag of Granny Smith apples. "Get either the letters from Diane to Claire or Samuel's journal. I'm dying to know what's in them and how all this stuff we're finding fits together."

The baby kicked hard in Megan's belly, forcing her to shift her weight until the discomfort dissipated. "This is not like me."

"I know. I've heard pregnancy is a little like *Invasion of the Body Snatchers*."

"It is, really."

Lucy reached for an apron, looped it over her head, and then tied the strands behind her. "Besides, I have an ulterior motive. When we deliver these pies, I'd like to pitch my idea of using Winter Cottage property as a wedding venue."

"You can definitely do that."

"I've been trying to figure a way into the world of wedding planners. They seem to be a very tight group."

"They can be."

"How did you meet this planner?" Lucy asked.

"She planned my wedding."

"Oh." Lucy ducked her head toward a utensil drawer as if she were avoiding looking at a bad car accident.

"You might as well go ahead and ask about the wedding."

Lucy measured the offer and replied with a grin. "I didn't want to be nosy, but it's killing me."

Megan retrieved Diane's letters from her backpack and sat at the kitchen table. Off her feet, her body instantly relaxed. "It was going to be one of the biggest weddings this planner had ever done. She was thrilled. My mother was thrilled. Helen appeared thrilled. A trifecta."

"But."

"I'll tell you, but please don't share this. You're the first person I've told."

Lucy crossed her heart with her index finger. "Yeah, I won't tell a soul."

"I discovered I was pregnant and went to tell Scott. I found him with my bridesmaid. They were each only partly dressed."

"Ouch."

"I got pretty pissed. I never cheated on him, and if he'd had doubts, he should have come to me instead of sneaking around. I deserve better than that."

"Yes, you do, sister."

"I cut Scott off completely. He tried several times to explain, but I wouldn't have any of it. The way I saw it, we would both move on with our lives. Clean break."

"But he didn't."

"No." Sadness chilled her skin. "And if I'd been just a little kinder, maybe things wouldn't have turned out the way they did."

"You don't know that. Accidents happen."

"Especially when a pilot is distracted."

"You don't know that either."

"I do. And so does Helen." Several of Scott's voice-mail messages had sounded desperate. "Helen is trying for the sake of the baby, but she still blames me."

"Helen was pretty terrific today," Lucy said.

"Helen was trying to bridge the gap to her grandchild. But once the baby is born, I think we're going to have a real tug-of-war over this kid."

"You'll work it out. It's nice the baby has family who want to be in her life."

Megan rubbed her belly. "Remember, Helen and Rick don't know about Brandy, and I want to keep it that way. I don't need any more pity."

"Brandy?"

"The woman with Scott."

Lucy narrowed her eyes. "Brandy. I don't even know her, but I don't like her. She'll never get an invite to Winter Cottage."

"Thanks."

"Why didn't you tell Helen about Brandy? She might understand you better if she knew."

"I was tempted. But the more I thought about it, I realized Helen has a lot of great memories of Scott, and I don't want to take that away from her."

"You're too reasonable, Megan."

Megan untied the faded red twine wrapped around the letters. "I think you're the first person who has ever called me reasonable."

"Who would say you weren't?"

"My parents; Scott; Helen; my brother, Deacon."

"What's the deal with your brother? Does he ever come to the Eastern Shore?"

"We both vacationed here with our parents, but he's not been back in years. He's the family's golden boy and setting the world on fire in the Buchanan Corporation, as I was supposed to do."

Lucy shrugged. "What did I say about plans?"

"I hear you," Megan said, grinning.

"So who was this Brandy chick to you?"

She gently laid out the letters based on the chronological order of the postmarks. "She was one of my bridesmaids and my college roommate."

"Ouch again. Has she called you since?"

"Several times. I blocked her number months ago." She fingered the first letter.

Lucy dug a paring knife out of the drawer and grabbed another apple from the bag. "And if we're getting personal here, what's Rick's deal?"

"He and Scott were friends."

"And Rick doesn't know about Brandy either?" She sounded skeptical.

"No. He never gave any hint that he did, and again, I want to keep it that way."

"I find that hard to believe. Guys share conquests."

"Rick would have said something to me. Yes, he was Scott's friend, but he's too honorable to have let me walk down the aisle knowing Scott was sleeping with Brandy."

"You know Rick has got a thing for you," Lucy said.

Megan chuckled. "He's loyal to Scott. He's looking after me because of the baby. And I don't want him thinking less of Scott. There's no point now."

Lucy filled a large metal bowl with ice water and squeezed several lemons into it. "There's smoke in that boy's eyes when he looks at you."

"He's always intense. Pay him no mind."

Megan reached for the first letter, dated December 2, 1902. The handwriting on the envelope was childlike, full of the loops and swirls so common with young girls. Diane would have been eleven when she wrote this letter to Claire, who would have been fourteen. Their mother had died in childbirth in 1900, and in the next two years, they had been sent away by their father to live with families on the mainland.

She began to read the little girl's words to her sister Claire.

> I fear the times will never be better. Mama is dead, and Papa has sent you away, along with Jemma, Sarah, the boys, and me. We will never be a family again. I am an orphan and *alone* in this world. Promises are like butterflies. Beautiful. Colorful. Easily crushed and broken.

"Claire hated leaving her siblings and their home," Lucy said. "I never understood why their father sent them away."

"Opportunity. The chances of them making a more successful marriage increased if they left the Eastern Shore."

"Maybe. But he kept the boys."

"Because he knew they would make their way on the sea as all the other men in the area did."

"Did you ever come across any information about Addie and Isaac Hedrick?"

"Addie's family was here before the Revolutionary War. Isaac's family migrated here in the 1870s from Eastern Europe."

"So they may have been Jewish?"

"Yes, I suppose so. There are communities of Jews who were persecuted in Russia in the 1870s."

"I didn't know that," Lucy said.

She peeled apples with the quick precision of someone who had once made her living in a kitchen while Megan read the letters following Diane from the Eastern Shore of Virginia to Baltimore and finally to Le Havre, France. The next letter picked up almost six months later and reported that Madame LeBlanc had died suddenly.

"How old was Diane when Madame LeBlanc died?" Lucy asked.

"Twelve."

"Natasha was about that age when her mother died. I can't imagine where she'd be if she'd been passed off to complete strangers in another city. Why didn't her father take her back?"

"Life could be very hard out here one hundred years ago," Megan said. "I'd like to think Isaac made a hard choice because he believed it was in her best interest."

Megan imagined all the dangers a young girl on the streets of a seaport city a century ago would have faced. She would have been alone, and though she referenced her ability to speak French, she had to have been overwhelmed.

CHAPTER SEVENTEEN

Megan

Wednesday, March 7, 2018
Cape Hudson, Virginia
8:00 p.m.

By the time Megan had read the twentieth letter, Lucy had peeled all the apples and cut them into thin slices. The apples now floated in an ice-water lemon bath while she mixed brown sugar, flour, salt, and butter in another bowl.

"Well, we know from the photograph that they did see each other again in Le Havre in 1909. Very unusual for two local girls to find themselves out of the state, let alone in a foreign country around that time."

"I've never been to Europe. It's on my bucket list."

"It's pretty amazing," Megan said. "Maybe one day I can take you and Natasha and give you the grand tour."

"We can put the spud in the front pack and make a real trip out of it."

"That would be fun." Megan wanted this to be her home but also realized Natasha and her daughter had a big wide world to explore.

Lucy lifted the crust from the board and laid it in a pie plate. After wiping her hands on her apron, she grabbed sugar, cinnamon, salt, and flour and, in a large bowl, mixed enough to make ten pies. "Are you sure they want all apple pies?"

"That was the order they gave me. They met at a cidery and bonded over an apple lemon-zest drink. It's going to be the signature cocktail for the reception."

Lucy scrunched her face. "Seriously?"

"I was going to have a signature cocktail. Our drink was a manhattan."

"You're a whiskey drinker?"

"I love a good glass of whiskey. Can't wait for the day when I can have one again."

Lucy did a double take. "There's a whole other Megan out there that I feel I don't know."

Megan rubbed her belly and shifted her weight. "As I said, I used to be a real person, Lucy. Now I'm a pod."

Lucy laughed. "I was a pretty swinging gal until I became the mother of a preteen and fell for a farmer."

"It might be a few years before we see Europe, but once the kid is born, we should line up sitters and have a night out, like adults. We can drink whiskey and listen to live music."

Lucy cocked her head, as if she pretended to think. "I don't remember what that's like."

"It's a distant memory for me as well."

Lucy nodded. "It's a date. When do these pies have to be delivered?"

"Friday in Norfolk."

"It's Wednesday evening. Assembly and baking tomorrow."

"I know. I'm cutting it close this time. I didn't think there'd be much to do at Spring House on Friday. Mr. Tucker and his crew are set to demo the kitchen and bathrooms then. It's going to be a mess."

"Megan, you're one of the hardest-working people I know."

"I have to be. My parents weren't thrilled with the history undergrad, but they covered the cost. When I announced my intentions to get a master's and PhD in history, the purse strings closed. Dad called it tough love and figured I'd come running back."

"But you didn't."

"I can be stubborn."

Chuckling, Lucy washed her hands. She drained the apples and then tossed the flour-sugar mixture into them, blending until each thin slice was coated.

"Don't put the filling into the shells right away."

"Not my first rodeo, grasshopper. I know. Let it sit and give off some of its juices. No one likes a soggy bottom crust."

"You got it."

With her back feeling better, Megan rose to wash her hands. She dug out a zester and began to rub it against the lemons as Lucy quickly rolled out crusts and assembled the first four apple pies.

Lucy rolled out several rounds of dough and then lined eight small pie shells and pricked the bottoms with a fork. All went into the oven for ten minutes.

Within the next hour, half the pie shells were baked and cooling on the counter, the sliced apples were marinating, and Lucy was rolling out the second round of crust.

As Megan filled the teakettle with water and set it on the stove, her phone rang. She recognized the number as local. "Megan Buchanan."

"This is Mrs. Appleton at the Eastern Shore of Virginia Historical Society. I'm sorry it's so late, but I've had a day full of tours and haven't had a chance to make my calls."

"Mrs. Appleton. How are you?" Megan and Mrs. Appleton had met a few times over the last few years while she was working on her dissertation. The historian was in her midfifties and had overseen the renovation of a mansion built by a shipping merchant in the 1790s in the town of Onancock. Mrs. Appleton didn't know much about Winter Cottage but had been as helpful as she could.

"Helen Jessup called and told me you're looking for information on Spring House."

Megan rolled her head from side to side, not thrilled that Helen was making calls on her behalf. *She's trying to be helpful,* Megan silently reminded herself. "That's right."

"I found some interesting references to Spring House. I've pulled several items, and they are available for you to review anytime. Helen said you're pregnant and need your rest."

Frustration ate at her. It was one thing for Helen to fuss over her pregnancy but another to insert herself into her work. "I'm still pretty mobile. And I'd love to come by and see what you have."

"I'm here all day tomorrow if that's convenient. I've found several firsthand accounts of your house and the people who lived in it. Some are first sources, so I can't let you borrow them, but you're welcome to photograph."

"That's fantastic. See you tomorrow."

CHAPTER EIGHTEEN

Megan

Thursday, March 8, 2018
Cape Hudson, Virginia
8:00 a.m.

Megan rose extra early and put the first batch of pies in the oven. She had an overpowering sense that she was cutting it close on time, and she needed to get these pies baked as soon as possible. By the time Lucy, Natasha, and Dolly hustled out the front door to school, Winter Cottage smelled of apples and cinnamon as the apple pies cooled on the counter.

When the kitchen was back in order and the baked pies were all counted, recounted, and boxed, Megan gathered her purse and water and headed over to Spring House, where Mr. Tucker was standing on the front porch talking to Helen. They appeared to be discussing the windows and the shutters, and Megan sensed that Helen was annexing her renovation project.

She parked and walked toward them, doing her best not to waddle. As she moved closer, she saw paint samples in Helen's hand, and as her irritation spiked, she imagined she heard Scott whisper, *Please, Meg. She's happy. She's smiling.*

Brushing what felt like a gnat away from her face, Megan dug a smile out from God only knew where. "How's it going?"

Helen turned and at least had the decency to look as if she'd been caught in the act. "Megan. You're early. I wanted to make sure the house was unlocked for Mr. Tucker. I still have a key that Samuel gave his brother years ago. Funny I should still have that."

"Thank you, that's thoughtful."

"Is there anything you need to say to Mr. Tucker?"

Megan cleared her throat. "Mr. Tucker, I think you have your marching orders."

"I do. Demo all of the exterior siding so we can see what we're working with. And please save anything that looks historical. When in doubt, save."

"It's wise you aren't around all the dust," Helen said.

"I'm actually headed to the historical society," Megan said.

"Did Mrs. Appleton have information for you?" Helen asked.

"She did." Megan held on to that smile as she put the house key back in her pocket. She pictured Scott asking her to look out for his mother. "Would you like to come and see what she's dug up?"

"I would love to," Helen said. "I think Mr. Tucker and I are finished here."

Mr. Tucker nodded. "Me and the guys are going to get right to it. It's going to be a messy few days."

"I'll check in at the end of the day," Megan replied.

"Understood," Mr. Tucker said.

"Shall I drive?" Helen asked. "I know you're quite capable, but this will be your chance to relax."

Megan mentally swatted away all images of Scott and settled into the passenger seat. "Sure. That sounds great."

The pristine shape of the car's interior was not a surprise; nor was the faint scent of air freshener, which reminded Megan of Helen's home. The coffee cup in the holder between them read MARINES in bold red letters, and she recognized it as Scott's. It had been his favorite. Helen's pink lipstick darkened the rim.

After Scott's death, Megan had heard from friends that Helen had continued to pay the rent on Scott's apartment for several months. Some said she would often visit the one-bedroom unit and sit for hours on the couch in silence. Finally, she had begun bringing in boxes and carefully wrapping up his belongings. After she'd washed and ironed his clothes, she had folded and boxed them before driving them to the Goodwill.

Scott's furniture had been typical bachelor fare. Helen had not been as sentimental about that and called a local thrift store to pick it up. She had boxed up all items that seemed to belong to a woman and mailed them to Megan's parents' house. There had been no note in the box, but there were several women's bracelets that Megan did not recognize. What hadn't belonged to her went straight into the trash.

Twenty minutes later, Megan and Helen arrived at the steps of a brick house built circa 1800. Designed in the Federal style, it had a center section and matching wings on both sides. Megan twisted the knob and stepped into the dimly lit entryway. A spiral staircase led to a second floor, and on the right was a parlor across from a formal dining room. The society had purchased the house in the 1980s and renovated it, and the group continued to raise funds for its general upkeep and operation.

"I've spoken to Mrs. Appleton a few times over the years, and she was a big help when I was writing my dissertation," Megan said.

"I must admit I can now understand your obsession with the past a little better. I'm very curious to discover more about the Jessup family."

Megan's phone chimed with a text, and she glanced down to see a note from Chloe. Local records indicate the entire Mandel family was transported to Auschwitz. No reported survivors.

Sadness gripped her as she knocked on the open door, the rapping of her knuckles echoing through the house. "Hello?"

Footsteps echoed from the parlor, and a woman dressed in jeans, a collared shirt, and tennis shoes appeared. Gray hair pulled back in a ponytail accentuated an angular face tastefully made up with rouge, a touch of eye shadow, and peach-hued lipstick.

"Megan Buchanan," she said, smiling.

"Mrs. Alice Appleton. Pleasure to see you again." Megan gripped her hand firmly and shook it.

"How is the renovation going?"

"We've just started phase one. So far so good. Mrs. Appleton, I believe you spoke to Mrs. Helen Jessup."

Helen's smile was gracious and genuine. "I didn't think you'd call so quickly."

"Thankfully we digitized the records a couple of years ago, so it's making searches much faster. I simply typed in *Spring House*, and I uncovered quite a bit of surprising history. As you know, our collection includes several journals and letters."

"Yes," Megan said. "I was able to access some of that information on Winter Cottage when I was writing my dissertation."

"I remember. How is the newest owner of Winter Cottage? Ms. Kincaid's arrival is still the talk of the town."

"She's great. We hope to begin renovations on Winter Cottage in the fall."

"Please keep us involved. It's a thrilling project," Mrs. Appleton offered. "We would love to scan whatever records you find and add them to our collection."

"We're still sifting through much of it, but once we have it sorted, I'll certainly give you a call," Megan said.

"So what do you have on the Jessup house?" Helen asked.

Megan and Helen followed Mrs. Appleton through the parlor to an odd addition that did not quite fit with the traditional Federal style. They sat in chairs angled in front of a desk that had come straight out of a modern furniture store. It was the furthest from historical she could imagine. Still, even a historical society's office had to focus on functionality. And judging by the stacks of papers on this desk, Mrs. Appleton was juggling a lot.

Mrs. Appleton laid out an article dated July 1, 1922, featuring Eric and Sally Jessup with their five sons. The family posed in front of Spring House and the summer kitchen located behind it. The article reported on Eric's recent actions to save sailors on a sinking ship in the bay.

Helen tapped the face of the second-youngest boy. "That was my late grandfather-in-law. And youngest of the five boys is Samuel." Samuel was the blondest and most dashing of the Jessup men.

Mrs. Appleton laid out a second article on the table. It was dated April 2, 1942. The headline read, SAMUEL JESSUP SAVES 100 NAVY SAILORS.

"I never realized he was such a hero," Helen said. She began to read out loud. "Merchant marine Samuel Jessup, while returning from a supply run to Great Britain, was witness to the torpedoing of USS *Jackson* by a German U-boat. He ordered depth charges dropped and destroyed the enemy vessel, and then he and his first mate repeatedly rowed into burning, oil-slicked waters to save the survivors."

She went on to detail the names of Samuel's crew and the injuries they'd sustained.

"My word," Mrs. Appleton said. "You would have never known."

Never once in all the times she'd seen Samuel had he ever mentioned the war. "Mrs. Appleton, we found quite a few artifacts in Samuel's desk drawer. Specifically, there were letters between Claire and her sister Diane. Nothing too far out of the ordinary, but we did find a French passport issued to an Elise Mandel and her son dated 1939. It states on the papers that she was Jewish. I don't suppose that name rings a bell. I just heard from a friend in France who tells me the entire family was transported to a concentration camp. I'm hoping she and her son made it to the Eastern Shore."

Mrs. Appleton scribbled down the date and name on a pad. "The name doesn't sound familiar, but if she moved to Cape Hudson, there would be some record of her or her son. I can dig around."

"Thank you. I would appreciate that."

Megan and Helen spent a few more minutes chatting with Mrs. Appleton before they left the historical society. As Megan settled in the front seat of the Volvo, Helen was on her phone. "Rick, this is Helen."

"Helen." Rick's deep voice echoed over the car's speakerphone and vibrated through her body.

"Megan and I are on the hunt for Elise Mandel. We found her travel papers at Spring House. Mrs. Appleton is searching the woman to see if she moved to Cape Hudson, but it occurred to me the sheriff's office might have some record of her. Do me a favor and see if your police files have any information on the woman."

"Sure. I'll look into it," Rick said.

"Thank you." Megan was annoyed she had not thought of the idea herself.

"Helen, I didn't think you personally were that interested in the shore's history," Rick said.

"My job now is to keep Megan and the baby as healthy and relaxed as possible. So where they go, I follow. And if that means helping solve a mystery, then call me Dr. Watson."

"I'll look into it," he said with a chuckle.

"If you'd rather I review the police files, I can."

"No, I have this."

"Excellent."

When the two arrived back at Spring House, Megan thought about the picture of the Jessups and the image of the summer kitchen in the background. She found herself scanning the land for the structure that had burned in the late 1930s. Helen came around the side of the car with her phone opened to the map she'd taken a picture of at the historical society.

Megan walked toward the edge of the grass, which had grown tall enough to reach her hips. Her fingers skimmed the green tops as she stared out over the land and the bay beyond.

"There's no telling what's in that grass, Megan," Helen warned.

"Aren't you a little curious about the kitchen? It was part of the history of this land," Megan said.

"Of course. But I'm practical. Let's focus on one thing at a time. Baby first. And then Spring House. Summer kitchen or whatever will have to wait."

"The foundation has been lost in all the underbrush. I'd love to locate it and get a better sense of the entire layout. It can't be that far ahead."

Helen stepped in front of her. "At least let me go first. If there's a well, or a nest of snakes, I'll go in first."

"Helen, you're going to ruin your shoes," Megan said.

"They're only shoes, dear," Helen countered.

"Helen, that doesn't sound like you at all."

"I'm tired of sounding and being like myself. I have closets full of shoes, but I have only one grandchild. Let's go, dear."

For all Helen's micromanaging, there were moments like this one when Megan saw the woman that Scott had adored. "Okay."

Helen pushed back the tall grass with her hands and gingerly stepped forward.

Megan followed behind like a kid on a treasure hunt. The soil was soft from last week's rains, but it was manageable.

"Twenty-seven, twenty-eight . . ." Helen proudly called out the small steps as they went.

By the time they had counted out the distance, there still was no evidence of any kitchen foundation. Helen held up her phone, trying to orient the picture with the view before her. "I don't see it," she huffed.

"It's got to be close." Megan looked back at Spring House. Realizing their angle might be off slightly, she moved east a dozen paces. Her foot caught on an unexpected stone, and she tripped. Her rounded belly threw off her balance, and before she knew it, she'd pitched forward.

Helen was at her side in a moment. "Good Lord. Are you all right?"

Megan reached for her belly. The baby jabbed hard. "The baby's fine. I just lost my footing, but I think I found the kitchen."

Helen helped her to her feet. "Can you stand? Are you sure you're okay?"

She brushed the dirt from the palms of her hands. "I'm fine."

Helen's face paled, and she looked as if she could get physically sick. "Good Lord. I thought you had fallen into a well."

"I didn't mean to scare you," Megan said.

Helen was not a hugger, and her pride was her armor. There was a reason why it did not make any sense for Megan to hug Helen, but Megan wrapped her arms around her anyway. The baby landed a solid elbow—this time right into Helen's stomach. "Jackpot."

The woman drew back. "Oh my word. She kicked."

Megan took Helen's hand and pressed it against her belly. "She does that a lot." To prove her point, the baby kicked again.

Tears welled in Helen's eyes. "This baby is a miracle."

Though Megan felt bloated, clumsy, and fat, she knew Helen was right. "Yes, she is."

Helen kept her palm on Megan's belly. "He loved you so much."

"I know." And in his way, he had. But Scott had been like Samuel. Love of a woman would never have been enough for him.

The clouds overhead grew darker, and in the distance, thunder rumbled. A raindrop hit her face and then another. "Let's get back to Spring House."

When they arrived, Mr. Tucker and his crew had stripped away the weathered white siding. What lay beneath were two log cabins joined together by a center section. Log cabins were sturdy and built to last if done right, but at some point, they had fallen out of favor and had been seen as outdated. Many had been covered in wood siding to give them a more modern look.

But she loved the humble building that now stood before her. It no longer had to pretend it was something else. It could embrace its proud heritage.

April 9, 1939
From the Journal of Samuel Jessup

My first mate, Billy, knows the waters off the coast of France well. For nearly a decade he sailed into Le Havre and picked up bottles of booze from a local couple named Gilbert and Diane Bernard. Diane, it seems, is Miss Claire's younger sister, and there was always an exchange of letters and trinkets on the docks. Billy took the bottles back to Norfolk, Virginia, and delivered them to Claire Buchanan, who paid him well for his troubles and risk. In those days, selling booze in the States was illegal, but that didn't stop Miss Claire from turning a fine profit. Billy has told me the best spots to drop anchor if I don't want no trouble from the law or the Germans.

The winds of war are blowing hotter. I'd like nothing better than to tangle again with one of them U-boats and send it right to the bottom of the Atlantic.

CHAPTER NINETEEN

Diane

Age 12

Tuesday, November 3, 1903
Normandy, France

As Diane stood at the cliffs and looked over the ocean, the stiff breeze ruffled the folds of her skirt and stirred up worries.

Since she had arrived in Normandy almost a month ago, she'd dreamed each night of the police arriving at the château. Grim-faced men dressed in uniforms placing handcuffs on her and escorting her to a darkened cell where Pierre waited. As always, his dark and unsettling eyes pinned her as he stood watching, his arm raised and ready to strike. She had nowhere to run.

Each time she awoke, she would pull out the planchette, hold it close, and ask her mother for strength and any kind of message to give her comfort. But no message ever revealed itself, and to her frustration, her loneliness grew. "You're worthless to me," she said to the device. "You don't do anything but sparkle."

The waves crashed against the rocks below as she extended her hand over the cliff and dangled the planchette. She was ready to release it and watch it fall to the rocks. It would be her last physical link to Madame LeBlanc, but something stopped her.

As tempted as she was, she could not seem to loosen her grip. It truly was her last connection to her mother. If she threw it away, her mother would be gone forever, and she just could not bear that pain.

She shoved the device back in her pocket. "Claire, where are you?"

The ocean waves crashed, the wind gusted, and seagulls squawked. But no one answered.

She cupped her hand over her eyes and stared out over the waves, praying Claire might be on the other side thinking of her. It had been so long since she had seen her sister.

The dog's barking made her turn, smiling in spite of herself. She and Oscar were getting to be close friends. Like her, he had a sweet tooth, and though Madame Herbert frowned on it, Diane gave him bits of piecrust. He not only sat beside her at meals now but also found his way into her attic room and slept on the edge of her bed.

"It must be getting close to suppertime," she said. The dog knew time better than most humans, especially when it came to meals.

Diane picked up the basket filled with the eggs she had gathered, and together they walked down the path away from the cliffs toward the château nestled into the side of a rocky hill. When she pushed through the back door, the scent of Madame's bread blended with a chicken roasting in the oven. Madame was sitting at the roughly hewn kitchen table snapping the tips of string beans for dinner.

Diane found comfort knowing that Madame spent most of her days in the kitchen. She walked to the sink, then cranked the lever up and down until water gushed out. She washed the eggs before she put them in a bowl. She then toweled off her hands with a red-and-white-checkered towel.

Diane sat at the table across from Madame and scooped up a handful of beans. She began to snap off the tips.

"I see you were able to gather the eggs," Madame Herbert said.

"Only a dozen today. The red hen didn't have any, and when I checked, she was fairly annoyed with me."

The woman chuckled. "That's Esme. She has always been temperamental."

"Always, or is it just me she hates? She doesn't mind when you gather the eggs."

Madame peered over the rims of wire half glasses. "I raised her from a chick. She's still getting to know you. And like Oscar, when she realizes you aren't going to hurt her, she'll relax."

Diane looked down at the red mark on the back of her hand. It was her most recent souvenir from Esme. Outside, the neigh of a horse signaled Gilbert's return from the orchard. He left each day long before sunrise, and so far, he had never returned from the fields before sunset.

She peered out the window to see him dismount. His boots were covered in mud, and he was scowling as he walked his black steed toward the stables.

"That boy has been working himself ragged," Madame said.

Diane looked away from the window, slightly embarrassed she had been caught staring. "What has he been doing?"

Bent, wrinkled fingers pinched off the top of a bean with an efficiency Diane's own mama had had. "There's always much to be done here. The work never stops. Just today he was rotating the oak barrels. It takes an artist's touch to make the kind of ciders and distilled liquors we do. So many of the vineyards and orchards were struck by the blight and nearly destroyed. But Gilbert and his grandfather saw to it that the apple trees remained strong. When there was no wine to drink, people turned to apples and us."

"His uncle, Mr. LeBlanc, wasn't a help?" Diane asked.

Madame Herbert scrunched up her face. "I can't speak ill of the dead, for they may come back and haunt me. Better I say nothing about Monsieur LeBlanc."

"The dead don't hear us." Diane was feeling surly, still annoyed with her planchette.

"Of course the dead listen in to our conversation. They also speak to us, but we don't always listen." She leaned forward, glancing from side to side as if to make sure there was no spirit lurking close by. "Monsieur LeBlanc liked the finer things. That is why he eloped with Gilbert's aunt while she was studying in Paris. He fooled her with sweet words and gestures."

"What did Émilie study?"

"She was a great artist. It was a good thing, for she was not suited for farm life. Her papa finally relented and permitted her to study in Paris for one month. One little month. The next we know, she is married to Monsieur LeBlanc and soon after that, dead from typhus. When Émilie died and Monsieur LeBlanc realized he would not inherit the estate, he quickly found himself another woman. The woman you knew as Madame LeBlanc."

"Was Gilbert's father heartbroken when Émilie died?"

"Gilbert's father died when he was very young. His grandfather raised him."

"Was his grandfather sad?"

"The old man never showed much emotion, but after Émilie died, he grew quieter and more sullen, if that is possible. He died when Gilbert was seventeen."

"Who took over the farm then?"

"Gilbert, of course."

"How long have you lived here?" Diane asked.

"All my life. I came here with my husband when I wasn't much older than you. My Louis was a winemaker at heart, and he worked closely with Gilbert's grandfather. I raised Gilbert after his dear mother died giving birth to him. And when my husband passed, Gilbert moved me up to this house, and here we live."

"If Gilbert didn't like Madame LeBlanc, why did he come to Le Havre?"

"For you, of course. She told him you were his cousin. She told him you were Émilie's child. If Gilbert is dedicated to anything more than this land, it is family." She tsk-tsked, shaking her head. "Madame LeBlanc and her husband were as clever as they were evil."

Diane could not imagine leaving this place. Here she felt safe. "Gilbert has not said a word to me since I arrived. Do you think he has forgotten about me?" She half hoped he had.

"I know he has spoken to Max several times about you."

"Why?"

"He wants to make sure that man Pierre does not find his way here."

She could feel Pierre's fingers tightening around her neck. "Will he?"

"Max asked around and learned no one had noticed Gilbert. Max also made sure he told everyone he saw that you two went east toward Germany."

On the heels of relief came the fear that Gilbert would tire of covering for her. "Perhaps Gilbert won't notice that I am here and I can stay. I am a hard worker and can help you with all the chores. I am good with chores, and the dog likes me just fine, I think. And like you said, one day Esme will come to trust me."

Madame glanced at the dog and arched a brow. "Oscar knows a soft touch when he sees one."

"But I am a help to you, no?" Diane insisted.

"Yes, child. It has been lovely having you here."

"When Gilbert decides to send me away, will you speak to him?" Diane asked.

Madame humphed. "Gilbert is like you. He develops a soft spot for any creature he puts under his protection. Once that happens, he is the most loyal of men."

"But he doesn't want me around."

"Perhaps not. But yet, here you sit." She scooped up a handful of beans and pinched the tops free with her thumb and index finger. "Have you written a letter to your sister yet?"

"I've written several."

"Then Gilbert will post them for you." Her old fingers worked quickly and efficiently, snapping off the ends of the beans. "Did you tell your sister about what happened in Le Havre?"

"I did in the first letter." Diane wanted her sister to worry their father so he'd realize he had made a terrible mistake.

"Claire will surely worry when she reads it."

"I know."

Madame Herbert snapped her beans, saying nothing as she peered over her glasses at Diane. "It is not so terrible here, is it?"

"No, it's not."

"You eat well."

"Yes."

"Oscar follows you everywhere."

"Yes."

"Perhaps you should write a happier letter. Save the bad news for when you see your sister in person."

The door opened and Gilbert appeared, his dark hair tousled from the wind and his tanned cheeks reddened by the cold. The dog rose up, tail wagging, and immediately crossed to him. Gilbert rubbed the dog between the ears.

He nodded to them both as he crossed the kitchen, washed his hands, and then tore off a piece of the cooling bread.

"That is for supper, young man," Madame Herbert said.

Gilbert kissed her on the cheek. "I know. Thank you."

He sat at the head of the table, and Diane could feel her fingers trembling just a little under his scrutiny. Fresh worries churned in her belly, and she feared her stay here was going to end. Why would he keep her around? She was not family. And she had been a part of a plan to defraud him.

"Good afternoon," Diane said. Her sister Claire had always acted older than her years, and Diane desperately wanted to appear braver and older right now.

"You look well," Gilbert said. "I think Madame Herbert is fattening you up."

"The girl eats all the time," the old woman chuckled.

"Should I eat less?" Diane said quickly. "Madame LeBlanc said ladies don't eat."

Madame Herbert huffed and muttered several words. "Perhaps ladies don't eat, but this woman does. You like eating, don't you?"

Diane nodded. "I do. Very much."

"Then eat!" Madame Herbert said. "I will have no hungry children in my home."

Gilbert poured a glass of cider and drank. "I understand you've been a big help to Madame."

"It is no different than when I worked at home with my mother and family," she said. "We are an ocean away, but it's all very much the same."

Gilbert regarded her as a man might a broken farm tool or a cracked wheel. "As to the matter of your sister and your father, I'll need contact information so they know you're safe."

"You're sending me away?" Diane could barely hold back the emotions she had locked deep inside her.

"I didn't say that," Gilbert said. "But they are your family. They deserve to know you're safe and well."

"My father is at sea, I suppose, but my sister lives in New York. She works for the Buchanan family. I have their address memorized."

"Good. Write her a letter, and I'll post it in Le Havre."

Mention of the city reminded her of Madame LeBlanc's lifeless body and Pierre. "Madame Herbert said your friend Max told everyone we went toward Germany."

Gilbert sighed. "He did, and that is a good thing. Though no one saw us together, there are people who saw you with Madame LeBlanc. The police were searching for you, but the idea of going as far as Germany for a slip of a girl is too much for them to bother with."

She paled. "What if Pierre doesn't believe Max's lies?"

"Max is very clever. If he spins a story, everyone will believe it."

"Has he seen Pierre?"

"There has been no sighting of him. What do you know about this Pierre?"

"Very little. When Madame LeBlanc went out in the evenings, he always went with her. A man once came to our house in Baltimore and was very angry with Madame LeBlanc. Pierre hit him several times and tossed him out. He never came again." She snapped a string bean in half.

"Did he ever hit you?" Gilbert's voice was quiet, but held a dangerous edge.

"Yes."

Gilbert drank another sip of cider. "He won't hit you again. You're safe here."

"So she shall stay here until her family can come and fetch her," Madame Herbert said. "And there is no rush for her to leave. Winter is coming in a few short weeks, and travel is terrible when the snows come. And I've gotten rather used to having her around the house. The help has been a godsend for a woman with tired, old bones."

"She belongs with her family," Gilbert insisted. "And your bones have plenty of energy left in them."

Madame shook her head. "Let the sister know she's well. And we'll see in the spring if she's to travel to New York or stay here."

"She cannot stay here forever," Gilbert said.

"Of course not." Madame waved her hands as if brushing the subject aside. "But for now, she's fine where she is."

Gilbert stared at the old woman. "You'll not make the final decision in this matter."

Madame Herbert shrugged and was not the least bit put off by his expression. "Of course not. You are head of the household. I will need more wood for the kitchen stove. Would you be so good as to bring some inside for me?"

He drained the last of his cider. "I am in charge of this house, Madame Herbert."

"Of course you are, dear."

Gilbert's expression reminded Diane of the time she had brought home a stray cat. Her father had not been happy, and he had demanded the creature leave his house at once. And then he had stared at the faces of his wife and children and known in an instant he had been overruled.

"Write your letter, girl, and I'll post it when I travel to Le Havre in two days." He looked at the dog and snapped his fingers as he walked toward the door. The dog did not budge from his spot by Diane.

"Not you too," Gilbert grumbled. "Damnation."

The word was barely audible over the slamming back door. "Is he going to send me away?" Diane asked.

Madame Herbert shrugged. "Certainly not during the winter. That would be barbaric."

"But when spring comes?"

She went back to snapping her green beans. "We will decide once spring comes, eh? You might be quite ready to be rid of us."

Diane did not want to go into the village, but Gilbert and Madame Herbert insisted. People had already heard whispers about a new girl

living at the château, and the sooner they met her at the Sunday service, the sooner they would accept her.

"Are you a Catholic?" Madame Herbert tucked a strand of hair behind Diane's ear as Gilbert stabled the horses near the church.

"Mama said we were Methodist."

Madame Herbert frowned and then glanced up at the stone spire of the church behind them. "I will take that as a yes. And if anyone else asks, say yes, and then make the sign of the cross like this." The old woman touched her forehead, belly, and then on either side of each breast. "These are good people and they are hardworking, but it's easy to become a little superstitious and untrusting this far from a big city. I'm a healer in town, so as much as they respect me, some fear me."

"Why?"

Her shrug was casual, and she fussed with the lace on the collar of her Sunday dress. "Who can say? Perhaps I am too good at my job."

"Can you teach me?" Diane asked.

"To be a healer? Why would a pretty girl like you want such a difficult job?"

"I want to be of use. I want to know." She wanted to be so needed that they could never think of sending her away.

"It is not easy."

"I am a hard worker."

A slight smile tugged at her thin lips. "Yes, you are."

Gilbert approached them, his long legs eating up the ground between them as his coat flapped open. He'd put on a fine linen shirt and polished his boots. And of course he was frowning. Always frowning.

Church bells clanged above their heads, echoing over the red clay rooftops and stone chimneys that puffed out snow from the fires in the hearths.

Gilbert carefully buttoned his jacket and looked beyond Madame Herbert and Diane toward a group of couples gathered at the church entrance. "There is already gossip about Diane."

"There is always gossip," Madame Herbert said.

"Those who wish to work at the château know that I don't tolerate it, but there are others who aren't so easily persuaded."

Diane looked toward the church entrance to discover that several women were staring openly at her. When her eyes met theirs, they turned and hurried into the church.

"Let us go in," Gilbert said.

He took Madame Herbert by the arm and nodded for Diane to walk beside them. When they stepped under the church's stone arch, she found herself standing at the back of an ancient sanctuary flanked by tall stained-glass windows featuring scenes detailing the betrayal and death of Christ. Morning light shone through colored glass, sprinkling reds, greens, and golds on parishioners garbed in blacks and browns.

Gilbert allowed Madame Herbert to walk in front of him, and he followed behind her with Diane at his side until they reached the first pew, which was empty. Carved into the pew's side was the letter *B*. Bernard. Claire had said once that the Buchanans had their own pew at their church in New York, but she'd never seen such a thing.

She stood beside Madame Herbert, and Gilbert took his place beside her. Madame removed a hymnbook from her purse and opened it to a well-worn page. The minister or, rather, priest came out and indicated that the parishioners sing that very hymn.

"It is always the same," Madame said.

Diane could speak French, but she'd never learned to read it, so as Madame's wobbly, loud voice boomed out the hymn in time with Gilbert's baritone voice, she did her best to mimic the sounds and mumble words a beat or two behind them. Standing in the front, she couldn't see anyone staring at her but often felt their rapt attention pressing against her back.

The service continued on, and when they were called to the front to stand before the priest, she cupped her hands as Madame Herbert did and ate the wafer. She drank from a cup of wine, swallowing hard as she struggled not to cough. The service continued, and by the time the priest said his final words, she had crossed herself for the tenth time. With great relief, she followed Gilbert and Madame Herbert out of the sanctuary.

They stepped into the bright sunshine, and the warmth on her face was soothing. However, the moment's peace ended quickly with the approach of two older, thick-waisted women. Both were smiling, but they reminded her more of wolves stalking prey.

"Madame Herbert," the first said as she kissed her on her cheek. "You look well."

"But of course. Let me introduce you to my cousin. This is Diane, and she is from Paris. Diane, this is Madame Locard and Madame Claremont."

"Your cousin?" the woman said, inspecting Diane. "I have known you for thirty years, and you never mentioned a young cousin."

"Ah, my extended family is large, and I lose track sometimes." Madame Herbert turned to Gilbert. "Gilbert was kind enough to allow her to visit us for a little while."

"How long will she be staying?" Madame Claremont asked.

"At least until spring," Gilbert said.

"Ah, how nice," Madame Locard said. "How old are you, Diane?"

"Twelve."

The older woman's expression sharpened. "I will have to introduce you to my son. He is fifteen. Of course, they would be properly chaperoned."

Gilbert jerked hard at his cuff. "We shall see about that. For now, Diane is still settling in."

"Madame Herbert, you made no mention of her visit last I saw you."

"Didn't I?" she said. "I must have forgotten."

"I will get the carriage," Gilbert said. "I won't be but a minute."

216

The women continued to talk over Diane, and several more women gathered. Some asked about Paris, and another decided that her accent was indeed Parisian. When the carriage rolled up with Gilbert at the reins, she gratefully helped Madame Herbert into her seat and took her place between her and Gilbert.

They waved to the still very curious churchgoers as he drove them out of town.

"Cousin?" Gilbert said.

Madame Herbert arranged a plaid blanket over her legs and Diane's. "I thought that was rather clever of me. They will accept her faster if they know she is family."

"And if she stays beyond spring?" he challenged.

"Then my poor distant cousin, her father, shall die a tragic death, and she will have to stay longer."

He grunted. "You two had better get your stories straight, because the inquisition of ladies will be in full swing by next Sunday."

Madame Herbert laughed. "I'm rather enjoying the challenge."

They rode along in silence for a mile, and Diane found herself relaxing back into her seat as they moved past the green, rolling countryside.

The sharp, panicked neigh of a horse followed by the shouts of a woman cut through the silence. Gilbert was instantly alert, and his grip on the reins tightened. Madame too was on alert and spared a quick glance in his direction. Diane's thoughts instantly went to Pierre. Had he somehow not believed Max's lie about them traveling east?

Gilbert snapped the reins, and the horses trotted faster. When they rounded the corner, they came upon an overturned cart. The driver lay on the road, the side of the cart trapping his leg. His horse, tethered to the cart, bucked and pulled, and each time he did so, the cart jolted and the man cried out in pain.

"That is Robert Françoise?" Madame Herbert said.

Gilbert stopped their own horse a safe distance away and set the hand brake before securely tying off the reins.

He jumped down and hurried around the cart toward the panicked horse, which was more a threat to the man than any injury. He approached the animal, speaking in a soothing voice and holding his hands out. The horse snorted and kicked as if to warn Gilbert off, but he held his ground and continued to speak to the distressed animal. Finally, he was able to reach the headgear and unfasten it. He set the animal free and watched it trot down the road.

Madame Herbert tossed off the blanket. "We must go to Robert."

Diane climbed down off the seat and held out her hands for Madame Herbert, who leaned heavily on her as she too descended. When Diane looked closer at Robert, she saw a bloody gash on his head, and his left leg was twisted at a horrific angle. "What do we do?"

"I always carry a bag of medicines in the back. Fetch that."

Diane ran around the carriage, located the rucksack, and carried it around, chasing after Madame, who was already marching toward the accident site.

Gilbert inspected Robert's head and leg. "We shall get you out right away, Robert."

Robert rolled his head from side to side. "It is like knives cutting into me."

Gilbert dashed past Diane to his own horse, quickly unharnessed the animal, and tied the reins to wagon wheels that jutted toward the sky.

"What do I do?" Diane asked.

"Talk to him." Madame had already laid out a blanket and was lining up her potions and odd-looking devices.

Diane rubbed her palms over her thighs and then, drawing in a breath, moved toward him. The coppery scent of blood grew stronger, and her heart thudded so hard against her ribs she was sure one would snap.

Robert rolled his head toward her, his green eyes brightened with panic and fear. "I'm going to die, aren't I?"

The anguish in his voice gave her courage to drop to her knees beside him. Her hands trembled, and she was afraid to touch him.

"Keep him calm," Gilbert ordered. "This might hurt."

"I don't want to die. I have a wife. Children."

Diane laid her hand on the man's shoulder and found what she guessed must look like a wobbly smile. "You are not going to die today," she said.

"I am. The pain is too great for me to survive."

She remembered how Madame LeBlanc could sound so sure when she lied to her customers. What had seemed so terrible to Diane then now seemed the best course of action. "I know for a fact you are not dying." She reached for his palm and traced the lifeline. "This line tells me that you will live to be a very old man."

The fear tensing his body eased a small fraction. "Only a witch would know that."

"I don't know about witches," she said. "But I know lives. And yours is going to be very, very long."

"Ready?" Gilbert said.

Diane tightened her grip on Robert's hand, which was rough with calluses and fresh blisters. "Yes, we need to get this cart away so this dear man can get on with his life."

"She says I'm not going to die, Gilbert," Robert said.

"Then you will not." Gilbert took his horse by the reins and moved slowly forward. The cart rocked. Robert tensed and screamed. Gilbert's jaw tightened as he kept walking until finally the cart rose above the man.

Diane grabbed the man by the shoulders. "You must help me, Robert."

He screamed in agony.

She pulled and tugged against what felt like deadweight. She could see that one leg was broken, but the other appeared intact. "Push with your good leg."

Groaning in pain, he pushed with his good leg as she pulled, and together they were able to move him clear of the wagon.

"We are clear!" she shouted.

Gilbert kept coaxing the horse forward, pulling the wagon until it rocked back and forth and then tipped forward onto the three remaining working wheels. Madame Herbert lowered her old bones down to the ground beside Robert and studied the injuries. Her smile didn't quite reach her eyes.

"The witch girl says I have a long life," Robert said. "Gilbert agrees."

"Then it is not my place to contradict," Madame Herbert said. "Diane, we must see that your bold prediction comes true."

"Yes, Madame. What do I do?"

"You and Gilbert hold his shoulders down while I set the leg."

She and Gilbert each pressed on a shoulder as the old woman moved around the body. She unlaced the man's boot and removed it, along with his woolen sock. "I shall count to three, Robert."

He closed his eyes, gritting his teeth. "Aye. Three it is."

Diane and Gilbert exchanged glances and pressed with all their weight.

"One." As Madame spoke, Robert's body tensed, and he strained against their combined weight. "Two." As he drew in a breath, the old woman pulled hard on the leg, and the twisted bones cracked back into place. Robert screamed, his eyes rolled back in his head, and he lost consciousness.

Diane's breathing was quick, and she thought for a moment she too would swoon. "Is he dead?"

"No," Madame Herbert said. "But we must get the leg splinted before he wakes up. Find me two large branches, and I will bind them to his leg."

Gilbert rose and extended his hand to Diane. "You did well."

She brushed the leaves off her skirt. "Thank you."

As he found a long branch and snapped it in two, he regarded her with a raised brow. "Let us hope that Robert forgets that you read palms and can predict the future, Witch Girl."

"I'm not a witch!" she said quickly.

"Whether you are or not is of no concern to me. I've no opinion on witches one way or the other. But the good folks of the village might think differently. I suggest you practice your hymns and the timing of your crosses before Sunday service next week."

———— ⚬⚬~⚬⚬ ————

When spring arrived after the long winter, Diane's prediction came true. Robert did live. And though she worked hard to learn the hymns and speak vaguely about her "family" in Paris, rumors about her persisted. No one called her a witch to her face, for all feared Gilbert. Several young girls who came to see Madame Herbert asked if Diane made love potions. Madame Herbert chased them all away.

In mid-April a letter arrived from Claire. Diane was thrilled to hear from her big sister. Claire informed her she had found a position for her in the Buchanan house. Diane was to be her assistant, and Claire would wire her money for the passage.

At first Diane was excited, but as she sat in her bed rubbing Oscar's head, she realized deep down she did not want to leave. Diane did not want any part of helping dress the young and very selfish Victoria Buchanan.

She had grown to love this farm, and she now helped Madame with all the chores. And when Madame's bones ached on rainy days and her hands were too sore to knead the bread, she taught Diane how to do it. At first, her bread was rather hard and chewy, but as the weeks passed, she showed considerable progress.

Gilbert announced one April afternoon, "I head to Le Havre tomorrow. You will want to post a letter to your sister, I think."

Tension rippled through her shoulders as she kneaded the dough. She did not have the courage to look at him. "I would like to stay here," she said.

Madame Herbert drew in a breath but did not speak as a long silence passed. Gilbert studied her. Finally, he reached for an apple tart and centered it on his plate. "Then you shall stay."

"Truly?"

"If you grow tired of us, you may leave at any time," he said.

The apples were ripening nicely in the summer's warmth. Gilbert and his farmhands would be harvesting them in two months. And each day Diane brought lunches to them all, just as Madame Herbert had done for decades.

Claire wrote to Diane, begging her to return to America, but with each passing week, Diane found it easier and easier to refuse all her sister's offers.

Life settled into the mundane. As always, she saw little of Gilbert. She worked in the house, taking care of Madame and the dog, baking bread, and cooking meals until one day, without anyone saying a word, she found herself in charge of the household.

Claire had written several times, insisting Diane return to the United States, but Diane always found an excuse why she could not leave. In the end she told Claire she did not wish to return, and finally Claire accepted her decision.

Madame LeBlanc's murder, which had been such a sensation, had nearly faded from her memory. However, from time to time, she would still dream of Pierre, and each time she did, she would wake with a start. She had not forgotten Pierre, and she feared he had not forgotten her.

CHAPTER TWENTY

Megan

Friday, March 9, 2018
Cape Hudson, Virginia
8:00 a.m.

Lucy loaded the coolers containing the pies Megan had finished baking the previous night at 11:00 p.m. in the back of Megan's truck. She slammed the tailgate closed, settled behind the wheel, and turned to Megan. "Helen knows we aren't going to be at Spring House today, right?"

"Correct." Megan pressed her fingertips to her temple. "Turns out she had to get back to Norfolk to check in with her grandmother-in-law. But she'll return in a couple of days to inspect Mr. Tucker's work."

"She's jumped back into your life with both feet," Lucy said. "How's that going for you?"

"Scott said she was like that when he was a kid. He called her Über Mom. It drove him crazy."

"Now she's Über Grandma."

"Which is helpful and overwhelming. I'm hoping as time passes, she'll ease up."

Lucy shook her head. "You're the exact opposite of Helen."

"Which is why I think Scott picked me."

The baby rolled to the right, forcing Megan to shift in her seat, watching as the rows of cornfields gave way to the expanse of the Chesapeake Bay Bridge–Tunnel. The twenty-three-mile drive across the bay into Norfolk. In the distance the clouds had thickened and grown dark.

"Are we still on for Natasha's party tomorrow night?" Megan asked.

"We are. Six o'clock."

"What's the final theme?"

"You saved the day, Megan. All the girls are thrilled about playing vintage games and getting their fortunes read. They have all decided not to dress up but to wear black and white colors only."

"How very mysterious," Megan said, smiling.

"Hank's also coming, and so is Rick. Both have offered to be on hand to scare off any boys who think they might show up and crash the party."

"Natasha must have been mortified."

"Scandalized. We'll do our family celebration at six. Hope you have black-and-white maternity garb."

Megan felt humbled to be included as family. "I'll find something."

They arrived at the venue marked by two large brick pillars, each sporting a sign that read PINEHURST. The property had originally been a plantation built in the 1840s along the James River. Like many old structures, it had found a new life as a historical museum as well as a wedding venue.

Lucy stopped the vehicle and snapped several pictures before she continued down the long dirt road that curled through a grove of trees lining the way. Each tree was several feet wide and stood over fifty feet tall, creating a graceful canopy of foliage.

Megan directed Lucy to drive around a bend and toward a large white event tent. Inside the tent were several bare, round wooden tables waiting to be dressed. On the other side of the tent was a pink food truck, and painted on the side were the words KIERNAN'S KAKES.

Memories of Megan's last visit to this venue had a familiar knot tightening in her chest. "Full disclosure, I was supposed to have my wedding here."

"Really? A little stuffy for you. Did Helen pick it out?"

"Not quite. Helen and my mother found it. I was working at a dig in Alexandria and didn't have time, so they took charge. You should have seen them. They were both so proud of their find."

Lucy shook her head. "It's a lovely place, but I don't picture you here."

"Neither did I. I was trying to wedge myself into a life that wasn't mine." Her mother's disappointment over the canceled wedding still weighed on Megan.

"I'm glad you came to the Eastern Shore," Lucy said. "I'm not sure what I'd have done with Winter Cottage or Spring House without you."

"Claire Buchanan reached out from the grave and literally saved me," Megan said.

"Back at you." Lucy shut off the engine and walked around to the back of the truck and lowered the tailgate. She grabbed the first cooler. "I'll get the other one. Just point the way."

"Straight toward the food truck."

Lucy carried the cooler to Kiernan's food truck. Megan had discovered the nomad baker and event planner at an event in Richmond when she was searching for a caterer. She had liked the woman's offbeat style instantly and asked for a catering proposal. Her mother had not been thrilled by Kiernan, but on this point, Megan had held firm. She'd learned later that Kiernan had refused full payment and accepted money for only the supplies she had already purchased. That gesture had saved Megan's parents at least ten grand.

Lucy set the first cooler by the steps to the food truck. "Be right back with the second cooler."

Megan peered into the truck but did not see anyone.

The sound of voices had her turning toward the river, where Kiernan stood with a tall, burly man who was erecting a second tent. Kiernan's red hair was pinned up into a loose topknot, and she wore a black T-shirt embossed with double *K*s. Top-Siders peeked out from jeans that hugged rounded hips and nipped in at a narrow waist.

"Kiernan," Megan called out.

The woman turned, her smile reflecting relief and joy. "You made it!"

"I didn't flake on you," Megan said.

Kiernan hugged Megan while patting her rounded belly. One thing Megan had learned was that pregnancy had transformed her belly into public property, with friends, family, and a few strangers all admiring it.

"Looking good, Mama," Kiernan said.

"I'm in the home stretch."

"Can't wait to see your pretty baby," Kiernan said.

Megan was excited too, but the idea that there really was a person she was actually going to be allowed to raise still freaked her out. "Thanks for the gig."

"When the bride said her man loved pies, you were the first person I thought about."

"I appreciate the work. I brought a friend along who's helping. Let me introduce you."

As they approached the truck, Lucy was setting down the second cooler. "Lucy owns property on the Eastern Shore. You might have heard of Winter Cottage. She's thinking about making it into a wedding venue."

Kiernan handed a check to Megan. "That's awesome. There aren't enough venues up that way. Do you have a card? I'm always on the hunt for new locations."

"No card yet, but I will soon."

Kiernan retrieved a card from her back pocket. "Text me a few pictures of your place and let me see what you have."

"I will."

"The cake is my signature, but we plan the entire show from soup to nuts."

Lucy took the card and tapped it against her palm. "Right now, we're launching into a redo of all the buildings on the property. It's not perfect now, but the grounds are always stunning."

"Super. A trip to the Eastern Shore might be nice."

"Perfect."

Megan tucked the check into her pocket, glad to have the extra cash. "Thanks again for the business."

"Ready for the rain?" Lucy asked.

"When I received Megan's text, I ordered a second tent." She looked up toward the clouds. "Weatherman says it's going to blow over."

"The old-timers at the café swear the rain is coming," Lucy said.

Kiernan reached for her phone and opened the weather app. "Clear skies."

Lucy held up her hands. "These dudes are never wrong."

Kiernan looked back at her tent. "I also have the side flaps, just in case."

Megan hugged Kiernan, and she and Lucy climbed into the truck. As they drove down the long driveway toward the main road, a feeling of relief and closure washed over Megan.

"What's the deal with Kiernan?" Lucy asked. "Is she doing well for herself?"

"I think she does okay. Her coordinating services start at five grand."

"Five grand. Wow."

"But she earns every cent. Even the most expensive weddings have drama."

Megan's phone rang, and when she saw Rick's name on the display, she absently moistened her lips and brushed back her bangs. "Rick, what's up?"

"I found no information on Elise Mandel, but I'm going to keep digging. I'll see you at Lucy's tomorrow night, right?"

"Yes."

"Hopefully I'll find something. I'm headed north right now. Sam Denver's boat sank, and I'm going to see if I can help him raise it."

"His boat sank? We didn't have any weather last night."

"High tide. He didn't secure the boat properly, and when the tide rose, the bow did not."

"Ouch."

"He's a mess. He's put his entire savings into restoring his baby."

"Then I'll let you go. Keep the mean streets of the Eastern Shore safe, Sheriff."

He chuckled. "Doing my best, ma'am."

Megan hung up, and an unwitting smile spread across her lips.

"Megan has a crush," Lucy teased.

Her face warmed, and she ducked her head. "Lucy, I'm eight months pregnant. He's being nice to me because of Scott."

Lucy laughed. "Keep telling yourself that."

When Megan and Lucy returned to Winter Cottage, Lucy headed back to school for Natasha while Megan settled in the rocker by the large windows overlooking the bay. She had been reading more of Diane's letters, but as much as she enjoyed them, fatigue got the better of her, and soon she drifted off to sleep.

Dolly's barking startled her awake. Rubbing her eyes, she sat forward and saw Diane's letters scattered on the floor. Groaning, she forced her big belly forward and began to gather them.

Rolling her head from side to side, she chased away the tension that buzzed around her. She put the letters back in a folder and stepped out onto the front porch just as Helen got out of her car.

"Helen, this is a surprise," Megan said.

"I know. I should have called, but I want to make sure there were no aftereffects of your fall."

"I stumbled. I didn't fall. And I'm fine."

"Good."

"Why are you smiling?" Megan asked.

"Because I'm very pleased with myself. I was too excited not to bring you this surprise."

Pressing her hand to her belly, she walked toward the car. "What do you have?"

"First an idea. It occurred to me as I was driving here. I have the perfect name for the baby."

"You do?"

"Scottie. That's a very cute name for a girl, don't you think?"

"Is it short for anything?"

"Scarlet or Scotlyn, both of which are lovely. I can picture her name on a business card right now. Of course her title will be president."

"Good to think ahead," Megan said. "Scottie Buchanan is cute."

Helen opened the back of her car. "Her name isn't going to be Jessup?"

"Her middle name will be Jessup. Her last name will be Buchanan."

Helen frowned. "A baby should have her father's name."

"Jessup will be her middle name."

"Of course you can name the baby whatever you wish, but I'm going to encourage you to change your mind about her last name."

"I won't, Helen." Anger bubbled up inside of her as she thought about anyone telling her how to raise her child.

"Scott is her father."

"And I am her mother." Megan considered herself easygoing, but she had limits. She shoved out a breath, not wanting to have this fight now. "You said you brought something."

"Yes," Helen said as if remembering the purpose of this visit. "I have a real surprise that I think we can both agree upon."

Helen removed the blanket and revealed a handmade hooded primitive wooden cradle made from teak. Three feet long and a little over a foot wide, it sat low to the ground on beveled rocking edges and was constructed with wooden pegs. Carved on the hood were an *H* and a *J*.

"It was Scott's cradle," Helen said. "It was passed down through the Jessup family. It's over a hundred years old and was built by Isaac Hedrick before he gave it to the Jessups when he gave them his sons to raise."

"I didn't realize you had the cradle."

"My in-laws gave it to me when Scott was born. We used it for the few months of his infancy. I would lay him in it as I cooked in the kitchen or folded laundry. Finally, he just got too big for it.

"Have a look at the headboard. See the *H* and the *J*? As you know, the *H* represents Hedrick. Your Claire from Winter Cottage and all her siblings would have lain in this as babies."

As Megan laid her hand on the smooth wood, peaceful energy rolled through her. "It's lovely."

Helen smiled, pleased. "I thought with your knack for history, you'd appreciate it. When you and Scott first got engaged, I mentioned it to him, but he didn't seem interested."

Whatever annoyance she'd felt toward Helen moments ago softened. This cradle was exactly the kind of antique she would be proud to use. "It's truly wonderful."

"Truly?"

Megan smiled. "Yes."

The sheriff's car pulled up. "I called Rick and asked him to come by and have a look at the cradle. He's so handy with any kind of construction, and I thought it best to have the cradle checked out before we put the baby in it. You just can't be too careful."

Rick parked, stepped out of his car, and then nodded to them before he strode over. His hair was damp, and he wore a button-down shirt showing just enough chest to trigger a few impure thoughts. Rick's jeans were worn, and they hugged his narrow hips.

His gaze went to Megan first, and for an instant, she held it before he cleared his throat and shifted his attention to Helen. Megan blushed, and her nerves tingled.

"Scott could hardly drive a nail into the wall," Helen said. "Whenever he needed anything hung, he'd call Rick, so that's exactly what I did."

Rick kissed her on the cheek. "You look younger every time I see you."

"And you're still a bad liar," Helen said, smiling.

He rocked the cradle gently in the back of her car and then ran his palm over the smooth wood. "Is this the cradle you wanted me to give the once-over?"

"Yes," Helen said. "As you can see, it's very old, and I want to make sure it's safe."

"It's handsome," he said. "And it looks very sturdy. Any baby would be fine in this."

"Excellent. I was hoping you'd say that. Could you take it into the house for us?" Helen asked.

Rick pushed aside the blanket, and with one steady pull, he removed the three-foot-long cradle. He easily carried it to the house and through the main hallway. "Where do you want it?"

"The parlor for now," Megan said. "Beside the rocking chair."

Megan and Helen followed, and when he set it down in front of the hearth, an odd sense of peace came over her. Megan ran her hand over the top, and her heart sped up as she pictured a woman sitting in a rocker beside it, humming. She smelled freshly baking bread and heard the rumble of boys' laughter around her.

"It's really lovely, Helen," Megan said.

"Did you notice the fish on the headboard?" Helen asked. She ran her hand over the carvings. "Twelve fish. All carved at different times. They represent almost all the children who have slept in this cradle. I never could get my husband to carve a fish for Scott." She frowned. "We really should have carved Scott's fish into the headboard."

"I can still do it," Rick offered. "And I can do one for the baby as well."

"That would be great," Helen said with a warm smile.

Megan knelt and traced the fish, thinking through the ancestry charts she had made on the Jessup and Hedrick families. The little fish were arranged around the *H*, each swimming in a circle. The fish at the top was carefully carved, but with each successive fish, the details became fainter. The fourth fish was barely legible; however, the fifth, sixth, and seventh fish were done with great care.

Megan thought about the fourth Hedrick child. That would have been Diane, the little girl who had almost vanished until very recently. She traced her fingers around the rough edges of her fish.

"When Scott's grandmother gave it to me, I was so certain I wouldn't use it," Helen said. "It seemed so old and unnecessary when I was surrounded by the most modern beds, rockers, and bouncy chairs. But I remember one night when Scott was about two weeks old. He would not go to sleep. I rocked him. I tried to feed him. I paced with him. Nothing worked. I remember sitting even on the floor of his nursery next to the cradle. I was too tired to stand, and out of desperation, I laid him in it. I held the headboard and rocked it gently. He fussed a few times and then suddenly stopped. Scared me to death. I was certain I'd done something wrong. But when I took a good look at him, I realized he was sound asleep."

Megan could feel Addie's and Sally's energy in the cradle. Both women had infused it with calm and love.

"Nicely done, Helen," Rick said.

There was a rough quality about his voice that made Megan wish he were not simply bound to her by duty and obligation. She wanted him to simply want her.

"Helen, we're having a party for Natasha tomorrow night," Megan said. "We'd like you to come."

"Oh no, I can't. That's her party," Helen said. "I wouldn't belong."

"Of course you would," Megan said. "Rick and I will both be there. It'll be fun. Lucy has now roped me into reading fortunes. You can help."

"Are you sure?" Helen asked.

"Very," Megan said. "Come. It starts at six p.m."

"All right, I will. I'm going to have to dash now. I need to run Grandmother to the doctor, but I'll be back tomorrow night."

"Perfect."

Rick remained behind as Helen drove off. "You're doing a good job, Megan. And I really admire how kind you are to Helen. I know she can take over sometimes, but she only wants the best for her friends and family."

"She wants me to name the baby Scottie."

"Do you like it?"

"It's nice, but I'm not so sure."

"What name do you like?" Rick asked.

She glanced down at the cradle's headboard, and again her gaze was drawn to the fourth fish. "Diane."

"Diane? The girl who wrote those letters?"

"Yeah. I'm not sure if there is anyone left who remembers her."

"I like it."

"Really?"

"Absolutely."

She drew in a slow breath. "When you see me, who do you see?"

"I see Megan Buchanan."

She shook her head. "You see Scott. You see duty. Honor."

He took her hand in his and carefully rubbed his thumb over her palm. "No, Megan, I see you."

A tinge of warmth rolled through her. "Hard to miss this bloated belly and round face."

He shook his head as his gaze centered on her. "I see a beautiful woman."

"You're being nice."

He held her gaze and began to lean toward her. She realized he was going to kiss her, and her body hummed with an excitement she hadn't felt in a long time. But before he could close the distance between them, his radio squawked. As Rick shoved out a sigh, a muscle in the side of his jaw pulsed as he responded and promised to be en route immediately.

"I've got to go."

"Saved by the bell," she quipped.

He shook his head. "This discussion isn't over, lady." And with that declaration, he was gone.

CHAPTER
TWENTY-ONE

Megan

Saturday, March 10, 2018
Cape Hudson, Virginia
10:00 a.m.

It was raining when Megan awoke. She spent most of the early-morning hours reading Diane's letters, but when she offered to help Lucy and Natasha decorate, they told her to put her feet up and rest.

Restless, Megan searched her closet for something to wear to the party but couldn't find anything that did not make her look huge. She considered a drive into Norfolk for a shopping trip to one of the maternity shops, but in the end decided she was not interested in battling the rain on the bridge.

Instead, she grabbed a raincoat, dashed into Cape Hudson, and stopped at a local tourism shop, where she found a large black T-shirt sporting a blue star, which fit the fortune-telling theme.

As the rain let up temporarily, she moved along the sidewalk toward the center of town. The lull in the weather was short-lived as fat raindrops soon found her cheek. Another and another fell, and she realized she was about to be caught in a downpour. She quickly dashed into Arlene's diner.

Bells jingled overhead as she stepped inside and wiped the rain from her face. The diner was empty, as it often was in the early afternoon. Her stomach grumbled, and though she had eaten breakfast a couple of hours ago, her appetite was again ravenous.

"Hello?" she said.

Arlene appeared at the double saloon doors, smiling as she pushed through. Her red hair was twisted into a knot, and a diner T-shirt hugged her ample breasts. "Megan. It's been a few weeks. Where have you been, girl?"

Megan sauntered up to one of the stools at the bar, remembering all the summers she and her family had eaten burgers and ice cream here. "Been working. Life is crazy."

"I can't wait to hold that little gal in my arms. Been a long time since I held a baby."

"Don't rush it." Megan plucked a sugar packet from the white holder and began to fiddle with it. "She'll be here soon enough."

Arlene poured her a glass of lemonade. "You sure about that? You're carrying that baby mighty low."

She drank. "Please, don't rush me into motherhood."

"You want the usual? Grilled chicken sandwich with fries on the side?"

Megan twirled the packet. "You know me all too well."

"You always loved those fries, even when you were a kid."

"Those vacations seem like a lifetime ago."

"Your mom and dad should be back soon, right?" Arlene asked.

"A couple of weeks."

"And Deacon, what's that scoundrel up to?"

"Making billions of dollars as a corporate attorney. A very big shot."

Arlene moved toward the grill top and dropped a piece of lean chicken on it. As it sizzled, she placed a handful of fresh-cut potato strips in the fryer. "Does that bother you?"

"No. Of course not."

"You sound like it does."

Megan drank more lemonade. "I love what I do. I can't imagine not doing it. But he is the favored son. Deacon took the conventional path, and my parents adore him for it."

"I bet they're proud of you."

Megan smoothed her hand over her belly. "Not so much these days."

Arlene flipped the piece of chicken, opened a bun, and set it on the griddle. "I hear Helen has bought a house in town."

Megan swallowed wrong and coughed for several seconds before she wheezed out, "Did she?"

"She didn't tell you?"

"Does it look like it?"

Arlene shrugged. "You know Helen. Heart of gold, but she can be more demanding than a general."

———— ⚬⚬⚬⚬⚬ ————

Megan dressed in her best black stretch pants and the new shirt she had purchased. Neither did anything to make her look the least bit attractive, so she shifted her focus to her hair, which she hoped would somehow make her look, well, less pregnant. She brushed her micro bangs back and pulled her hair into a high ponytail, but she still had a face that looked like a chubby full moon.

"Why do you care?" she muttered. "You're really being goofy." Turning from the mirror, she made her way into the hallway, where Lucy was waiting with glitter that she sprinkled on Megan's hair.

"You look beautiful."

"Do you really think so?"

"I do. A very beautiful fortune-teller," Lucy said. "And I'm the chief manager of the party, clothing consultant for Natasha, and wrangler of six tween girls."

"Luceee," Natasha yelled, "I think I ripped my dress."

Lucy looked at Megan. "I'd trade jobs with you, but I like you too much."

"I'm here to serve. You may now call me Madame LeBlanc."

"From the letters?"

"Why not? She sounds mysterious and dangerous."

"Of course, a historical reference."

Smiling, Megan made her way down the center staircase past the white and black floating balloons tied to the banister.

The center hallway of Winter Cottage was filled with more balloons that led partygoers to what had originally been a parlor. This was the room where her great-grandfather and his wife would have retired after dinner for drinks with friends and to enjoy cards, music, and lively discussions. She could only imagine their reaction to a half dozen girls giggling and running about.

Attached to the parlor was a large storage closet, which they'd also decorated with a table, chairs, and more balloons. That would be Madame LeBlanc's domain.

Megan opened the front door to Rick and Hank. Both men were dressed in khakis, button-downs, and loafers. Both carried coolers.

"You two are quite the pair," Megan said, stepping aside.

"How goes it with the party girl?" Hank asked.

"Lucy is currently dealing with a broken-zipper emergency. No tears or yelling yet."

Hank shook his head. "Lucy is a saint."

"Agreed. Is that the ice?"

"Yes," Hank said.

"I'm cake and ice cream," Rick said.

"Wonderful. Gentlemen, go into the kitchen." She followed behind to a table set up with sodas and punch. "Leave the ice there, and let's get that cake set up on the table."

"Yes, ma'am." Rick handed her the ice cream, which she put in the freezer. When she turned, he had set the cake in the center of the table. It had candles circling the word GOTCHA and a picture of Natasha, Lucy, and Dolly.

"How was she able to keep it a secret?" Megan asked.

"She was at my place most of the night working on it," Hank said. "She got only a few hours of sleep."

"Tell me it's her chocolate cake?" Megan asked.

"You're in luck. It's also Natasha's favorite," Hank said. "I have a present for Natasha in the car. I'll be right back."

"I like the glitter," Rick said.

"Tonight I'm going to be Madame Megan LeBlanc, the world-famous fortune-teller."

"Sounds fancy. What kind of fortunes are you going to read?"

"I have the planchette that we found at Samuel's house. And there's an old party trick I used to do when I was in high school. Give me something of yours, and I can hold it while telling you secrets about yourself."

"That sounds interesting." He fished his keys out of his pocket and pulled one off. "Show me your stuff, Madame LeBlanc. Tell me what this tells you about me."

She laughed, taking the key and curling her fingers around it into a tight fist. She shrugged, smiling and feeling very comfortable around Rick. She ran her hand over the smooth metal of the key's flat edge and then along the ridges of the side. "You're a man who is very nostalgic," she said. "This key holds sentimental value."

He arched a brow. "That the best you got, Madame LeBlanc? You'll have to be more clever if you're going to fool a bunch of tween girls."

She tightened her hold on the key and drew in a breath. She thought back to the night that she had met Rick and Scott. The men had just come from a poker game, and she had overheard Rick say he had won a house. Like any good card reader, she watched his body language closely, ready to take her cues from him. "You won this key."

His gaze sharpened. "Keep going."

She realized her educated guess was correct. "You won this key in a poker game. Atlantic City. No. Norfolk. It fits the lock of a cabin, which you won." She thought back to all the things he'd said about luck and winning. "The key is a reminder to you that you make your own luck."

He stared, accepting the key back from her. "You got all that from holding it?"

"Of course. I am Madame LeBlanc. All things are possible in my world."

"It's pretty damn close to the truth," he said quietly.

She laughed. "I have a great memory for details. I'm sure Scott told me something about the key or the cabin at one point. Just good detective work and memory."

He turned the key over in his fingers. "That would be one hell of a memory."

"Steel trap." She tapped her finger against her temple.

He put the key back on his ring. "Only I never told Scott the story."

"You must have forgotten. It's understandable." She knew she had heard him speak about the cabin and had assumed he'd told Scott.

He shook his head. "Nope. I'm damn sure of that. I'd planned to invite you to that cabin."

"When?"

"Right after you laid me out on your worldview of politics. I'd just won the cabin for a weekend getaway. When I saw you, I imagined you there wearing only my shirt."

Heat rose in her cheeks. "The wrong kind of sparks flew that day. You walked away."

"You challenged me. And after I thought about what you said and remembered how I like a challenge, I wanted to see you again. But then I found out Scott had asked you out, and that was that. I never used the cabin."

Her stomach did a few somersaults. "Oh." She cleared her throat. "Why did you keep the key?"

"As a reminder to strike while the iron is hot."

He faced her and was only a few inches away. The baby rolled over her bladder, reminding her that she was not exactly the woman he had met before. When the doorbell rang, she pulled her gaze from his and moved to answer the front door. "I better get that."

Her cheeks felt flushed as she walked down the hallway to the door, and when she opened it, she found Helen on the front porch holding a bright package tied up in a pink bow.

"Helen, welcome." Megan hoped her flushed face had cooled. "This is the calm before the storm."

"You look lovely."

"Thank you."

"Did you get a chance to put your feet up today?"

"Spent the better part of the afternoon sitting on the couch, blowing up balloons."

"I can see that."

Hank climbed the front steps as Rick came around the corner, crossed to Helen, and kissed her on the cheek. "You look terrific."

"Thank you, dear."

Hank also kissed her on the cheek. "I'm glad you could make it."

"It was sweet of you all to include me." She held up her present. "I've never bought for a young girl before. I hope I got it right."

Megan took the gift and set it on a long table with the others. "I know she'll love it."

Lucy and Natasha came down the stairs. Lucy was wearing a long, slim-fitting black dress that accentuated a thin waist that Megan had never known on her best day. Her hair hung loose around her shoulders, and she wore dangling silver earrings. Natasha also wore a black dress, but hers skimmed her legs just below the knees. It came with cap sleeves and a sweetheart neckline. Her hair was pinned back in a sophisticated twist, revealing a pair of pearl earrings Megan had lent to her for the evening.

Hank whistled. "My goodness, you ladies look fine."

Lucy smiled and kissed him quickly on the lips, lingering for only a split second but long enough to transmit love and the promise of later.

Natasha looked at the gift Helen had wrapped and the smaller one from Megan. "Are these for me?"

"They are," Megan said.

"Can I open them now?"

"Nope," Hank said. "I've got burgers to cook on the grill, and you're helping me."

Natasha rolled her eyes but did not look as put out as she pretended. "Fine. I'll be the perfect hostess."

While she helped him start the gas grill, Lucy dashed into the kitchen and quickly reappeared with a plate of neatly made patties. Rick, Megan, and Helen followed her outside to the lawn overlooking the bay.

The sun dipped low in the horizon, ready to skim the water. The grass was still wet from the afternoon shower and served as a reminder that this time of year could be so unpredictable. However, this evening the weather was perfect.

Megan lowered into an Adirondack chair and stretched out her legs. More and more she was sitting. She wondered why pregnancy was not as effortless as she had expected. One friend had run a half marathon in her third trimester, while another had worked as a floor nurse right up until she delivered.

"So, if you need a babysitter, I can help," Natasha said. She handed Megan a glass of lemonade. "The fire department is offering a CPR class, and I'm going to take it. You can never be too prepared."

At this point, Megan had bought the basic supplies. She figured she'd get the rest once birthing classes started the next week. "That's very responsible of you. Maybe I should take it too."

"Probably not a bad idea. Babies are tricky little things," Natasha said.

"You think so?"

"I do." Natasha spoke with the seriousness of an old sage as she sat in the chair beside her. "Did you ever take those delivery classes?"

"They don't start until next month." She seemed to be dropping the ball at every turn. "I still have time."

"Lucy and I will help you. You're not in this alone."

"Thank you."

Hank looked up from the grill as he flipped the burgers and he and Rick shared a laugh. Rick said something she could not hear and took a long pull on his beer. She thought about that cabin in the woods and what it would have been like to spend the weekend there with him.

"So Helen says the baby's name is Scottie," Natasha said, bringing Megan back to the present.

"That has not been decided." Megan's tone sounded harsher than she had intended, so she managed a smile. "I'm partial to Duchess Agatha Fairy Princess."

Lucy laughed. "Duchess Fair Weather is nice."

Natasha's tone turned serious. "What about Diane?"

"Funny you should say that," Megan said. "I was thinking the same just the other day."

Natasha grinned, then shrugged. "It's a good idea, right?"

"Yeah." The name felt more and more right. "I like it."

"Did you ever figure out what happened to Diane?"

"No."

"It doesn't seem like she'd just stop writing."

"My guess is there are more letters, but we've just not found them yet."

"I wonder why they weren't all together," Natasha said.

"Maybe someone had a secret."

"Burgers are ready," Hank said.

She tried to rise out of the chair but found her equilibrium had subtly shifted since just a few days ago. As Natasha rushed off, Megan pushed forward a couple more times, not much different from one of those beached turtles whose legs flapped as it tried to right itself.

A firm hand took hold of her arm and with steady pressure lifted her out of the chair. She looked up to see Rick smiling.

"I know," she said. "Not a pretty sight. Just another indignity on the road to motherhood."

"It's cute," he said.

"Said the man with the trim waist and the ankles that aren't swollen."

He didn't release her hand immediately but held it, and she let him as if they were both pretending that she needed the support.

She finally pulled her hand away. "Thanks."

"Sure. You doing all right?"

"Other than balancing the biggest job of my life and pregnancy? Doing great."

"You're overdoing it."

"Probably. But I want this job to work out. It's going to lead to other opportunities, and if baby wants to eat, Mama's got to work."

"By the way, I found nothing on Elise Mandel. I even checked with buddies in Virginia and Maryland State Police Departments. There is no record of the woman ever living here."

"Really?"

"Vanished into thin air."

They walked over to the table now filled with a collection of salads and freshly grilled burgers and hot dogs.

She made a plate and sat at the table. Rick sat beside her. They all chatted and listened to Natasha's stories about school and her take on each of the girls who were coming.

Lucy checked her watch. "We still have a half hour before everyone arrives, so if you all will be so kind as to retire to the dining room, I have a surprise planned."

Natasha's eyes brightened even as she tried to play it cool and look as if this were no big deal. Everyone gathered around the long dining table that was as old as the house while Lucy vanished into the kitchen. When she returned, she was carrying a cake now lit with dozens of candles.

She set it in front of Natasha. "Kiddo, I received word from the judge today. It is official. You're a Kincaid."

"For real?" Natasha's voice was a faint whisper.

"For real," Lucy said, beaming.

"So, like, you're my mother now?" she asked.

"Technically, but still your sister."

"That's so weird," Natasha said.

"It's going to take some explaining if anyone presses, but mother or sister, we're family in every sense of the word now."

Tears welled in Natasha's eyes as Megan snapped pictures with her phone. The girl ran to Lucy and hugged her close as a sob rolled through her body.

Lucy kissed her on top of the head and said, "Better blow out those candles."

Natasha sniffed, rubbed her eyes, and blew out her candles in one breath. Megan removed the candles and cut into the cake, serving them all generous slices. After the plates were clear, Hank cleared his throat. "How about some presents?"

"Yes!" Natasha shouted.

Hank handed her Helen's gift first. "Start here."

"What is it?" Natasha asked.

"Open it," Helen said.

"What do you say?" Lucy said.

"Thank you, Mrs. Jessup."

"You're very welcome, my dear."

Natasha ripped off the bow and opened the box. Inside was an antique handheld mirror. Natasha held it up, admiring her reflection. "It's so pretty."

"Every young girl needs a way to admire herself," Helen said. "My grandmother gave it to me when I was about your age. It seemed silly to save it for what might be. Right now is what counts."

"It's beautiful, Helen," Lucy said.

"I hope she can pass it on to her daughter one day," Helen said. "Whenever you look in this mirror, always smile."

"Why?" Natasha asked.

"Because even if you feel awful," Helen said, "that smile will be your protector."

Natasha looked in the mirror and flashed a youthful smile, the kind that could not be forced. Then she stuck out her tongue and waggled her eyebrows before giggling.

"See?" Helen said. "Like magic."

"Thanks again, Mrs. Jessup," Natasha said.

Natasha opened her next gift. She ripped off the paper, letting it fall to the ground, and then opened the box. It was empty. Natasha held it up, dumbfounded. "What's the deal?"

"It goes with the earrings you're wearing," Megan said.

Natasha's hands went up to her ears. "For real. I can keep these?"

"They're all yours," Megan said.

Rick's gift was not wrapped but enclosed in a paper bag. Natasha giggled, and when she opened it, she found a pocketknife. She eyed it with excitement as Rick gave her clear instructions on how to hold it and reminded her she could never take it to school. She promised several times and proudly tucked it in her pocket.

Finally Hank handed her a medium-size brown box. Again, no wrapping, but it was securely taped. Natasha reached for her pocketknife and carefully cut the tape. She opened the box and found a bike helmet.

Natasha settled it on her head and then used Helen's mirror to inspect it. "It looks super cool, Hank. Thank you."

"The rest of it's on the front porch," he said.

"It?" she asked.

Hank's expression was stoic. "Have a look."

Natasha clipped the bike-helmet strap in place, ran to the front door, and yanked it open. Resting against the front of the house was a new red ten-speed bike. She looked back at Hank, her gaze wide with wonder. "This is for me?"

"All yours, kid."

Natasha ran back to Hank and hugged him tightly. "I can't ride it right now or I'll get all sweaty. But I will ride it later and forever."

He unfastened the strap and carefully removed the helmet. "I get it. You've got to look great for the party."

Natasha touched her hair. "Is it messed up?"

"Nope, it's perfect," Hank said.

"This is the best party ever!" Natasha said.

As she chatted with Lucy and Helen about her gifts, Megan patted Hank on the back. "Well done, cousin."

"I like to think I hit the nail on the head."

"I meant to tell you I've been reading through Samuel Jessup's journal. Did you know he actually met Victoria Garrison when he was an adult?"

"Great-Grandmother lived in Africa with her husband for a time, as I remember."

"Yes. Apparently, Samuel ferried her and Edward back to the States in 1939."

"She would have been in her early forties then. I think she had my granduncle Jeb about that time," Hank said.

She thought about Samuel's journal but did not recall any mention of the boy. It was not likely the child had traveled separately, and of course Samuel might not have interfaced with the child during the voyage.

Several cars came up the long drive. "Let's get this party started," Lucy said. "Everyone, take your places."

"Where would you like me?" Helen asked.

"You're helping Madame LeBlanc in her shop," Lucy said. "The menfolk are crowd control and security."

"No teenage boy will pass that doorstep," Hank said.

Natasha rolled her eyes. "That's so lame."

"Who is Madame LeBlanc?" Helen asked.

"Moi." Megan smiled as she crooked her finger. "Come this way."

"What is it that I do?" Helen asked.

"I'll sit in the room, and you escort the young ladies in. Have them give me an object, and I'll offer some insight."

"Sounds fascinating but not too scary to send a young girl running in hysterics." She looked around the parlor as they passed through. "All the years I drove by this house, I never saw the inside."

"Let me give you a quick tour."

"That would be lovely." They began in the parlor, made their way down a back hallway to what would have been the servants' dining room, and next to that, George Buchanan's gunroom and office. Upstairs, Megan told Helen about the different rooms and who had inhabited them. Helen took it all in.

"This project is much larger than I ever imagined. It could take years to restore Spring House and Winter Cottage, as well as the lighthouse. You and the baby could be here for a long while."

"It's a lovely place to grow up," Megan conceded.

"I'm thinking about schools. Mark always felt like he came up a bit short when it came to formal education. He could repair any engine with his hands but had no taste for the bookwork."

Megan held up her hand. "Stop, Helen. Let me deliver the baby first. Then we'll worry about her education."

Helen studied her as she had always regarded Scott when they'd disagreed. She might appear to give in, but she always doubled back around until she got her way. "Well, on the bright side, with your parents returning and me, you'll never want for a babysitter."

"That's true."

They returned to the small room where Megan was to read fortunes. When she pulled the planchette from the box, Helen's interest was piqued.

"You found that in Samuel's desk?" she asked.

Megan held it out to her. "Yes, it's a very intricate piece."

"And heavy." Helen smoothed her fingers over the inlaid red-and-white-glass gems. "Have you had it appraised?"

"Not yet. But it's on the list of things."

"And what's it supposed to do?" The stones just then caught the evening light and sparkled.

"Spirits are supposed to communicate through it."

Helen handed back the planchette. "I don't believe I would ever ask it any questions. I think I'd be afraid of the answers."

April 9, 1939
From the Journal of Samuel Jessup

There's all kind of talk that the Germans are on the move. A few of the crew are from Poland, and they been hearing stories from their families that it ain't going to be much longer before the Germans bust out of their borders and start a real fight just like they did in 1914. You'd have thought they'd have learned a lesson from the last time they tussled with us, but I guess they are stubborn. I'd bet my last dollar that they'll go for the coastlines in the next year. If I was them, I'd do the same. Without ships like mine, Europe will be cut off from the world, and it won't take much to starve her fuel supplies and force her into submission.

I got the crew on high alert. Every man is ordered to carry a sidearm while we dock in Le Havre and until we are well free and clear.

CHAPTER
TWENTY-TWO

Diane

Age 18

Wednesday, September 1, 1909
Normandy, France

Diane pulled the rough blanket over her head, fending off the morning chill of an early winter. She had been working the last two weeks alongside Gilbert in the orchard, picking apples. They had been racing against the cold rains that Madame Herbert had warned would damage the harvest.

Finally, very late yesterday, they had unloaded the last of the bushels into the barn, where Gilbert would extract their juices.

Over the last six years, Diane had grown several inches taller, and her hips and bosom were now rounded. Madame Herbert had taught her all her knowledge of healing, and the villagers always expected Diane on house calls. Last week, on a day Gilbert had extra help in the orchard, Diane and Madame had attended the birth of the Locard baby. The birth had been hard, and when the child was born, he was small, not breathing, and blue. While Madame attended the mother with other women from the village, Diane had rubbed the baby's breastbone and blown air into his mouth. This had gone on for several minutes, and she'd not realized how silent the room had become until the child's eyes popped open and he cried. The women breathed a collective sigh of relief.

The village still whispered about her magical talents, and some called her Witch Healer. But it seemed they had all agreed that if she was a witch, she was at least their witch.

Diane had begun to notice the stares from several of the men in the village when Gilbert, Madame, and she drove in for Mass. Gilbert noticed this new attention too and did not like it in the least.

Oscar grumbled. He did not care how much the apples had required of her. He wanted to go outside. Now that he was getting older, he had no patience for waiting. Drawing in a breath, she tossed back the covers, looking down at the dog's gray snout. Like Madame Herbert, he did not rally quickly on rainy, cold days. It promised to be an early, hard winter for them both.

Diane rubbed his head and then quickly dressed. "I will hurry, my dear Oscar."

In the last year, she had taken to holding on to Oscar's collar as they moved down the narrow stairs. His bones were rickety and his balance uneven. There were moments when he imagined himself a pup and would make a sudden, quick movement. So Diane's charge was to keep him from tumbling down the stairs.

The house was quiet as they crossed the cobblestone floor of the kitchen. She lifted the heavy iron lock and opened the door. A blast of cold, damp air rushed at her and cut through the wool fabric of her dress. The sky above was dark and threatening. Fat water droplets began to fall as she watched Oscar sniffing around.

Diane turned to the stove and, using an iron rod, teased a fire from the embers before tossing in several logs from the woodbin. As she stared at the neat stack of wood, she pictured Gilbert piling fresh logs last night in anticipation of the rains. He was always diligent.

She set the hot water to boil as she ground coffee beans and placed them in the top of the brass coffeepot. As the water heated, she cracked a dozen eggs and mixed in handfuls of cheese and a few of the roasted vegetables from yesterday's lunch. All went into a shallow pan and into the oven. The kettle whistled, and she poured the hot water into the pot. This was her favorite time of day, before the house began to stir. The dog scratched at the back door, and she let him in. She quickly grabbed a towel from her apron and dried off his fur, wet from the rain, flinching when he tried to shake.

"Ah, you and your hair," she said. "What am I going to do with you?"

She filled his water bowl and chopped up meat and roasted vegetables for his meal. As he began to eat, Madame Herbert pushed through the doors to the kitchen, leaning heavily on her cane.

"I hear the rain," the old woman said.

"You were right. It is colder than normal too." Diane pulled out a chair for her and beckoned her to sit.

Madame Herbert slowly lowered into her seat, now cushioned with a thick pillow. Her arthritis had grown worse in the last year, and moving about the house was now a daily challenge.

Diane set out three porcelain cups and poured coffee into two. She put cream and sugar into Madame's cup and set it in front of her before sitting herself. "Did you sleep well?"

"Ah, terrible. But then, that is the way I always sleep. Never get old, Diane. It is not fun."

"If I can help it, I shan't get old, Madame Herbert."

The old woman swatted away the naive comment of youth and then sipped her coffee.

"Gilbert and I worked with the hired hands, and we harvested all the apples. We only had a few hours to spare."

"Gilbert finally came home about one in the morning. You know I hear every creak in this house and have never been able to sleep until he's inside and the door is locked behind him."

Diane had become attuned to Gilbert's presence but was surprised she had not heard him come in last night. "I didn't hear a thing."

"You were exhausted. And young people need more sleep than old people."

"Gilbert says this year's crop is going to be one of the best in a generation. He says we might actually turn a real profit."

"That would be a comfort."

Bent, wrinkled hands embraced the warm cup as Madame Herbert raised it to her nose and savored the scent. She took two sips. "A letter came for you yesterday. I would have told you when you came in, but I was dozing, and it slipped my mind." She reached into the pocket of her apron and pulled out the envelope addressed to Diane.

The letter was from Claire, and as always, excitement tingled through her. Claire had been traveling with the Buchanan family for nearly a decade, and she had seen many marvelous sights. Whenever Claire could buy a postcard, she tucked it into the envelope. Diane now had a collection of fifteen cards from all over the world, including London, Rome, and Moscow.

Carefully, she pulled back the flap and removed its contents. *Dear Diane.* Claire's crisp, neat handwriting reminded her of her mother's, and the tug of home was always strongest when she read her sisters' letters, especially Claire's. Though her other sisters, Jemma and Sarah, wrote, it was infrequent, and their lives did not seem nearly as exciting as Claire's.

Madame never asked about the letters, but as Diane had grown to love the old woman, she had started to share some of them with her. Madame now looked forward to Claire's letters as well.

I have just arrived with the Buchanans in England.
We were blessed with smooth sailing and crossed the
Atlantic in record time.

Claire went on to detail some of the places she had seen and the outfits she had created for Victoria Buchanan. She told Diane how she still found herself chasing after Victoria, who at fourteen hated the constraints of society. The girl was increasingly fussy about her clothes and often made Claire remake a line of stitching or redo a hem. Claire also had news of their sisters and brothers. "It says here George Buchanan has finished his hunting lodge near Cape Hudson. She says it is larger than twenty homes on the Shore combined. And they use it only a couple of months out of the year when they go bird hunting."

"Just for hunting birds?" the old woman scoffed.

"Ducks from the bay are quite the delicacy."

She grunted. "A duck is a duck. Leave it to the wealthy to make some ducks fancy and others not."

Diane remembered walking with Claire and her mother to watch as the railcars brought in the first of the lumber for the big house that Claire called Winter Cottage.

In the final line, her sister stated she was coming to Paris in mid-September. She was traveling ahead of the Buchanans, and she would be in Le Havre for a night and hoped Diane could meet her there.

"My sister is coming to France. She wants to see me in Le Havre." Diane had not returned to the city since the day she had fled it with Gilbert. Even after all these years, the idea of returning chilled her bones.

"I traveled to Le Havre when I was younger with my husband. Several times we would stroll through the finer areas because I liked to see the way the ladies dressed. Always too impractical for the life I led here, but I liked to see it nonetheless." Madame Herbert gently swirled her coffee as she did when she was deep in thought. "Of course, you must go see your sister."

Diane had not seen any of her family in almost nine years. Whatever anger she had for Claire and even her father had faded with time. She understood now why they had done what they'd done. Her life was good now, and if not for their decisions, she might not ever have found it. "I would enjoy that very much."

"Gilbert is going to Le Havre on business. He'll take you. And I'll be sure he sends a case of his best Calvados to give to the Buchanans. It would be good for his business to have a rich family's favor."

"Gilbert would be too proud to peddle his Calvados to my family."

"You're right, of course. The peddling will be your job. If you put in a good word with your sister about our liqueur, then maybe Claire will pass on that information to the steward at the Buchanan house. It would be quite nice to have a wealthy American client."

The idea of spending time with Claire was a tantalizing carrot, and she was proud of the liqueur that Gilbert made. "Claire would buy it from me."

Madame Herbert's lips curled into a sly grin. "You are a clever girl. I've always known this since I first laid eyes on you."

Diane dropped her gaze to her sister's beautiful handwriting. "I can write a note to Claire. She should be in London."

Madame slurped her coffee, pleased with herself. "Ah, this could be very good for us all. Gilbert sells Calvados, you see your sister, and the farm perhaps gets a little richer."

Diane wrote to Claire that morning, and Madame had one of the local boys post the letter later that day. Diane did not have long to wait before she heard back from Claire, and soon the two had a date to meet at a café not far from Max's shop. Madame lent Diane a red scarf that she had kept wrapped in paper in her dresser drawer, as well as a wide-brimmed hat and gloves to match.

Nervous excitement raced through Diane the day Gilbert pulled his motortruck in front of the château. His expression was somber—as it had been since the day Madame Herbert had announced her plan.

Diane, wearing Madame Herbert's scarf, hat, and gloves, hugged her and scratched Oscar between the ears before she climbed into the truck. She was excited but also worried about seeing Claire. She had changed so much in the last nine years, and surely Claire had as well. As she smoothed her hand over the fresh calluses from the harvest, she wished the cloth of her dress were a little finer.

Gilbert started the engine, and they set out on the drive to Le Havre. By the time they had arrived at the inn around the corner from Max's shop, it was late afternoon. As she climbed out of the truck, she looked around at the tall gray buildings that had not changed since the day Madame LeBlanc had been murdered and they had fled moments ahead of the police.

Tension rippled through her as she looked around at the faces of the men and women on the streets. She did not recognize any, but the same types of characters—including shop owners, rough men, even the girls on the streets—remained. What had become of Pierre? Had the police discovered what he had done, or had he escaped?

"He's not here," Gilbert said.

She looked up at his brooding features, searching for an explanation. "How do you know?"

"I've seen men like him before. Like a cockroach, they scamper away when there is trouble. And Max would have told me if he'd surfaced."

"He may have returned. Madame LeBlanc said once he was from this area."

"Even if he did, you have changed too much for him to recognize you."

"I hope you're right."

"I am. Go to your room and sleep. I'll meet you down here in the morning and escort you to the café and to your sister. And while you visit, I will inquire with Max about Pierre Laurent."

She had every reason to trust Gilbert. Whereas she was letting fear drive her, he relied on logic. Still, despite his assurances, Diane's sleep that night was deeply troubled. She dreamed of Pierre, his hands tightening around Madame's neck and then her own.

—— ❦ ——

Diane woke early and took extra time washing her face and styling her hair as she had seen some of the women in the city wearing theirs yesterday. She wrapped the red scarf around her neck and positioned the hat carefully on her head. When she inspected herself in the small mirror, she saw a young woman looking back at her.

Gilbert was waiting when she came downstairs, and when he saw her, his stern expression soured.

"Do you think I look nice?" she asked.

"Yes," he growled. "You look as if you belong in the city."

Ignoring the tension in his tone, she accepted his arm, and the two walked through the city to the café. They stood on the street corner as she searched the crowd for Claire. Intent on finding the girl she had left at the depot in Cape Hudson, she missed the lovely young woman who approached her.

"Diane?"

Diane recognized the voice instantly and turned toward the young woman wearing a burgundy jacket and skirt trimmed in brocade. Her sister's skin reminded her of peaches covered in cream, and her eyes were sharp and direct, just like their father's. Her face was lean, her cheekbones angled, and her lips full and smiling. If not for the auburn highlights in her hair and her eyes, Diane might have overlooked her altogether.

"Claire?" Diane said as she stepped away from Gilbert.

Claire closed the distance between them and wrapped her arms around her. "Those eyes will always give you away, no matter how old you are."

Diane raised her arms and hugged her sister tightly. Emotions she had long locked away roiled up inside her, welling in her eyes and spilling down each cheek. She had not touched anything remotely like home since she had left nine years ago, and to be this close to what she'd once had was so pleasurable it ached.

"You don't smell like the bay," Diane said.

"I've not been to Cape Hudson in quite some time, but Lord, how I miss it. You smell like the ocean."

"There is a hill above the apple orchard that overlooks the sea. The land is far too rugged to be like home, but the ocean is close, and it smells exactly the same."

Claire drew back and gently brushed a tear from her cheek and then one from Diane's. "That was so long ago."

"Right now it feels like yesterday." Remembering Gilbert standing behind them, she said, "May I present Monsieur Gilbert Bernard. He owns the orchard where I work." And then in French, Diane said, "Gilbert, this is my sister Claire."

Claire extended her hand to Gilbert, but her smile was not as quick as it had been for Diane. Her older sister scrutinized the man as if she were a dowager inspecting a footman. Gilbert held her gaze as if he expected and even welcomed such scrutiny.

"It is a pleasure to meet you," Claire said in French. "Diane speaks very kindly of you, Madame Herbert, and Oscar."

Mention of the dog prompted a small smile from Gilbert as he nodded slightly. "She runs the house and most of the estate now. We would be lost without her." Gilbert straightened his shoulders. "I think it is time for you two to visit."

"Would you like to join us at the café?" Claire asked.

"I think this is your time to catch up," he said. "Diane, when should I return?"

"I'm not sure," Diane said.

"I shall take good care of her, Monsieur Bernard," Claire said. "I shall deliver her back to your inn before the end of the day."

He hesitated and looked to Diane as if he did not like the idea of leaving her. But finally he nodded. "Of course."

"Thank you, Gilbert," Diane said.

Very formally, he touched the brim of his hat, turned on his heel, and left them alone. For a moment, she felt a sense of loss, but it was quickly overshadowed by excitement when Claire brushed a stray curl back just as their mother had done when Diane was little.

"You are so grown-up," Claire said in disbelief.

Diane glanced quickly in the direction where Gilbert had strode off, but he had vanished into the crowd.

"So much time has been lost. Mama never wanted it to be this way." Sadness passed over Claire's eyes, like clouds in front of the sun, but just as quickly the darkness lifted. "We cannot dwell on what is past. We only have now."

Diane realized several of the people around them were openly staring and clearly wondering who these two women were. "I think we are upsetting everyone's morning coffee."

"That is too bad for them," Claire said. "It has been too long since I've seen you for me to worry about convention."

Giddy laughter rose up inside Diane. With Claire at her side, she felt the boldness she had enjoyed as a young child running along the beaches of the Eastern Shore. "If we cannot give people something to talk about, then who will?"

Claire laughed, hooking her arm into the crook of Diane's. "Perhaps we should at least try to appear respectable, or we might find ourselves the center of gossip or, worse, earn the attention of a gendarme."

Mention of the police sobered Diane's mood a fraction. "I suppose we should take care."

Claire leaned her head into Diane. "You are right, of course. We don't have the luxury of not caring. We serve at the pleasure of our employers, who expect impeccable behavior."

Her sister's sobering words did not quell the excitement that she felt right now. To have her sister with her, and to have a piece of who she had once been, felt too good to let worry dampen it.

Claire led them inside the café, and with the grace of a fine lady, she told the maître d' that they wanted a quiet table.

Judging by the expression on the maître d', Claire was considered a woman of importance. It was her innate talent with the needle and thread as well as her bearing that allowed her to create the illusion of a grand lady.

Diane tugged at the red scarf Madame Herbert had lent her. This morning, she'd felt quite elegant in the piece, but now, compared with Claire's accoutrements, it seemed plain and provincial.

The sisters settled at a table in the corner, and the waiter quickly brought them two cups of coffee and a plate of macarons. Madame Herbert had taught Diane how to make more rustic pies and tarts, but neither had mastered the very delicate pastries made by the chefs in the city. This morning's fare would cost Diane all the coins she had stuffed in her bag, but it would be worth it.

Claire sat back, regarding her as Diane sipped coffee that tasted divine. There was so much goodness crammed into this moment that she wished some of it could be saved, wrapped up, and parceled out later when her spirits were low.

"You look beautiful." Claire's eyes widened.

Diane raised her head, licking the cream from her upper lip. "No, it's you who looks beautiful. I thought for a moment you were one of the Buchanan ladies."

"No, far from it. I'm good at creating an illusion and making the best of what I have. But you are stunning."

Diane picked at the red scarf, noticing a small hole. She reached for a cookie, unable to resist.

"If I were to dress you, you could pass as the wealthiest woman in the city. Men and women would be falling at your feet to meet you."

"Until they heard me speak and realized I don't know much about anything."

Claire leaned in. "Madame LeBlanc promised to see to your education. She told Papa there were schools in Baltimore and Paris that you could attend."

For years, she'd maintained the pretense that her life was going well so that Claire would not worry. "There was some talk of sending me to a school, but in the end, there was no time for books. She handled most of my instruction herself. Surely the Buchanans did better by you."

Claire frowned. "I spend my days sewing and looking after Victoria."

"In your letters you make it all sound so wonderful."

"I'm not complaining. I've seen things I never would have if I'd stayed in Cape Hudson. But I've learned that travel and seeing the big world is not all that the books Mama read us promised."

"Ah, the girls in the stories manage to leave their wretched worlds and find wealth and happiness."

"I suppose there are not enough princes to go around to save girls like us."

Diane bit into the cookie, savoring a sweetness that did not quite cut through the bitterness she felt. "What of Jemma and Sarah and the boys? I don't receive many letters from any of them."

"The boys are terrible at writing, and I have received a few letters from Jemma and Sarah. The girls still live on the farm in the Shenandoah Valley, and they assure me their lives are good. The boys are fine. I trade letters with Sally Jessup often. Stanley is eleven, Joseph is ten, and Michael is nine. All three boys help Mr. Jessup with the boats and are becoming quite skilled watermen. When Papa is in port, he sees the boys. Sarah and Jemma have not seen him since he sent them away."

It stung to know their father kept up with his sons but not his daughters. "Jemma and Sarah must remember Mama?"

"They do. And they mention in their letters some of their fondest memories. Stanley remembers a little. But Michael and Joseph don't have any recollection of her. In their very few letters, they call Sally their mama. And to Sally's credit, she does love those boys."

Again she resented her brothers because they had been spared the feeling of loss she and Claire felt over losing their mother. "Have you seen Papa?"

"No. There was talk at one time of me going to see Winter Cottage, the Buchanans' hunting lodge on the Eastern Shore, but in the end Victoria changed her mind, so we didn't go."

"You're still trying to herd all the Hedrick ducklings, just as you did when Mama was alive." Their mother had been quite sick with her last two pregnancies, and Claire had stepped into her shoes as mother hen. But despite all Claire's work, she could not keep her ducklings corralled.

They both sat in silence for a moment and ate their cookies before Claire said, "Was it hard for you when Madame LeBlanc died?"

Diane was glad now she had sugarcoated the woman's dark demise. It would do no good to burden Claire with the information. "When I was in her care, she was not the most affectionate woman. I was quite lucky Madame LeBlanc sent me to live with Gilbert and Madame Herbert."

"Mrs. Lawrence was sorry to hear of her death. They were close at one time."

Diane stiffened. "How did she hear?"

"Through an old acquaintance of Madame LeBlanc's. Pierre Laurent."

Diane set her cup on the saucer, her taste for the treat instantly vanishing. "I didn't realize he'd been in contact. Did he mention me?"

"No. If Madame LeBlanc had wanted him to know her plans for you, she would have shared them with him herself."

Stillness settled over Diane. Madame LeBlanc had spoken of her cousin but never mentioned his name in front of Pierre. Perhaps she had been planning to leave Pierre behind for a long time. "So he doesn't know I live at Château Bernard."

"No." Claire eyed her closely. "You're pale."

"No, I'm fine."

"Should I know more about this Pierre Laurent?"

Diane relaxed back in her seat. There had been no sign of Pierre in six years, so it seemed foolish for her to worry. "No. He is of the past, as is Madame LeBlanc."

Claire did not speak for several moments as she continued to study Diane until, finally, she broke her silence. "There is talk of Mrs. Lawrence marrying Mr. Buchanan one day. However, the current Mrs. Buchanan has not obliged them. She's very much alive."

Diane raised her brow. "Mrs. Lawrence says this to you?"

"A woman says many things to her dressmaker. Though you are the only person I have told this secret to, so do not share it. My discretion is why Mrs. Lawrence likes me so much."

"And what of Victoria?"

"Don't ever mention this marriage to her either. She gets quite moody at the thought of another woman taking her mother's place."

"Has our papa found a new wife?"

"Not according to Sally Jessup. He's content to sail with the merchant marines."

"Which is what he did before."

Their mother had been the driving force in the family, and she'd kept the children safe, the house maintained, and the gardens tended during Papa's long absences.

"Mrs. Lawrence is still open to me hiring an assistant. You have declined several times before, but I have to ask again," Claire said. "Would you come work with me?"

"Sewing for Victoria and doing whatever you needed?"

"You are one of the few people I trust, and it would be heaven to have family with me again."

"Even if I'm all thumbs with a needle and thread? I can assure you my sewing skills have not improved." Still, to be asked and know she had not been forgotten meant the world, even though it would mean another family and another carved-out space that did not exactly fit.

Claire smiled over the rim of her cup. "I'm sure we can work around that. The Buchanans are rich enough to keep as large a staff as they'd like."

"I've grown accustomed to the orchard. I discovered I have a talent for making things grow. I like to dig my hands in the rich soil."

"But with me you can travel the world."

"I have made it several thousand miles from Cape Hudson, and it seems to me the world is much the same everywhere. I have no desire to travel farther than where I am."

"Ah, stubborn as always. Tell me you're not turning me down because I have offered. I know things didn't work out as I promised at Mama's funeral, but it will be different this time. If you travel with the Buchanans, we will see places and people you could never see in a small town in America or France. I promise you I'll not send you away again."

The last words were barely a whisper and choked with sadness and regret. "I know you meant well and still do, but neither one of us really has control of our lives."

"That's not true," Claire countered.

"And if Mrs. Lawrence were to end her relationship with you, then where would you go?"

"Then I would put on my best outfit and attend Sunday service at the most prominent church in New York. I'm quite sure I would have orders to create dresses for women in society within the month. I'm very good at what I do, and I can teach you all that I know. Perhaps one day we might even own our own shop."

The idea had great appeal. The two of them owning a business in America was tempting. She would then have the means to visit Virginia and see her brothers and sisters. But choosing Claire meant leaving behind the château, the apple trees, Madame Herbert, Oscar, and even the sour-faced Gilbert.

"What would you do if your Mr. Bernard asked you to leave the château?" Claire challenged.

Diane had no answer. The idea of leaving the orchard churned up a melancholy she had not felt since her mother died. "He wouldn't send me away."

"How do you know that?"

"I know. Loyalty runs so deep in Gilbert, it is fused into his marrow and bone."

"Is there more between you two?"

Heat rose in Diane's face, warming her cheeks. "No. He's an honorable man."

"But a man."

"It's not like that." Suddenly annoyed, she asked, "How long are you in Le Havre?"

"Two days. Then I'll take the train to Paris. By then Mrs. Lawrence's and Victoria's trunks will have arrived. I would like you to come to Paris. I want you to meet Mrs. Lawrence and Victoria. We can begin planning our own enterprise together."

"I have never longed to see Paris."

"Ah, I think you don't know what you're missing. You can tell Mr. Bernard that you're coming to visit me. Perhaps you will stay with me a couple of days or weeks, and then we'll see."

"I'm eighteen, Claire. I believe the days of you looking out for me are over."

Claire leaned forward, and when she spoke, her voice was heavy with emotion. "You and our brothers and sisters are my children, my life. I will always put you first. It is my greatest wish that we will all be together again."

Diane had always known that the Hedrick brothers and sisters would never gather as a group again. "Mama expected too much of you when she asked you to take care of us."

"I promised her."

"She should not have asked that of you. You were a child yourself."

Claire laid her hand over Diane's. "You know she never would have left us willingly."

"She gave Papa two sons, and yet she needed to try for another child. She knew by then that pregnancy was a risk. She knew the dangers, and yet she tried for another baby."

"She loved us."

A bitter seed that had burrowed in Diane long ago took hold and sprouted. "Did she?"

Claire hesitated as if she too had sensed this truth but could never voice it. "How can you say that?"

"You know it as well as I do. You can't tell me you don't blame her."

Claire dropped her gaze to the brocade on her cuff and traced it with her gloved hand. "She loved us."

"I'm not saying she didn't. But she was so anxious to please Papa, and he was never happier than when he held his own son in his arms. He kept the boys close. The daughters he cast off."

"For our own good."

"Or perhaps for his own good. Out of sight, out of mind."

"I can't believe that."

"Then you're a better woman than I, Claire."

Claire stared at her, her eyes flaring with an anger that reminded Diane of when they were young girls. Unlike then, she would not be bossed around.

Diane dropped her gaze to her half-consumed coffee and the treats she had barely touched. "I was so excited to see you today. I never intended to bait you into an argument."

"It's like it always was, eh?" Claire said with affection.

"I thought I had moved past all this because I am truly happy where I am."

"Of all the children, you were the one that fought me the most. The world tried its best to change us, but it seems we're exactly as we've always been."

Diane laughed, seeing the truth. She imagined them in their eighties, meeting again and finding something to argue about.

Claire ordered more coffee and macarons, and the awkwardness of their meeting passed as they settled into their old relationship as if they had never been apart.

"I have a surprise for you," Claire said.

"A surprise?"

"There is a photographer around the corner. He has agreed to take our picture."

"Picture?"

"Yes."

Claire pulled out the picture taken of the four sisters with their mother. Diane was the baby in her arms, Jemma and Sarah stood on her left and right, and Claire stood behind her, a small hand resting on her shoulder. Tears glistened in Diane's eyes as she stared at her mother's face. "Remember this?" Claire asked.

Diane studied it closely, stunned to see her mother's face and how young she had been. "I had forgotten what she looked like," she whispered.

"I try to remember the sound of her voice, but I can't," Claire said.

Diane slowly tried to hand back the picture, not sure if she really wanted to remember what was gone forever.

"You keep it. I have more memories of her."

Diane pushed the picture toward her sister. "No. You should have it. You're the one who will make sure the world doesn't forget us."

"I promise you." Claire pulled several francs from her purse and handed them to their waiter. And when Diane dug for her coins, Claire refused them. "No, this is my treat."

They walked down the cobblestone street, arm in arm, laughing and mindful of the stares.

The photographer's shop was located on a side street sandwiched between a bakery and a millinery. The studio was small, and inside, its walls were draped in heavy fabric. Light flickered from a dozen small gas lamps that added touches of brightness in an otherwise dreary room.

Claire introduced herself and Diane to the photographer, who said he had been expecting them. He seated them on a settee. The photographer ducked his head under the thick black cloth and then came around and positioned their faces toward the camera. "Look at me, ladies. And smile. You are pretty and too young for such somber expressions."

They both smiled, holding the pose as he exposed the lenses and counted to fifteen. He reloaded the large glass-plate negative in his camera and took another picture.

When the session was done, Claire and Diane hugged and agreed the picture would be mailed to their father, so that he would not forget them.

The sisters held hands and leaned close as the carriage rocked over the cobblestones, as if knowing that talk of working together and owning a shop one day was just that—talk. They both sensed that life was soon going to take them in different directions.

Diane kissed Claire goodbye, and she stepped onto the cobblestones. As the carriage rolled away, she waved to her sister, who leaned out the window until the vehicle rumbled around the corner and out of sight.

As Diane stepped through the front door of the small inn, she felt a lightness of spirit and a boldness she had not really known since before Mama had died. When she walked into the lobby, Gilbert was there sitting by the fire, a glass of untouched wine in front of him.

She smiled as she tugged the tips of her gloves and removed them. She sat across from him. "Only you could be in Le Havre and look so glum."

"It smells in this city," he said.

She made a face as she reached for his wine and took a sip. It was too sweet, and it sat on the back of the tongue in a most unpleasant way. "Your cider is certainly much better."

"Yes." He looked up at her. "When do you leave?"

"Leave for where?" Diane asked.

"With your sister and the rich family she works for. I didn't think you'd stay with us forever and knew this day would come."

"Are you happy it has?" she asked.

"It's not my place to have an opinion," he said.

"You always have an opinion, Gilbert. Do you wish for me to leave?" She felt her own breath catch in her throat as she waited for his answer.

He gulped down half the glass of wine and winced. "No, I don't want you to leave."

If this day with Claire had shown her anything, it was that her own future was indeed not secure. She loved living at Château Bernard, but her place there relied on the whims of Gilbert and Madame Herbert. "And what would you have me do when I return to the château?"

"What do you mean?"

"I think it's time I secured my future."

He looked perplexed. "You have a secure future."

"No, of course I don't. The baker's son has affection for me. And the miller has spoken to me at church several times. I could perhaps make a marriage of either of them or the tanner's son. Then I would know for certain where I belong in this world."

"They are all idiots, and you would be bored silly within a month," he growled.

"Perhaps. But I would know I have a place that is all mine."

His gaze sharpened. "You belong at Château Bernard."

"As what? Maid? Cook? Nurse? Apple picker?"

He looked up at her, his gaze full of an emotion she had not seen before. "We should return to the orchard now. The city makes you crazy."

She drew in a breath, staring at his expression for any sign that he did not truly mean what he had just asked of her. "Not crazy. Curious."

He curled his fingers into fists as if he were clinging to sanity. "What is your place at the orchard? You are the orchard now. It would not exist without you. I would have died two years ago if you'd not nursed me."

She had been so terrified during those dark days when the fever had taken him over. Where would she have gone if not for him?

Gilbert drew in a breath. "Marry me."

She laughed, believing he was joking, but his gaze held no hints of teasing, and very quickly her smile faded. "Why do you want to marry me?"

His brows drew together. "I think we would work well together."

Her very practical Gilbert was never one for nice words. He was always direct and to the point. But in a world filled with meaningless pretty words, she found she rather liked directness.

The idea of marrying him had indeed crossed her mind many times. When he had been ill, and she had sponged down his body with cool towels, she had been very aware of him as a man. When the miller had taken her hand a month ago after church, she'd wanted it to be Gilbert's fingers wrapped around hers. When the tanner had tried to kiss her, she had turned her cheek, annoyed that Gilbert had never tried to kiss her. No matter which young man put himself in her path, she saw only Gilbert. "Just like that, you want to marry me."

"Yes, I do." He reached in his pants pocket and pulled out a small piece of cloth. Carefully, he unwrapped it to reveal a small gold band. "It was my mother's," he said.

"How long have you been carrying this?"

"Weeks."

She held out her hand, and he carefully placed it on her palm. She curled her fingers around it. "And when we are married, what would I do? Continue on as I have?"

He cleared his throat. "I assume there will be children."

Heat rose up in her cheeks. "And if I don't want children?"

He studied her, more puzzled than worried. "Why wouldn't you?"

As much as she had dreamed of sharing the marriage bed with Gilbert, the idea of delivering a baby terrified her. "My mother had seven children. She died having the last."

"That was a long time ago. And there's a doctor in town. I would like to have children, especially if one is a girl, and she looks like you."

The idea of holding a baby in her arms held a faint appeal, but it also brought back memories of an absent mother, a father's disappointment, and younger brothers who took the lion's share of the attention. Her fingers pressed the gold into her palm.

"Perhaps not right away," he said. A frown wrinkled his brow. "But I would want a child one day."

"Perhaps one or two. But until then, you would have to be content with just me. Would that do?"

"Yes," he whispered before he cleared his throat. "That would do very nicely."

She slid the ring on her finger and discovered it fit perfectly. She came up to him, and, grabbing the rough fabric of his lapel, she pulled him toward her and kissed him. He sat stock-still, but his lips were soft, and he smelled faintly of soap and fresh air. After a moment, he rose, and his hand came up to her waist. He pressed her toward him, deepening the kiss.

Her senses exploded, and all the restless nights she had lain awake thinking about touching him culminated into a desire that left her breathless. She had always been reckless, making decisions too quickly.

"Is this marriage crazy? I know I'm older," Gilbert said.

"Ten years is not such a difference." She reached for the half glass of wine and drank the rest. "All right, I'll marry you. When?"

"Now. Today. And then we will deliver that Calvados to your sister and be done with this town."

She smiled and leaned forward, kissing him on the lips in full view of everyone in the inn.

The next day, when Diane and Gilbert delivered the case of cider to Claire's hotel room, she greeted them with a smile until her gaze caught the glimmer of the gold on her finger.

Claire took her sister's hand, studied the ring for a long moment, and then looked in her eyes. "Impetuous."

"Perhaps." But Diane was worried. She wanted her sister's approval. "Do I have your blessing?"

"Monsieur Bernard, you will take very good care of my sister," Claire said.

He met her gaze head-on and nodded. "I will."

"Then I wish you both a long and happy life together," Claire said.

___ ⚬⚭⚬ ___

Pierre had been detained in a Paris jail cell. The police had arrested him when a woman claimed he had beaten her. But in the end, he had been able to reason with the magistrate and paint the woman as hysterical. The magistrate had eyed Pierre's dark suit and silk vest and concluded he was a man of means and not someone to tangle with.

After his release, he took the first train back to Le Havre and visited the inn where he had learned Claire Hedrick was staying. Over the years, he had continued to write Mrs. Lawrence, and finally, she had begun jotting notes to him. One of which spoke of Claire's trip to France.

If he had not been such a fool, he would not have arrived late in the port city. He made his way through the inn and found the manager.

When he described Claire and a story about them being siblings, the manager finally admitted that she had left several days ago for Paris.

He had inquired about Diane, and the manager remembered her but could not say where she had gone. Ah, he had been such a fool!

It was mere happenstance that he was walking by the photographer's studio and spotted the picture of the two young women. It had been six years since he had seen Diane, but the instant he saw the picture, he knew it was her. Those eyes.

In the six years since he had seen her, not a day passed that he did not think about how Madame LeBlanc and Diane had cheated him. Madame LeBlanc was dead and couldn't tell him what she'd done with the gems she'd stolen from her marks on the ocean liner. But Diane could. He could see now he was fortunate that he'd been stopped from killing the girl.

The photographer had been pleased his work had caught Pierre's attention and had happily accepted three francs for the copy.

He asked around the area for anyone who might have seen the women. There had been a waiter who had served them. But in the end, he never found Diane.

Pierre took the photograph back to his small apartment. He set it on the marble mantel above his fireplace, so that it was the first thing he saw when he entered his apartment or when he awoke in the morning.

Over the coming years, he would stare at the photograph for hours. Sometimes he would talk to it, explaining in great detail what he would do to Diane when he finally found her. Other times he spoke sweetly and kindly, as if the woman were his lover. Once he became so angry he nearly threw it in the fire. But in the end, he did not destroy it. It was his obsession.

Diane might have forgotten him, but he never forgot about her.

CHAPTER
TWENTY-THREE

Diane

Age 23

Tuesday, September 15, 1914
Normandy, France

Over the past five years, Diane and Gilbert had enjoyed many blessings. They'd learned each and every curve of the other's body, and their physical pleasure grew each time they lay together. At first, Diane hoped they would not have children. She wanted Gilbert all to herself, and she wanted the time to learn more about the orchard and how the cider was made. Gilbert was a patient teacher and she a quick learner. And now she was his partner in every sense of the word.

There were days around her monthly flow when she would become melancholy and wonder if God was punishing her for not truly wanting children. Or perhaps it was because she had helped Madame LeBlanc with her dark arts, or never told the police about Pierre. Whatever the reasons, she did her best not to dwell on it. She consoled herself with the knowledge that the orchards had flourished and grew still more productive each passing year.

Two years ago, Madame Herbert had passed away in her sleep on a winter morning, and a day later Oscar followed. Gilbert had seen to it that they were buried side by side in the family graveyard beside Madame Herbert's beloved husband.

Diane and Gilbert had lain together that night, needing to love each other and to savor the sweetness of life. For several more months their life remained good, even as the flames of war burned hotter.

Gilbert read the papers weekly, and when they were in town, he and the other men felt the pull of duty. Though the trees were bursting with sweet apples and looked like the best crop in over a generation, she worried the war would take him from her.

"The government is drafting men to fight," he said.

She stood at the counter, kneading dough, and it was a struggle for her to keep her voice even. "You are too old. Leave the fighting for the younger men."

The paper crinkled as it did when he neatly folded it in quarters. "I'm thirty-three and in my prime, or so my wife tells me."

She dug the heel of her hand into the dough with extra force, annoyed he was joking while she was petrified. "I don't want you to leave. I need you here."

He rose and walked to the stove, wrapping his arms around her narrow waist, and kissed her on that very tender spot behind her ear. "You can run this place as well as me. And I will return very soon. They say it will be over before the fall harvest."

She wiped her hands on her apron and faced him. "How does anyone know when a war will be over? Wars are like cyclones on the water. Powerful, destructive, and damn unpredictable."

He laid his hands on her hips and tugged her toward him. "I shall return to you."

But her husband had already promised that he would never leave her. Diane laid her hand over his chest. His heart beat steady and sure under her fingertips. He was her life. She could not live without him. "Maybe if you leave, I shall return to America."

He arched a brow, not the least bit threatened by the statement. "You would leave this place? You would leave our home?"

She looked away, unable to stare into those beautiful eyes. "I might."

He laughed and hugged her to him, and despite her fears, she allowed him to pull her close. "You love me. You love the orchard too much to leave."

"But you *are* leaving," she said.

"I'll come back to you." He spoke with such surety. Such confidence. But there was no way he could be sure.

"Swear it."

"I swear."

She wanted to believe he would keep his word to her, so she forced a smile for him when he boarded the eastbound train the following day. She stood on the platform until the train pulled away from the station and its whistle grew silent in the distance.

It would be years before he kept that promise and returned to her. But when he did, he was not the same.

April 10, 1939
From the Journal of Samuel Jessup

We received word from Gilbert Bernard today via the harbormaster in Le Havre. He'll meet us on the docks late tonight. He's got several passengers for us to take. He warned it would be dangerous, which suits me just fine.

CHAPTER TWENTY-FOUR

Megan

Wednesday, April 11, 2018
Cape Hudson, Virginia
10:00 a.m.

"Bad news," Mr. Tucker said.

Work at Spring House had progressed at a steady pace over the last month. Old and crumbling layers were stripped away from the walls while the kitchen and bathrooms were demolished. Though there were still weeks of work ahead, drywall was going up the next day. The restoration had turned a corner and would soon really take shape.

"I thought we were finished with the bad news," Megan said.

"The guys were clearing the land around the property, and they found an old septic system. The wheel of the backhoe ran over it, and it cracked."

"I didn't know there was a second septic system on the property."

"No one did. We are going to have to remove the old tank and fill in the hole. It's not only an environmental issue, but it's also a safety one. Don't want anyone stumbling into it down the road."

"No, we don't."

"I also had a chance to poke around the old kitchen house, and it looks like I found a door to a cellar."

"Old root cellars weren't uncommon."

"Maybe, but we're going to have to excavate it and figure out what we got. Again, a safety hazard."

"Okay, close up the tank, and let me know when you get that cellar open." She checked her watch. "I've got to get going. Helen is picking me up. We have our second birthing class."

"I thought you two got into a tussle during the last one."

They had. Lucy was her birth coach, but Helen had insisted that she attend. The instructor had given Megan a baby doll to hold, and the toy had been in her arms less than a minute before Helen took it from her. Megan, suddenly really annoyed, had grabbed the baby doll back, but Helen had refused to release it. The doll had ripped.

Mr. Tucker went back toward the house surrounded with a collection of power tools. Megan's stomach cramped, and without thinking, she began to rub it as she had done the better part of the last couple of nights. She dialed Lucy's number.

When Lucy answered, Megan walked away from the construction noise as the sounds of girls squealing on the other end rumbled over the line. "You must have more news from Spring House."

"I do." She rubbed her belly and shifted her stance.

"What stack of cash does the money pit demand today?" Lucy asked.

"Educated guess is at least five grand." She gave her a rundown on the discoveries.

Lucy sighed. "Well, you did warn me there would be a few nasty surprises."

Megan crossed her fingers. "I think that we've identified all of them. We really should have a functioning house by September or October."

"Good. I'm anxious to get that house put together and get into a real routine." A bus engine rumbled in the background.

"How is the field trip going?" Megan asked.

"For the first hour it was fine because all the kids went right back to sleep. Now we're approaching Richmond, and the beasts are stirring. I suspect it's going to be a wild day."

"It's going to be a pretty day today, so the canal walk will be nice, and the governor's mansion is always interesting."

"So you keep telling me," Lucy said. "Already looking forward to a glass of wine when I get home tonight."

Megan chuckled. "Text me pictures."

"Will do. How goes it with the baby?"

"She's still in the oven," Megan said.

"Good. See you about seven tonight."

"I'll be here."

As Megan walked toward her car, her belly cramped again, only this time the discomfort wrapped around her belly toward her back. She took several deep breaths until it finally passed. Her doctor had said not to worry about contractions unless she had more than four in the same hour. But what was a contraction? Were they all like this, or were they worse? Surely last night's backache didn't count, right? She tried to remember the birthing movie Helen had brought by Winter Cottage and insisted she watch.

She took another step, and a fresh pain gripped her belly. When it passed, she checked her watch. It had been thirty seconds between pains. But two was not four, and she figured it had to be what her doctor called Braxton Hicks pains. She checked her watch and considered calling her mother, but it was the middle of the night in Australia, and if she called, there wasn't anything her mother could do.

No sense freaking the woman out when she was half a world away. Besides, everyone said first babies were always late, not early, so the chances that she was really in labor were slim. Right?

Megan settled behind the steering wheel of her car and instantly felt a little better. Tipping her head back, she closed her eyes. "Baby, you cannot be early. I'm not ready to be a mother. I'm just *not* ready."

The baby kicked and shifted in her belly. A hard rap on the glass startled Megan as she turned.

Helen was standing there, her face tight with worry. "Are you all right?"

She sat forward as she hissed in a breath. "I'm not sure."

"What do you mean, not sure?" Helen opened the door and laid her hand on Megan's belly. "It's hard as a rock. That means you are having a contraction."

"I haven't had that many."

Helen dug her cell phone out of her purse as Rick pulled up. He parked beside her car and with one glance was frowning. He knew something was not right.

Focusing on her breathing, Megan smiled at Helen. "I think I'm fine now." Her body felt relaxed, and she felt pretty good now. "Yes, definitely better."

"Is everything all right?" he asked, eyeing her and then Helen.

"If I hear *bad news* and *Spring House* one more time, I might go crazy," she said.

Neither he nor Helen appeared amused at her attempt at levity.

"She's having contractions," Helen said.

"Honestly, it has to be a false alarm," Megan said. "I still have at least a week or two to go." Her belly cramped. In the last ten minutes, this was her fourth cramp. *Damn it.* She refused to be in labor.

"You okay?" Rick asked.

"She's not okay," Helen said.

Megan winced, knowing her life was going to change now whether she wanted it to or not. "I think Helen might be right. It could be a contraction, but I'm not sure."

"I am sure," Helen said.

"It's got to be a Braxton Hicks contraction," Megan countered. "I read all about it. That's the kind of contraction that isn't the real deal, but definitely uncomfortable."

"I know what they are," Rick said. "And Helen could be right, and it could be the real deal. You might be in premature labor."

"How would you know about premature labor?"

"I'm a town sheriff. I'm officially a jack-of-all-trades."

"And I've given birth," Helen said. "Women know these things."

"How many have you had?" Rick demanded.

The intensity of their gazes revved up her nerves. "Three, or was it four?"

"Four!" they shouted at the same time.

"Might have only been three."

"In the last hour?" He rubbed his hand over the back of his neck.

She checked her watch. "The last half hour."

He ran his hand over his short hair and muttered under his breath. "Both of you get in my car."

"Excellent idea," Helen said. "Use the sirens."

"Why?" Megan asked. "This could be a false alarm."

"The doctor can tell us at the hospital," Rick said.

Helen ran to her car and grabbed a bag. "I took the liberty of packing an overnight bag for Megan. I was afraid with her crazy schedule, she would forget."

"I didn't forget," Megan said. "It just seemed too early."

"It's never too early to be prepared," Helen said.

"I have to meet with the countertop and flooring guy tomorrow," she said.

"Helen and Megan, get in my car." He reached for his radio, and, pressing a button, said, "Martha, I'm logging out. I'm taking Megan Buchanan to the hospital."

"Is it time for the baby?"

"Don't know. But she's having contractions. Four in the last half hour."

"Ooh, that's the real deal," Martha said. *"Let me know how it goes."*

"Ten-four." He opened the car door. "Get in."

"I don't have my purse," Megan said.

"Sit," Helen said, handing the overnight bag to Rick. "Where is it?"

"Front seat of my truck." Her belly tightened. *Make that five contractions.*

She settled into the front seat and hooked the seat belt as Rick got behind the wheel and Helen grabbed her purse. She got into the back seat, slid to the middle, and fastened the belt.

Rick started the engine. "Are these the only contractions you've had?"

She leaned against the seat and paused. "It was a rough night."

His jaw pulsed as he threw the truck into gear. "What does that mean?"

"Uncomfortable."

Helen leaned between them. "They said in the birthing class that premature babies represent twelve percent of births. This is a thirty-six-week baby, so her lungs might not be mature."

Megan flexed her fingers, willing the fear and tension away. "Helen, I don't need the grim statistics right now."

"I'm just being honest," Helen said.

Rick picked up speed and flipped on his lights and siren.

"The lights aren't necessary, Rick. Seriously, I bet this is a false alarm." Another cramp had her shifting and pressing her hand to her belly.

He drove faster. "If I had two sirens, I'd put them both on. You're in labor, and this kid isn't waiting."

As the lights flashed, she glanced back at the house and saw Mr. Tucker come out on the porch. Between him and Martha, the town would all know soon enough. "Please don't make this a big thing."

"You're having a baby," Rick said. "This is a *big* thing."

"Women have been having babies for thousands of years," she said.

"I have a confession. It's my first hospital run with a pregnant woman, so I'd rather err on the safe side if it's all right with you."

"And it is my first and only grandchild," Helen said.

Megan drew in a deep breath.

Rick muttered a curse. "Should you call Lucy? I thought she was going to help."

"Right now she's arriving in Richmond on a field trip with Natasha's class."

"That's two hours away from Norfolk," he said.

"She rode the school bus with the kids. She's out of pocket on this rodeo."

"Who's next on the bench?"

"Me," Helen said. "I've trained to be her birthing coach too."

"We had one class," Megan said.

"One is better than none," Helen replied. "And I have had a baby, dear."

Megan dropped her head against the headrest as she shifted and tried to get comfortable. "This really could be a false alarm. In fact, I bet we all have a good laugh about it. I feel like I'm wasting your time."

"I can call ahead to the hospital," Helen said.

"Can you just wait until we know if this is the real deal or not?" Megan said. "I don't want to get Lucy all torqued up, and then there's no spud to show."

As the highway rushed past, she winced. "We should be there in plenty of time."

Rick cursed under his breath as he drove past the marshes and toward the Bay Bridge–Tunnel. No one spoke as he crossed the seventeen-mile expanse and wound around the beltway toward the hospital. Several times Megan shifted in her seat and did her best to hide the pain.

"How are you doing?" he asked.

"Feeling pretty good," she lied.

"You're pale as a ghost, and you've touched your belly and grimaced four times since we got in the car," Helen said.

"That much?" she said. "I didn't notice."

Twenty minutes later, after using his lights to cut through traffic, he rolled up to the hospital emergency entrance.

"Stay put," he said.

"I can walk."

"Sit down," Helen said.

"She's right, damn it!" Rick said.

"Fine. Sitting!"

He dashed through the sliding doors of the emergency room. As the seconds ticked, fear rushed through her.

"I'm right here," Helen said. "No need to worry."

Tears welled in her eyes. Rick and Helen would see her through this crisis, but once they had seen Scott's baby safely into the world, then what?

Minutes later, Rick appeared with a nurse and a wheelchair. He opened the truck door and unlatched her seat belt. He took her by the arm and lifted her, helping her settle into the chair.

A nurse, who didn't appear nearly as panicked as Rick or Helen, laid her hand on Megan's shoulder. "This is your first baby, isn't it?"

"How can you tell?" Megan asked.

The nurse unlocked the wheelchair's brake and nodded toward Rick with a grin. "Rookie Daddy and Grandma."

"Grandma," Helen said. "I think I'm too young to be called Grandma. We'll have to come up with some other name."

Megan was about to tell the nurse Rick was not the baby's father when another pain gripped her belly. She sucked in a breath as the nurse pushed her through the front door of the emergency room, while Rick parked his cruiser.

"We'll get you checked into a room," the nurse said.

Minutes later Helen was helping Megan out of her clothes and into a gown. As the nurse settled her into a bed, Rick walked into the room. "I have your paperwork filled out. You're all set," he said.

"Thanks," she said.

Helen tugged up her blanket. "Much better."

As the nurse started the IV, she said to Rick and Helen, "If you two are going to stay, you better get washed up and put on those gowns. While you do that, I'm going to check to see how much she's dilated."

"Right," Rick said. He turned away, stripping off his jacket. He rolled up his sleeves and reached for a gown.

Helen slid a gown over her outfit and pushed up the sleeves to her gold bracelets.

"Daddy and Grandma, you got her here in the nick of time. Mama is nine centimeters dilated and completely effaced."

Helen sucked in a breath.

Rick stared at the nurse.

"That means it's go time, Daddy," the nurse said. "I'm grabbing the doctor because we don't have much time."

"Right, thanks," Rick said.

"How could I be that far along?" Megan said. "I thought labor was supposed to take hours."

The nurse grinned and patted her on the shoulder. "Not in your case, sweetie."

"Are you sure?" Megan asked.

"Very. You're going to be a mama real soon."

Megan closed her eyes. She wanted to be a good mom, and she wanted to do this right. But already she had been caught by surprise by the kid.

"I called Lucy," Rick said. "I put a call into a buddy at the state police. He's picking her up."

"Thank you," Megan said. "I really don't want to do this . . . alone." The last word came out with a rush of breath as she breathed through another contraction.

"Take a few deep breaths. It'll make you feel better," Rick said.

Megan expelled several breaths. "Whoever said breathing helps has never been in labor."

"I know, dear," Helen said. "I almost punched my doctor when he told me I should be feeling better. Scott was a ten-pound baby."

The doctor appeared at the door, moving with quick, purposeful strides. He settled on a seat at the end of the bed and examined Megan.

"Ms. Buchanan, I think you might be setting a speed record today." The doctor looked at Rick and Helen. "Dad and Grandma, get up behind her shoulders and be ready to hold her hands."

"What about drugs?" Megan said. "Don't I get an epidural or something?"

"Mom," the doctor said, "we're beyond that now. The nurse is going to put a sedative in your IV to take the edge off, but this baby is coming in quick."

"I'm not ready," Megan said. An overwhelming sense of panic washed over her.

The doctor laughed. "You can take it up with your daughter when you see her."

Another contraction silenced her reply, and soon all her words and thoughts were washed away in waves of contractions that came faster and faster. Her focus narrowed to the arrival of each contraction, the pain and the brief respites and the urge to push.

It was not long before the doctor told her to push, and Rick and Helen were gripping her hands and whispering words of encouragement.

"You're doing great, Meg," Rick said. Until now, the only one who had called her Meg was Scott.

"You're so brave," Helen said.

"Now do this!" Rick sounded like a marine captain who belonged on a battlefield and not in the delivery room dressed in scrubs that read DAD on the back.

Sweat dampened her forehead as the pressure built. She thought about Scott and all the hard words they had shared the last time they had seen each other. *God, I'm so sorry, Scott. I really wish you could see this.*

When the final push came, even the guilt was shoved aside as her entire focus centered on the baby.

Breathe. Breathe. Breathe.

She gritted her teeth, holding Rick's hand tight, and when the doctor told her one more push, she put all her energy into the push. She felt the baby slide from her.

The doctor grabbed the baby and suctioned her mouth out. Suddenly, Megan was not focused on discomfort or the future or any project. All her thoughts shifted to the tiny, wrinkled, pink creature in the doctor's arms who was too silent.

CHAPTER TWENTY-FIVE

Diane

Age 28

Saturday, September 6, 1919
Normandy, France

Diane and Gilbert's daughter was born in the château in the middle of one of the worst storms to hit the region in generations. The wind outside roared over the roof, tearing tiles as it swept past and banging the shutters against the stone house. The apples were ripe, ready for the picking, vulnerable and exposed to the elements. And they were both helpless to do anything.

Though no bombs had dropped on their land, there had been few men to help Diane with the harvests during the war. For four years, she'd spent endless hours alone, picking and hauling apples in the hopes of saving their livelihood. Occasionally, some of the very old and young came from the village to help her, but in the end, many of the apples had simply fallen to the ground and rotted.

It had been raining the afternoon Gilbert had returned to her after the Great War. The trees were heavy with unpicked, rotting fruit and nearly choked by tall weeds. The war had nearly destroyed the orchard and Gilbert, who was frightfully thin and wearier than she had ever seen him. She wept as he walked up their long driveway, and she ran toward him. When she embraced him, she hugged him with all her earthly strength. The rains soaking them both to the skin, they had stood in that spot, unable to move for the longest time.

That night Gilbert's eyes had been for only her, and they had made love with desperation that stretched the bounds of passion. They both had a frantic need to reaffirm their lives.

Diane had gotten pregnant with Adele that first night.

And now she held the fruit of that love, their daughter, whose pink face and heart-shaped lips took Diane's breath away. Her hair was black as gunpowder, and her petite fingers curled into tiny fists as if she were ready for a fight.

Diane was now soaked in sweat, and her body still ached from the screaming pain of her daughter's birth. She had not been this helpless since the day Pierre had wrapped his hands around her neck and tried to squeeze the life from her. She would have been in a panic, if not for Gilbert.

But her husband had saved her—and their daughter—as he helped her through the long, painful birthing process.

"Hold your daughter," she said, handing him the baby.

Her husband cradled their baby in trembling hands still red and scarred by an exploding German shell. Four long years of war had left her husband so accustomed to death and dying that holding this new life was almost more than he could bear. He was afraid to celebrate his daughter's birth, because loving always led to loss.

Living with Madame Herbert for so many years had taught him basic birthing skills, so he understood if he laid the child on Diane's stomach, her body would soon contract and expel the afterbirth.

Diane laid a hand on her child and watched Gilbert as he untied one of his shoelaces and looped it around the umbilical cord. He double knotted it before reaching for a pocketknife and then dipping the blade in a bowl of rainwater collected in a chipped earthenware bowl. He cleaned the knife as best he could and then wiped it quickly on his sleeve before he carefully severed the cord.

He shrugged off his shirt and swaddled their child in the plaid cloth. "The war has nearly ruined us. She deserves so much more."

"She has us. We have always been enough for each other. And we will be enough for her."

He placed the girl in her mother's arms, and Diane hoped intuition would take over. The baby scrunched up her face but quickly settled into the warmth of the flannel.

"I will be right back. Are you okay to be alone for a moment?" Gilbert wrapped up the afterbirth.

"Yes."

As he dashed outside with the afterbirth, Diane dropped her gaze to her daughter's face, taking inventory of her fingers and toes. Almost immediately, she recognized her mother's nose and the shape of Gilbert's face. This child was the very best of them both.

Outside an animal scurried in the darkness as Gilbert returned. He listened closely and reached for the rifle he'd kept propped by the window. Hungry, displaced soldiers were desperate enough to take, even kill, for what little he had.

She held the baby tighter. "Make no mistake, my girl," she whispered as she tucked Gilbert's shirt close to her daughter's small chin. "I will always love you. Always protect you." The baby yawned and nestled close to Diane's breast, unconcerned about words that were only soft sounds to her.

The baby then cried, and Diane shushed her. "What is it?"

"She is hungry, no doubt."

"Yes." She remembered all the times she'd watched Madame Herbert angle a new mother's breast toward a baby's mouth. She looked up at Gilbert, who stared at her helplessly, and feeling a blush cross her face, she reached for the buttons on her worn blue cotton dress already straining against her full breasts. She didn't like the dress, but she made do because it had accommodated her growing waistline.

She freed her breast and exposed a pink nipple and angled it toward the baby's mouth. Immediately the baby rooted and then latched on as endless babes had done since the first child was born. But the newness for Diane caught her off guard, and she sucked in a breath, shocked at the odd sensation shooting through her body. Small fists kneaded her breast, and the baby began to suckle. "She is eating."

"Like her father, she has a strong appetite," Gilbert said.

They sat in silence as they enjoyed this very precious moment. Finally, she looked up at her husband, noting already his brow creased with worry. "How bad is it outside?"

The storm had ripped across the land last night, delivering yet another blow to them. "We will survive," he said finally. "Some trees are gone, but most are fine."

"Wait until the sun rises, and then we can look." She took his hand in hers. "We will be fine now. It is written in the stars."

He sat on the edge of the bed, running his hand over her thigh. "You speak with the surety of a sorceress, and for once I am going to believe you."

"I am a witch," she said, smiling.

"Your lavender-blue eyes bewitched me a long time ago. I have no choice but to follow you."

Tears burned in his eyes, and he couldn't seem to summon the energy to straighten his stooped shoulders. He was a proud man who loved his apples as passionately as he did his wife and child. She knew he feared the storm would take what little the war had left behind.

"We will save what we can and replant what is lost," Diane said.

"You make it sound simple."

"We will love the land as we love each other and our child. And the trees will flourish. We and this land are two halves of one whole."

"What will you name her?" he said.

"Adele. For my mother." She had chosen the name months ago when the child quickened in her womb.

"Adele."

The child's namesake had been a sea captain's wife, and she had died before her thirtieth birthday. Diane worried the name choice might be an inauspicious omen but cast her doubts aside and chose to believe God would not take back a child who was such a great blessing.

CHAPTER
TWENTY-SIX

Diane

Age 48

Saturday, April 8, 1939
Normandy, France

Adele would prove to be their only child, but she was so perfect that neither Diane nor Gilbert ever longed for another. She grew up in the orchards, riding among the trees on her father's shoulders when she was small. As she grew older, her favorite toy was the planchette, which to her delight sparkled in the light. And as she grew into a beautiful woman, she dressed up in the scarves and clothes Claire sent.

God had chosen to give them only one child, but she was indeed his finest work.

From the moment of her birth, their little family had grown strong. Diane often said that the orchards were so intertwined with their lives that each needed the other to survive. She could never say where one life ended and the other began.

They had not only survived the storms, but in the last few years, Gilbert's reputation as a distiller had grown to the point that Château Bernard was well known not only in the region but also the country.

"What do you think of the apples?" Gilbert asked.

Diane turned and smiled into the face that was now deeply lined. The dark hair was also graying, but the sharpness in his gaze remained. "Still sour."

He plucked an apple from the tree, bit into it, and then spat it out. "This worries me."

"Perhaps as soon as the summer heat arrives, they will sweeten."

"Maybe."

She crooked her arm in his, and the two began to walk down the narrow grass path separating the rows of trees. "You're scowling more than usual."

He patted her hand resting on his forearm. "Am I?"

"What is it?"

"I have heard from Max."

"But he writes to you regularly. What has he said now that bothers you?"

"The Germans have arrested his son-in-law in Germany. His daughter, Elise, has fled Germany and is in Le Havre."

"And Elise's son? How is he?"

"Well," Gilbert said. "Elise is also pregnant again. She's due any day."

Gilbert and Max had both tasted war up close, and both now feared it. Neither man was filled with swelling pride or imbued with a surety that the fighting would end quickly.

"Max is worried that it will be a matter of time before the Germans march across France to the Atlantic."

Gilbert had often said that since the Great War, Germany had been starved and chained up like a mad dog. Each year it had grown angrier and stronger, and it was a matter of time before it would throw off its chains and seek full retribution from the last war's victors.

"I've heard from Claire," Diane said. "She asks us again to visit America. She reminded me that America is calling home some of its diplomats, and according to her last letter, Victoria and her husband,

Edward Garrison, were planning to leave North Africa and returning to New York. She said the USS *Mayhew* will be in Le Havre by April 10. We could go to America for a while and visit Claire. It would nice for Adele to see where I grew up. Elise and her son can come with us. Max too, if you think he'd ever leave France."

"He'll never leave," Gilbert said.

She regarded her stubborn husband. "You and Max are cut from the same cloth. Neither of you will leave France."

He studied her closely. "That doesn't mean you shouldn't."

"I'll never leave my home. It took me too long to find it and too much work to save it. But Adele is different. She must leave and go to Claire until we know it's safe for her," said Diane.

"Our daughter is stubborn like her mother," Gilbert said.

And her grandfather. "Years ago, my father sent me away, and it broke my heart. There were times when I thought I would die from the loneliness."

Gilbert stopped, cupped her face in his hands, and kissed her.

She kissed him back. "If my father had not sent me away, I never would have found you or had this wonderful life. I understand now he did what he had to do to save me. And now I'll have to do the same for our daughter."

Gilbert hugged her close, and for several moments, they stood, clinging to all that they loved.

"Adele would never go without us," she said.

"Max is having a wine tasting on the eleventh to win the favor of the local authorities. I wasn't planning on going, but now I see we must. It's been over a year since Adele has seen Le Havre, and she would enjoy the trip. Once we are in the city, if the *Mayhew* is in port, then we will find a way to see Adele, Elise, and the child aboard."

"Our daughter would go if Elise and the baby needed help."

Diane had not been to Le Havre since the day she had last seen Claire in 1909. After that visit, she'd been stalked by nightmares of

Pierre that had not left her for months. Since then, she had rarely left the village, content to stay in her orchard and far away from Pierre. The idea of her sweet Adele visiting Le Havre sent a shiver through her.

Diane nodded and set about packing the few things she would need. In her room, she pushed her hand up under her mattress and pulled out the wooden box that she had taken from Madame LeBlanc's apartment so many years ago. She opened the lid and stared at the gems sparkling in the planchette. She'd stopped believing long ago the living could speak to the dead as Madame LeBlanc had claimed. But Diane had also learned its true secret and would send it along with Adele to protect her during the hard days that were sure to come.

———— ⚭ ————

Adele was thrilled at the chance to visit Le Havre, and she chatted constantly throughout the day and well into the night. However, uneasiness stalked Diane. Gilbert was not a man who liked to show off, but in this case, he spent the next day selecting his very best bottles for Max's competition. It was as if he sensed this would be their last outing as a family.

"Mama, could we do some shopping in Le Havre?" Adele asked. The girl was nineteen now and blessed with thick ebony hair that curled with a slight wave, a peaches-and-cream complexion, and a bright, wide smile that made the boys in the village look twice.

"I don't see why not," Diane said. "It's been years since I was in the city, but I'm certain there are still shops where young ladies can browse."

Their old truck rumbled over the dirt roads and into the heart of Le Havre. Funny, after all these years Diane would have thought she would remember more, but the streets and people were as foreign to her as when she had first visited.

Gilbert made his way through the city streets. Adele chattered, pointed to several shops, and giggled at the thought of eating pastries from the city.

However, the deeper they traveled into the city, the more silent Diane grew. When they reached the area near Max's wine shop, her thoughts shifted to the past. Even after all these years, she could picture Madame LeBlanc's pale face and the savage bruises around her neck as she lay on the floor of their apartment. A chill swept through Diane as she wondered what had become of Pierre. He was a roach, as Gilbert had once said, and she felt certain he had survived.

Gilbert pulled into the alley behind Max's shop, and just as they had a long time ago, they walked through his front door. Bells jingled over their heads, and the familiar scent of wine, cheese, and oak barrels greeted her.

Max appeared behind the counter and tossed up his hands. Though he smiled broadly, there was no missing the lines of worry etched deep in his face. "Ah, my most favorite people in the world!"

He hugged Gilbert, kissing him on both cheeks, and did the same with Diane and Adele. "Once I told the other winemakers that you were attending, they agreed to the competition. There are twelve in all, and I believe one of the newspapers might even attend. Several of the winemakers are determined to put the cider maker in his place."

Gilbert scoffed and then laughed. "Let them try."

"Adele," Max said, "my daughter has arrived. I am anxious for you to meet her."

Adele smiled, and she pulled her gaze from a crate of wine shipped in from Bordeaux. "How's she feeling?"

"Not well," he said. "She's been in bed most of the day."

"Is she ill?"

"I'm not sure. Her stomach aches, and she complains of a headache that grows worse by the day."

"And her son. How is he?" Diane asked.

"Sleeping now but unsettled," Max said.

"Help me unpack my crates," Gilbert said to Max. "It will give two old men a chance to catch up and discuss the future."

Max held Gilbert's gaze an extra beat, and he seemed to sense there were things that needed to be said without Adele listening. "That would be welcomed, old friend."

Diane led Adele up the winding back staircase to the second-floor room where they found Elise lying in a large bed. Her one-year-old son slept on his back next to her. His breathing was heavy and even, a sign he was in a deep sleep.

Diane sat on the edge of the bed and touched the young woman's forehead, now damp with sweat. "She has a fever."

"Is it the pregnancy?" Adele whispered.

"I don't know."

"We passed a pharmacy on the way here. It's just down the block. I could see about some medicine."

Diane didn't like the idea of Adele wandering the city alone, but it was clear this girl would need more help than she could provide. She dug several coins from her pocket and pressed them into her daughter's palm. "Go quickly, and do not speak to strangers. This place is not like home."

Adele kissed her on the cheek. "Yes, Mama."

———— ⚜ ————

As Pierre sat in the café and stared over the top of his newspaper, *Le Matin*, he caught the gaze of a woman sitting at another table. Pierre smiled and was pleased to see her blush. Even at fifty-three he knew his smile still had the power to charm.

The woman held his gaze long enough to tell him she was interested. She was not his idea of a great beauty. Her hips were too thin and her face unremarkable, but sometimes a man had needs to attend to.

He turned his attention back to the paper, flipping to the editorial page featuring a piece that spoke of Germany's industrial success and its desire to collaborate with its French neighbors, who enjoyed a flourishing cultural life.

Germany, he would wager, would flex her muscles very soon and cross the border into France. However, she would not be bearing a laurel wreath. If Madame LeBlanc had taught him anything, it was how to read the winds of change and to be charming to the right people. That skill had carried him higher than he had ever imagined. It would see him through whatever conquest Germany had planned.

His gaze was then drawn to the image of a wine merchant who was holding a regional wine competition. It was not the contest or winner that was of such interest to him, but the man who owned the shop. His name was Max Shubert.

In all these years, he had not forgotten the shop where Diane had gone for supplies that last day. He had followed her long enough to see her vanish into the store, and then he had raced back to find Madame LeBlanc alone. He glanced at his hands, remembering how they had tingled when he squeezed her neck with the rope. Even to this day, he regretted hurting her, but then again it had been her own fault. She had tried to cheat him. He knew, despite her denials, she had stolen several priceless pieces from the foolish Mrs. Howard.

Suddenly restless, he folded the paper and looked up toward the woman. He had no interest in her now and was most anxious to visit Shubert's shop. Pierre rose, tossed several coins on the table, and walked briskly across Le Havre toward Shubert's wine shop.

When he reached the corner across from the shop, he saw a young woman leaving. She had lovely hair and a delightful figure that forced him to pause and watch. As she crossed a street, a car honked its horn, startling her, and she looked back his way. His breath caught in his throat when he saw her face.

All these years, he had imagined Diane in many incarnations. What would he do if they met again? He imagined time would have changed her, aged her. But now as she stood before him, he could see that she had aged barely a half dozen years. She was as he had always imagined her fully grown into womanhood.

Old needs to possess and control her rose up like a leviathan from the ocean. He didn't know what she remembered from that long-ago night, but whatever it was, he could not risk her coming forward and publicly calling him a murderer.

In truth, the idea of killing Diane made him as giddy as a young boy with a new toy.

CHAPTER
TWENTY-SEVEN

Diane

Age 48

Monday, April 10, 1939
Le Havre, France

Adele returned with a few tablets the pharmacist said would help with Elise's fever. Diane crushed the tablets into a fine powder and mixed them in water before helping the thirty-year-old woman sit up and drink.

"What is wrong with her?" Adele asked.

"A fever, but from what, I do not know. Many things can go wrong when a woman is pregnant."

Adele nibbled her bottom lip, a habit she'd had since she was a young girl. "What are we to do with her?"

"Papa and Mr. Shubert will return soon, and you and I are going to help this girl and her young son get to a boat waiting for them in the harbor."

"Why?"

"Her husband was arrested in Germany, and Max fears she might again be in danger."

"Why?"

"Because it is a matter of time before the Germans are marching into France."

"But the men in the village say France can hold her lines."

Diane pressed her hand to Elise's forehead. "I don't believe that, and neither does Papa."

"What will we do if the Germans come?" Adele said.

"That is a problem for another day. First we must get this girl to the pier and onto the boat." Downstairs the door opened and closed, followed by a steady beat of footsteps on the stairs.

"What about the unborn baby?" Adele said.

"We have delivered babies in the village before."

"You have." Adele frowned. "Does that mean you're getting on the ship?"

Diane's own father had never told her that he was leaving her for good when he took her to the LeBlancs' home. She had hated him for that deception for many years, and now, she was about to do the same to her own daughter. What mattered was that Adele got on that ship and sailed to the safer waters of the Chesapeake Bay.

Gilbert appeared in the door. "It's time to go."

Grateful she did not have to answer her daughter's question now, Diane rose and crossed to her husband, quickly explaining Elise's condition. He nodded grimly, ordered Adele to pick up the baby and the small bag of diapers and bottles beside his cradle, and then he and Diane helped Elise up, and together they walked her down the stairs to the waiting car in the alley.

Max sat behind the wheel, his gaze ahead and his fingers gripping the wheel. "How is she?"

"Not well." Diane scooted into the back seat. With Gilbert's help, Elise was laid across the seat and rested her head in Diane's lap.

Elise moaned softly. "My baby."

"Both are fine," Diane said, stroking her hair. "Stay calm, and we'll get you all to safety."

"There was a man watching the shop," Max said.

"Who?" Gilbert asked.

"I don't know," Max said. "But I have a few friends that are watching him."

Adele sat in the front seat between Max and Gilbert with the sleeping boy in her arms. She looked back at Diane and shook her head as if she knew their lives were going to change forever.

Almost an hour later, Max pulled the car up onto the dock beside the *Mayhew*. The car ride had been tense, the silence broken only by Elise's moans and the baby's heavy breathing.

Max shut off the engine, and he and Gilbert stepped out. The moon was full and illuminated the calm waters of the harbor.

"We'll be right back," Gilbert said to Diane.

She smiled at him, not sure it was possible to love a man more than she did. "We'll be waiting."

The two men made their way down the dock and were greeted by another sailor. Under the light of the full moon, the three men spoke, and then the sailor vanished before returning minutes later with another man.

"Who are those men, Mama?" Adele stared out the front window toward the approaching men on the dock.

"They're going to help us," Diane said.

"Who are they?"

"The tall one, I think, is Samuel, the ship's second mate. He's a very good friend of your aunt Claire's."

"But we aren't going with them, are we, Mama? It's just Elise and the baby that are going?"

"We cannot send Elise off alone, Adele. She's going to deliver this baby very soon."

"But there must be a ship's doctor."

Diane closed her eyes, feeling unshed tears sting her eyes. She was grateful her daughter still stared ahead and was not looking her in the eye. "I must ask a very hard thing of you, Adele."

"What is that?"

"I need you to get on that ship with Elise and her son. I need you to take care of them and see to it that they get to America safely."

Adele twisted in her seat, and her stark blue eyes were filled with disbelief. "I cannot leave you and Papa."

"It will not be forever, Adele. You'll visit with your aunt, and once the winds of war have blown over, you'll return to Papa and me."

"How do you know there's going to be a war?"

"I just do."

The car door opened, and Gilbert and Max helped a nearly unconscious Elise out of the car. Max tried to lift his daughter but was not strong enough. It was the seaman with broad shoulders and a firmly set jaw who took Elise easily in his arms. The front door opened, and the other seaman, who was short and had thick auburn hair, extended his hand to Adele. At first Adele did not take it, but Diane beckoned her to do so.

Diane scooted out of the car and grabbed the small rucksack she had packed for Adele. They all made their way to the ship. Max kissed his daughter and grandson on the head, and the seaman carried her aboard the ship.

Adele stood stoically by her parents' side. "I don't want to leave."

"You have to leave," Gilbert said softly.

"But there's the harvest at the orchard and the bottling. I've promised several of the girls in the village to help with a summer dance. I can't leave."

Diane hugged her daughter closely. "I love you more than anything. But you must go. Take this bag. There's a letter in it for Claire and things I want you to have."

"But you should come with me," Adele said.

Diane shook her head as she smoothed a lock of her daughter's hair back. "We can't. Your father and I have to stay."

"But why?"

"Because war is coming," Gilbert said. "And we can't abandon our home."

"But I can stay and help," Adele said.

"If you do, Elise and her son will likely die, and we won't be able to do the work that will be needed of us," Gilbert said.

"You're too old to fight, Papa," Adele said.

"There are many ways I can still help," he said.

Diane kissed her daughter on her cheek, and then Gilbert took his daughter into his arms.

The seaman cleared his throat. "We need to go now, or we'll miss the tide."

Diane and Gilbert walked their daughter up to the gangplank and stood as they watched her climb aboard the ship. Diane looked up as a woman appeared on the deck. She was blonde, finely dressed, and Diane knew instantly it was Victoria.

Victoria, the young girl whom her sister Claire had cared for and guarded secrets for, raised her hand and nodded. Diane slowly raised her own, realizing she was turning her life and heart over to a woman she had never met. "Take care of her," she said.

"I will." Victoria turned toward Adele and tried to escort her belowdecks.

But Adele ran to the railing of the ship. "Mama!"

Pain Diane had never felt racked her body as she turned with Gilbert and began to walk away from the ship. Tears welled in her eyes and streamed down her face. Had her father felt this way when he had walked away from her?

Gilbert's chin was set, and his gaze nailed directly ahead, but he intertwined his fingers with hers and held her hand tight. "Don't look back. We must do this."

"It won't be forever," Max said. "It will not."

When they returned to the car, Diane did look back to see her daughter still standing on the deck. She wanted to follow her child, protect her.

Samuel stood guard at the end of the gangplank and was turning when car lights flashed over them. The car parked beside theirs, its engine still running and headlights cutting through the night air. A man climbed out.

At first, Diane could not make out the man's face, shadowed as it was by the headlights. But when he stepped forward, she saw the glint of a gun and then his triumphant expression.

A familiar feeling of dread cut through her body as he approached. It was Pierre, and he was grinning just as he had years ago when he'd pushed her down the stairs.

CHAPTER TWENTY-EIGHT

Megan

Wednesday, April 11, 2018
Norfolk, Virginia
1:00 p.m.

The doctor was silent as he cleaned out the baby's mouth and nose and then rolled her on her side and began to rub her between the shoulder blades. Megan waited for the cry that would assure her the baby was okay.

More silence coiled around her, and she looked up to Rick's and Helen's faces, hoping to see some kind of reassurance. Instead, Rick's expression was stony, as if he was already bracing himself. And Helen's eyes glistened with tears.

"What's going on with the baby?" Megan asked.

Helen tightened her grip and stood stock-still, just as she had at Scott's funeral.

The doctor did not answer. He rubbed the baby harder between the shoulder blades. The silence stretched.

And then the room echoed with the baby's loud wail. The doctor and nurse both relaxed as he handed the baby to the nurse.

"It's a girl," Dr. Monroe said.

"Can I see her?" Megan asked.

"Give the nurse a second to check her out. She's a little thing."

"Is that bad?" Megan craned her neck, trying to see the child, who had vanished with the nurse off to the side.

"We like the babies to go to term, but sometimes they'd rather come early," the doctor said. "Judging by that cry, she has a good set of lungs."

Megan watched the nurse's back as she measured, poked, and prodded the now-screaming newborn. Megan was mindful of the doctor delivering the afterbirth and cleaning her up, but she was anxious to hold her baby.

"Next time you have a baby, Megan," the doctor said, "don't cut it so close."

"I didn't realize I was," she said.

The nurse turned, a pink bundle nestled in the crook of her arm. Excitement, worry, and fear collided as the nurse came closer and then laid the baby in Megan's arms. The child fussed as she rooted her face close to Megan's breast. Her hair was dark and her skin a light pink. She had Scott's nose.

Rick laid his hand on her shoulder. "You did a great job, Megan."

Megan looked up and smiled at Rick, and then her gaze flickered past him to Helen. She was pressing the sleeves of her gown to her eyes and releasing a breath. The tension she had carried for years relaxed.

"Thank you," Helen whispered.

—— ❧❧ ——

Helen ran to make phone calls, and when she returned to the room twenty minutes later, the baby had been whisked away to the prenatal ward, where the neonatologist was performing a complete examination.

Rick had gone down the hallway to check on the baby for Megan as a nurse monitored her IV.

"Megan." Helen looked pale and drawn as she crossed the room and kissed her on the cheek. "Where is the baby? Why is she gone?"

"She's fine," Megan said. "The doctors are checking her out."

"Can I see her?" Helen asked. "I want to hold her and assure myself she is real."

"She's in the nursery," Megan said. "You can see her through the glass, I think. Rick is there, and the doctor is examining her."

"But she really is all right?" Helen asked. "She didn't breathe at first. I've never felt so afraid."

"She looks good. And she has a great set of lungs."

"She's so early." Helen shook her head. "I knew you were doing too much."

Tension rippled through Megan, and all the hopefulness she had felt when the baby was born faded. She had been overdoing it for weeks, which she realized now was selfish.

The nurse cleared her throat. "Ma'am, you should go and have a look at the baby."

Helen looked up at the nurse, annoyed. "Yes. I will."

Megan swallowed a lump in her throat as she watched the woman leave. "Her son was the baby's father. He died last September."

"Well, I'm your nurse, and you're the only one I'm worried about right now. You doing okay?"

The rush of adrenaline, the pain, and the emotion had hit Megan so fast that she wasn't quite sure. "I'm fine, I think."

"Sometimes babies just come early, Megan." A knock on the door had her looking up to see Lucy standing there. Her blonde hair was pulled up into a ponytail, and she was wearing a green shirt that read CHAPERONE.

"Lucy, nice shirt—can I get one?" Megan asked.

Lucy dropped her backpack in a chair, crossed the room, and hugged her. "Are you okay?"

Megan relaxed into the embrace, gripping Lucy's shirt. "I'm good."

Lucy drew back, smoothing Megan's bangs into place. "I hear it all went pretty quick."

"Who knew I'd be so good at delivering babies?"

"Your buddy Rick sure has some pull with the Virginia State Police. One of them met us at the Virginia Museum and whisked me away. The kids were so thrilled, and we ended up taking a quick selfie with the officer. I'm officially the coolest mom at the school."

"Mom. Does it feel weird to be describing yourself that way?"

"You have no idea how insane it sounds. But life is change, and I'm okay with it. You will be too."

"Do you feel fine about raising a child?" Megan asked.

Lucy smiled. "Hell no. But Arlene tells me that mild hysteria is normal, and once you're a mother, you never feel like you've figured it out."

"Seriously?"

"Seriously." Lucy fished out her phone and dialed Megan's mother's number. "Grandma, this is Lucy Kincaid. Nope, everything is fine, but your daughter just had a baby girl, and I think you two should have a chat."

Megan accepted the phone as her mother's squeals echoed from the receiver. She squeezed Lucy's hand. "Thank you."

"Anytime, kid."

She raised the phone to her ear. "Hey, Mom."

"Megan, how are you?" Her voice sounded rough with sleep, but Megan had never heard a voice that sounded so good to her.

A nurse stood by Megan as she nursed the baby for the third time. It had taken several tries before the nurse had helped Megan maneuver her nipple into the baby's mouth yesterday and for the baby to figure out she needed to latch. The second and now third attempts at nursing were proving to be a struggle.

The baby finally clamped on her nipple and suckled just as Helen arrived carrying a car seat and a diaper bag filled with clothes. "I've been to three stores. You would think there's one local store that would have all the things a baby needs."

The baby startled, clamping down hard on Megan's nipple, and when Megan jumped, the baby cried. Megan was at a loss for what to do, but the nurse calmly maneuvered the baby back into position. However, with Helen watching, Megan could not quite relax. The baby pulled harder, as if sensing her tension, but they were both trying to make this mother-daughter thing work.

The nurse laid her hand on Megan's shoulder. "You're doing fine. I'll be right outside if you need me."

Helen set down the car seat and bag in a chair and came around to look at the baby. "She looks so pretty. I swear she's a carbon copy of Scott."

The sound of Helen's voice distracted the baby, and she cried. This time Megan tried to angle her nipple back toward the baby, but for whatever reason the kid would not latch now. All the pictures Megan had seen of happy, tranquil, breastfeeding mothers felt more like a pipe dream. The baby cried and fussed as if she had just figured out she had a rookie mom.

"Just turn the nipple down a little," Helen said.

"I know. I'm doing everything that the nurse said. It's just not working."

"Maybe I should go get the nurse. I don't want the baby going hungry."

"She won't go hungry." Panic rose in Megan's throat. This was something she wanted to figure out, because the day would come when she would be doing it alone.

"She needs every bit of nourishment she can get. She was only six pounds, one ounce. And babies always lose weight the first week."

"I've got this," Megan lied. She wanted so much to prove to Helen she could do this one thing.

"I'll get the nurse."

Before she could tell Helen to wait, the woman was gone. "Come on, kid. You've got to work with me. I know you aren't an old pro at this either. It's a team effort." The baby rooted her mouth around but still did not latch.

Seconds later Helen returned with the nurse, who reminded Megan that breastfeeding would take a little time. Megan guided the baby's mouth forward and the kid suckled.

"See, just a bit of expert advice," Helen said.

Megan thanked the nurse. She wanted to savor this moment with her daughter, but Helen still hovered. "What did you buy, Helen?"

"Ah, I bought you a car seat, a month's worth of diapers, formula just in case, a breast pump, and . . ." She continued to list off items, but Megan lost count.

"That's very generous. You didn't have to do that."

"Of course I did." Helen smiled down at the baby.

"I understand the baby had a good night," Megan said.

"That's what they told me. I noticed over her bassinet in the nursery, it read Baby Buchanan. I felt certain you'd end up using the Jessup name."

Megan didn't want to fight about names right now. "I haven't thought about names."

"Well, it's a good thing you have me. I spoke to the staff, and they agreed to write Jessup on the card. I don't want anyone getting confused about who my little angel is. Are we agreed her name is going to be Scottie?"

She smoothed her hand over the baby's tuft of dark hair. "I'm not sure about the name, Helen."

"What name are you considering?"

"I keep coming back to Diane," she said.

"The girl who wrote the letters?" Helen asked.

"Yes."

"Seems an odd choice, don't you think? You never knew the girl."

"I kind of feel like I do. Her sister Claire is the reason we're all here now."

"Diane Jessup," Helen said, testing the name.

"Diane Jessup Buchanan," Megan said.

"The baby deserves her father's name."

"And she has it. As well as her mother's."

Helen stared at her a long moment. "You've clearly had a long night."

"Yes, I have."

Helen removed a small stuffed animal from one of the bags and rubbed its soft fur. "I spoke to Grandmother last night. I'd like to bring her by to see the baby."

"We would enjoy that," Megan said. "I want my daughter to know her family."

"Perhaps at Winter Cottage in a few days?"

"Perfect."

"And just so you know, I plan to speak to Lucy," Helen said. "I think it would be an excellent idea if I move into Winter Cottage. There are plenty of spare rooms."

"You think Lucy will agree to this?"

"I can be very persuasive. Fear not, she will say yes, and I'll be there for the baby day and night."

Two days later, the nursing staff and doctors pronounced Megan ready to go home with her new baby. She wanted to argue that they had made a mistake and that she was not nearly qualified enough to care for a child. But the nurses assured her over and over that she would be fine. As Lucy drove them all home, Helen sat in the front passenger seat and Megan in the back next to the car seat. Somehow, along the way, Megan had agreed to let Helen stay at Winter Cottage for a couple of weeks.

They arrived back at Winter Cottage, where Hank and Natasha greeted her with a bouquet of pink balloons. Lucy cooed over the baby while Hank stared at the child as if he wasn't quite sure what to do with his latest cousin. Natasha regaled them with statistics from CPR class and showed them numerous YouTube videos.

By the time mother and baby had settled in their room, Megan was exhausted and her nerves were shot as she lay back on her bed and closed her eyes. It seemed like only seconds later, the baby's cries jerked her awake.

Helen, who had made herself at home in the room beside Megan's, was at the doorway. "Is Baby Diane all right?"

"She's just hungry." Megan picked up the baby and felt the heft in her diaper. "And wet."

"Let me change her."

"No, I have to do this, Helen."

"You're exhausted. I lost track of how many diapers I've changed."

Megan carried the baby over to a table now outfitted with a changing pad and laid the crying, wiggly girl down. Helen hovered close, pointing out when Megan had the diaper upside down and when she didn't tape the tab on the side tight enough. Finally, Helen whooshed her aside and within seconds had the baby properly diapered.

"See?" Helen said, cradling the baby close. "That was easy, wasn't it, Diane?"

And this was how it went for the next few days. Megan lost track of her days and nights and began to wonder if a person really could die from sleep deprivation and being smothered by a too-helpful almost mother-in-law.

Thankfully, Megan physically recovered very quickly. Five days into motherhood, the sun was shining, and she was anxious to get out of the house and walk.

Helen had insisted on babysitting, pronouncing it too cold for the baby to be outside.

"She'll be fine," Megan said. "It's seventy degrees, and I'm going to wrap her up in that awesome outfit you bought her. Besides, aren't you supposed to be checking on Grandmother Jessup today?"

"Really, Megan, I think you should stay inside," Helen said.

Megan laid her hand on Helen's. "It's okay. The baby will be fine. All will be well."

Helen's brow furrowed with worry. "I'll be back as quick as I can."

"I'm looking forward to meeting Grandmother Jessup."

After several more bits of advice, Helen finally drove off, and Megan released the breath she'd been holding for days. "Okay, kid, it's just you and me. We're going solo, and we're walking to Spring House to see how the framing is going. You okay with that?"

The baby nestled close to her, and she took that as a yes. Outside the sky was a brilliant blue, the clouds white and wispy. As she walked, she kept her hand on the baby's bottom and moved slowly at first for fear the pack might slip off. But the pack held, the baby slept, and with each step Megan felt a little better and more confident.

When she arrived at Spring House, Mr. Tucker and his men had reframed the rafters in the roof, and the shingles for the new roof had arrived. Inside, the new plumbing was being roughed in, and the electrician had begun rewiring the house to code. To have three contractors working on the project at one time was nothing short of a minor miracle on the Eastern Shore.

Mr. Tucker came out and greeted her. "I heard you had a project of your own going."

"I did. This is Diane."

He smiled at the baby. "I have six of my own. Nothing better."

She wasn't exactly sure when this little baby had totally stolen her heart. But Diane had managed it, and Megan knew there was no going back. "You're right about that. How goes it with the house?"

"Right on schedule. I want your approval to bring in a landscape crew. A buddy of mine has a crew on the Eastern Shore tomorrow, and they're looking for a half day's work. He could clear around the foundation of that kitchen house and see what you have there."

"Can he text me a quote?" Megan asked.

"Already asked." He pulled out a business card and handed it to her. Handwritten on the front was a quote for three hundred dollars. "He'll clear all the land around it."

"I don't want the apple trees damaged. It's important that we save them."

"I've told him that."

"Then let's do this. I'm curious about what's over there. What about the basement? What's the status?" Megan asked.

"There is some water damage, and it's filled with boxes that will have to be cleared out. There also appears to be a padlocked door."

"A padlocked door?"

"Most likely more storage, but if you want the basement resealed and the floor dug out so we can have more headspace, the door is going to have to be opened."

"Once you've got the room cleared, go ahead and open it," Megan said.

"Will do." Mr. Tucker gave her a quick tour of the house, and she was pleased by the progress. The cabinet, granite, and floor people had been scheduled, so it was now full steam ahead. "I'd take you into the basement but don't know if the air is good for the baby."

"Understood. I'll come back tomorrow without her."

"By then we should have the door opened, and you can get a first look at what's likely old junk."

She laughed. "One man's old junk is often my kind of treasure."

When she arrived back at Winter Cottage, Rick's truck was parked out front. She had not seen much of him in the last week. He'd stopped by the hospital the day after the baby was born, reminded her if she needed anything to call, and then he had vanished.

He was not dressed in uniform and looked really nice in his jeans and button-down blue shirt. Aware that she was now wearing nipple pads and her maternity pants, she brushed her bangs from her eyes and thought maybe he would not notice the heavy scent of milk that followed her everywhere.

"Long time no see," she said.

"I brought you a present," he said.

"Baby Diane is one lucky girl."

"The present is not for the baby. It's for you. I got the lowdown from Lucy on what Helen has bought the baby, and I know the kid is set for at least a year."

A thrill of excitement rocketed through her. "Perhaps even two years."

"This gift is just for you."

She brushed her bangs from her eyes. "Come on inside, and I'll make you a cup of coffee."

"Where's Lucy?" he said as he stepped inside.

"She's meeting with a wedding planner. The extra tent that the planner put up saved the day."

"Never mess with Arlene's predictions."

"So I'm learning."

He dropped his gaze to the baby. "Hard to believe someone so small could strike such fear in me. My nerves were buzzing for days after she was born."

She shifted and tugged back the pack so he could see her face. "I suppose she wanted to make a dramatic entrance."

"She's going to be a heartbreaker."

She walked into the parlor and carefully lifted the sleeping baby out of the pack and laid her in the cradle now lined with a soft pad Helen had ordered custom made. The baby nestled into the folds and relaxed.

"How long she sleeps is anyone's guess. But I just fed her, so I think I have a solid hour."

His gaze crossed quickly over her full breasts. "Motherhood agrees with you."

"I feel like I've been hit by a truck." She sat on the settee, and he took the chair to her right.

He reached in the paper bag and pulled out a long, thin box. It wasn't wrapped, nor did it have a bow, but Rick had never been the kind of guy who fussed over frills. "I remember you mentioning Ragland's Mariner Antique Shop in Norfolk, so I stopped by and picked this up for you."

Excited, she shifted in her seat. "Sounds mysterious."

"Full disclosure, Duncan suggested this for you. He seems to know the items you gravitate to. It's not much, but you said you weren't a fan of flowers."

The fact that he'd even bothered to ask Duncan meant more to her than she could say. She accepted the box, smoothing her hand over the surface. Carefully, she lifted off the lid and peeled back the tissue-paper lining.

Inside was a wet-plate photography print of Spring House, and in the background was Winter Cottage while it was still under construction. A finely dressed man and woman stood in front of Winter Cottage, both appearing to survey the construction work.

"Duncan discovered that your great-great-grandfather hired a series of photographers to document the construction of Winter Cottage. He said the photograph you bought a couple of weeks ago was taken about a year earlier than this one."

She smoothed her fingertips over the edges of the image, staring at the couple in the distance. "This is my great-great-grandfather and his soon-to-be second wife, Elizabeth Lawrence. Wow. Thank you, Rick."

"I'm glad you like it." His voice sounded relieved and a little pleased.

"I love it." When she looked up, he was staring at her in a way that made her body hum. How was it that he could just look at her and make her want things?

Desire and energy made her forget that her hair was not really combed, makeup might be a thing of the past, and that she smelled like milk and baby. She wanted so much to lean in and kiss him. But if she did, whatever pull there was between them might just evaporate as the reality of their lives would tug them in different directions.

Rick held steady, not moving forward or backward. If a kiss was going to happen, it would have to be her doing.

She had a newborn, a job that would keep her crazy busy for several years, and an almost mother-in-law who was going to be a fixture in Diane's and her lives for the long term. She was nobody's rose.

And still, she leaned toward him slowly, waiting for him to pull back. But he stayed put. He was as steady and sure as the lighthouse on the property.

Her lips were inches from his when the front door burst open and slammed shut. The baby startled awake and began to cry. Megan drew back in time to see Helen appear. Her gaze slid between the two, and her eyes narrowed as if she knew they'd been about to kiss.

Helen stiffened and shook her head. "What's going on here?"

Megan drew in a breath. "I was about to kiss Rick."

Helen crossed the room and readied to pick up Diane. "I'll take the baby."

Megan stepped in front of her and cradled Diane in her own arms. "She's my child. I will take care of her."

"I don't think the child should be in this room with you two now," Helen said stiffly.

"Why?"

Helen straightened. "You are disrespecting my son's memory. He's barely been dead a year, and you have forgotten him. He never would have done this to you."

And in that moment, Megan reached her breaking point. All her actions to protect Scott's memory were forgotten. "Of course he would have done it to me."

"How can you say that?" Helen's voice was bright with anger. "You were never good enough for my boy. I tried to raise you to his standards, but I can see I wasted my time."

"His standards! Your son cheated on me! He betrayed me!" She patted the fussy baby, trying to soothe her cries and hold back her own tears.

Helen shook her head. "How can you say such lies?"

"They aren't lies," Megan hissed. "I caught him in bed with my bridesmaid Brandy two weeks before the wedding."

"It's a lie," Helen said. "Scott would never do that. Rick, tell Megan she is wrong about my son!"

When Megan looked to Rick, she expected to see the same disbelief she saw on Helen's face. Instead, there was no hint of shock.

Rick looked at Megan. "I'm sorry, Helen. But Megan is right. Scott was cheating."

Megan stepped back, swallowing a hard lump in her throat. "You knew."

"Yes," he said.

"This is not true," Helen said.

Rick's gaze didn't waver from Megan. "I'm sorry. I wanted to tell you. Scott and I fought over this several times, and I told him to get his act together or I would go to you."

"But you didn't, did you?"

"I would have made him tell you before the wedding," he said.

Tears streamed down Megan's face, and Helen stared at them both in horror.

"Very convenient to say that now." Megan turned and, holding Diane close, walked out of the room toward the staircase. "Both of you get out of this house. I want nothing to do with either of you."

CHAPTER
TWENTY-NINE

Megan

Friday, May 4, 2018
Cape Hudson, Virginia
3:00 p.m.

The days following her fight with Rick and Helen had been a blur for Megan. Her time was spent caring for Diane and overseeing the work at Spring House. It wasn't lost on her that as the old house was coming together, her life was falling apart. Helen had moved out, and she had tried to call Megan several times, but Megan ignored the calls. And when Helen had shown up unannounced, Megan had refused to see her or let her see the baby.

It was a warm spring day when Megan received a call from Mr. Tucker, who had finally cleared enough debris from the cellar so he could inspect it. During his inspection, he'd found a padlocked door, which he assumed led to an old root cellar. He had asked if she and Lucy would like to be present when he opened the door.

Her curiosity was too great not to see what he might have found, so Megan had left the sleeping baby in Natasha's care, and she and Lucy met him at Spring House.

They found Mr. Tucker on the front porch directing two men carrying Sheetrock up to the second floor. He greeted them both and informed them the electrician and plumber were almost halfway finished. The place was shaping up nicely.

"That's terrific," Megan said, mentally calculating how much both tradesmen were charging. "What about the flooring?"

"Arrived yesterday, and it's in the front parlor. It'll have to sit for several days while it acclimates to the temperature and humidity."

"Perfect. And the cabinets?" Megan asked.

"They've been ordered and will be here in two weeks. That'll give us time to finish the Sheetrock and the flooring."

"Perfect." Megan stepped into the house, now open and flooded with light. "Hard to believe it's the same house."

Mr. Tucker shook his head. "Left on its own for another few years, I don't believe the house would have made it."

"I appreciate the update," Lucy said. "But I'd like to see what's in the basement. Been thinking about this all night."

Tucker motioned them toward the kitchen and then toward a set of stairs that led to the basement. "Watch your head. We haven't dug out the basement floor yet, so the ceiling is still low."

"What are the chances that you won't just hit water when you start digging?"

"I've taken several soil samples. We should be good to go down the extra two feet. Doesn't seem like a lot, but if you do that, then you've suddenly got one thousand extra square feet of very usable space."

"No telling what you'll end up using the house for," Megan said.

"I only twitched a little when I saw the estimate, but the way I figure it, Claire wanted all this saved properly, and saving doesn't come cheap."

"No, it doesn't," Megan said.

The three descended the wooden staircase to the dirt floor. Mr. Tucker had strung a series of utility lights that illuminated the center section of the basement but left the corners dark and ominous. He reached for a set of bolt cutters leaning against the wall.

"I don't do spiders or rats," Lucy said.

"What about snakes?" Mr. Tucker asked.

Lucy stopped midstride. "Seriously?"

"Just kidding," he said, grinning.

"Jokes are permissible on the first floor and outside. Not in dark basements," Lucy said.

As they bantered back and forth, Megan's attention shifted to the door Mr. Tucker had mentioned.

Mr. Tucker snapped the lock with one snip and handed it to Lucy. "I'll admit I'm a bit curious myself."

"Any idea what it could be?" Lucy asked. "Perhaps a dead body or two?"

Megan shook her head. "All bets are off with this property. But I'm hoping no dead body."

Lucy laughed as she passed the lock to Megan. "I have to admit, life has been mighty interesting since my arrival in Cape Hudson."

Megan held the cool metal in her hands, turning it over slowly as she searched for any markings that might tell her more about it. It was old, likely dating back seventy-plus years, and it was very possible it even predated Samuel's arrival in the house.

Megan tightened her fingers around it, but no real impression came to her. "Please open the door."

He tugged on the door, and the stiff and rusted hinges squeaked and groaned in protest. He reached for one of the lights hanging on the ceiling above and shone it into the room.

From floor to ceiling, racks were filled with hundreds of dusty bottles. Taking the light from Mr. Tucker, Megan stepped into the room. The light swept over toward the tall shelves filled with dark-green bottles that all lay on their sides. She removed one bottle and wiped off the dust from the label. It read CHÂTEAU BERNARD, the name of the orchard where Diane had landed after she had vanished from Le Havre.

"What are all these doing here?" Lucy said.

"Diane said Claire bought these from the orchard as early as 1910 and well through the early 1930s until the end of prohibition."

"This is where Claire kept her bootleg stash," Lucy said with appreciation.

Megan moved to other bottles. "Claire inherited Winter Cottage but no money from the Buchanan estate. All the monies went into a trust for her son, so this would have been an effective way for her to make cash. It also would have helped her sister earn income during a time when the French economy was depressed."

"Makes sense," Lucy said. "Whatever small allowance George Buchanan was giving her stopped after he and his wife died in a car accident in 1920."

"We know she had extensive connections in the merchant marines who traveled regularly between Europe and America," Megan said.

Mr. Tucker scratched his head. "From the Eastern Shore, it would have been easy to ship cases of liquor into Norfolk or as far north as Baltimore."

Megan nodded. "There was no arrest record for Claire, so if she was selling booze, she never got caught."

"She was a smart woman," Lucy said.

"When her son inherited the company in 1938, Claire gained a great deal of say in the company's management," Megan said. "And from what my father said, she was a very good businesswoman. However, when her son, Robert Jr., took full control, he was not as successful a manager."

Lucy moved along the rows of bottles, spot-checking the dates. "All the pictures I've seen of Claire are of a very proper woman who always dressed her best. I'm still trying to reconcile her as a bootlegger. That woman never ceases to amaze me."

Megan pressed her hand against the label of a bottle, hoping for some kind of impression of Diane, but there was none. "We still don't know what happened to Diane."

"We might not ever know," Lucy said.

Megan carefully replaced the bottle. She just could not accept the fact that someone did not know what had happened to Diane.

When Megan returned to Winter Cottage, she discovered Helen's car parked out front. A surge of annoyance shot through her, and she pictured Helen barreling past Natasha straight toward Diane.

Fury growing, Megan walked up the front stairs, through the front door, and followed the sound of Helen's voice to the parlor.

Helen met her in the hallway, cutting off her advance, holding up her hands in surrender. "You can be as mad as you want at me, but I brought Grandmother Jessup with me today. There's not going to be many more days when she can make a trip like this. Please talk to Grandmother Jessup. She has no part in what's between us."

"Where is Diane?"

"She's in the parlor. Natasha is standing guard over the baby. She's quite protective."

Megan rolled her head from side to side and drew back her shoulders. "This doesn't mean that you and I are square."

"I know that."

"Okay." She walked into the parlor and found Grandmother Jessup sitting in her wheelchair by the tall bank of windows, the azure sky and Chesapeake Bay at her back. The woman's pale-white hair almost glowed in the sunlight, and though her face was deeply wrinkled and her shoulders stooped, she smiled as she looked at Diane in the cradle.

Natasha rose from her chair by the cradle and quickly crossed to Megan. "They just got here. I didn't let them hold the baby."

"You did a good job. Thank you so much," Megan said.

Natasha grinned. "I'm pretty good at babysitting."

"Yes, you are. Would you mind stepping out while I visit?"

"Sure. But call if you need me."

"I will." She patted the girl on the shoulder.

"Grandmother Jessup," Megan said, "this is a lovely surprise."

"I hope we aren't intruding," she said with surprisingly clarity. "But I wanted to see my great-great-granddaughter."

Megan reached into the cradle, lifted out the baby, and laid her in the woman's arms. The baby cooed and yawned.

"It's been so long since I held my own child in my arms," Grandmother Jessup said. "But a mother never forgets this feeling."

"I hope I never forget."

"Can you sit beside me awhile?" Grandmother Jessup asked.

"Of course."

The older woman whispered, "Helen has always meant well. Though she can be a bit bossy, she's always been singularly devoted to her husband and son. I respect that."

The blunt assessment sapped some of Megan's anger. As annoyed as she was with Helen, the old woman before her spoke truth.

Grandmother Jessup smoothed her hand over the tufts of dark hair on Diane's head. "Helen told me about the letters, Samuel's journal, and the box with the planchette."

"What do you know about them?" Megan asked.

"A great deal." The old woman shifted as she tried to reach into her pocket.

Megan took the baby so Grandmother could pull out a small booklet made of brittle paper. On the outside were the words RÉPUBLIQUE FRANÇAISE PASSEPORT.

Megan placed Diane in her cradle and tucked her blankets around her. She accepted the identification papers and read the name Adele Madeleine Bernard, born 1919 in Normandy, France. "Of course, your accent is French."

She nodded. "My parents were Gilbert and Diane Bernard."

How many letters had Diane written, gushing about her child she adored so much? "You're Adele."

"I've been called Grandmother for so many years. It's nice to hear my name again."

Megan raised her gaze, searching the old woman's face for any traces of Diane or Claire, and discovered a keenness that Adele's mother and aunt had shared in the picture taken in Le Havre so long ago. "Claire sent a ship to Le Havre in April 1939. Was that for you?"

"She had many friends along the Eastern Shore, and she asked Samuel if he would come and fetch me. He, of course, did and brought me back to Cape Hudson."

This matched up with her ancestry research. "When I was doing the Jessup family tree, I found your marriage certificate to Aaron Jessup in 1944, but I could never find your birth certificate."

"In those days it was not so important to have a birth certificate when one married. Many, especially here on the Eastern Shore, were born at home, and there was no record other than the family Bible."

"You speak English very well. Almost with no accent."

"My mama taught me to speak English. And we spoke it at home often. She always wanted me to be able to talk to Claire if the time came. And when the time did come, I moved here, never to return home again." She smoothed manicured fingers over the back of her wrinkled hand. "Helen said you found the planchette."

"Yes. It was hidden in Samuel's desk."

"Bring it to me."

Megan glanced at the sleeping baby, torn between picking up the baby and possibly waking her or leaving her alone in the room.

The old woman smiled. "I can watch her for a minute or two."

"I'll be right back."

Megan quickly ran upstairs to her room and retrieved the planchette as well as the dreidels and the identification papers for Elise Mandel. She had so many questions for Adele.

She rushed back into the parlor to find Diane still sleeping and Adele smiling down at her. Breathless, Megan took the seat beside Adele.

The old woman took the planchette and smoothed her hand over it, running her index finger along the edge as if she were searching. "When I was six or seven, my mother sent me to fetch a shawl from her trunk, and I found this hidden at the bottom. I was immediately fascinated by it and took it to her to ask its meaning. I'd heard whispers in the village that she was a witch, and I wasn't sure what to think of this."

"Did she mention Madame LeBlanc?"

"Yes. She told me the entire story of how she and her sisters were farmed out by their father after their mother died. My mother was given to Madame LeBlanc."

"Madame LeBlanc was not always good to your mother. Perhaps Claire and your mother didn't want you to know this."

"No, I suppose not." She traced several of the gems embedded in the top. "To prove to me that the device wasn't mystical, Mama showed me its secret that she discovered by accident. Would you like to see it?"

Megan smiled. "Yes, I certainly would."

Adele's eyes twinkled with mischief as she pressed a section of the wood on the top edge. A strip of wood popped free, and the top separated from the bottom. "This is the reason Madame LeBlanc and Mama worried that Pierre would chase after her."

Encased in the small velvet-lined interior were diamonds of various shapes and sizes packed in so tightly there was barely any space between them. They sparkled in the light.

"Madame LeBlanc was a con artist and a thief. Mama realized on that last cruise across the Atlantic the woman had been stealing from all her clients, but she never saw the gems until she found the secret latch."

Megan traced her fingertips over the glistening gems. "They must be worth a fortune."

"They were worth a fortune in 1903. I can't imagine what their value is now."

"Why didn't you sell them?" Megan asked.

Adele shook her head. "My mother suffered for those stones. I wanted nothing to do with them."

"What happened to Pierre?" Diane asked.

Adele's triumphant expression darkened into sadness. "Samuel killed him."

"What?"

"I was standing on the deck of the ship watching my parents walk away from me when Pierre arrived on the dock. Pierre had a gun. I saw my father step in front of my mother, and I could hear angry voices, though I couldn't make out what they said."

Megan could feel stress and fear build in her, as it must have in Diane Bernard all those years ago.

"I turned to Samuel and asked for his help. He moved so quickly I barely saw him duck into the shadows. When he reappeared moments later, he had gotten behind Pierre. The gun was pointed at my parents, and Samuel did not hesitate. He stabbed Pierre in the neck and killed him instantly. He called to another sailor, and the two carried the body on the ship. Later they dumped it at sea."

Megan felt a sense of vindication, knowing that Pierre had not escaped justice. "And what of your parents? They escaped Pierre, but I can find no record of them."

"I didn't find out what happened to them until 1943. Samuel sailed often to European ports during the war. He smuggled supplies for the resistance as well as into England. He took terrible risks, but no matter how great the danger, he refused to back down, even after he was badly injured when a U-boat sank his ship in 1942 near the coast of France. He made it to the coast and was saved by resistance fighters. It's then that he learned what happened to Mama and Papa." Adele shook her head. Even after seventy-five years, it seemed like it still hurt her to speak the words.

Megan laid her hand on the older woman's arm. "I can tell from your mother's letters to Claire that your parents were deeply in love."

"Ah, they were. When I was little, and after they'd sent me to bed, I would hear them laughing. When I peered out my bedroom door, I could see them dancing in the kitchen." She drew in a breath. "Max was transported to Dachau in late 1940, and after that my mother and father joined the French Resistance. In 1942 they were caught smuggling guns hidden in a cider cask. According to the sources who spoke to Samuel, my parents were shot where they stood."

Megan's throat tightened with unshed tears. "I am so sorry."

Tears glistened in her blue eyes. "It was quick. And they were together. I am grateful for that." She reached for Elise Mandel's travel papers and opened the booklet to the woman's picture. "I had forgotten what she looked like."

"What happened to her?"

"I have kept so many secrets. For most of my life, they weighed heavily on me, but now telling them won't hurt anyone, I hope."

CHAPTER THIRTY

Adele

Tuesday, April 11, 1939
Le Havre, France
Midnight

By the time they were out to sea and the lights from the shore had vanished, Elise was crying in pain as her contractions overtook her small, slender body. The baby boy was also crying, and no matter how much Adele rocked him, nothing would soothe him.

Her heart beat so fast, she could barely breathe as she tried to figure out what to do with the laboring woman. She had helped her mother several times but never delivered a baby alone. She patted the boy on the back and reached into Elise's carpetbag until she found the silver dreidel. She shook it in front of the boy until it caught his attention.

Elise moaned in pain. She had not regained consciousness since they had left Max's home. Holding the boy, Adele pressed a trembling hand to Elise's forehead and noted it was hotter than ever. The doctor's pills were not working.

There was a knock on the cabin door, and it opened before she could respond. She turned and found Samuel. His clothes were still wet, his thick cable sweater stained with Pierre's blood. "There is no doctor on the ship," he said.

She bounced the baby boy and was grateful when he took the toy and began to chew. "I don't know what to do."

"I have spoken to Mrs. Garrison, our only other female passenger," Samuel said. "She has agreed to help."

Mrs. Garrison stepped around Samuel and set down a bowl of hot water and several towels on a small table. She gently touched him on the shoulder. Blonde hair was pulled into a soft bun, and her high cheekbones and vivid blue eyes reminded Adele of the film star Jean Harlow. She wore a plain black dress and had rolled up her sleeves.

Mrs. Garrison looked at Elise and for a moment appeared to be lost in thought before she cleared her throat and said, "Adele, I am Mrs. Garrison, and together, we will do this."

"Thank you." The baby cooed and drooled on the toy in his hand.

Mrs. Garrison smiled at the baby and gently ran her hand over the side of his blond curls. "Give the baby to Samuel. He will see that the boy is fed and cared for while you and I attend to his mother."

Adele studied Mrs. Garrison's creamy skin and neatly trimmed nails. "You have delivered a baby?"

Mrs. Garrison rinsed her hands in the water and dried them with one of the towels. "I have seen babies born."

"Can we get you anything else, Mrs. Garrison?" Samuel asked.

"No, Mr. Jessup. You may leave us now. This is a job for women."

Samuel took the boy, who appeared fascinated by his knit cap. When Elise curled on her side and gripped her belly, Samuel and the boy quickly departed.

Victoria stripped Elise's shoes, her knitted stockings, and then her clothes. After covering the woman with a blanket, she stacked pillows at the top of the bed and with Adele's help pulled Elise up to elevate her head.

"Do you have children?" Adele asked.

"No. My husband and I were not blessed." A faltering smile flickered on her lips. "Go on—wash your hands. I think it will not be much longer."

The baby boy arrived two hours later in a rush of screams and blood. He had a strong, lusty cry, but Elise did not respond to the sound of her newborn son. She was unresponsive, and her eyes had rolled back in her head. Mrs. Garrison wrapped the baby in a large, clean towel and held him close for a long moment.

Elise began to scream again, and, though she was not lucid, her body was again convulsing and straining as if trying to expel another child. "There should be an afterbirth," Mrs. Garrison said.

"But her pains are so violent," Adele whispered. "I helped my mother at other births, but I've never seen anything like this."

Mrs. Garrison pressed her fingertips to Elise's neck. "Her pulse is racing."

"She was sick before we arrived."

Victoria pushed up the woman's legs, and this time, they both saw the crown of another head in the birth canal. "Another child!" Victoria grabbed the shoulders and pulled. A small baby boy slid out. His complexion was blue and his body still.

As blood gushed over the sheets and blankets and Elise's face grew even more ashen, Mrs. Garrison raised the baby up by his feet and rubbed him hard between the shoulder blades. For several moments, the child did not make a sound, and Adele feared the child was lost.

Mrs. Garrison laid the baby on his side and cleaned out his mouth with her finger. She then covered his mouth and nose with her mouth and blew in several quick breaths. "Come on, little one."

"How do you know to do this?" Adele asked.

"I saw it done once." She rubbed her knuckle firmly into the center of the baby's chest.

Finally, the child twitched and began to cry. Smiling, Mrs. Garrison wrapped the boy in another towel. "Elise, you have two sons. You must open your eyes for them."

Elise's breathing had stopped. When Adele touched Elise's neck, she felt no pulse. Mrs. Garrison laid the baby aside and shook the woman. She tipped her head back and blew air into her lungs just as she had done with the infant moments ago. But Elise did not respond.

She was dead.

CHAPTER
THIRTY-ONE

Megan

Friday, May 4, 2018
Cape Hudson, Virginia
4:30 p.m.

"Victoria's first son was born in 1938, and her twin boys were born in 1939. She kept all three of Elise's children and passed them off as her own," Megan said.

"The decision was made that night when Elise's body was buried at sea," Adele said. "Everyone aboard ship was there, and we all said a prayer for the lost girl. I went back to my cabin and was sitting with the babies when Mr. and Mrs. Garrison came to see me. They were willing to raise the babies, but they wanted the world to know the children were theirs."

"I always wondered why Victoria's children never laid claim to the Buchanan monies."

"Claire was waiting for us on the dock when we arrived in Norfolk. She and Mrs. Garrison spoke privately, and I assume a deal was struck."

"Samuel knew."

"Yes."

"When Mrs. Garrison refused to take the dreidels or the identification papers, Samuel took them both. He said he would keep them for the children if they ever wanted to know about their heritage. One day, he said, the secret would come to light."

"He knew by then that Victoria was his biological mother, and he thought the boys would need a connection to their past."

"Yes."

———— ❧❧ ————

Later that afternoon Helen drove Adele back to Norfolk, and Megan fed Diane again. As she laid the baby in the cradle in the parlor, the front door to Winter Cottage opened and closed.

Lucy and Hank appeared in the door, and when they saw the baby sleeping, the trio stepped into the kitchen. "Lucy tells me you found out something about my ancestry."

"I did. Adele, Grandmother Jessup, told me." She laid out the dreidels and Elise Mandel's travel papers and began to retell the woman's story. "From how Adele describes it, she hemorrhaged to death. Maybe if you relay the story to an ob-gyn, they can explain better about what happened."

Hank ran his hand over his hair, staring at Elise's face. "She looks like my sister, Rebecca."

"I've not seen Rebecca in years," Megan said.

"My grandfather was the oldest of Victoria and Edward's children. Dad and I planned to see Grandpop next week. Can I take these to show him?"

"They are yours to keep," Megan said. "Maybe your father and grandfather can figure out if you still have family in Germany or France."

He studied Elise's picture for a long moment. "Thanks, Megan. This means a lot."

"I'm glad I found it."

Hank hugged Lucy close and then kissed her.

"I have one more surprise." Megan picked up the planchette and popped the latch. She carefully opened it and watched as their eyes widened.

"Diamonds?" Lucy said.

"Stolen over a century ago by a con woman on a cruise ship," Megan said. "Adele showed me the latch."

Lucy looked at Hank, shaking her head as if she could not believe it. "Did she ever sell any of these?"

"She said she never touched them."

"Are they traceable?" Hank asked. "Can we return them?"

"Loose stones are nearly impossible to trace. I think Madame LeBlanc knew that." Megan smiled. "Those diamonds will send Natasha to any school she wants to attend."

"I don't know what to say," Lucy said.

"I'll leave it all to you now." Megan checked on the baby, and, confirming she was still sleeping, she stepped out onto the back porch. The sun was setting low in the sky, and soon it would dip again behind the horizon. The sound of footsteps approached, and she turned to see Helen.

"I took Grandmother Jessup back to Norfolk. She was quite exhausted."

"I'm glad I got a chance to meet her," Megan said.

"I am truly sorry, Megan. I have said things to you that are unforgivable."

"You're right," Megan said.

"I've been so angry since Scott died, and you've caught the brunt of that. I'm so sorry." She ran a trembling hand over her hair. "I know my son wasn't perfect. But I loved him."

Megan knew Helen could be difficult, but she loved her son. Now that Megan had Diane, she understood the power of a mother's love for her child. "Can you do a favor for me and watch the baby? I want to run an errand."

Helen drew back, tears glistening in her eyes. "Of course."

"I won't be gone long."

"Take as much time as you need."

Megan ducked inside, grabbed her purse, and a minute later was driving off Winter Cottage property toward the main road. She drove north on Route 13 and took the turn to Rick's house. When she turned into his driveway, she was glad to see his truck parked there.

She parked beside it and got out of the car, smoothing damp palms over her jeans. She knocked on the front door, but there was no answer, and she thought maybe he was not home. But then came the sound of a hammer banging behind the house.

She hurried around the side and down the sandy path filled with crushed oyster shells. His shipment of siding had arrived, and he was now stripping off the old. He wore faded jeans, a weathered blue T-shirt, and work boots as he raised his hammer. He seemed to sense her, and he turned. His expression was an unreadable mask, but she could see the tension rippling through his body.

"Megan, I should have told you about Brandy," he said.

"Why didn't you?"

"I didn't know how. But I swear, I wouldn't have let you walk down that aisle, knowing what I did. I was just doing my best to make sure I wasn't going to blow up your wedding for the wrong reasons."

She took a step toward him. "Telling me about Brandy wasn't a bad reason."

"I never wanted you to marry Scott." His voice was rough with emotion.

"Why not?"

"Because I wanted you for myself." He tossed his hammer aside and rubbed his hand over his head. "I can't tell you how many times I wanted you to give up on him and come to me. But I knew Scott loved you, and I couldn't betray that trust."

She closed the distance between them and took his hand. "I'm tired of trying to figure out Scott's complicated idea of love."

Rick tightened his hold around her fingers. "I can promise you, my view of loving you is far simpler. All I've ever seen when you're around is you. No one else."

"Diane and I are a package deal now."

"I wouldn't have it any other way. I love that kid like she was my own."

Megan rose up on tiptoe and kissed him. He rested his hands on her hips. "Let's see how it goes, Sheriff Markham. You might get tired of me."

Pulling her close, he kissed her again. "No way in hell, lady."

April 8, 1939

My dearest sister,
I am entrusting you with my heart and soul, my precious daughter, Adele. Gilbert will not leave France, and I cannot leave him or the village when I know in my bones that darkness is coming soon.

Each time you see Adele, remind her that her mother and father loved her more than life. Tell her to find love, to make beautiful babies, and to live well. If she finds half the happiness I have found with Gilbert, then she will be truly blessed.
Love,
Diane

April 18, 1939
From the Journal of Samuel Jessup

The ship docked first in Baltimore, where Mr. and Mrs. Garrison departed with their sons. Miss Claire met us on the docks. She and Mrs. Garrison spoke only briefly, and no one could hear what they said. But the women hugged. As the Garrisons entered a waiting car, Miss Claire went to Adele and wrapped her arms around her. "You are home," she said. "Finally home."

I left them on the docks, my mind already turning back to my ship and the cargo that would soon stock it for my return trip to Europe.

ABOUT THE AUTHOR

Photo © 2017 Studio FBJ

A southerner by birth, Mary Ellen Taylor's love of her home state of Virginia is evident in her contemporary women's fiction, which includes her novels *Spring House* and *Winter Cottage*. When Mary Ellen's not writing, she spends time baking, hiking, and spoiling her miniature dachshunds, Buddy, Bella, and Tiki. For more information about the author, check out www.MaryEllenTaylor.com.